I hate reality,
but it's still the only place
I can get a decent steak.

WOODY ALLEN

*Die Wanderratten*

There are two types of rat:
The hungry and the fat.
The fat are happy at home,
But the hungry have to roam.

HEINRICH HEINE

# The Hungry and the Fat

# TIMUR VERMES

# **The Hungry and the Fat**

*Translated from the German by*
*Jamie Bulloch*

MACLEHOSE PRESS
QUERCUS · LONDON

First published in the German language as *Die Hungrigen und die Satten* by Eichborn Verlag in der Bastei Lübbe AG in 2018

First published in Great Britain in 2020

This paperback published in 2021 by

MacLehose Press
An imprint of Quercus Publishing Ltd
Carmelite House
50 Victoria Embankment
London EC4Y 0DZ

An Hachette UK company

A CIP catalogue record for this book is available
from the British Library.

ISBN (MMP) 978 1 52940 056 4
ISBN (Ebook) 978 1 52940 053 3

3   5   7   9   10   8   6   4   2

Designed and typeset in Minion by Patty Rennie
Printed and bound in Great Britain by Clays Ltd, Elcograf S.p.A.

MIX
Paper from
responsible sources
FSC® C104740

Papers used by MacLehose Press are from well-managed
forests and other responsible sources.

# Part One

# Part One

# 1

The under-secretary cannot decide. Granite, they said, is the toughest material out there. Or what about artificial stone? Not that he's particularly fussed – as under-secretary he has other things on his mind – but Tommy has made it quite clear that he doesn't want to make all the decisions alone. Which is why the under-secretary, coffee in hand, is now poring over a pile of catalogues and comparing materials. Natural stone? Laminate?

"Laminate for the work surface?" the under-secretary said. "Isn't that for floors?"

"We'll get to the floor."

"So what's the advantage? Can't we just have wood?"

"Just wood!" Tommy snorted as if the under-secretary had suggested climbing Mount Everest in flip flops. He was standing in the hallway in his shorts, the "Hello Kitty" rucksack across his shoulders. But not even the cat's ghastly head could mar the flawless arse below. Then the flawless arse turned and gleaming white shorts approached on two slim, tanned legs with a spectacular fuzz of blond hair. As Tommy sauntered past he picked up something, which looked like

3

an extremely thick and extremely boring magazine, and let it slap down on the table like an enormous paper steak. "Have a read of this," he said, "and see what normal people have to deal with. I can't keep spelling it out for you. I've got to go now, and by the way the wallpaper won't choose itself."

"But . . ."

"Be happy that I've already narrowed down the choice. We'll make the final decision on Saturday morning, half ten, at the wallpaper shop. It's in the diary."

"Outlook or Calendar?"

"Both. Gotta go now. Happy governing! And say hi to Volker!"

The under-secretary certainly won't be saying hi to Volker. And again he curses the moment he agreed to move in with Tommy. They'd had a wonderfully practical arrangement – him in Berlin, Tommy in Hamburg, happily reunited every fortnight. He was able to meet who he liked in the evenings, have backroom conversations until all hours, hook up with someone (though that was seldom, to be honest) or bring people home and chew over a few strategies until half past three in the morning. That wouldn't have to change, Tommy insists, and perhaps he's right. You could easily bring five politicians home without waking your partner if you've got enough space to put the bedroom a fair distance away. And now they're going to have a fabulous two hundred and fifty square metres, plus roof terrace. Throw in a jacuzzi and Tommy can spend more time doing what he does best.

Which certainly isn't cooking.

Granite is superb, the under-secretary reads in the paper-

steak, but natural stone stains easily. And absorbs liquids. Granite is also hard blah, blah, blah . . . Weighed down by his catalogue misery, the under-secretary glances at his mobile, hoping to be saved by a message. But there are none. He taps on the calendar: two meetings, two interviews. No emergencies. He thinks of Tommy's bottom in the white shorts and the phrase "summer recess" springs to mind. There's nothing going on, and he ought to be glad about that. It wasn't always thus.

That summer and autumn when the stupid cow opened Germany's doors to refugees. The events on New Year's Eve in Cologne. The hiding they took for the Turkey deal. And then another hiding after the putsch. One crisis meeting after another, seemingly with no break in between. He can't remember whether it was September or October when he came home and Tommy said, "The way you stink makes me wonder who's still keen to negotiate with you." He didn't change his clothes for four or five days at a time, but now that the uproar has more or less subsided, the refugee numbers have dropped, and they're mentoring or reducing or upskilling this new stock – or all of these together – he can cut back on the overtime and finally pick up a decent book.

But instead of that he's reading kitchen catalogues.

"Wood is a living material," it says. Exactly. Good old wood. The disadvantages: vulnerable to moisture, fruit and vegetable juice, blood. You simply have to be careful not to cut yourself, he thinks, before realising that they're not referring to the cook's blood here.

There's been so little to do recently that he was even able

to chair a transport meeting. The summer break is looming; he can already sense the election campaign in the air. Little more is going to happen. If governments do anything at all, it's straight after taking office; they need to show their voters that the election has achieved something. But after two or three years all the nice, simple tasks are complete. What's left is arduous and risky.

Laminate. Not good for hot pans. How clever, a work surface that can't cope with hot pans – who thinks these things up? But what should they have instead? What copes well with heat? Steel? Glass?

My kingdom for a national crisis.

It would be far simpler if Tommy decided. At the moment, however, they're not just discussing a domestic cooker, but a domestic crisis too. Fortunately it's quite specific and hasn't affected other sectors, but still, they have to ensure it doesn't spread. The domestic crisis is called "The under-secretary is so brilliant at delegating" and it means he needs to involve himself a little more in household affairs. Recently Tommy let him know that he regarded himself as the under-secretary's life companion, not just another ministerial tart. Then Tommy wanted to know whether the two of them could agree that he, Tommy, wasn't just a ministerial tart, otherwise, Tommy said – and he was saying this in the nicest possible way – otherwise they could end this here and now.

And that means everything is going to get a bit trickier. He had thought that the new kitchen would simply involve getting more chipboard from the D.I.Y. store. He even enjoys the occasional visit to the D.I.Y. store. The subtle aroma of wood and solvent, the neatly ordered shelves. All those tins of paint. Screws. Brackets. Screwdriver sets. Spanner sets. Not that he's especially handy, but if you've got a spanner set, one of each size, and a screwdriver set, one of each size, doesn't that give you the feeling of satisfaction, of being prepared for every screw life can throw at you?

Dekton. The miracle substance. You can slaughter a pig on it and detonate an atom bomb, and then, in fifty thousand years' time, when the earth has been re-inhabited by mutants, those mutants will clear away the rubble and say, "Hey! A Dekton work surface. Almost as good as new!" This is an exaggeration, of course; Chernobyl has shown that you can re-inhabit nuclear areas far more quickly and without such rapid mutation. As far as he's concerned, this phasing out of nuclear power is not entirely crazy; he's chatted to a few people from Vattenfall who seem to have their heads screwed on. But he doesn't want to know about the environmental impact. Of this Dekton stuff. Environmental impact is a big deal for Tommy: "After all, we're leaving this to our children."

"We're gay."

"You need to get out of your bubble. That bloody party of yours is making you incredibly narrow minded, it really is!"

His mobile rings. Finally. The driver.

"I'll be down in a sec."

He needs to be quick now. He's often noticed that he finds it easier to think when he's under pressure. He doesn't have a clue about kitchens. Tommy has very precise ideas and wants to have a kitchen that looks impressive should the minister happen to come around. And if one day the under-secretary happens to become a minister himself, who knows who might be paying them a visit? That cute prime minister from Sweden?

Mmm.

Briefly the under-secretary pictures Svensson in a pair of boxers. Then he snaps out of it and becomes the professional politician once again. He picks up his smartphone, compares prices, then chooses the most expensive. Tommy will say "typical" and complain that he's a show-off (ten minutes), that you can get it better and cheaper (two minutes), then he'll suggest his own and go on about the choice of colour (thirty to forty-five minutes), and the under-secretary will just have to make a bit of a fuss (five minutes, ideally fifteen) before giving in.

No doubt it could all be done quicker. But sometimes you have to embark on these kinds of detours, and in this respect dealing with Tommy is no different from dealing with his ministerial tarts.

But he can't tell Tommy this, of course.

# 2

Nadeche Hackenbusch leans back contentedly. She knows that the first ripples can be felt long before she arrives at the T.V. company. Like shockwaves, like the wind before a storm, that rustling in the trees that sounds different from the normal breeze. Like the humming of railway tracks before a train approaches.

Logically it should begin when Sensenbrink instructs his secretary not to put though any unscheduled telephone calls, and yet again tells her to remind everyone who's coming to the meeting, so that everybody shows. But well in advance of that moment her name is already buzzing down the corridors like a rumour. Employees sense a phenomenon like this as animals sense an earthquake.

"You lot have got a tough day ahead."

"Is she coming on her own?"

"So? Full company meeting again?"

The time when she used to flit from meeting to meeting in different departments is long gone. To begin with she felt important, until she realised that you're more important if you meet the same people in fewer meetings. Last year, when it became apparent that the first series would hit record viewing figures, she managed this for the first time. There was only one single meeting for the second series, which everyone had to show up at. And the date wasn't suggested to her; she chose it herself. Of course she went for July.

"Why 'of course'?" asks the new girl beside her in the limousine.

"Because it means some of them will have to interrupt their holidays," she says, flipping open a pocket mirror and checking her make-up. A fluid, gliding movement, hand into the bag, hand out with mirror flipped open as it's raised, a glance during the brief pause between the mirror coming up and going back down, hand with mirror glides into the bag, all in all under two seconds.

"Doesn't that piss them off?"

"Sure. But that's like, the only way to get respect. The important people, the people with money, the people who make the decisions – those are the ones you have to treat badly. Not the little people. Write that down, please."

The new girl jots it on her pad. Nadeche Hackenbusch doesn't yet know whether this is going to be a self-help book or her memoir, but it's one of her favourite phrases and it has to be in there, whatever. She puts her hand in her bag again and plucks out a fifty-euro note. It happens so smoothly, maybe she has a special section for fifty-euro notes. She leans forwards and puts the note into the driver's hand. "Before I forget, this is for you." She sinks back into her seat.

"You need to treat the little people well," she says. "That's what my mum always said. I come from a humble back-ground, you see. My mum was a very simple woman."

"Oh, wait a sec." The new girl leafs back through her pad, then says, "Your mother married a businessman – do you really want to depict that as a humble background?"

"My mum was a *very* simple woman," she clarifies. "And I will never forget my roots. You have to know who you are. Only those with roots are proper people."

She pauses briefly. When nothing happens she widens her eyes and nods towards the writing pad.

"Sorry," the new girl says. "Only . . . those with . . . roots are . . . proper people."

She notes with satisfaction that her words are being writ-ten down. "In the beginning I only used to give ten euros," she says. "Then I thought that might be like, a bit stingy. So I gave twenty euros. But then I thought that might *still* be stingy. And I mean, it's silly to give a tip if you end up think-ing it wasn't enough. I might as well not bother. So now I give fifty."

"And you don't think fifty's stingy?" the new girl asks.

Nadeche doesn't like the undertone. Is she being ironic? Critical? Sar . . . whateveritis?

"Anybody who doesn't think fifty's enough is like, prob-ably after a hundred. And a hundred's greedy."

"But fifty isn't?"

Nadeche Hackenbusch makes a disapproving sound with her lips. "How much do you give, then?"

"I dunno," the new girl says. "Five, maybe? It depends on the fare."

"Absolutely not." She shakes her beautiful head. "I can already see that I'm not going to be able to explain it to you. Just try to get it down in some form and we'll look at it later. Maybe we'll edit it out altogether."

"The bit about the tip or the important people?"

This new girl won't last long. Thank God her handwriting's good; whoever replaces her will have no problem reusing the notes.

"I don't know yet," Nadeche says, gazing absentmindedly out of the car window. "Maybe both."

"Shame I'm not being paid by the hour," the new girl says ruefully.

"You signed your contract."

Nadeche checks the time, then grabs her mobile. "Madeleine? Look, it's me. We'll be there in ten minutes. Could you call and let them know? So that when . . . Exactly. Actually, no, I fancy a cappuccino today . . . Super . . . Sweetener. You're a real love!"

Outside, the city flashes past. She likes this. Some of her old friends shook their heads when they found out how her life had changed. The interviews, the living in the public eye, an endless willingness to be photographed or spoken to. Plus the fact that this wasn't just a burst of fame, it's remained pretty constant ever since. She, however, was in thrall to her new life straightaway, and she still loves it. It's a world she feels comfortable in, as others might in their local pub. Not least because the corollaries of her fame mean she can always be sure she's on the right track. The fact that there's always someone hovering around her leads Nadeche to believe that she must be leading an interesting and enviable life. For her, journalists are like canaries in a mine. So long as one's still hopping around, everything's O.K.

She glances at the new girl.

"Take this turning, please," she says to the driver. "I just want to see what they've built here."

"But then we'll be late."

"We're not in any hurry," she says softly.

Which is why, half an hour later, she relishes Sensenbrink's apology that her cappuccino is cold. "A fresh one, please. Pronto!"

"Only if it's not too much trouble!" Nadeche Hackenbusch says.

Once again they've opted for the large conference room at the very top of the building. With a view of all of Hamburg. They meet in a hotel, the very best in town, rather than in one of those shabby studios in Cologne or Unterföhring in Munich, where square tables are shoved together beneath outdated designer lamps. She likes it like this. Place settings and those three-tier stands for nibbles, biscuits and cakes. The T.V. companies can boast all they like about their catering departments, but in the end you just get canteen coffee and supermarket biscuits. No, she wants linen serviettes, she wants attentive waiters all wearing the same outfit, she wants to see other people spending money on her. For a brief moment she thinks she ought to dictate this to the new girl at some point. Or to her successor.

The cappuccino arrives soon after Sensenbrink has launched into his presentation; he's going to have to start from the beginning, which is a good thing, she thinks, as not everyone was quiet first time around. Besides, she loves staring at the logo of her programme: "Nadeche Hackenbusch: An Angel in Adversity". They added a cutesy doe with dungarees and slightly too large breasts. The doe looks like her, even though she'd never dream of wearing dungarees.

"The ratings are epic," Sensenbrink says, fading in some graphics, "and they're still heading north. We're getting the old codgers and the young ones. This topic is still our secret sauce and nobody else's. Of course it helps that nobody believed in the format to begin with."

"Apart from me," she insists. O.K., she didn't have another offer at the time, but there's no television show that isn't better with her, and because of her.

"It's hard to believe nothing's staged," a blonde woman says. She's met the blonde many a time, but can't remember her name. The blonde is young, thirty at most, at the very most, and yet at the last meeting she said several things that made the others sit up and take notice. Kalkberger? Kalkbrenner? It sounded a bit like something you might find in a D.I.Y. store. She'll make a note of the name next time. But Nadeche can't tell for sure how the remark was meant. Was it sarcastic? Sceptical?

"I suggest you check again," she says harshly.

"No, no, I don't doubt it in the least," the blonde says. "The authenticity is what makes the programme stand out. Some of those scenes, they practically stink through the T.V. screen. I'm sure I can speak for everybody in the room when I say we're full of admiration."

They all rap their knuckles on the table in appreciation. She smiles and makes it look bashful. "I can assure you I want everything to stay authentic in future too. After all, the key point is that these people need our help."

"Yes, but I couldn't do it." These words come from a quiet, shy mouse of a woman at the far end of the table. "I get annoyed with myself for thinking this, but I couldn't pull it off. Sometimes I think how cute these refugee kids look – but that episode from a couple of weeks back."

"Ow, exactly. The one with the teeth . . ."

"Ugh, the teeth episode."

Nadeche sees Kärrner smiling. Kärrner rarely says a word, even though it's his television company. He controls meetings with his face.

"That's how it is . . ." she says.

"Sure, but the teeth of those kids were practically black!"

"That was the one time I thought for a brief moment that you might be fiddling it," the blonde says. "That you'd cherry-picked some especially bad cases. I honestly didn't believe it could be as bad as that."

"Oh, but it is. You just need to take a look at the parents' teeth. People like that, you really need to start from scratch."

"And then they give their kids handfuls of sugar cubes . . ." The mousy lady is beside herself. "I could have screamed at the telly."

"I know," Nadeche says sympathetically. "Oral hygiene, it's like, mad. And it's not like they all lost their toothbrushes fleeing to Europe – they never had them in the first place.

They think toothpaste is some kind of sealant. So we have to step in and help."

"Spot on," Sensenbrink says. "That's our reach-out. But the great thing is: we've hit a nerve. It's not just the ratings that tell us this, it's also the reactions on Facebook. So sometimes it's ugly, but at the end of the day: it shocks. It leaves the viewers speechless. It's no coincidence that the first thing people think of is the teeth episode."

"The dentist's visit to the hostel . . ." This comes from an executive somebody or other who's remained anonymous so far. Shaking his head, he puffs up his fat cheeks and slowly exhales. "The way he peered into their mouths, one after the other, and then grimaced – there's no way you can act that . . ."

"He didn't need to act," Nadeche Hackenbusch says. "What he found was terrible. Things happen that I'd never have believed possible. There are children younger than four whose mouths smell like a septic tank."

The bigwigs in the T.V. company exchange glances. They purse their lips and raise their eyebrows to acknowledge the gravity of the situation. She wonders whether this is the time to drop her fabulous phrase right into the middle of this silence. The phrase that always makes such a splash whenever she utters it to a newspaper or into a camera, and everyone is taken aback by how such a beautiful woman can be so thoughtful and have such a grasp of economic relations. But then the possibly critical blonde gets in before her and says:

"And this in one of the richest countries on this earth."

She even says "this earth", which always sounds more reproachful than "the earth". What a bitch!

"Frau Karstleiter is so on point," Sensenbrink responds. "But this is what's growing our business. These images may be hard to stomach, but they shock people in a way it's almost impossible to do these days. It signposts us exactly the way to go: where it hurts."

"We're there already," she says energetically. "If you like I'll show you my feet after a day's filming."

There is warm and sympathetic laughter all around, including from Sensenbrink. "I think we're all well aware of the A1 effort you're putting in. You eat, drink and sleep 'Angel in Adversity'. And it's your baby – its success is totally dependent on Nadeche Hackenbusch. It thrives on your commitment, your authenticity, your willingness to get your hands dirty and your feet sore. But – and please forgive this play on words – despite the punishment those feet have already sustained, today we'd like to propose that you go one step further."

"It's the first I've heard of it." She tries to wrinkle a few lines of anger on her brow. If there's one thing she hates, it's people trying to control her. She knows how difficult it is to become independent and remain so. She knows best what's good for her, and she knows that advertising people, management consultants and media people like to do the same things they've already done to others. But unless she goes her own way she won't remain the one and only Nadeche Hackenbusch. She's not risking much; her position right now is too good for someone to put the screws on her. All the same, a little frown ought to signal that Sensenbrink's treading on thin ice. But then she realises that it'll only make her look silly. You can't have everything: wrinkles *and* Botox.

"Of course. You won't have heard anything about it yet, the idea's fresh out of the wrapper," Sensenbrink says hastily. "But don't worry, you know we don't decide anything here without running it up your flagpole first—"

"I have the final word," she says, somewhat too defiantly.

"Yes, sure, you have the final word, period. What would 'Angel in Adversity' be without *the* Nadeche Hackenbusch? Nonetheless I beg you to listen to the proposal. We believe we've got a once-in-a-lifetime opportunity here . . ."

Reassured by Sensenbrink's tone and efforts to placate her, she smiles her priceless smile – which even the *Frankfurter Allgemeine Zeitung* once described as "overwhelming" – and says, "O.K, then."

She sees Frau Karstleiter stand up, go to the front of the room and place her notes on the lectern. She shows slight signs of tension, not only because she's talking to Nadeche Hackenbusch, clearly, but because the scope of the project is huge. A pretty good sign.

"Not only has the second series of 'Angel in Adversity' been a huge success," Karstleiter begins, "the programme also exhibits enormous potential for growth. Viewer surveys have shown that Nadeche Hackenbusch represents honest commitment. The public particularly likes the shift away from one-off features. Because we're always filming in the same hostel, the viewers are able to see the overall improvement in the refugees' situation. We ought to take advantage of this momentum and enthusiasm. And so, Frau Hackenbusch, with a third of the series yet to be broadcast, we'd like to finish with a special. Perhaps even a multi-part special."

Nadeche frowns as best she can. This just sounds like more. And, as she knows only too well, more is not always good. Once, for television, she shared an apartment with models. This was ramped up in pre-publicity, but it turned out to be appalling, downmarket television. Someone had wanted to plug the gap between series of "Germany's Top Model" with model-related stuff. Although she was gone after the second episode, she remembers the ghastly award ceremony. Not the Lanxess Arena, not the Allianz Arena, not New York or Paris, but beside a pool at a four-star dump in Mallorca, with no audience at all. It was so miserable, they might as well have handed the winner her ugly prize at a bus stop. This is why Nadeche says sceptically, "To be honest, that sounds a bit cheap."

"Not as far as the budget's concerned," Karstleiter immediately assures her. "We're making more money available than for the normal episodes. We're taking this very seriously."

The comment about the budget works. More budget means more for her.

"We want to strengthen our product rather than weaken it. We want Nadeche Hackenbusch to get to the heart of the matter. We want you to go where a lack of toothbrushes is the least of people's problems. To the largest refugee camp in the world."

This catches her off guard.

"Are you crazy?"

"What do you mean?"

"Do you know like, what's going on down there? People are being shot!"

"People aren't being shot," Karstleiter says.

"How do you know that?"

"They wouldn't be able to amass all those refugees if people were being shot."

"If people weren't being shot there wouldn't be any refugees. Take a look at the news!"

"Frau Hackenbusch, Frau Hackenbusch, we don't see any cause for concern," Sensenbrink chips in, "the whole place is teeming with military and blue helmets and aid organisations!"

"I don't believe that. Where did you get that from?"

"Well I can't reel the programmes off the top of my head, but why else would all those refugees be ending up there? I think if you peel the onion—"

"I don't have the time to be glued to some news channel. Put me together a dossieux and I'll have it checked out."

"Frau Hackenbusch," Karstleiter says gently, like a broad-shouldered orderly holding out a straitjacket, "do you really think we'd send you somewhere dangerous? We'd be risking just as much as you."

"I see it a bit differently."

Sensenbrink looks at Kärrner, who pulls an unenthusiastic face. He clears his throat and then says firmly, "Perhaps we ought to look at the whole thing from a different dugout. Nobody here's trying to deny that the risks are greater than for some studio filming in Ossendorf. And so the crucial question is whether it's worth it."

"I can give you the answer right now: no way!"

"Sure, the idea went down here like that too," Sensenbrink says, now with incredible earnestness. "But just for a moment see us as the partner. *Your* partner."

No matter how much she baulks at this, no matter how reluctant she is to have anything taken out of her hands, Nadeche cannot stop Sensenbrink getting his foot in the door and forcing it open a crack.

"First and foremost, of course, we're thinking of our own interests, but we can't deny that sometimes our interests and your interests are on the same hymn sheet. And just let me disambiguate: if we're discussing these risks with you, it's only because we see opportunities. For us – I'm not going to keep the kimono closed on that one – but for you too. Just think how you and we can synergise with this special. It's the perfect storm. At a stroke you're going to leave all those home-furnishing and renovation formats in the trolley park. The blind date and missing persons' programmes—"

"These days I don't reckon anybody thinks the B-listers fronting those shows are in my league," Nadeche says truculently.

"We don't need to make comparisons," Sensenbrink says, coming to her defence. "But just incubate this for a moment: it will prove your seriousness to an extent never seen before. Nadeche Hackenbusch goes where others do not dare. Like Antonia Rados."

"Antonella who?"

"Antonia Rados. The R.T.L. woman who always pops up in war zones."

"Never heard of her."

"It's not important. Let's just say it would put you in Günther Jauch territory," Sensenbrink says patiently. "There's been only one like him in Germany before. Do you remember Margarethe Schreinemakers?"

Of course.

Everyone using Botox remembers Schreinemakers. Best T.V. slot, three, four hours, advert breaks as long as an entire soap, no problem if it overran. That was the heyday of infotainment. And everyone would have loved to take home what Schreinemakers took home.

She should have have paid tax on it all, or something like that. But this won't happen to Nadeche; she always pays her taxes. Last time she just said, "Right, I want 2.5 million after tax and all that. You must have someone in your accounts department who can sort it."

They did.

"You'd be the new Margarethe Schreinemakers. But with the radiance of Angelina Jolie," that bloody Karstleiter now adds.

Could Karstleiter tell from her face that the Schreinemakers comment had worked? She tries not to give anything away, ever; she's not an amateur, after all. But Sensenbrink had hit a nerve and now this Margarethe Jolie, it takes root in her head straightaway. That and the fact that as Angelina Schreinemakers she'll still be able to command screen presence when the day comes that she actually needs

Botox. Because up till now it's just been a precautionary measure. Pyrolactic.

She doesn't make any promises, of course. She handles this visit to the T.V. company with the confidence she's renowned for. But when she's back in the limousine, once more dictating a section of her life philosophy to the new girl, Nadeche is unusually lacking in concentration. She's almost annoyed by this, and yet her mind keeps turning to the trailer for the show, as if it's already in the can. The earthy voice that says:

"And Nadeche Hackenbusch's next guest this evening: His Holiness."

# 3

The refugee is trying very hard to walk normally, which isn't easy as it doesn't feel normal. He can't yet tell if his gait looks more natural. The others are staring and it's making him nervous. He ducks his head slightly, but from the reaction this gets he realises it's a mistake; he must look like a stork with a hunchback. So, a change of plan: chest out, head up and a broad grin.

That's better.

He's got be careful to not start waving graciously at everyone, like the old queen of England.

Should he have done it earlier? He couldn't have. Not that he spent a long time thinking about it. And he isn't even sure it's right. But he can't change it now.

Then he begins to relax; the grin turns into a smile. He lets himself sink into his new role. They're looking at him, of course. What else would they be doing? If every day is exactly the same as the previous, any slight variation is exciting. What's interesting is that his air of self-confidence is eliciting other reactions: less giggling, more encouraging nods. Two children follow him, just like they sometimes run behind cars. More might have joined in, but then an actual car does arrive and the cloud of dust it throws up scatters the children.

The refugee toys with the new situation. A girl catches his eye and he responds with a dance step. She laughs. It feels good. It *was* right. It was worth it. He should have done this earlier. Turning the corner, the refugee sees Mahmoud.

Mahmoud is squatting on the floor, watching a group of girls. The refugee thrusts his hands into his trouser pockets and stands beside him. Mahmoud doesn't move a muscle.

"It's pointless," the refugee says to him.

"You don't know that," Mahmoud says without looking up.

"I do. You shouldn't be staring like that."

"I'm staring like everyone else."

"Exactly," he says. "Everyone stares at Nayla, everyone stares like you do. How's she supposed to see that you're special?"

"It's got nothing to do with Nayla."

"Who then? Elani?"

"Maybe. Maybe not."

"That would be even more stupid. Elani will think you're staring at Nayla too. And then Elani will think you're like everyone else."

Mahmoud looks up at the refugee. "Got a better idea?"

"Why don't you just go over, real cool, so Nayla starts thinking about how to get rid of you. And when she opens her mouth . . . then you turn to Elani."

Mahmoud looks at the girls again. After a moment

he says, "That's your routine. You're a talker. I'm more of a watcher. My strength lies in my gaze. Where are those shoes from?"

Mahmoud hasn't looked down once. Maybe his strength really does lie in his gaze.

"You can save a bit of cash if you don't smoke," the refugee says, offering Mahmoud a cigarette.

Mahmoud takes one and says, "But you save even more if you scrounge." Still on his haunches, he puts the cigarette behind his ear and turns to the refugee like a car mechanic inspecting damage. "They look nice," he says approvingly, "they even look genuine. If I didn't know that you can't get genuine ones here, I'd say—"

"Of course you can."

The refugee rolls the packet of cigarettes into the left sleeve of his T-shirt. It's important to keep them on show; in any camp cigarettes are indispensable, even for non-smokers. Everyone wants cigarettes, if not for themselves then their parents, siblings or for a friend like Mahmoud.

Mahmoud impatiently taps the refugee's leg. Then he shakes it until the refugee lifts his foot so that the shoe mechanic can inspect the sole too. "Great colour. Who did you get them from? Mbeke? In that case they're not genuine."

"That's for sure."

"What did I tell you? Not genuine."

"No. They're not from Mbeke."

"Who then? I know Ndugu isn't dealing in shoes anymore."

"They're not from Ndugu."

"Then they're definitely not genuine."

The refugee laughs.

Mahmoud straightens up. "Go on. Tell me!"

"O.K. . . . Zalando."

"Zalando doesn't sell shoes."

"Maybe he's making an exception."

Mahmoud looks at him. Nobody knows Zalando's real name. All they know is that he works for the organisation and he's German. And that if you ask him a favour, he always gives the same answer. "Why are you asking me? Am I Zalando?" What a stupid thing to say, when nobody knows his real name. Maybe he is the famous Zalando after all.

"So you're not going to tell me," Mahmoud says. He plucks the cigarette from behind his ear and holds it out to the refugee, his eyebrows raised.

The refugee takes a lighter from his pocket. If you want to make people happy with cigarettes you need to be able to light the cigarette too. Otherwise they'll look for someone with a light and you won't have that useful conversation. They'll stop listening or forget half of what you're saying. Mahmoud and he wander down the dusty street in silence. Mahmoud looks at his smartphone.

"In Berlin they're eating potatoes and pigs' trotters now."

"Who wants to go to Berlin?"

"Not me."

"Me neither."

"It's lovely here!" Mahmoud exclaims.

"It's magnificent!" the refugee says, throwing out his arms. "The most beautiful stones in the world. Free sun. What have they got in Berlin that we don't have here?"

"Blonde women," Mahmoud says, then takes a drag of his cigarette.

"So what? Who wants blonde women?"

"Me. To try out."

"But Mahmoud!" The refugee steps in Mahmoud's way. "Blonde women are the devil's own creation. If you let blondes into your house you'll reap bad luck. You'll fall ill. Your crops will wither. Listen to your old father: a blonde woman will curse you and all your goats will starve."

"What luck! My goats have already starved. So now I'm owed a blonde."

"You've never kept goats."

"Even more unfair! I might get two blondes now."

They both laugh.

"So, where are the shoes from?"

"I bought them."

"New?"

"New."

"Where did you get the cash?"

"You've got cash too."

"Sure. But I'm not going to spend it. At least, not on something as stupid as shoes."

"On what then? A smuggler?"

"You bet your arse. Only a premier smuggler, mind."

"Hear ye, one and all!" the refugee mocks. "A premier smuggler, no less!"

"Well, well, well. Someone else with travel plans."

This is Miki, standing behind his bar on the camp highway. He cobbled it together from planks and chipboard, and a few scraps of corrugated iron and the bonnet of an old Mercedes provide the shade. The original plan was to paint it all one colour. But you know how it is, someone pops by for a visit, it rains, your best friend won't help because you're fooling around with his wife, and before you know it five years have gone by and you find yourself waiting for the bar to fall down so you can build a new one. But this one's too stable for that.

The bar isn't so small that Miki can run it undisturbed, yet it's small enough that the gangs aren't always breathing down his neck. But without gang protection, he doesn't always get electricity for his fridge.

"Well, I *am* going to leave!" Mahmoud stops. "I mean, this shithole isn't everyone's dream destination."

"Don't be so sure," Miki says. Reaching beneath the bar, he throws an ice cube across the street. "How about a cold drink before the big trip?"

The refugee is about to catch it, but Mahmoud snatches it out of the air and stuffs it in his mouth.

"Thanks, I've got one."

"Come on," the refugee says, "I'll treat you." He nudges Mahmoud over to Miki's bar. "Two beers. Export. And have one yourself."

"Thank you, kind sir," Miki says loftily, placing three bottles on the counter. Mahmoud is taken aback.

"New shoes, export beer. Have I missed something?"

"Don't know yet," the refugee says. "Just drink. Perhaps it was a mistake to buy you one."

"Beer is never a mistake," Miki says, taking a large gulp. It's very hot.

"Have the smugglers dropped their prices, by any chance?" Mahmoud probes.

"Yours won't have," the refugee teases him, then leans to-wards Miki. "Mahmoud is saving for a premier smuggler."

Miki looks at him wide-eyed.

"Exactly," Mahmoud says. "No way is this man heading off in some dark, cramped lorry."

"What then?" Miki leans against the fridge. He takes the only beer glass from the shelf and starts to polish it.

"This man is going to settle down in the shade till the smuggler comes. In a white Mercedes. With cream-coloured seats. Then the smuggler springs out of the driver's seat. He's wearing a uniform like those men who work in expensive hotels, and he's carrying a parasol. He runs around the car, holds the door open for me and says, "Please, get in, Bwana Mahmoud!"

"He runs around the car to hold the door open for you?" Miki holds the glass up to the sun.

"So it is written, O non-believers. I get into the car and we cross the border. He drives at a leisurely speed and asks whether I like the view through the window. 'I can take a dif-ferent route if you like, your wish is my command, Bwana Mahmoud,' and I say, 'No, this is fine. Just make sure we don't get there too early.'"

"That mustn't happen, of course not," Miki mocks.

"Yes, yes, make your silly jokes . . . you haven't got a clue. You know nothing about Germany. But I do, and let me tell you, Germans don't like it if you turn up early."

"If you turn up *late*," the refugee corrects him.

"And early."

"Rubbish!"

"That's what the smuggler says too, but I say, 'It's not rubbish. Think how awkward it would be for their new Merkel if I get there and he hasn't got my room ready yet.' So I say to him. 'Let's cross the border again.' And he says, 'We can cross the border as many times as you like, Bwana Mahmoud. But the new Merkel rang earlier to say that he's emptied two hotels for you. You have to choose one.' And then . . .'" Mahmoud takes a swig of beer before casually replacing the bottle exactly on the wet ring on the wooden table, "then I say, 'I'll take whichever hotel has the bedroom and toilet on the same floor.'"

"Good plan," the refugee says. He clinks his beer against Mahmoud's and Miki's bottles and drinks.

"It is good," Miki says, "but you're wrong. If there's anyone who's not going to end up in a dark, cramped lorry, then it's *this* man." He jerks a thumb towards himself. "Because this man's staying here. Here, in the shithole. But you, my dear friend, you'll be ripped off and your corpse will be shoved out into the desert. On a cream-coloured handcart."

"Spoilsport," Mahmoud says.

"But the best thing is: I'm already where you want to be. Because here the toilet is on the same floor, in any direction. You won't find a floor like this in the whole of Europe:

fifty square kilometres. It's the largest suite in the world!"

"Hahaha!" Mahmoud says. He's no longer looking at Miki or the refugee, but up at the endless blue sky beyond the tents. His fantasy may have been over the top, but it was lovely, the refugee thinks, and if Mahmoud looked them in the eye he would only see that Miki is right. Too much time has passed since Germany opened her doors. Since they still had a woman as their Merkel. Anybody within striking distance at the time had won the lottery. But that moment's not going to repeat itself. They've been here for a year and a half now, and these months will be followed by many more.

The refugee turns and leans his back on the counter beside Mahmoud. It is afternoon and the faster, stronger children are coming back from collecting wood. When the refugee first noticed them in the camp, they would be finished by lunchtime. But when millions of people need fuel – wood, twigs, dung, whatever – it takes longer to find. Millions, and growing by the day. The equation is simple: new people arrive, but nobody can leave. In the past, the influx of people was moved on, to Morocco, Libya, Egypt, or back to their home countries. But that was in the past. Before Europe closed its borders one by one.

A sand-coloured dog saunters up. There is not much dog left of him, in truth; he's little more than a fur-covered, panting basket on legs. He scours the ground, his eyes skimming the sides of the street. He can see there's nothing worth sniffing around here. He stops and turns to the three men at the bar. He only has one eye, but in the camp that's enough. Nobody beckons the dog, but nobody's hurling stones at him either. The dog makes the effort to wag his tail. Miki flaps a hand at him wearily. The dog stops wagging his tail and continues on his way. This is how Europe thought it could deal with the refugee question.

When the people came aboard boats, Europe tried to close off the Mediterranean. And when Europe realised that you can't close a sea, that you can't even keep watch over a twisting coastline, umpteen thousand kilometres long, they moved the border back onto land, but this time in Africa. They paid Egypt, Algeria, Tunisia and Morocco, and gave some to the Libyans too, although less of course. Because even now they don't know who to hand over the money to in Libya. But this wasn't enough for the Europeans. Not least because the north Africans kept wondering out loud what might happen if they didn't keep quite so vigilant a watch over the borders. It was something they'd learned from the Turks, having seen how much respect and recognition you can earn if you play around with the refugee button. So the Europeans spent more money and drew their next line south of the Sahara. Which is precisely why Mahmoud's dream of premier smugglers isn't even funny anymore. Because now there are *only* premier smugglers.

"I'll let you in on a secret," the refugee says, without looking at the other two.

His eyes wander across the camp, the endless camp. He's often walked to the outer edge. You can do that if you've got plenty of time on your hands. On one side you see nothing, and in the nothingness there's dust and sand and stones and more nothingness in between. And on the other side you see tents and tent-like huts and hut-like tents and tents with patches and tents with holes and abandoned tents and tents bursting with people, and if you've nothing else to do you can ponder which view is the more desolate. If you can't decide, you go to bed and come back a few days later. You could also come back the next day, but anyone with even half their marbles doesn't inflict that on themselves.

"I'll let you in on a secret," the refugee says again.

"Huh?" Miki is making squeaking noises with the glass.

"About the shoes."

"There's a shoe secret?"

Mahmoud points silently to the ground. Miki leans right over the wobbly, creaking counter and the refugee feels the plank of wood dig into his back.

"Wow! New shoes!"

The thing about the people smugglers was the biggest lie of all. It was said they wanted to combat the smugglers. But governments can't combat people smugglers. It's the same with drugs and prostitutes and alcohol. The only thing governments can influence is the price. Every police officer, every warship they dispatch only ever ends up raising the price, and this is exactly what happened. Prices rose and they're still rising. Few people can afford the tariffs these days, which means that the smugglers can work less for more money. Not only that, but now they don't have to give away so much of it because they don't need to involve third parties anymore.

In the past, when the inflatable dinghy option still worked, it was an organised mass market with loads of jobs throughout Africa. There was always a need for people who passed on information, communicated meeting points, recruited clients for transports, acquired life vests. A boat full of people requires all manner of errands and a skipper. And so even someone without a penny to their name could earn themselves the crossing by being prepared to act as navigator on the dinghy. It was a fair opportunity for all involved, because any idiot can steer a rubber dinghy. But now?

Now, rather than dispatching eighty people in a dinghy they send off eight in a light aircraft. Or an old helicopter. The pilot is an expert. Although the aeroplane and helicopter need maintenance, and that's another job for experts. These days the smugglers employ only experts. And the now-redundant helpers swell the refugee camps.

"I've come to the conclusion that it's pointless to save," the refugee says.

"Are you giving up?" Mahmoud asks.

"That's not what I'm saying. What I'm saying is, saving is pointless."

"A good attitude." Miki claps him on the shoulder from behind. "Another beer?"

"I said saving is pointless. Doesn't mean getting smashed is a good idea."

"So how are you going to get the cash together?" Mahmoud says.

"No idea. But tell me again how it's supposed to work."

Mahmoud falls silent. What should he say? No matter how much beer Mahmoud guzzled, the refugee would still be right. Just as the smugglers' prices are going up, the chances of earning the money inside the camp are sinking. Even though the camp now has two million inhabitants. Enough for an entire city. But it can never become a city.

For the ailing country that is home to this camp has enough cities that don't work already. It has a government that wasn't in power three years ago, and which probably won't be in power five years from now. It keeps being attacked by two other groups that could just as easily be in power, and in all likelihood will be soon. The only reason the camp exists and continues to grow is that it offers something you can't get anywhere else: security, however scant.

The security comes from U.N. and European money. In return, the government currently in power helps to protect the camp, to its own advantage: money, development aid and deliveries of defensive weapons continue to flow. Essentially, they're leasing one of the most barren areas on earth for a profitable sum, which is why the two rebel groups strive even harder to assume power themselves, to rake in their share of the refugee harvest.

As a result the camp has scarcely been touched in fifteen years. There is enough security for survival, but not for a future. You can get along in the camp, like Miki. One day you might even be able to buy a new second-hand fridge for your beer, if you dare believe in that much of a future. But nobody's going to build a factory here. Nobody's going to invest money in this mass of tents, which might disappear in a fortnight. And nobody will offer work here, because there are no prospects other than dust and sand and drought.

Here a man can earn nothing, and a woman earns only

in the unique way that women have been earning for millennia. But even the most beautiful woman in the world couldn't earn enough to keep pace with the smugglers' prices, which the Europeans have ratcheted up by closing their borders. This is true for everyone in the camp, including Mahmoud. It's even more true of Mahmoud, in fact, because nobody wants to shag him.

"Saving is pointless," the refugee says soberly. "Because even if you do save, every day the gap between what you've got and what the smuggler demands is widening."

"It doesn't have to be a premier smuggler," Mahmoud says.

"Does that make any difference?"

"What difference will new shoes make?" Miki puts his beer glass back on the shelf. "You're not actually going anywhere."

"But I walk better."

And that's the truth. Most people here wear flip-flops or slippers, and the children wear nothing on their feet.

"It's not as if you have to walk that far here."

"But at least walking doesn't cost anything."

The refugee reflects for a moment. Maybe he's onto something, some association he can't yet pin down.

"Well?" Mahmoud looks expectantly at the refugee.

"Look, I can't afford a smuggler because I don't have the money. But I do have time. I've got all the time in the world. I've been here for a year and a half. If I'd walked only ten kilometres a day in that time, I'd be five thousand kilometres from here by now."

To begin with Mahmoud can't think of anything to say. Miki is silent too.

"Five thousand kilometres . . . not bad at all." The refugee is thinking as he's talking, or vice versa. He doesn't know where he's going with this, but he has the feeling there are other useful thoughts scattered about. "Five thousand kilometres. Free of charge. And I'd still have the money that would have gone to the smuggler."

"Sure, and maybe a bit extra too," Mahmoud grumbles. "What are you actually living off on this march of yours?"

"You're right, I have to eat and drink. But think how much I could eat and drink for the money I've saved?"

"They say Berlin's pricey," Miki warns, but now he sounds more curious. He wants to know where these ideas are leading. He gives the refugee another beer.

"Hey!" Mahmoud protests. "What about me?"

"You come up with a bright idea and you'll get one too," Miki says.

"So, I've got a little less money and I'm five thousand kilometres further on—"

"What about the borders?" Mahmoud reminds him.

"I could get guides. They don't cost much."

"Yeah right, they'll be just waiting to give you a special price. Well, if I were going to offer a special price it would be to my premier smuggler. They come back, you see? Special price for regular customers."

"I haven't worked it out in that much detail . . ." the refugee admits.

"And then Mr Special Price is standing by the European

border installations. They tell you you come from a fabulous country and don't know just how lucky you are to live there. And that's that, goodbye."

"O.K., O.K. . . ."

"Great," Miki says. "And I just gave you a beer for that!"

"I didn't promise a miracle!" the refugee says, trying to fob them off, but it's too late. He had an idea, was interrupted at the wrong moment, and now it's gone. He tries to pick up the threads, he closes his eyes and wills his stream of thought to come back. Just like dreams you can return to if you do it right.

"I've got no money, but I do have plenty of time," the refugee repeats. "And I've got two feet—"

"We've heard this already."

And then the idea is gone for good. Angrily, he picks up his beer and takes a swig before Miki thinks of putting the bottle away again. He does this sometimes. If you turn up to Miki's late in the day and drunk, you might be served a bottle that's only half full.

"But one thing's for sure," he says. "Whether I save or not, I'll never keep up with the transport prices."

"Come on," Mahmoud consoles him. "It only looks that way at the moment. Maybe prices will fall and we'll be back on track."

"They're not going to fall," the refugee says assertively. "Europe doesn't want us. Nobody wants us. And the less someone wants you, the more expensive the journey becomes."

None of them can think of anything to say to this. But

to underline his resolve, to emphasise once again the validity of his initial idea, he buys another round of beers. And while they drink and brood, he is assailed repeatedly by the thought that a unique opportunity has just gone begging.

# 4

Because the chair hasn't arrived yet, the atmosphere in the meeting room is reminiscent of a classroom when the teacher comes in late. Which is astonishing, because this class is called the federal government. To be fair, it is the summer recess. Parliament is having a break, virtually everyone is having a break, and the federal government only meets once a fortnight. The chancellor is on holiday, as is the vice chancellor, not to mention most of the ministers, which is why they send their deputies even though they have nothing to say. There are people here today who find themselves at the cabinet table for the very first time. They've all been here before, of course, and tried out the black chairs, including the one in the middle, they've taken selfies with their finger on the chancellor's call button, but not all have been sent here on previous occasions specifically to sit in these chairs and actually do something useful.

In this instance the word "useful" is perhaps a bit of an exaggeration, as today they're basically just going to run through the agenda. And not even that if the minister for the environment – the longest-serving among them and chair of the meeting – doesn't turn up.

The under-secretary scans the room for familiar faces. Lohm ought to be here. Like Lohm, he is one of the youngest; only Amsel from the Greens is younger. In spite of this the under-secretary has been in this room more often than most, more often even than Lohm. Leubl, minister of the interior, sends him as a matter of principle, and not only in summer either.

"Because I know you're always thinking beyond the agenda," Leubl said the first time.

"It's very kind of you to say so, but the others do that too—"

"Do me a favour and spare me the loyalty, would you? At least when it's just us. You're the only one I actually chose. I've got Rogler because the minister president still owes him something. Schwanstatt is a pompous old bag on a Women's Farmers' Association and Christian Democratic Employees' Association ticket. If I sent her out I could be sure she'd get lost on the way home, and believe me, nothing would make me happier. The only reason I allowed those two to be forced on me was to get you into the bargain."

"I never knew—"

"You were thinking that this old man was gaga, were you? He bought three lottery tickets and drew two blanks?"

Leubl gave him such a stern look that he opted to keep his mouth shut. Then Leubl sat at his desk, opened a file and began to read. Without looking up, he said, "So, if I can't make cabinet, you're my man. Or if I don't fancy it. I expect you to gear yourself up for the job."

And the under-secretary *is* prepared, even though there's not much to look at today beyond a report on energy research. Not even energy transition, but *research*, which is about as important as the film the teacher sticks on for the class on the last day of term.

Eager tweeting fills the room with its silence. In theory at least, because Karsdorff-Gundelingen and Gröner from the ministry of transport haven't yet worked out how to switch off the keyboard sound on their phones. There is a barrage of clicking, letter after letter, the technology and method about as useful as a white stick for sighted people, and the only thing one can be sure of is that neither could leak information to the press from under the table. He can't think who would want to swap information with them in the first place. K.-G. is as stupid as she looks, and Gröner is such a henchman of the automobile industry it's embarrassing. Not only is he as thick as two short planks, he's also pig-headed. All the journalists, even those from *A.D.A.C. Motorwelt*, refer to him as "Groaner".

The under-secretary waves at Grevensen, who he respects. For forty-five years Grevensen has been exuding Social Democratic cordiality in North Rhine–Westphalia. He began with the Young Socialists, on the left wing, but not a radical. You can only really appreciate the significance of his grassroots work when you talk to him in private, share a glass of wine in his M.P.'s apartment and check out his jazz collection. And when you see that he devours all the American writers and a load of French ones in their original languages, and admits to you how difficult he finds it to listen to the appalling drivel of his party comrades, the slogans repeated over and over, their unbearable complacency, and what an unbelievable struggle it is for him not to flee, screaming, from a colliery band.

"The songs are so fucking tedious. And that sluggish tempo! As if they were all trumpeting asthmatics! Brass-band music as a driver of social integration is all well and good, but do they actually have to perform it? I spent six years watching my children regurgitate their scripts in the school theatre, so if you're talking about support for culture, then all I can say is I've done my bit!"

Then they thrust this young candidate in front of his nose. But to make sure he keeps his trap shut and actively praises his successor to boot, he's been given a three-year finale in the ministry of justice. And this is precisely what the under-secretary likes so much about Grevensen. Many people would view this as a first step into retirement, as early leave, and they'd start drinking at eleven in the morning so that their well-paid time passed more quickly. But Grevensen plays the game to the final whistle like a pro. He'll definitely have read the material for today. He'll have checked to see whether there are any clauses in which, unintentionally, positions are revealed, admissions made, little things let through on the nod. He's dead certain to have asked colleagues whether he'll find any dealings or remarks from their own department in it. And he'll have realised that the material is in fact as dull as it looks. Which is more than 80 per cent of the people here have, including the two ministers who've actually turned up in person.

The under-secretary's mobile lights up. WhatsApp.

"Have you heard? N.H. now advertising washing-up liquid!"

From Lohm, of course. There's only one answer to that.

"Headline news."

No sooner has he pressed "send" than the next message has arrived:

"Even more fairy than Fairy."

"You're such a closet queen. Where are you?"

Lohm bursts into the room with broad, cheeky grin and winks at him. He returns the gesture by rolling his eyes in a friendly/bored way. They've known each other since they were law students. Lohm was good-looking in those days, even after he joined the Greens, and back then their dress sense was as dubious as it is today. And he was pretty smart too. You could always have a good laugh with Lohm. But totally hetero, unfortunately.

It was while they were still at university that Lohm advised him to actively play the gay card. He was one of the first the under-secretary had confided in. And Lohm was proved right. In Guido Westerwelle's F.D.P. it would have been a doddle; they had a slight tradition of homosexuality, the minor extravagance of a 5-per cent party which is little more than a fringe group. In the C.D.U., on the other hand, it's something else altogether. You need balls.

"Yes, but you've got them," Lohm said.

"You don't have a clue what you're talking about."

"Don't I? I drive a 1978 Porsche 911. I fill it with leaded petrol, not because it needs it, but because it likes it. I'm currently building my own home, way out of town, with triple garage *and* carport so that my 1965 Jeep can stay nice and dry even when my girlfriend turns up with her Alfa Spider. What do you think the Greens make of someone like me?"

Lohm was right: the under-secretary does have balls.

He could have opted for the easy route. But he wanted to be taken seriously and so went down Grevensen's hard path, with the difference that he didn't caress the party's soul in the process. He did the rounds of the local associations, he spoke to everyone and told them all he was gay before drinking them under the table or fleecing them at cards. That evening when he was in his mid-twenties, when he took a parliamentary party secretary, the deputy secretary-general and a special advisor to the cleaners in a game of Schafkopf, was the stuff of legend. When it was time to settle he said, "I'll accept cheques but not blowjobs. And I'm not just talking to the lady here."

Ever since, Lohm has been teasing him with all the latest gossip about Nadeche Hackenbusch. Because, for reasons he can't fathom, Nadeche Hackenbusch is regarded as a gay icon. This seems to happen regularly. Marianne Rosenberg, he read again recently, is still puzzled as to how and why the honour was bestowed on her. After all, there were others who sang "He belongs to me". But with Nadeche there's really no connection between her and the gay community. You just have to look at her – the way she moves, speaks, behaves in general – to realise that she's as straight as they come, and that her only exceptional feature is her inordinate phoniness. Tommy watches her show on television – what a dreadful woman. Apparently she's doing something meaningful at the moment, but nobody should harbour any doubts that the entire thing is first and foremost a vehicle for Nadeche Hackenbusch, who's using it to get better T.V. slots and more lucrative advertising contracts. He knows people like her, and she doesn't look like the type to be satisfied with any old niche programme. Oh no, Nadeche Hackenbusch wants to make it to the big time.

Here comes the minister for the environment. Normally the journalists would be asked to leave the room at this point, but there aren't any here today – another sign of how uneventful the meeting is going to be. A playgroup for the ministry for the environment and the ministry of economics. Although it looks as though the minister of economics isn't here either. This must have been arranged to allow the other two to shine. Two under-secretaries snicker; the minister of the environment glowers at them.

The under-secretary wears his pensive listening expression so he can inconspicuously observe what he's really interested in: unusual behaviour. He knows there will inevitably be an objection from the ministry of economics, because the document is missing the paragraph about support measures, and he'd be amazed if Klein didn't milk this, to draw the attention to himself again. Klein loves the sound of his own voice.

At some point the minister of the environment will crack a joke about her husband. He's expecting this, but he's watching for anything that's different from the usual. Anything that tells you someone is abandoning a position, implying that they've negotiated a deal with someone. Or that they might even be signalling a complete change in policy direction. But today there's seems to be nothing to discover. He checks the time. With luck the session will be over in an hour. An hour and a half if Klein delivers a lecture and everybody's smart enough to refrain from responding. Unfortunately, at least two of the individuals in the room today make that doubtful. But there's no way it can run beyond one o'clock so he texts Lohm: "Lunch?"

And Lohm texts back: "Ethiopian? Congolese? Nigerian? African is obligatory today!"

"Huh?"

"Haven't you set a Google alert for your sweetheart? N.H. is going to Africa."

## 5

Astrid von Roëll is sitting in Africa, freezing. With the temperature outside at thirty-nine degrees, the *Evangeline* reporter tries unobtrusively to stretch the three-quarter sleeves of her cardigan to four-fifths sleeves. The air conditioning inside the off-road vehicle is switched to fifteen, and she's struggling against both the temperature and her stinginess: the cardigan was slightly too expensive – even slightly way too expensive – and she doesn't want the delicate sleeves to go baggy. She wouldn't care so much were she not sitting opposite Nadeche Hackenbusch, whose expression shows not the slightest hint of discomfort. And Astrid von Roëll doesn't want to come across as someone who didn't know that African off-roaders have air conditioning too. So she's trying to sit there casually, as if her favourite thing about foreign travel is this marvellous difference in temperatures.

As she watches Nadeche Hackenbusch tap something into her smartphone, Astrid endeavours to work out her secret. After all, Nadeche is wearing only a shortish denim skirt, an elegant yet simple top beneath a denim jacket, and canvas plimsolls. It all seems very down-to-earth, apart from the rhinestones, which are trashy, but Astrid has seen one of the labels and she knows you wouldn't get change out of four thousand euros for the outfit, not if you include the shoes and other bits and bobs. But despite the price, this get-up doesn't have an in-built heating system. How is it possible? How can she stand it? Is she wearing invisible thermal underwear?

What an extraordinary woman.

Astrid von Roëll has been monitoring Nadeche Hackenbusch's career from the outset. Her beginnings in that talent show, the embarrassing slip-ups – of course they sneered at first, in the planning meetings. Such naivety. She remembers that at her goddaughter's school, girls would insult each other with the words, "You're such a Nadeche!" or "You total Nadeche!" She went out in the fourth round, of course, having survived the third only because she'd got such brilliant ratings; the YouTube videos were cult viewing and the T.V. execs needed to sell advertising, after all. Her looks and her refreshing genuineness were tailor made for this. Legs that practically went up to her ears, almost too long, in fact, meaning she was always slightly gauche, not completely uncoordinated but often on the verge of crumpling like a very young calf. A most versatile bosom which, depending on the situation, could be thrillingly exaggerated or discreetly hidden beneath clothes, as now. That sensational face, which even back then was breathtakingly beautiful, and yet as normal as that of the assistant at the bakery next door. A smile like a sunrise, a large mouth that was never at rest and spouted an unbelievable amount of rubbish, albeit with an implicit honesty. How could anyone think that giving

Nadeche her own programme might be a good idea? Surely they could see she couldn't deliver lines to camera. Even now she still can't: she's got no idea what it's supposed to sound like. You can play her clips of hundreds of presenters, but she can't hear the difference. Which is why she sounded ever more distorted with every desperate attempt. More uncertain and less like herself. This went down badly; the viewers noticed too. At first the ratings were middling, then dreadful.

The media industry can be cruel to women. And Astrid von Roëll knows this better than anyone. She's been with *Evangeline* for sixteen years now, but she never fails to be shocked. What happened to Esther Schweins from "R.T.L. Saturday Night"? Or Tanja Schumann? They used to be so funny, but now? All the guys from the programme have found other homes, but what about the women? Schumann had to resort to "I'm a Celebrity . . .", as if there hadn't been enough misery in her life. Nadeche had definitely made a better fist of it.

Astrid von Roëll can't recall Nadeche ever having disappeared from the television screen altogether. That's down to her extraordinarily eventful life. Her marriage to the national hockey player, her first child (a boy called Scheel), her divorce, her unfortunate singing career at the same time as her affair with YouTuber LeBretzel ("stress on the final syllable, please"), her separation after that rape and the second pregnancy that was the result, almost like the perfect punchline, and the discussion about abortion alongside the trial that ended in a dubious settlement. Then came the happy birth of her second son, Bonno, named Beckham-style after where he was conceived, and the book on motherhood, which Astrid worked on as an advisor, although sadly uncredited. Only when the book flopped was Nadeche ripe for "I'm a Celebrity . . ." But just at that moment came "Angel in Adversity".

The car has leather seats, which take an unbelievably long time to warm up. Good for the connective tissue, at least, Astrid consoles herself. With a sleek movement Nadeche slips her mobile into her Louis Vuitton bag. In the past there were women who looked the height of elegance with a cigarette holder – the smartphone is Nadeche Hackenbusch's cigarette holder.

"What have you brought along for the filming?" she asks, leaning towards Astrid.

"Quite a lot of H&M. They're doing loads of adverts at the moment. Some Hallhuber, and then a couple of suitcases of Doris zu Wagenbach."

"Oh my God!"

"You know how it works with us."

"Doris zu Wagenbach!" She emphasises her contempt to perfection. "Chuck a quilt and a clown into a shredder and there's your evening dress. I have no idea why you're so obsessed with her."

"The editorial office sees her as the up-and-coming fashion—"

"—the up-and-coming fashion talent? Wagenbach? I like your editorial office, but you know how they traipse about. Has your deputy editor worked out how to do up his shirt yet? Every time I see him he's got a button open. And we're lucky it's only the shirt we're talking about. For God's sake, the man works for *Evangeline*! Can't someone tell him?"

Astrid von Roëll tries to stop her teeth from chattering. "We only have to take a couple of pieces from the collection, the rest can go back to where they came from. And we've got plenty of Hallhuber too."

"Hallhuber. Jesus. Oh well, better than nothing." Nadeche slumps back in her seat and breathes out audibly. She stares out of the window. Beyond the tinted glass, a local vanishes into the blue-yellow-grey dust. They can't see much. Their car is the third in the convoy, and the two in front have stirred up clouds of dust. "But I'm relying on you. I don't want it to sound like I'd wear this crap myself."

"Sure," Astrid assures her. "It's just for the filming."

"Yes, but it's awful, isn't it? I mean, like, these are poor people, really poor. They don't have a roof over their heads, they don't have anything to eat. And we come along from one of the richest countries on this earth and what do we bring them? H&M and Doris zu Wagenbach! These people must feel like the lowest of the low."

"It's not as if they usually wear Dior," Astrid tries to appease her.

"Precisely. They usually wear shite and now they can wear crap too."

"But H&M isn't—"

"That's exactly why this planet will, like, never be at peace. There's just no sensitivity for the poorest of the poor!"

"We've got Hallhuber too . . ." Astrid reiterates helplessly. She feels a slight retching in her throat. It's bloody cold in this fucking car, she's been on her feet for twenty-seven hours and she's really tried her damndest. She knows that Nadeche Hackenbusch hates Doris zu Wagenbach, because of the shop@Home thing. Because Wagenbach got Nadeche's slot after sales of HackenPush-ups fell. It was nobody's fault, large breasts were simply no longer in such demand, but Nadeche thinks that a Wagenbach plot lay behind it. And because she, Astrid, knew this, she made an extra effort to get something nice from Hallhuber. It wasn't easy at all. She had to ring the brainless intern on the fashion desk three or four times until she had it wrapped up – and now this angry outburst. She's not normally like this, but for a moment she thinks she might cry. Then Nadeche says, "It's just like this fucking car."

Oh, right.

So she's not to blame for the bad mood, but the car.

At moments like this it really pays off that Astrid has been up close to Nadeche Hackenbusch throughout her career. She would even go as far as to say that Nadeche is her discovery. Ever since she was given her first show on Kabel Eins or Vox or R.T.L.2: "Balderdeche", which became a fiasco. Today Astrid knows everything there is to know about Nadeche. In interviews and features she's documented this wonderful Cinderella story so often, this incomparable rise to stardom, that she feels as if she's gone through all that muck together with Nadeche, the entire length of that stony path, the difficult years after school, the tiny shared flat in Hamburg, the worries about not being able to pay the rent. For may it never be forgotten: Nadeche Hackenbusch, star and role model to hundreds of thousands of girls and young women, comes from a very modest background. And all this time she, Astrid von Roëll, has been at her side. Even during the rape case, a really vile affair with an extremely difficult burden of proof, as with all rape cases. Once again it was very evident how quickly the victim can become the perpetrator. The poor status a woman has in court and in public. Just because in the middle of the trial it transpired that she had been away filming at the time the crime allegedly took place, which led to many in the media doubting her story.

As if you're able to check the date in the middle of being raped.

"Judges in Germany are still living in the 1950s," Astrid von Roëll wrote in a piece at the time. Also: "In a year that has 365 days, the law cannot possibly depend on the coincidence of a correct date." Her piece elicited many readers' letters and comments on the website, and a very large number of women offered their thanks.

"What's wrong with the car?"

Astrid is toying with the idea of winding down a window to let in some African heat, but there's just too much dust. And she doesn't want to give the game away, even if her lips have turned blue. How does Nadeche manage it? "I think it might be new. I'm not so sure about the others, but this one . . . it even smells brand new."

"There's a spray what makes it like that. They always try to pull a fast one on you. But I was expecting that."

"So what's wrong with it?"

"Er, hell-o? The colour?"

"The colour?"

"They were like, you're going to be the new Schreinemakers. So I was like, I want a car with a zebra pattern. Like on 'Daktari'."

"It's a great idea, I thought so the moment I saw it."

"It's great when it's in black and white. But black and *pink*?"

"I thought it had to be like that because it's your show and pink is—"

"Would Schreinemakers drive around in a pink zebra car?"

"I—"

"I may be a bimbo, but I've got eyes in my head. And I can see what non-bimbos drive around in. Daktari saves animals. He spends the whole day thinking of nothing but animals and people, and that's why he drives around in a black-and-white zebra car like everyone else in Africa. Meanwhile I'm like, stuck in a pink box, as if the colour is the most important bit."

These are the moments that really thrill Astrid von Roëll. It's at moments like this that she's a true Nadeche Hackenbusch fan. The fact that Nadeche spots those little details which she'd never have spotted herself. At moments like this she feels that a star isn't a star purely by chance, but because they notice things that pass others by.

"So what are you going to do?"

"They've got to change it. And fast. The production manager's going to have to get hold of a different car, right away."

"Is that even possible?"

"There's no such thing as impossible. And I want to see

the final cut. I swear, if that Cindy von Marzahn slut is on the screen for even a second the shit's really going to hit the fan. ProSieben has already been talking to my agent. They're desperate to have me. But don't write that."

Astrid gives a professional nod. This is the kind of stuff *Evangeline* readers love. Women who are striking-looking and yet not stupid, but assertive. Hard as nails, yet sensitive, as men ought to be more often, whereas in real life only women ever are. A few are, at least. And that's why she's perfect for "Angel in Adversity". Because she gets stuck in, because she's experienced life from the very bottom, because she's a role model for the weakest, because she fights for the little people, for women, for children and, at the end of the first series, for that little dog too. Because she sees what it's like inside the hostel and says straightaway, "There's no such thing as impossible."

They should say that in editorial meetings now and then.

She herself can say it in editorial meetings soon, since they're discussing her promotion to the chief editorial team. At the moment her business card says "Editor at Large", like in the big U.S. publishing houses, but soon that could be "Chief Editorial Member", very soon, in fact. Or, even better, "Chief Editorial Member at Large". It's high time too: she's good at leadership, she's an excellent decision maker. She even styled her corner office herself and everyone thinks it's great.

And of course it's no coincidence that Astrid is responsible for Nadeche Hackenbusch. For she and Nadeche are kindred spirits, of sorts. Astrid can be as hard as nails too, and journalists are capable of virtually anything because they see and hear so much. With that kind of experience you can become a Politician at Large, or a Manager at Large. She might not be quite as stunning as Nadeche Hackenbusch, but she's superb at expressing things in words and that's why Nadeche respects her. She doesn't articulate this all the time, but Astrid is aware of it all the same. And that's why she, exclusively she, is sitting here in the car with the star presenter. After all, Nadeche reads what's written about her and she remembers who is fair and who is mean, like the people at *Gloria*, or that spiteful lot from *G-Style* with their sneaky snaps of celebs without make-up. If you provide a refreshing contrast to that rabble, a good rapport develops naturally. And yet you have to watch out.

For her colleagues are also keen to piggyback on someone like Nadeche Hackenbusch. Every few weeks someone comes to the editorial meeting proposing a Hackenbusch story, most likely a load of rubbish. And Astrid immediately says so: "That can't be true, Nadeche would have told me." She says the name as casually as that, "Nadeche", so everybody knows how close the two of them are and how impossible it would be for a Hackenbusch story to happen without her getting wind of it. The editor-in-chief then tasks her, of course, with checking the story, and she discovers it's utter garbage. Or at least completely different. Like the one about the second pregnancy which her colleague Grant was desperate to hog for himself: "Nadeche Hackenbusch at nine weeks". Bullshit.

It was ten weeks.

"Lou" Grant permanently whining, "But she *is* pregnant, she *is* pregnant," because of course he wants to be in the byline. "You can't just leave me out! That's not possible!"

"There's no such thing as impossible." She'd say it just like that. And let him talk it through with a Chief Editorial Member at Large. "Lou" Grant with information worth the square root of nothing.

The square root of minus nothing!

Astrid's anger has almost warmed her up, but it's more that she can no longer feel her frozen toes. She'd love to slip off her shoes and put her feet up on the seat, but she's had these shoes on for twenty-eight hours now, and who knows . . .

"Look!" Nadeche exclaims. "Greenhouses!"

This is why it's a good thing they're not doing a live programme with her. What at first glance look like greenhouses are in fact white tents in the shape of half barrels. U.N.H.C.R. is marked on them clearly, in large blue letters. In fact it's hard to miss.

"Bingo!" she says. "U.N.I.C.E.F. We should be there soon."

But soon doesn't come. Tents stand in endless rows in this nothingness. They never stop, even though the convoy of vehicles is by no means dawdling. You wouldn't be allowed to drive this fast in a built-up area in Germany and yet the tents refuse to come to an end. They don't get any wider or taller. In a place like this you expect to find something like a centre, a church, a castle, a bridge over a river. But here there's nothing. There wasn't anything here before either, and that's why everything's the same, just a dense layer of tents on the dusty, dried-up, scorched land. The view extends across the tent roofs and into the endless distance, a ruffled sea of white canvas with dark figures moving between the waves, hundreds and hundreds of them, with groups of small children breaking away from them, running to accompany the convoy for a while, as schools of dolphins might a ship.

Astrid looks at Nadeche, who is glued to the tinted window in astonishment, transfixed by the immense, overwhelming size of the camp, its limitless expanse making immediately clear that this isn't just a bigger version of the refugee hostel; it's something else altogether, a tent city for a population the size of Berlin or Paris. The most dreadful thing, Astrid thinks, is that despite the enormity it's going to be hard to find seven or eight passable locations for fashion shoots with refugee women. Or even one, for that matter.

Eventually the car comes to a stop. The sliding door opens. Astrid closes her eyes. Her mouth opens as if redeemed and she abandons herself to the wonderfully warm air that floods into the car. She wants to launch herself into it, frozen stiff as she is, she wants to sink into it, into this divine, sunny warmth. Swiftly she packs her bag, ready to get out as soon as Nadeche has left this ice palace on wheels. A hand floats inside the car, a white hand, and from the watch on its wrist Astrid recognises the location production manager trying to help Nadeche out, and Nadeche takes it for granted that there is a hand to grab. She wouldn't be surprised if someone laid their coat on the dusty ground before her. She stands up lithely, like a polar bear she must be immune to the cold. You come across them sometimes, people with a particular metabolism or whatever, not often but it does happen, like that Icelandic fisherman in the film who survived for hours in the sea. And Nadeche Hackenbusch must be one of those rare, adaptable human beings, Astrid thinks, just as Nadeche vents her complaint:

"Why didn't you warn me it was going to be such a long drive? Your silly heated seat almost like, melted my arse."

# 6

It was pure luck. Or natural destiny, but who can distinguish between the two apart from Allah? For anybody who'd been in the camp long enough could have got this job. And pretty much everyone did try to get it.

It took two hours at most for every last soul in the camp to know that an angel was coming from Germany: Malaika, as they say in Swahili. An angel from the television. They all swapped links for Malaika videos on YouTube, and they said that Malaika helped the poor, even though all you saw in the videos was Malaika and an elegantly dressed man talking into a microphone, or Malaika dressed as a village trollop having a bucket of iced water poured over her, probably as a warning to other village trollops. But the narrow selection of videos was because the angel came from Germany. The angel was unknown in countries where English or French was spoken; you needed to know the German words to find more clips. People searching for a German angel who helped poor people only ever got the ex-Merkel, who was a woman.

"Malaika is beautiful," Mahmoud says, trying to sound like an expert. "She's the most beautiful woman in the world."

"She's not as beautiful as Scarlett Johansson."

"That's because you only know Scarlett Johansson from photos. Where they make her up to be beautiful. Scarlett Johansson in Africa looks like a gnu."

They're drinking beer at Miki's and the refugee is paying. For he's landed the job that everyone was desperate to get. All of them were aware that the television Germans would bring work and money. Rumours were even circulating that there would be work for women too. But that was nonsense because no women had applied to the Germans. Not even the Germans can alter the fact that women are just as loathe to get a slap in the face as anyone else. But it was also clear that the good Germans would pay their helpers more than any people smuggler or small-time gangster. The refugee's main reason for applying is that he's hoping he might be able to afford a smuggler to take him to Europe.

Much of what they say about the Germans is true. For example, they really are well organised. To begin with he saw as little of the angel as the others did, for the angel had helper angels facilitating her search for experienced assistants. They had arrived at the camp a week before the angel did herself. Of course Ali and his boys paid a visit to the Germans too, and they pretended not to know each other so as to improve their chances. Mojo the Blue had dressed Salif in something he took to be a suit, as if the angel was on the lookout for a president. Shaquan the Liar, loopy Pakka, old Gbil who tries to make out he's some sort of sage – everyone who had their own pair of legs was there, and even some who didn't. The angel had three assistants who took the men's names and photographed them in an old-fashioned German way: with instant cameras rather than smartphones. But this is something you see all the time: the Germans prefer driving around in old V.W. buses or on old motorbikes or old bicycles.

Apparently Mojo was convinced that the Germans wouldn't look any further once they'd seen his man. Salif can speak French, he said, they're going to love Salif. But the Germans weren't interested in Salif's amazing French. They were far more interested in the refugee when he told them he could speak English. It had already crossed his mind that the Germans had always won their wars against the French, but lost the ones against the U.S. and the British. You respect the language of the victors, never that of the losers.

Then they took some video footage, which went well too. Many of the men were uncertain, but he was far too curious to lack confidence. He laughed a lot, in part because he'd taken a shine to the young assistant and because she laughed back. But very soon he wasn't laughing half as much; something had caught his attention.

There was another woman present who few had noticed because she was unremarkable looking, already very wrinkled. He noticed her because she was saying nothing, yet keeping a watchful eye on all that was happening. The Germans may be rich, but they think everything through carefully, and if they're spending money on a wrinkly old lady then she must be important.

This woman looked at him sympathetically as he talked to the dark-haired woman about his homeland. Before his turn he'd seen a huge black man play the protector type, which hadn't gone down well with the ladies. The dark-haired woman looked intimidated and tried to be done with him as quickly as possible, while the elderly lady just stared at her mobile. So he went for the opposite approach. If everyone else shouts loudly, speak softly. And then the dark-haired woman asked him about his homeland. He looked her in the eye, but only briefly, to avoid coming across as intimidating, as the large black guy had. Then he lowered his voice and said, "My homeland is far away from here. But always very close too."

Although he wasn't looking directly at her he could see that the elderly lady had put down her mobile. She'd taken a pen and jotted something on the sheet of paper with his instant picture clipped to it. And instead of going back to her mobile she kept looking at him. She must have heard something she liked. He pretended not to have noticed. He spoke his name into the camera, said how old he was, what he could do. He claimed to know everybody inside the camp, said that he could speak French too (which the Germans would hardly be able to verify), that he was fluent in thirteen African dialects (they wouldn't be able to check this either), and unlike most of the others he didn't profess to know German. He'd watched Lamine the nitwit offer up a fluent "Angemerkel" by way of proof, then seen Lamine's instant picture disappear straight into the wastepaper basket. It had come as a surprise that an idiot like him had been photographed in the first place, but the Germans couldn't have known that Lamine was the only person inside the camp that the children liked hurling stones at more than the dogs. He was easier to hit and didn't bite.

He didn't say much as he didn't want to come across as a windbag, rather a man in whom an angel could trust. He plumped for the Boateng type, not Kevin-Prince Boateng, but his brother, who was calmer and more controlled, someone the Germans wouldn't worry about despite the fact that he's black, someone who could even become world champion alongside them. They obviously had problems with young men too, so he made himself older. By seven years, no more, which meant that for television he was now thirty-one. First he got onto their shortlist. Then each one of them was taken in turn into a room with a camera. He didn't know whether the angel really was sitting on the other side of the camera; they just told him he should imagine she was. He said his name. And then, almost on a whim, he went up to the camera, cool, calm and Boateng-composed, and said softly, "A man's name means nothing to the lion."

Then he turned and left the room.

# 7

"'A man's name means nothing to the lion' – what the actual hell is that supposed to mean?"

Sensenbrink looks around the room. Some of his colleagues rapidly tap the phrase into their phones. Sensenbrink sighs.

"Can't he just keep his trap shut? Finally we get someone who looks like he might be the real goods and then he starts talking bollocks."

". . . the ideal first name for those born under the sign of Leo . . ." one assistant says quietly.

". . . for more than ninety years the name LOEWE has stood for quality in consumer electronics . . ." a man's voice reads out.

"It's got to be some African proverb. There must be a www.africanproverbs.com.," Sensenbrink says.

"Already tried that."

"Doesn't matter. The question is: what does he mean by it?" Beate Karstleiter remarks. Sensenbrink gives her a friendly nod. Karstleiter may be a bootlicker, but at least she can guess what he's thinking. There are enough people in this company who rush to show their obedience, but then their obedience rushes off in directions that aren't helpful to anyone.

"He's saying that our questions aren't important."

"Or that we're not lions."

"Of course we're not lions. But is that a good thing or a bad thing?"

"Bad. Surely everyone wants to be a lion. Lions are proud and strong."

"Maybe not in Africa. There, lions could just as easily be dangerous and wicked."

"Which would make us harmless and good. Because we're not lions."

"Oh, for Christ's sake . . ." Sensenbrink looks around. Discussions like this ought to be shut down at once; they produce nothing but crap.

"Well, the lion doesn't actually do anything. It's the lioness who does all the work. She hunts."

Exactly. All this gender crap. But what can you do? People want to talk, talk, talk so they can put themselves in the picture. You can't forbid them from speaking. If you did, they'd stop working altogether.

"He did say 'lion', in English. Not 'lioness'."

"I thought it was lionelle . . ."

"Like Mrs Messi?"

Now it's getting too silly. Sensenbrink applies the brakes. "Let's have the next one!"

The assistant says something into a mobile. The lion man goes out and another man comes into the room, wearing shorts, sliders and mirrored sunglasses. There is something visibly uncertain about him; he walks into the room as if fearing an ambush. A voice from the still-open door seems to tell him that a camera is transmitting his picture. He immediately stands up straight. The voice says something else, and he pushes his sunglasses up onto his head.

"Christ alive! Where did they drag this pimp up from?"

"Look at the trousers!"

"What the . . .?"

"Are they taking the piss?" Karstleiter says. "Ask them what the hell's going on."

The assistant mutters something into her headset, then says, "Apparently he was quite different in their preliminary chat."

"Quite different . . . quite different. Are they blind? What's that on his wrist?"

"That can't be real, can it?"

"Is that a Rolex?"

"Yeah, but it's a fake."

Sensenbrink bends over to his microphone. "Tell me, are you doing any kind of checks before you shove them in front of the camera? It's bad enough that he shows up at your end looking like that, but imagine what *we're* thinking when we see him preened like a pimp? Why did no-one tell him to take that fucking alarm clock off his wrist before we got a glimpse of him? Do you know how much this whole session is costing? Dedicated line, equipment, half of management sitting around here. Yes, sorry. I'm sorry too. Sorry, my arse! Just do your job. Next!"

They see the pimp turn towards the door and hurriedly take off his watch.

"What's going on? What's he doing? Fuck his stupid watch! He ought to have thought about that earlier . . ."

Now an elderly lady appears on the screen, angling the microphone on her headset closer to her mouth. "He says it's not his watch," she says, trying to appease Sensenbrink. "He says he just borrowed it to—"

"Yeah, yeah, too bad! Tough shit! We're a private T.V. company, not the Salvation fucking Army. No brain, no gain!"

All of a sudden the pimp drops to his knees and starts to cry. He blubs a few words into the camera: "angel" and "I can *aider*" – it becomes less and less intelligible. Inside that small room a bear, a mountain, a brick shithouse of a man collapses into a heap. He rips off his shirt to reveal a disconcertingly scarred chest.

"Oh, for fuck's sake."

"Now he's a victim too."

"But we can't take him just because he's a victim."

"Fuck-a-doodle-do."

"Woah, that's pretty major."

"I can't see."

The pimp clasps his hands in front of the camera, he says "*famille*", and looks imploringly at the elderly woman and into what, on him, looks like a little camera bag.

"Oh no!"

"We weren't looking for a cry-baby."

Sensenbrink can see the mood shifting. Now it's time to make a decision.

"Guys, nobody wants to punch the puppy, but we're still in the business of making entertainment. I specifically asked for a tough guy. Not someone from an aid organisation, but a real refugee. A sensitive type who's witnessed a whole heap of suffering, but it hasn't broken him."

"Nor robbed him of his humanity," Karstleiter adds.

"Precisely. Hard, but with a heart. And I'm afraid me no see no 'hard' here."

"And no English either."

"Huh?"

"We asked for English," Beate Karstleiter reminds him. "But I thought I heard French there."

"Oh, right. Yes, exactly! Why's the cry-baby blubbing in French?"

The elderly lady tries to help the sobbing giant to his feet. She asks him something, to which he yells "English" several times, but unfortunately more often "*anglais*".

"Fuck me, get rid of him! Get him out! Out! Out! We haven't got all fucking day. Jesus, Hackenbusch's English is bad enough. She can only speak French when she . . ." Sensenbrink struggles to find a way to finish his sentence.

Two production staff haul the crumpled hulk out of the room. He appears to resist briefly, but at the same time tries to look good for the camera. They can hear a faint yelling, a sad yelling, as if someone or something wonderful had died. For a moment the room on the screen is empty. An uncomfortable silence fills the office back in Germany too. Sensenbrink puts his arm over the backrest, turns around in his chair and addresses his team.

"That was a bit harsh, but I can't help that. This is where the rubber hits the road. We're making a programme about refugees, not stand-up comedy. This kind of stuff is going to happen all the time. So, if anyone here thinks it's not quite their cup of tea, they have my sympathy. But they need to stand up now and say they can't nut up. I hear there's a job going at that new show, "Pet Swap", or whatever it's called. But let me tell you, this is a blue-ocean opportunity, a once-in-a-lifetime thing, there's never been anything like it. You'll be talking about this to your grandchildren!"

Nobody gets up. Eyes drift around the tale. "I'm not leaving," someone says quietly to another, "how about you?" Nobody drops out. Satisfied, Sensenbrink turns around.

"Well, I just can't bloody wait to see who they've got for us next . . ."

A man in a skullcap steps in. He seems a little older. His shirt hangs down over his trousers – it's not a kaftan, but it looks a bit like one. Sensenbrink leaps to his feet.

"For fuck's sake, what's *that*?" Grabbing the microphone again, he talks to Africa directly.

"WHAT. IS. THAT? What's that on his face?"

Meaningful glances around the table.

"Exactly," Sensenbrink bellows, incensed. "And *why* is there a beard? I can't have someone with a beard. How would that look? You don't need to be fucking Albert Einstein to work that one out. As soon as your average house-wife switches on, she'll be saying, "Hey, look at Nadeche Hackenbusch! Is she casting terrorists now?"

An embarrassed silence hangs in the room. Further

glances are exchanged, heads are shaken, but this time in disappointment, disgust and incomprehension. "Those idiots from the on-site production team," their looks now say, or, "If you want something done properly . . ." Everyone in the room realises that they've sent the biggest failures in the company down there.

"I even *said* that. I said *no terrorists* . . . This is really beginning to rub my rhubarb! The beard thing is oh-so-fucking obvious! *No terrorists* means no terrorists and also nobody that looks like a terrorist! No fucking caps and no fucking beards . . . What? Why another one?" Sensenbrink takes a deep breath and, straining to control his temper, says, "Yes, you've understood me perfectly. Lose the beardies. Right now. Including those hipsters with suicide vests. And now send me in the next one who looks half-way normal."

Sensenbrink yanks out his headphones and tosses them onto the table.

"Coffee?" an assistant asks.

"Please." He starts massaging his temples. "How much longer is Suzanne on maternity leave?"

"Nine months."

Sensenbrink wearily scratches behind his ear, even though there's no itch.

"I'll pay for her babysitter and nanny and whatever else if she jumps on a plane and sorts out those cockwombles."

"We've already been there. She wants to be a good mother to her child."

"The kid'll turn out shite anyway. They all do these days, what with smartphones and the Internet. The last kids who didn't become total ignoranuses grew up in the eighties. Give her a bell and tell her she can name her salary."

"What, now? Really?"

"No, of course not. Ask them what the hell's going on down there. Are they having to give birth to the bloody candidates first?"

A slim black man enters the room. Probably in his early twenties, he gives a friendly smile.

"Hello?" he says with a wave at the camera. Then he says his name and starts talking about his family, his homeland, life in the camp, his friends, and Sensenbrink looks around the room to see if anyone else has stopped listening. He signals to an assistant to end this performance and bring in the next candidate. She mutters something into her mobile, upon which the man stops mid-flow, waves again at the camera and leaves the room. He's replaced by another young black man wearing a T-shirt so tight it could have been borrowed from a child. He's in good spirits and gives the camera a friendly wave, before starting to talk in a relaxed manner. Sensenbrink mutes the volume.

"Something's not right."

"The T-shirt's too small," Beate Karstleiter says. "But we can change that."

"I didn't want to interrupt," the assistant says hurriedly. "They told me they're sorry, he would have come in with no shirt at all. They told him to get one quickly and he came straight back in that one, they're really sorry, they're gutted, but—"

"No, it's not the T-shirt," Sensenbrink says. "The guy's

too cheerful. Just like the one before. What's going on down there? Are they handing out drugs or what?" Sensenbrink turns back to the screen. The young man is talking to the camera without pause.

"They say they're all like that," the assistant explains. "They're happy because there's an opportunity. Of a job, even just of something happening."

"Think about it! I can't sell this to the viewers. The show's called "Angel in Adversity", not "Angel at the Comedy Club". If anyone's going to bring light into the darkness here, it's Nadeche Hackenbusch. And that means it's got to be dark, get it? Christ on a fucking bike. And at Nadeche's side we've got to have someone who sees that it's dark too. Not some light entertainer. What about the first guy?"

"Lion man?"

"Get him back. I don't give a fuck what he meant. At least he meant something. It sounded sort of wise. What was it again?"

"Even the lion doesn't know what his name is."

"The man doesn't know what the lion's name is."

"No, it was bleaker than that. Slightly menacing. The man doesn't have to know what the lion's name is."

"Play it back!"

On the screen the man reappears in front of the camera.

"Is this now live? Is he back?"

"No, this is the recording."

"A man's name means nothing to the lion," the man says again.

"Yes, that was it!" Sensenbrink says, clenching his fist. "Now *that* is bleak."

"It's got something."

"It's like . . . like a nameless grave. It's kind of spooky too."

"But not frightening. He says it very soberly."

The image changes. The young man must be back in the room with the camera. "At least he's got a decent pair of trousers on," Sensenbrink says. "We ought to get him a pair of jeans too, but they mustn't be too new. And not top of the range either. Let Grande sort it out! Get them to tell him that we liked what he did. But he needs to unpack that thing with the lion."

They watch the man being given instructions. He moves calmly and nonchalantly; for a fleeting moment Sensenbrink fancies he knows him from somewhere.

"I think he's great," Sensenbrink hears from behind him, a female voice with a hint of a Swabian accent – Engerle. "He totally reminds me of Boateng when he was still playing. Lighter skin, of course. And without the daft glasses." Sensenbrink likes the comparison. Some positive associations, at last.

The lighter-skinned Boateng looks at the camera and says in English, "What lion?"

"You know, with the name of the man and that stuff!"

For a brief moment the man looks as if he doesn't have a clue what Sensenbrink's going on about. Then he smiles and says, "It's good. It's good you want to understand Africa. Let me help you understand Africa. It's a very great task." He pauses, then says with a smile, "Africa is like a woman . . ."

Sensenbrink raises his eyebrows. Africa is like a woman?

That sounds suspiciously trite. Is this Boateng character taking the piss?

". . . and like a zebra."

A few people in the room are now laughing sympathetically, women included. Sensenbrink laughs too. "Well, bugger me! He knows my wife! Do you know my wife?"

Boateng stares at the camera lens in confusion. "I don't know your wife, Sir," he hastily assures him.

"Sweet!" Engerle sighs, and someone else raises this to "Übersweet".

"O.K., let's park that, thank you," Sensenbrink says. "We'll take him. If we have just one of these wise sayings per programme, it'll be more than enough."

"He could get a cult following," Beate Karstleiter adds for all of those who haven't yet understood. "He'll be like that bimbo from 'Wife Swap' with her 'strawberry cheese' – but a clever version. We should get him under contract right away."

"Including book rights," Sensenbrink insists. "Will you make a note of that?"

The assistant passes on the message, chairs are pushed back, people gather up their belongings. The lighter-skinned Boateng has turned to leave the room when Sensenbrink says, "Wait! Wait! Could you angle the camera down for a moment?"

The instruction is relayed. The lighter-skinned Boateng comes back. The camera moves downwards.

"There we go!" Sensenbrink says, satisfied. "Finally, someone with decent pair of shoes."

# Hope for Africa

**This is a first: Nadeche Hackenbusch and EVANGELINE are giving refugee women a future. And never has the "Angel in Adversity" looked more beautiful than today**

By Astrid von Roëll

It's like a fairy tale from the *1,001 Nights*. The little girl, rejected and scorned, who's forced to sell sulphur matches all day long, who's unfairly treated at home, kept hidden by her stepmother and never allowed to meet the prince. But this girl is living a dream. She will become the best match-seller of all time to help other girls. And she is in Africa, the Dark Continent, between poverty and hope, between war and nature reserve. Nadeche Hackenbusch has allowed her very personal dream to come true. The dream of a strong woman who has set out to change this world of ours for the better. The dream of a woman who nobody believed capable of anything.

"I come from a humble background," she says in her exclusive interview with EVANGELINE, "and I know what these people here are going through." She's wearing a plain white blouse with her distressed Hallhuber jeans. "Nothing special," she smiles modestly. "It just needs to be practical. I'm also wearing sturdy shoes because of the scorpions and snakes. But here it's not about fashion, it's about people." Nadeche Hackenbusch has now been in Africa for twenty-four hours and just by looking at this woman one can see how much she has already been affected. Her emotions are ensnared, in flux, as if in a large vortex. Stirred up. Peering out of the window of the small hut we have retired to, she tells me, "I mean, I'm a woman too."

But what an admirable woman. A woman looking straight ahead like a captain, right at the front at the wheel of the great locomotive of life. But of course it's about fashion too.

Together with EVANGE-LINE, Nadeche Hackenbusch is going to give young refugee women back their self-esteem. There are well over half a million women here, many of them young mothers, some still children of mothers. They are alone in a hostile environment. "This is a world none of us know anymore," Nadeche Hackenbusch tells us. "A world of civil war and Boko Haram. And yet people live in this world too. I want to remind these women that they're still enchanting creatures, they can still be beautiful."

She will choose thirty of these young woman to showcase German fashion alongside her. To make a statement against violence, misfortune and poverty. Young fashion for a new world, bolstering courage for a new future that is building a bridge towards us, in distant Germany. Courageous fashion for courageous women, from Hallhuber to the top designer Doris zu Wagenbach, who told EVANGELINE in Munich, "The suffering of these women moves me profoundly."

On the hunt for her "manne-quins", Nadeche Hackenbusch roams the entire vast, endless camp. And she witnesses scenes for which words will never prove adequate. When flies settle on a hungry child she doesn't hesitate to swat these pests away with her own hand. With tears in her eyes she tells me, "Yes, these children need food. They need a home. But when they have these, what then? People are more than just food and a roof over their heads. People need their dignity too. Our world has stripped these people of their dignity and in some way I'm giving them a little of it back. That's the least any of us can do."

In spite of her ample heart, however, the "Angel in Adversity" knows that choosing her models is both tough and challenging. "I'd love to be able to take them all," she says amidst the forest of outstretched hands. "But I'm afraid that's just not possible. And it wouldn't be good for these women either. They don't just want to be taken, these women are proud and don't want my pity. They

## "Here it's not about fashion, it's about people"

want to show that they're good and are capable of achieving things." Something confirmed by her latest discovery, beautiful Ashanti, 17: "I want to achieve something so I can live in Europe," she says.

"That's so brave," Nadeche Hackenbusch tells her, visibly impressed. "These women are such great role models and refuse to give up, even though unfortunately Europe can't take anyone in at the moment." And yet Nadeche Hackenbusch cannot just wave goodbye to those candidates who don't make it through the tough selection process. Many women, she has realised, lack the essentials here.

"It's not just make-up, soap, shampoo – such everyday items for us in one of the richest countries on this earth. Lots of women here don't even have a bra, and though I can't help in every way, at least in this respect I can." She has brought along more than 2,000 of her exclusive HackenPush-ups, which she gives away without great fuss. "It's not much," Nadeche Hackenbusch says, her feet firmly on the ground. "A bra might not be able to solve all the world's problems.

But it's a small step, just like those waving lucky cats back home, powered by solar energy. A small step, but one that still needs to be taken by someone. I'd never want a lucky cat that runs on petrol."

It's another Nadeche Hackenbusch we are getting to see here. Motherhood has already turned her into a more thoughtful woman, with both feet firmly planted in real life. She laughs just as much as before, but

**"And yet people live in this world too"**

her eyes are alert and take in the world in all its beauty. Her experiences here have matured her further, supplementing her sensuality with a sensitivity she never had before. Is there a new love behind all this?

It shouldn't come as a surprise. For Nadeche Hackenbusch would not be the first woman to be enchanted by this mysterious continent. Africa – the very name has a thousand meanings which not even our smartest boffins will ever be able to explain. Ancient legends, stirring lives, tales of love and death and the most irresistible emotions from the darkest depths of human history. That is why this country is also known as the Dark Continent! In Africa, Meryl Streep found her Robert Redford, here the ravishing Juliette Binoche fell victim to the charms of the Hungarian Count Almásy, Sigourney Weaver sacrificed her life in the mist-shrouded rainforest for the poorest and most endangered apes in the world. And now – is it the turn of Nadeche Hackenbusch?

Who knows what the future holds? Sometimes it feels as if she's laughing

## "People are more than just food and a roof over their heads"

differently here than at home, despite the bitter poverty, the horrific stories, all the snakes and scorpions. Not more loudly nor more often, but more joyfully. Can this be true? And who would deserve it more than this admirable woman?

Dusk gradually creeps up on the camp, which shines in the glow of its fires in the simple beauty of poverty. Night is overtaken by the sounds of Africa; from somewhere in the distance comes the roar of a predator. Is it a tiger? Perhaps hunting a young elephant? Africa is merciless, but hope shines through and here love warms the hearts of both rich and poor in equal measure.

# 8

There's so much to learn from Nadeche Hackenbusch. Especially as a woman. This is of course what continually amazes Astrid von Roëll. The self-assurance, the unconditional commitment. Of course, she shouldn't forget that Nadeche Hackenbusch is ten years younger than her. Officially at least, although in fact – but she would never write this – the difference would be twelve years if she hadn't slightly adjusted her own age to reflect reality too. In fact if you were a pedant and checked the birth certificates (irrelevant – they're only pieces of paper) you'd end up with a difference of six years, or maybe eight. And yet, when she sees the confidence and assurance with which Nadeche Hackenbusch goes about her business, Astrid invariably gets the impression that *she's* the younger of the two.

Take, for example, the audacity with which Nadeche spent the first two days in her tent. Doing nothing at all. This is no small achievement, when you consider that a television company has transported tonnes of equipment across thousands of kilometres, as well as camera people, staff and Astrid herself – from Germany's leading celebrity magazine – and all this effort just for Nadeche Hackenbusch. Sure, as an *Evangeline* reporter she's aware that a certain degree of preferential treatment for stars, management or the press isn't just normal, but sensible, justified and appropriate. But – to put it bluntly – paralysing the entire operation for two whole days? She would never have dared to do that.

And of course Astrid von Roëll was angry too. Not only because she was obliged to concoct the first story in its entirety, including the refugee model Ashanti, 17. But also because on the first day she had to look for models on her own. Without consulting Nadeche, because the editorial team back home had already scheduled the model piece. And then she had to sit in Nadeche's posh tent with seventy or eighty photographs, which was hard enough in itself since Nadeche was permanently on the phone. To begin with she cast an indifferent eye over the pile of photos and then simply chucked them aside, as if they were junk mail.

"Listen sweetie, no, that's like, impossible. Please cancel that at *once*. I *can't* decide that now. And I *won't* decide it now. It doesn't matter, have them send photos of everything ... *No!* ... They're just to give an initial impression, but I still won't be able to make a decision ... I'm not going to make that sort of decision from photos! ... They should make sketches and I want a photo of *every* sketch beforehand. And afterwards too ... Yes, of course, of course you can have an opinion from a sketch, they can incorporate all my suggestions and then we can take another look. They're no different from the others: they give you one of their two favourite ideas and you're supposed to like, leap at one of them. Well, that's not how it works with me! I want to see *all* their ideas! . . . Yes, *even* the ones that aren't finished, and the ones they've already thrown away. Don't let them screw you over, there must be some they've scrunched up. Or ripped up and stuck back together with sticky tape! That's how you know they've really been in the bin. You call me the moment you've told them this, and *you* tell *me* what they say. Then we'll see. Loveyouloveyouloveyou!!"

Nadeche Hackenbusch ostentatiously taps the screen of her phone. Call ended. She drops the mobile onto the table. "Men," she says, smiling. "Basically they're the only children Germany's got enough of. Shame there are no nursery places for them."

She slumps back in her vast corner sofa. Astrid von Roëll catches the look in her eye, which says that Nadeche Hackenbusch's day-to-day life is utterly gruelling, but also that she's happy it's just the two of them here alone, like sisters who haven't seen each other in months. Astrid's anger is blown away in an instant. She can see how exhausted Nadeche is. She picks up the discarded pile of photographs and sits at the other end of the sofa. Rolf Benz – as the programme's credits read: "'Angel in Adversity', powered by Rolf Benz." With an aniline leather cover, Astrid notes, as Nadeche pours herself water from a large jug with pebbles in it.

"No, I'm not pregnant."

"Pregnant?"

"You've seen the jug and you're thinking: there's a heliotrope in the water – is Nadeche pregnant again?

But heliotrope isn't just for pregnant women, it gives every-one energy. They should put heliotrope in like, all the water here. Let me tell you, it's one of the first things I'm going to do in this camp. I'm going to see what sort of stones they've got in their water."

Astrid is momentarily distracted. The stone thing in the water is new, at least as far as Nadeche Hackenbusch is con-cerned. But she's aware of the principle, she's often thought about trying it out herself and some of the editorial team already have. So many famous people have died of cancer recently, it sort of makes you think.

"I was just thinking about the sofa. Aniline shows up everything."

"Sure, but aniline needs that."

"Aniline needs stains?"

"Sweetie, an animal doesn't have any stains. An animal's got a skin that's marked by its life. Everything that happens to this skin is life. And the animal still has a share in this life. The cow is here with us."

"Kind of."

"No, it really is. And that's why it doesn't matter if you spill water here, or wine. They're not stains, they're life."

Astrid longs to have her own tent kitted out like this. She doesn't have air conditioning either, just a fan with a dodgy connection.

Nadeche breathes in deeply, as if about to take a major dive. Then she says, "O.K., let's have a squint at what we've got here." She picks up the pile of photographs and casually goes through them. "No . . . no . . . no," she says, and with every "no" a polaroid glides onto the Rolf Benz table. "Oh no, that's really not good." Nadeche works her way through half the pictures and says, "I can already see we're going to have to start from scratch."

The anger which had just abated surges inside Astrid anew, now creeping up her chest and into her throat, where it lodges. Were she in the editorial offices she'd make a scene that others would watch through the glass partitions like groundhogs, but she can't do that here. Here where Nadeche, her friend, is treating her like the lowliest intern, and where she has no option but to appeal to this friendship.

"Come on, Nadeche," she says, pointing to the remainder of the pile, "you can't just say that. None of us can see into the future." Then, assuming a jocular expression, she squeezes out "not even you".

"Look, I don't need to be able to see into the future. You can do better than this." She takes a sip of water and asks sweetly, "So, when are you going to be promoted to management? They can't like, make you wait for ever."

It's lovely to have Nadeche on her side, of course. But somehow it doesn't feel like it.

"Oh well, you know," she says, distractedly, "either they've got to wait for a woman to leave or they have to appoint an extra man to balance it out. And they don't have one."

"What about Lou Grant?" Nadeche says, looking by turns so serious and amused that Astrid can't help giggling, because both of them know that Lou Grant really is a total waste of space. And yet Astrid's eyes keep wandering to the pile of photographs that Nadeche hasn't looked through yet, which she spent an entire day working on, without the help of an assistant. She had to approach people herself, complete strangers who couldn't speak her language, she had to use hand gestures to ask their permission and to try to explain to all of them what it was about, and she even drew a highly complex map, because if you want to find these people and their tents again you have to sketch roughly where they are. Thinking back on her day, it was a shedload of work, and the whole thing on foot. Never in all her years at *Evangeline* has she done as much by herself. And even if Nadeche isn't aware of this, she can't just chuck the pile of snaps in the bin.

"At least have a look at the others," she says.

If you were being generous you'd call it a request. But in truth it's like a defeated lion rolling over beside the victor, or bringing it an antelope leg or something. Nadeche looks at her tenderly and says, "Honestly, Astrid, I don't need to look at them. I can tell they're going to be useless."

That is like a kick in the shins, which hurts more than a gentle kick ought to, and it takes Astrid a few seconds to work out why. Because she wasn't expecting it, not from a woman. From a man, maybe, but not from a woman. At the very least she expected Nadeche to look at the pictures, even just out of politeness. Solidarity.

"Yes, but . . . you never said what you wanted!"

And now she's sitting here, having to justify herself. This isn't teamwork or partnership or anything.

"Come on, let's not like, get into a tizz about this, it's no use crying over spilled milk. Good things take time, after all."

"Nadeche, that's not possible. The editorial team are

waiting for the photographs! Do you want them to print blank pages?"

"There's no such thing as impossible! And I've never seen *Evangeline* with blank pages, they'll think of something. You know what? Let's just do a different story: Nadeche Hackenbusch's recipe for success. I'll dictate it right now and you scribble it down."

Astrid von Roëll thinks she might vomit. She knows exactly what they'll say in the editorial office. They'll be fuming. Then they'll see if they've got anything better. Then they'll conclude that at least they've still got Nadeche Hackenbusch in their mag – and an exclusive interview at that – and they'll print it. And none of this would be quite so bad if the readers knew what really went on, for instance if she wrote that Nadeche Hackenbusch's recipe for success is to dawdle and string everyone along until they're so far at their wits' end that they'll broadcast and print everything Madame Hackenbusch is kind enough to toss at them; that they'll bite every bullet, including the first-class tickets with which the angel flies to adversity; and that Nadeche Hackenbusch is a cunning, egotistical bitch whose behaviour is not one iota better than a man's.

And just how much Astrid von Roëll admires her for this.

Because Nadeche Hackenbusch goes that one step further, and that step is not one she herself is prepared to take.

She writes none of this, of course. But rather that Nadeche Hackenbusch has her excellent genes to thank for her looks. And that there's a heliotrope in her drinking water. Along with a rose quartz, a rock crystal and an amethyst.

# 9

Marion watches Nadeche critically examine her own reflection. Marion examines it too, just as critically. The face is still pretty good, she thinks. You can say what you like about Nadeche Hackenbusch, but she takes good care of herself. She gets plenty of sleep, she doesn't smoke, doesn't drink, there are no sins that need covering up. And she doesn't have much done, unlike Vladimir Putin, who now looks like his own latex mask. She'd love to know who's giving him advice.

Nadeche looks perfectly content. In the past Marion thought this was down to satisfaction with her work, but now she's not so sure. It's more that Nadeche is satisfied with herself. It's Marion, of course, who has been turning in reliably good work for eleven years. Nadeche no doubt thinks that she herself has been responsible, because she always insists on Marion for her make-up. Many might not consider this to be much of an achievement, but look at Putin. Even celebs can have a face like a turkey breast wrapped in clingfilm.

They've known each other ever since they were flatmates, and Marion managed to carve out a career on the back of

Nadeche's success, behind the scenes. Everyone benefits. And Marion knows she just doesn't have the body to be a model. Her shoulders are too broad, her bum too narrow . . . the perfect physique for a stripper in a gay bar.

And then there's her face.

It's definitely pretty, in a way, or . . . distinctive. She doesn't like her nose, but she's also somehow grateful for it. It's almost an advertisement for her trade, because the way she's able to make it look small demonstrates how good she is. Sometimes Marion can see people she meets for the first time trying to work out how much nose is hiding beneath the shading. And those who work it out know that she can work on a rotten banana until it looks like a fresh radish.

Not that Nadeche Hackenbusch is in need of any such magic. But Marion's art ekes another 5 per cent out of her gorgeous natural features, maybe even ten. And the figure goes up every year. For make-up is not merely a matter of expertise, but of experience. Marion knows Nadeche's face. That unevenness, there, where her left cheek becomes her left nostril. Or that point on her forehead which is always shinier than the rest under spotlights. Marion knows exactly the eye shadow that works best, and the tone of lightening which looks too artificial.

"Those two days paid off," Marion says, darkening the cheeks with wonderful subtlety. If you didn't know she was enhancing these, you'd never guess. Here is another advantage. Different make-up artists work on problem areas slightly differently, whereas Marion always does it the same way. And that's why you can scarcely see what's not real, even if you compare press photographs from the past few years. Marion has made a philosophy out of this. "You have to stick with the same story," she says. "If you've been narrating a Western the whole time, you can't suddenly bring on an astronaut's helmet." This isn't her invention, of course; in Hollywood they've been following this principle for years, but in Germany, where every actor needs to keep an eye on the money, it's a different matter.

"You've got such a great complexion," Marion says modestly. "You don't really need me at all."

"Of course I do," Nadeche says. "What would I do without you? With my face like a criminal's?"

"You'd find another stylist." Marion turns away and bends over the small make-up box. This is another thing that Nadeche loves about Marion: rather than lugging around crates of stuff she can make do with a handful of things in the tightest of spaces. She's made Nadeche up in the back of a taxi, in a barely accessible wardrobe and once in a Portaloo, by the light of a flickering torch.

Nadeche looks in the mirror and her eyes meet Marion's.

"Never," she says seriously, as her reflection smiles affectionately at Marion. "I'd never go in front of a camera again."

Marion is touched and smiles back, and for a moment she thinks it may be meant truthfully. On the other hand, two days have been quite enough, as evident not merely from Nadeche's complexion, but from the general sense of unease too. Or from Grande's voice as she knocks at the door and tries to winkle out something akin to a timetable. Grande is usually a rather calm and laid-back production manager, but as the hours and days have passed her voice has become increasingly strained. And higher. At the end of the first day, she said, "Shouldn't we be thinking about planning the first few days' schedules?"

Marion, who had just arrived, remembers Nadeche's answer: "Have you noticed how beautiful it is here? We like, only have this one world and we pass through it so thoughtlessly. We should start by making some features, and you don't need me for those."

"But we ought to—"

"And these marlboros!"

"Marlboros?"

"Haven't you seen them? Those huge birds? Awesome! We need footage of them landing in a tree. You must have seen them. They're all over Google! Don't get so stressed, just go outside too! We're only human, all of us."

"Fine, but—"

"No machinery. Just people."

"Yes, sure, but—"

"And the trees have to bob up and down."

"What?"

"The trees. When they land the trees have to bob up and down, so you can see how big the marlboros are."

"Oh, you're talking about *marabous*."

"That's what I said."

"But for now—"

"Sorry, I've got to make an urgent call. Don't forget, though! Take a look outside. They should film the leopards too. And the tigers!"

After choosing the colours Marion didn't have much else to do, except be a companion for Nadeche. Since Grande has been coming at ever shorter intervals she's also noticed that unease within the team has reached the right level for Nadeche. And this is what it's all about. You need to cause the maximum amount of unease, for only then can you appear as the knight in shining armour. Ideally when chaos, panic and helplessness have reached their absolute zenith. If you do it right, if you then confront the team – the camera people, the assistants, lighting crew and set builders – with politeness and friendliness, if you exude overwhelming kindness and a willingness to help, you will see a certain radiance in people's faces. They'll look at you with nothing but gratitude.

Marion opens the hairdressing cape and carefully flicks it so that no make-up, no powder gets on the clothes. Nadeche Hackenbusch stands up and checks her hair. Unfortunately her request for a separate hair stylist fell on deaf ears, but if she is to be the new Schreinemakers – so she's promised Marion – this will become standard. Marion will have an assistant. Nadeche turns to her make-up artist.

"What do you think?" she says, opening her arms like a show master. "Is this alright?"

Marion nods, then screws up her eyes. "Perhaps the rhinestones aren't quite—"

"What do you mean? They're great!"

"Sand-coloured jeans, fine. They're expensive, but you can't tell if you wear a boyfriend shirt over the bum like that. T-Shirt not see-through so none of those repressed guys gets any funny ideas, you can't see the nipples, everything nicely hidden. No earrings, no bangles, very nice. The old Swatch, cool but not flashy. The trainers are right too, but the rhinestones . . . I don't know. I don't know that design at all—"

"I stuck them on myself. Good, eh?"

"Sure, but here? Now? These people are really poor."

"Come on, it didn't bother anyone in the hostels back home."

"That may well be, but . . . I mean, I think it's all well and good for you to have a bit of R. and R. and all that, but I've had a look around this camp and there . . . I've never seen anything like it. *So* poor."

"Television thrives on contrast!" Nadeche says, now back at the mirror and gazing at herself with satisfaction. She's been missing this contradiction, and now she knows for sure that she's doing it absolutely right. "People don't want to see any old bag who's just as poor as the people she visits. This isn't 'Cinderella in Adversity', is it? Are you coming?"

With an economy of movement, Marion packs up her cantilever beauty case. She checks the make-up table and peers into the silver box that looks a bit like a princess's toolbox. Then she flips the box shut and follows Nadeche to the S.U.V. The heat is as absurd as the ice-cold air that hits them as they get into the car. Already inside are Grande and Astrid von Roëll, who says, "I've already switched on the seated heats."

"What a darling," Nadeche says. "What would I do without you?"

Grande's facial muscles tense and she says, "It's not far. We could walk it."

"Maybe we could," Nadeche says. "But an angel like, needs wings. By the way, when are they going to be resprayed?"

The car eases away. Only now does Marion notice that a dark, good-looking man in the front passenger seat is attempting to say hello to Nadeche. But she's ignoring him and Marion guesses why: the T.V. company's chosen a man for her, but Nadeche prefers to work with women. She casts a glance at Grande, who should be mediating between the two of them, but Grande is shirking her responsibility by staring into her smartphone. Maybe, Marion thinks, this is the actual reason for the triumph of the smartphone. Whereas children can close their eyes if there's something they don't want to see, adults have always had to face up to things . . . until now.

So it comes as quite a surprise when Nadeche puts down her mobile and stares out of the window, almost like a child. Grande frowns. It's almost beyond belief that her star hasn't stepped outside in two days.

The streets inside the camp all look the same. It's hard to tell which block they're in, which area, or even if they've just been driving in circles for ten minutes. The car pulls up outside a building made up of several containers and extended with tents. A mass of people are queuing there, lots of women with children, older children with smaller ones. Clearly an attempt had been made to erect a canopy over the area outside the building, to shelter those waiting, but the numbers must have grown and then they stopped cobbling more onto the cobbled-together roof construction. Marion sees people squatting in long lines, in that peculiar latrine position. She's familiar with this from the refugee hostel where Nadeche filmed; people squatting in the corridors, or wherever they can get a decent wi-fi connection. But she doesn't understand how they do it for even a minute without one of their legs going completely numb.

First the passenger gets out and then the vehicle turns, so that Nadeche can get out in front of the entrance and the camera. Marion sees the camera team, and beside them in canvas trainers is the passenger Nadeche ignored throughout the drive there. He looks relaxed, wearing the shirt Marion and Nadeche chose for him – not one of those garish things Africans love to wear, but a dark-blue shirt, not too fitted, even though he could easily carry that off as he's got the sort of figure people love to dress. Marion is desperate to get out too, to see how Nadeche gets on with him. But she doesn't want to be in the way of the camera team. Astrid has got out the other side, as has Grande. Marion stays in the car.

She's already done a recce of the building and there's nowhere you could set up a make-up station. She picks up the make-up box from beside her feet, opens it and prepares everything for her work. Cotton wool, tissues, cape. Experience tells her that it will be an hour at most before Nadeche comes back for a touch up. In this weather Marion reckons it'll be less.

Through the open door she sees Nadeche approach the young man. He offers her his hand, casually and yet attentively, as if he's been taking lessons from Barack Obama. From behind she can't see Nadeche's reaction, but she can see the way he moves – a natural talent. You'd even watch him open a bottle of water. She leans back and goes through her e-mails. An unusually large number of questions have appeared on her cosmetics blog today, and when she's finished with them she sees that Nadeche isn't back yet.

Marion checks the time. Way over an hour. That's unusual. She looks through the windows in all directions and sees nothing but refugees, dust and sun. She thinks about asking the driver, but he's busy with his mobile too. There's wi-fi outside the hospital, which explains the presence of all those refugees who aren't in the queue. Marion gets out, stretches, thrusts her hands into her jeans pockets and walks, stiff-legged, around the car.

The hospital has electricity too. There is an accumulation of mobiles attached to chargers, and bundles of leads creep along the ground like wiry plants. When people come to fetch their mobiles, others leap up and grab the coveted slot. Plugs are the new waterholes, it occurs to Marion. Two little girls come up to her and laugh as they tug at her trouser legs, but in these two days Marion has learned that you can only offer help at fixed times and fixed places – otherwise those in need will demand it everywhere and at any time. Back home Marion has a dog, so this wasn't particularly hard to learn.

She goes back to the car to fetch some sun cream. She hadn't anticipated having to reapply today, but she can't sit in that bloody freezing car anymore.

The girls don't leave her alone. They seem bored. Marion crouches to show them a little clapping and counting game. "*Aramsamsam*," she sings to them, and because they seem to really like this she continues: "*Bei Müllers hat's gebrannt, brannt, brannt*". Soon the girls can sing it really well, but

Nadeche is still not back. The girls are already making up a new version in which they warble "ulliulliulli" in an impressive, but also slightly awful two-part harmony. Marion gets up and wanders to the hospital entrance to peer inside. There are no signs of any disquiet; the sick wait there with the patience of a saint.

Ought she to be worried?

Can you attack a camera team and a star presenter without making a noise?

Or abduct them?

Unlikely. She could give Nadeche a bell, but she's bound to have switched her mobile off for filming. Marion circles the hospital building, which turns out to be bigger than expected. There are barely any windows to look through. But nor does anybody appear agitated. People come and go, always carrying the same things: sacks of flour or grain, water canisters, long bundles of sticks. Sacks, canisters, sticks. Sacks, canisters, sticks. A goat. Sacks, canisters, sticks. By the time she's back at the car she hasn't heard from Nadeche Hackenbusch for two and a half hours.

She calls Grande. Voicemail. Who else could she ask? And she can't just leave. If Nadeche needs a touch up and she's not there all hell will break loose. She returns to the vehicle and closes the door to have a drink. The children mustn't see her drinking the clean, bottled water. She rearranges a few of her make-up tools, then puts them back in their original positions. The air conditioning is working flawlessly, as are the heated seats. The car must have a battery the size of a fridge. It's all rather pleasant, in fact.

She sits up with a start. How long has she been asleep? What's happened? Hearing a shriek, she pushes open the door and stumbles into the bright light. Children are pouring out of the hospital, a camera assistant is moving swiftly with the backwards-walking cameraman in tow, guiding him around obstacles and tent posts. Then Nadeche Hackenbusch appears and with her the passenger. Her sleeves are rolled up, her shirt is open and there are stains on the T-shirt beneath. Sweat, dirt? It could be blood too, but not much. She doesn't look unhappy, but not especially enthusiastic either. If Marion had to describe her expression she'd say: different from normal. Serious. Like someone with a job to do. Like a politician with a full diary, not a party politician, but someone working in overseas aid. Her hair is all over the place. In the background Marion can see Grande, who seems out of breath. Nadeche turns to say something to her, waving her arms assertively. Marion catches her eye and gestures in an attempt to find out whether her make-up skills are required, but Nadeche shakes her head. Then she sits on the floor and the passenger follows suit.

To begin with Marion loses sight of her; Nadeche has almost entirely disappeared into a cluster of children, but from the cameraman's face she can tell that the situation isn't threatening. As he endeavours to hold her in the picture, his assistant keeps a few angles free for him. Marion approaches to find out what's going on. Astrid von Roëll is now beside her, but she's taking photos on her smartphone and trying to jot things down on a little notepad.

Nadeche is sitting with her designer jeans in the dust.

Her left foot is resting on the passenger's thigh and she's laughing. The children laugh too. The passenger is holding a knife, which he's using to remove the rhinestones from her shoe, one after the other. He passes them to Nadeche, who hands them out as fairly as possible.

One stone per child.

He's being careful, but he can't help making holes in Nadeche's trainers. She doesn't seem to care. He raises his eyebrows, but she gestures to him to keep going, grabbing a child with the other hand to take the rhinestone out of its mouth. Marion recognises the little girl. She's laughing and singing, "*Müllerhatzgebanbanban*". Then she puts the stone back in her mouth, but only until Nadeche protests.

The rhinestone process doesn't come to an end until Nadeche takes off her ruined shoes and tosses them away. Squealing, the children leap after them. The passenger gets up. He offers Nadeche his hand and she allows him to pull her up. She slaps the dust off her bottom, then takes her socks off too. For a moment it looks as if she's going to embrace the passenger, but instead she gives him her hand before heading back to the car in bare feet. Marion watches as a woman comes up to her. Nadeche turns to the woman, who thrusts a pair of those cheap sliders into her hands. Nadeche makes a gesture of payment, or more accurately non-payment, she pats her pockets, she doesn't have any money on her, only her socks. The woman declines the socks, these sliders are a gift. Embraces.

Nadeche gets to the S.U.V. Astrid joins her, then Grande, they reconvene in the car. Grande looks under great strain.

Astrid is scribbling as if her life depended on it. Nadeche sinks into her seat as if she never intends to get up again. She closes her eyes.

"What was that all about?" Marion says.

Nobody answers.

Grande takes a deep breath but doesn't speak. Her eyes still closed, Nadeche says, "Ten minutes' rest as soon as we're back. Then I want a meeting. We're going to like, plan some schedules for the next few days."

"I've already—" Grande says.

Nadeche sits up straight and opens her eyes, and with a clarity and focus Marion has never seen before, she says, "*We* are going to plan some schedules. And get *him* to join us. I want him to be there."

Grande is keen to add something; she takes another deep breath, but then simply nods. All that can be heard is the car's engine and Astrid's scribbling, interrupted occasionally by the hasty rustling of paper when she starts a new page, as if she were losing valuable letters every second.

Slumping into her seat, Nadeche closes her eyes. "Marion," she says. "Would you please take off my make-up?"

# Nadeche Hackenbusch: her greatest nightmare

**Hardship, poverty and violence. During her selfless work in the heart of the Dark Continent, the German superstar comes face to face with her own tragic past**

### By Astrid von Roëll

It is often said that women are the stronger sex. When it comes to pain, women are braver. Than men, for example. But how much suffering can one woman endure? For nobody can put up with infinite suffering, not even Nadeche Hackenbusch. Over the past few days this courageous woman, still a young woman, has – one cannot put it any other way – gone through nothing short of hell.

Nadeche Hackenbusch has been in Africa for weeks now. Around the clock she is busy with preparing every detail of her programme "Angel in Adversity". This is the Nadeche Hackenbusch who remains hidden to the public, the Nadeche Hackenbusch you only meet behind the scenes of the glittery world of the rich and beautiful. A disciplined worker, a woman who mans up twenty-four hours a day and more, but never complains. "As a woman you've always got to be a bit better than the men," she once told EVANGELINE, but as ever there was no trace of bitterness there, only real enthusiasm for the challenge. This is so typical of Nadeche Hackenbusch. Always a good person, a role model, but a woman too. Over the past few days, however, even she has had to acknowledge the limits of what a human being can endure. In the heart of Africa she is suddenly facing her greatest, her darkest nightmare.

The beginning of the day provides no clue as to what she might expect later on. It's one of those mornings when the African sun shines equally for everyone. Lionel, her young, good-looking guide, accompanies her to the local hospital. Throughout the camp there is sheer delight at a visit from the angel, who tirelessly lends a helping hand wherever she can. People aren't living on the other side of the moon here; thanks to their smartphones and the Internet they know almost everything about Nadeche Hackenbusch and the fantastic work she has already done in Germany. They are amazed at how modestly she arrives, her plain, sand-coloured jeans, the simple T-shirt beneath a shirt with rolled-up sleeves. "I pinched this from Nicolai," she tells me in her wonderfully relaxed manner. "He's going to get a big surprise when he sees it on T.V."

A black doctor greets the helping angel from distant Germany and offers her his hand. Closeness between people can be so simple. "If only the politicians were more like the people," he jokes gratefully, and Nadeche Hackenbusch gives a hearty laugh. He shows her the rooms inside the hospital, humble but clean, as is so often the case with simple people. But shortages are evident everywhere. "Not enough," he says frequently, "not enough," pointing out of the window at the long queues of those seeking help. It is so typical of the German angel's hands-on attitude that at once she says, "We'll try to film this as quickly as possible so you can get straight back to your patients!"

In Africa the enchanting way in which she talks to normal people is winning hearts. This infirmary bears no comparison with a German hospital. Here it's

**She's a good person, a role model, but a woman too**

full, with two to a bed, sometimes even three children sharing. Don't bother looking for white sheets here, or pretty pictures on the walls or reading lamps. The electricity even cuts out occasionally, and yet for Nadeche Hackenbusch this is no second-rate hospital. "These people are trying their best," she acknowledges. "They're doing a magnificent job in their own way. They're working in very modest circumstances and yet infant mortality is lower than one in five." In a flash she takes the initiative, drafting plans, organising projects.

Repaint the children's ward in bright colours to counter the greyness of everyday life. Set up handicraft classes. "Back in Germany we did this with a chain of craft shops, Fanta-Si! I'm sure they'd help out again." Time and again her wonderfully practical, fresh perspective on things takes everyone by surprise.

"In Germany we don't know how good we have it," she laughs, "but here you're soon jolted back to reality." And how true this is. After the children's ward Nadeche Hackenbusch discovers a room of young girls. Is this fate?

This is a group of girls who escaped the clutches of Boko Haram only a few days ago. Many are silent, some say nothing at all, but two of them are in high spirits, bizarrely cheerful. It may sound strange, but there is almost a hint of despair about their laughter and beaming smiles. This is one of the rare moments when Nadeche Hackenbusch sits beside one of the quiet girls and asks the crew to switch off the camera. When the girl says nothing, she says nothing either. Lionel wants to leave with the camera team, but Nadeche asks him to act as translator. He squats on the floor, not too close, just close enough to hear what's being said. If anything is being said.

She doesn't touch the girl, she just sits beside her like a big sister. Minutes pass. And then she nudges the girl's foot with her glittering trainers. Once, twice, three times. On the fourth occasion the girl nudges her back. She says something, so softly that Lionel shifts closer because he can barely understand her. He asks a short question in his gentle voice. She smiles, points at him and Nadeche, then he translates: "Beautiful shoes. We both have beautiful shoes."

"How are you?" Nadeche asks.

"Fine," she says. "Now."

Occasionally one is fortunate to meet special people and Lionel is one of these special people. For what the girl now says is something a girl would only ever disclose to her big sister, but Lionel manages to translate as if he were not even in the room. The abduction. The fear. The imprisonment. The men. Sometimes just one. Sometimes two. How she started thinking some were less bad because they left her in peace afterwards. Better than those who wanted her to spend the night with them because supposedly Allah had brought them together. The men who felt ashamed of their weakness the next morning and beat her because she had bewitched them. At this point, anyone with a heart can have only one question in mind: "How can Nadeche Hackenbusch bear to hear this?"

For here in Africa, the land of the tiger and the marabou, there is probably not a single woman who can empathise as intensely with this bitter misfortune from the depths of her heart.

Remaining courageous, she places her arm around the girl's shoulder, no doubt pondering her own terrible summer. Her apparent happiness with LeBrezel. Then that horrific night. The endless days in court. The war of opinion in the media. What felt like a second incidence of rape when justice ignored her suffering with the heartless claim that "No" only means "No" if you actually say it. And that now, however justified she may be, she is prevented from giving expression to her accusations under the threat of a 500,000 euro fine. It is the harsh, bitter, intolerable confrontation with her own past that makes Nadeche Hackenbusch, this strong, stunning, self-assured woman, reach out for a hand that momentarily affords her support. The hand of Lionel, a quite special man. And one can see clearly how here, in the heart of the Dark Continent, the distressing story of a young woman briefly unites two long-suffering hearts that are both ready for greatness.

**If only the politicians were more like the people**

# 10

It is a week before the refugee realises that the money won't be enough.

He's taken his beer from Miki's dimly lit bar and is leaning wearily against a shack, gazing up at the vast, starry night sky. He puts the fairly cold bottle against his forehead. That can't be right, he thinks. He earns well, very well in fact, and he works hard. And yet it seems as if his goal is growing ever more remote. He rubs his eyes. They feel sticky, as if they won't open or close properly. They began early, those Germans, and they worked the whole day. Today he was out collecting firewood with them. Because Malaika isn't just a gorgeous woman.

To begin with he thought she was just gorgeous and he wondered what a beautiful woman like her was doing in such an ugly camp. That's why he started by taking her to the infirmary. The angel would have probably made her way there without him, but it was the only place he reckoned was sufficiently clean for such a gorgeous angel. An angel, moreover, whose own car wasn't clean enough for her. He himself had heard that the angel wanted a white car.

Thinking back on it now, it's as if he met two angels in one that day. He recalls driving to the infirmary with the angel in the angelmobile. The angel was talking or incessantly tapping on her white-gold glittery angelphone to communicate with the angelworld. Only at the very last moment, when they pulled up at the infirmary, did the angel say something that sounded like the end of a conversation. Then he got out and the angel said they'd have to do it all over again, because she thought it would look better if he came out through a different door. The angel had a real look of concern, as if she had to inform someone that the entire infirmary had burned to the ground.

And then there was the other angel. The one who calmly sat down beside the girl who had escaped. Who listened to stories that no angel ought ever to hear. The angel who came out of the infirmary.

Who said nothing save for a single sentence, which she first kept repeating in German. Who turned to him, her hand on his forearm, and then said in a voice that no longer sounded anything like the voice of an angel, "This must different go. *Total*. I swear."

That was a week ago. Since then she hasn't visited another building; she'd rather walk about with people. She fetches water with them. She tries to cook with what people have here and she's collected firewood with Munira. This way of working must be highly unusual for Germans, he could see how her colleagues became impatient. If they'd had their way, after ten minutes on foot they'd have all got back into the clean car with its zebra stripes. Because in a region where almost nothing grows and two million people are out looking for firewood every day, you don't find wood ten minutes' walk from the camp perimeter. But the angel didn't want to get into her car. She wanted to go with Munira, and if Munira had to walk for two or three hours to find something to burn, the angel was set on doing the same.

"She go three hours?" she asked him again. "Real?"

"It's true, Malaika."

The angel's helpers protested.

At which the angel let the full fury of heaven thunder from her mouth.

He'd never seen someone crush five men using their voice alone. Let alone a woman. But that's what happened. The angel simply fetched a different, no doubt more comfortable pair of shoes from the car, and from that point on it was clear that they'd be walking the whole way. Which nobody regretted more than Munira; she'd have loved a ride in the angelmobile.

This is precisely how the refugee had imagined a German angel to be. Not merely good, but good through and through. She didn't just carry a bit of wood for the camera; the angel carried as much wood as Munira herself. He'd have bet anything that the angel would give up after a hundred paces, but she lugged the wood just as Jesus the Christian did his cross. Twice she vomited into the dust with exhaustion, but she never gave up.

And the Germans are just as thorough about the money.

He sips his beer. Little Saba approaches him. "Mtu?" she says. This is the name the children have given him. Everyone's been giving him a name recently. The Germans call him "Lionel"; he'd rather not ask why as he doesn't want to be complicated. The children say "Mtu" from *Mtu kwa malaika* – the man with the angel. Saba puts on her cutest smile, but if he gives in now he'll have every last child in the camp around his neck. He shoos her away, wearily, kindly, yet firmly. He tells her that he's already given Saba's mother a bit of help. Now he needs some peace, he needs to think. On his own. There are some things you can't talk about with anyone. Not even with Mahmoud.

These Germans are so thorough.

They put an astonishingly large sum of money on the table, it's true, but they won't be fleeced. The middle-aged woman they call Grande pays him daily. They never string him along, never fob him off; at the end of the day he always has the agreed sum in his hand in cash. But there's no advance either. And that's the snag. His money would be enough for a smuggler if he got it all in one go. But it's virtually impossible to save money.

Money isn't a problem if you have as little of it as everyone else. Nor is it a problem to have more money than others, so long as you can keep quiet about it. But if you can't keep it quiet, like him, *Mtu kwa malaika*, "the man with the angel", then you have to give the others a cut. Because you're the one who's making money out of the camp and other people's lives. And if you don't give them a cut, they won't let you do it anymore.

So he pays for the beers at Miki's. He gives Mahmoud and a few others little jobs. Finding stories. And he gives Mojo the Blue his share. In theory. He offered it to Mojo and Mojo was surprised. But then told the refugee to keep the money, they'd come up with a good solution soon. It won't be like this for long, though.

He could take money from other refugees for having brought the angel to them, of course. But if the Germans found out they'd give him the chop. And if they didn't, if he could actually earn more money, Mojo would muscle in and he'd have to set up his own gang to protect himself from Mojo. That costs time and money, and he has no desire to become a gang boss. What good would that do anyway? Mojo the Blue has been doing it since childhood; he'd last two days at most, and then someone would find him with his head down the latrine.

In any case his time to earn money is limited, because sooner or later Mojo the Blue will muscle in. He's just waiting to see how carefully the Germans are monitoring what goes on. But once he's checked it all out, Mojo will politely take him aside and tell him that all future meetings with the angel can only take place for a fee. And with Mojo's agreement, of course. Mojo will let him know what these meetings will cost. Or, better put, how much he'll have to give to Mojo.

And if that gets out the Germans will give him the sack.

Or he'll refuse and Mojo will have him killed.

Terrific.

He pushes the tip of his index finger into the neck of the bottle and gently flips it out. Pop. No, it is what it is. Even though he has the best-paid job in the entire camp, he's in exactly the same financial position as before.

Pop.

And one day Malaika will leave. And he'll grow old here and die. Unless . . . she takes him with her. But that money-dragon Grande ruled this out on day one.

"This *isn't* a ticket to Germany – understood?"

Why should she, anyway?

Maybe out of friendship?

But the likelihood is low. The Internet isn't exactly pulsing with stories of German camera crews taking home the sub-jects of their reports from Africa. The only possibility would be for a health issue. Someone with an illness, ideally a little girl who can only be operated on in Germany.

Unfortunately he's in rude health.

There must be another excuse, that . . . that his life is threatened. By . . . Mojo the Blue, of course.

That might work. It's actually a really good story. Why is he in this situation? Because the Germans and the angel came here. Because they got him into trouble. Because they put him in this delicate position, caught between money and violence and Mojo. And now they have to help him out of it. Him and maybe Mahmoud too.

The risk with this story is that it might wake some sleep-ing dogs which would better be left to lie. If Malaika finds out that deals like this are being done here in the camp she's bound to ask if he's been working for Mojo the whole time. But it's worth the risk. He just mustn't talk to her too soon.

"Mtu!" Sabu says, sitting on the ground beside him. Her talent for being able to look even cuter is highly impressive. She looks cute from the start, but she holds plenty in reserve, which means she can keep turning it on. There's no smarter child here. Should he be helping out someone like her?

"You can have my beer."

"Really?"

"The bottle, I mean. When I've finished."

Saba waves dismissively. "What am I going to do with a stupid bottle?"

He drains it and puts it in front of her.

"Take it to the Germans."

"And then?"

"They might give you some money. I've heard the Germans give money for bottles."

"They give money for empty bottles?"

"So I've heard."

He can see that she has her doubts about this.

"How much?"

"No idea."

"Tell me!"

"I don't know. A bit. Less than a beer would cost, of course. Otherwise everyone would bring them unopened bottles."

Saba lifts up the bottle. "So I bring them this empty bottle and they'll pay for it? You're crazy."

"Try it," he said kindly. "It's worth a shot."

"Why would they want the bottle?" Saba persists. "What are they going to do with it?"

"I don't know. German things. Maybe they'll just fill it up with beer again. Maybe Germans have too much beer and not enough bottles."

Saba looks sceptical.

"The bottles go onto a big ship, the ship sails to Germany and all the Germans are happy," he says. "Then they dance their German dance."

"How does the German dance go?"

He gets to his feet and leaps around a little, slapping his thighs. It looks like an elephant trying to move like a heron. "That's how it goes. Like at the Oktoberfest."

"It's a silly dance."

"Yes," he says, dropping beside Saba. "You can't choose your dances. Everyone has to dance like their parents. Everywhere in the world. Your parents' dance determines how your feet move. You dance like your parents too."

This makes sense to Saba.

"But why hasn't anyone taken their bottles to the Germans before? Everyone throws them away. It's really stupid!"

"Because nobody here knows the Germans very well. It's worth a shot, no more than that. I can't guarantee anything. You need to try it yourself."

Saba gets up, bottle in hand. "O.K. . . ." she says hesitantly, sticking her thumb into the neck of the bottle. It goes pop.

"Can I do my own dance for them?"

He pictures Saba going to the Germans with the bottle and dancing. Then he says, "Do the German dance. And say something in German. Do you know any German?"

"*Hatzgebanbanban*?"

"What's that supposed to be?"

"A German song. Everyone's singing it now."

"O.K., if everyone's singing that, then say something else."

"I don't know . . ."

"You want them to remember you, don't you? Say: Oktoberfest!"

"Ottobafes?"

"Exactly. Do it!"

Saba leaps around clumsily, a little elephant on a heron's legs, slapping her legs at random. Then she presents the bottle and says "Ottobafes" as a fanfare. He nods. Perhaps it's not so far-fetched after all.

The Germans might just find it cute.

# 11

A clean desk, a clean house. Joseph Leubl likes things to be neat and tidy. Other people might find that boring, but he's been keeping it this way for fifty-seven years, ever since he's had his own room. Having grown up with four brothers he knows what a pigsty looks like and he also knows that he doesn't want one. He never leaves his office until all the jobs on his desk are done. And when he gets home, his house mustn't look as if there's more work to be done here.

He gets out of the limousine and says goodbye to the driver, who will be collecting him again tomorrow morning. Then he walks along the claret flagstones in the lawn to the house. He likes these flags, he likes how they're edged in moss and the way those tiny red beetles, similar to lice, scuttle over them in summer. The flagstones remind him of his parents' house; he brought them to Berlin specially, after he and his brothers sold the property. Whenever he sees them he thinks of the lawn sprinkler in the sun, the fragrance of damp grass and the feel of hot, wet stone beneath his feet. He had them sunk into the lawn just as he remembered from his childhood. The tufts of grass need to cushion the stone edges;

people shouldn't have to worry about stubbing their toes. Otherwise you can't run across the lawn. Otherwise children can't run across the lawn. Both his daughters used to do a lot of running. The memory pleases him; he knows of children who don't go outside at all anymore, unless you scatter Pokémons around the city as bait.

He goes inside and savours the smell he misses elsewhere, even though he doesn't notice it at home.

"I'm home!" he shouts from the hallway.

Leubl has had to do this ever since the limousines became quieter and the windows better insulated. He scared the living daylights out of his wife a dozen times until he got used to calling out whenever he arrived home. He hangs his coat on the rack and, in his mind only, hangs up a hat as well. He hasn't worn one for more than thirty years, but the thought of it is still part of his coming-home-from-work routine. He removes his immaculate shoes and inserts shoe trees, with which he lifts them onto the rack. After putting on a pair of felt slippers he walks across the tiles into the living room and kitchen. Leubl can hear his wife clanking around in the fridge.

He gives her a kiss on the cheek.

"How was your day?"

"The usual. The fountain's broken. I called the installer, but he can't come till next week."

"That's O.K."

The kitchen is separate. He doesn't like this modern fashion of all the living areas flowing into one. He doesn't want his kitchen overlapping with the sitting room and the sitting room drifting into the garden via a glass conservatory. The children's room shouldn't be in the bedroom and the toolshed shouldn't be in the garage, even if the garage has been empty since they've had the official car.

He goes to the fridge to get a beer. Not a pils, not a wheat beer, not a low-alcohol beer. Not a V.I.P. beer. Nor one of those rustic beers that's carted in from some remote village. And – heaven forbid! – certainly not a craft beer. He hates these new-fangled brews which start off so bitter, as if they'd burned in the copper, then suddenly taste of mango. Or mandarins. Compost beer. He wants a beer of the sort his father used to drink when he came in from the fields.

He drinks lager.

Leubl opens the bottle and pours the beer into his half-litre glass. He's about to take it into the sitting room to watch the news when his wife says, "Binny's here, by the way."

He doesn't respond. But he's not thrilled.

He likes an orderly life. He tiptoes into the sitting room. It's empty. He puts the beer down on the tiled coffee table and slumps onto the sofa. He's relieved to have a few precious minutes alone in the sitting room. There aren't many evenings like this, in the quiet summer period, although he takes more liberties than any other minister. He came into politics from the outside; he doesn't have grassroots party support and never has done. He's there because they need him, and if you don't have grassroots support you don't have to bother cultivating it. In any case he stopped trying years ago. He's seventy-five years old and doesn't have that much time to gift away.

Leubl sees two thin legs come down the stairs. Followed by a skinny midriff in shorts and two breasts that weren't there a couple of months ago.

"Hi, Grandad!"

"Binny!"

"Hmm?"

The minister raps his knuckles firmly on the table and looks at her impatiently.

"Sorry."

She plucks out her earphones, coils the cord around her smartphone and places it demonstratively on the bookshelf. Leubl nods, appeased.

"Well?"

"Well what?"

She slumps into an armchair just as he did. Strange, this identical movement, but with him you can see that he's shattered, whereas she's just in a huff.

"Looking forward to your holiday?"

"Nah!"

"Are you having a spot of bother with Mum?"

"Two weeks in the arse end of the world with no wi-fi? Moist! What am I going to do in Nowheresville?"

"You know that I was born in Nowheresville, don't you? And that Grandma was born just down the road. I'd live there still if I didn't have to be in Berlin."

"Huh!"

She kicks off her slippers and clamps her toes to the edge of the coffee table. Catching the expression on his face, she swiftly takes them off again. Her feet slap on the floor tiles.

"The minister of the interior always get wi-fi if he wants it."

"Don't be like that. Your mother just wants to spend as much time with you as possible."

"That's the worst part."

"I'm not sure you understand. It's because she knows there won't be so many more holidays with you."

"Really? Why's that then? She's not ill, that's for sure."

Leubl frowns.

"Sorry."

"You shouldn't joke about things like that. What I meant is that your mother was once your age too. The last time we went away together was when she was fifteen."

"Thank God!" This is his wife, coming in with the tray.

"Oh yes, Grandma's all very relaxed about it now. But she cried her eyes out at the time."

He gets up and sits at the head of the dining table with his beer, Binny sits opposite, Grandma in between. She sets out the plates, butter, bread basket, tomatoes, salami, the vegan spread and the glasses. Binny picks one up critically.

"Nobody's going to believe me when I tell them the minister of the interior drinks out of old mustard jars."

"Why shouldn't we?" Grandma asks as she cuts the tomatoes into quarters and grinds pepper over them.

"They're so lame, they've even got Mickey Mouse on them. You can't get uncooler than that."

"That's fitting, then," Leubl says, buttering a slice of bread in preparation for some salami. "Of all the cabinet, the minister of the interior is always the least cool."

"Really? Why?"

"Because he's in charge of the police." He bites into his bread. "The minister of the interior is a bit like Germany's caretaker."

He watches his granddaughter scrape a sort of greyish-brown mortar from the vegan jar, before cladding a slice of bread with it. Expertly, you might say. He offers her a lettuce leaf with his fork.

"Here, you can use this for wallpaper."

"Joseph!"

"To be fair, I don't make any comments about your murderous salami, Grandad."

He lays the lettuce on his bread.

"The salami murderer issues a formal apology."

"Fine, but for that you can lowkey tell the stupid minister for transport that he needs to get decent Internet access to Doofhausen, sharpish."

He laughs. He doesn't mention how delighted he is that her mother doesn't go along with all that Internet and mobile nonsense. Nor does he admit how awful the Internet access really is in the area. Or that he regards the transport minister as the only member of the cabinet who is without question 100 per cent inept.

After supper Grandma gets up to clear the table. He takes the rest of his beer back to the sofa. Eight o'clock on the dot. The evening news is his last bastion.

"Can't we watch something else?"

"Aren't you at all interested in the news?"

"I know it all already. I've got the app."

"Well, I don't and nor does Grandma."

Jens Riewa appears on the screen. Today he's been dressed in an unflattering shade of blue, which means he sometimes disappears against the graphic overlays.

"Yeah," Binny says. "Here comes the assassination."

He gives her a warning look, but at the same time he's amazed by all the things she picks up on. She can, in fact, correctly predict almost all of the day's news, even those items he assumes must bore her.

"They're proposing a new electoral law," Binny says. "To give sixteen-year-olds the vote. That would mean I could vote next year."

"And what would you vote?" Grandma Leubl asks.

"A.f.D."

A moment's silence. He keeps a stiff upper lip and says, without looking at her, "Because of Mum."

"Exactly. She hit the roof. Had a screaming fit. Beeeee-neeeeee, how could you?"

"What about my party?"

"Forget it. You're not shit enough."

"Is that supposed to be a compliment."

"No. I mean, you're shit too."

It occurs to him that at her age he wouldn't have been allowed to say "shit", but it hardly bothers him. What does that say about our times?

That his period of grace is over. As soon as the weather finished, Binny grabs the remote control. He doesn't complain, he knows that Grandma Leubl is on Binny's side. And he knows too that it's quite an accolade to have Binny watching television with them. Normally she sees everything on the computer, on demand.

"So what are we watching?"

"Nadeche Hackenbusch," Binny says. "I'm not gonna lie, this is even something for you two."

"The one with the . . . ?" he says, intimating breasts.

"The one with the refugees!"

What he sees on the screen is indeed astonishing. He knows this cheap model, of course, pretty much like all the other cheap bimbos. But this time the cheap model has been sent to one of the world's hotspots: the largest refugee camp on Earth. This, however, isn't the usual misery television with some listless family living in a mouldy ruin, this is real hardship. Binny and his wife sink inaudibly into the background as he watches, in amazement, the bimbo model, accompanied by a terrifically handsome refugee, talking a lot of nonsense, but also making the occasional comment that verges on the sensible. The bimbo model, he learns, was on this programme yesterday. And will be on again tomorrow, and daily for the next fortnight, broadcasting from this wretched place. What he sees makes him more uneasy by the minute. He crosses the room to the telephone and dials from memory the under-secretary's number.

# 12

It's payday.

"Sensenbrink speaking."

"Kasewalk, *Süddeutsche Zeitung*. We're delighted you've made time for us."

"It's not unlimited, though – lots of balls in the air and all that," Sensenbrink advises him, pumping a Boris Becker fist beneath the table. Kasewalk is top five. Maybe even top three. If you want a report in a paper, it's got to be the *Süddeutsche*, the *F.A.Z.*, the Sunday *F.A.Z.*, the *Welt* or – who knows? – maybe the *Spiegel* too. But in the end it's the *Süddeutsche* and the *F.A.Z.* that really count, and if Kasewalk calls then you can assume that they're keeping at least half a page free, maybe more. And this is for a daily piece with Nadeche Hackenbusch, who the *Süddeutsche* wouldn't have even shown its arse to a couple of months ago.

"I'm just about to go into a meeting. What can I do for you?"

"It's about 'Angel in Adversity', obviously. Or A2, as I hear you lot call it. Is that right?"

"Who's been spilling the chickpeas?"

"You've cracked the ten-million-viewer mark and the numbers are still rising. That's the kind of figures you get for the cup final, and you're doing it every day. Are you surprised by the success?"

"Well, A2 was already champions league before."

"But not on this scale."

"That's true. And here's the subtle difference. There are series which are successful and then they try to stuff too much tuna in the taco. There's an offshoot, then another one, but to be honest it's just the same soup diluted with plenty of water. The A2 special is different."

"To begin with there were critics who didn't see it that way. Some of them writing for this paper."

"But who's right now? I mean, I'm an old hand at this game and I know best when I'm diluting something and when I'm not—"

"What have you diluted?"

Sensenbrink laughs and Kasewalk joins in. The old sly-question trick, but nonetheless Sensenbrink feels a warm glow. The *Süddeutsche* is playing the sly-question game with him! Kasewalk from the *Süddeutsche*, half a page – Sensenbrink has to swallow; he feels loved. He shakes his head, surprised at himself, but he can't put it any other way. He's enjoying this. When was the last time he was rung up by a newspaper? And now it's all kicking off, the interview, the attention, everything. He means to enjoy this; he leans back.

"Not A2 at any rate. To continue with the metaphor, we haven't just added more water, we've got more ingredients too."

"And what are these ingredients?"

Finally, the right questions. This isn't someone just after sales figures or a broadcaster statement. Someone wants to know his opinion because he, Sensenbrink, is now a somebody: the creator of 'Angel in Adversity'. Not of 'Angel in Adversity', the trashy programme, but 'Angel in Adversity' the surprisingly good show. This interview tells him that it's no coincidence and it's not because of Nadeche Hackenbusch. It's because of Sensenbrink. It's Sensenbrink's interview.

It's Sensenbrink's payday.

"More vegetables, more fat, more meat," Sensenbrink expands. "But not of the 'Now with 15 per cent more potato chunks' kind. The main thing is that the viewers are noticeably closer to the action. A2 used to be pre-produced and broadcast once a week. Naturally the viewers have to manage their expectations. After thirty years of commercial television they've learned that formats like this are optimised for the small screen. They have to be."

"You exaggerate conflicts, hype problems, increase the drama—"

"I'm not going to confirm that, but what I will say is that producing the A2 special on a daily basis means we can't optimise to anything like the same degree – the viewers get the raw material, if you like, but it's also more kosher, the real deal. And they know it."

"Aren't they used to that? I mean, 'I'm a Celebrity' is filmed and broadcast every day too."

"Sure, but the viewers know full well that the jungle's a totally phoney set-up. C-listers sitting around on their arses for money, and to spice things up a bit they need those artificial trials. Don't forget, the so-called personalities can drop out any time they like. With some of them you even know beforehand that they'll be buggering off as soon as they're allowed. Nobody can do that on A2."

"Apart from Nadeche Hackenbusch."

"Well, you could say that about the news too. Any reporter can go home whenever they like. That doesn't make the wars they report from any safer. No, the people Nadeche Hackenbusch reports on don't have any alternative. They were in that camp yesterday, they're in it today and they'll still be there tomorrow."

"Reporters don't have flings on the ground, do they?"

There we go. That's all part and parcel of this, it's the crucial question. Kasewalk has to ask this so he can tell his boss that they're shedding light on the background to this story rather than merely offering Sensenbrink an elaborate platform. And Sensenbrink knows the score too, because he's so damn professional. There needs to be a bit of disruption in the mix, and then Kasewalk will be happy. Quietly he leans back in his chair and puts his feet on the desk. He saw someone do this once in an interview on H.B.O.

"With all due respect, what are you insinuating?"

"We're not insinuating anything."

"Then maybe you should put your question differently."

"Fine. From some of the scenes in the A2 special, one might conclude that the relationship between Frau Hackenbusch and her colleague extends beyond the purely professional."

"And which scenes are you thinking of?"

"The 'Month's End' episode. The family that has literally nothing—"

"—and doesn't get anything either. That's the norm in those camps, that's reality when you're living your life on rations. This is how the cycle goes. On the first five days everyone's got something to eat. On the next five days you visit friends to spare yourselves a meal. And then come the fifteen days when everyone's starving. Frau Hackenbusch had no idea about this, nor did any of the team – even me. When you see and experience this in real life, it hits you hard. So I think it's perfectly normal that even a strong personality like Frau Hackenbusch should need another human being to lean on."

"She could have leaned on the camera team, but she went for Lionel."

"Are we really going to spend our time discussing who Frau Hackenbusch leans on and when? If this shows anything at all, it's professionalism, because the cameraman mustn't let the camera wobble."

"How about the episode with the dirty water . . . or the little boy who died of fever?"

"I'm hearing you. The short scenes where Frau Hackenbusch reaches for Lionel's hand, his shoulder. Speaking as a T.V. guy, let me tell you quite frankly that we're amped when we see moments like this – they're pure gold. Not just for us, for any broadcaster. Despite this we neither ask for them nor orchestrate them. But if I get one on camera I'm not going to be so stupid as to cut it, am I?"

"Because it's more meat in your soup."

"Exactly. The viewers are drawn in closer. And seeing as you ran it up the flagpole, this is true for the relationship between those two as well. I can't tell you what's going on between Frau Hackenbusch and Lionel, you'd have to ask them that. But at the end of the day, it's genuine. We don't script anything, we don't know ourselves what's happening on an emotional level."

"You don't know what's happening on your own show?"

"No, I don't. And I'm perfectly happy to take responsibility for the fact that the tension is working. I mean, this is something you can *only* do with Nadeche Hackenbusch. As your questions make quite clear."

"How so?"

"Because if this was anyone else you wouldn't be asking. It wouldn't interest you whether what happened in the programme was real or not. But with Nadeche it's different, because she's done a lot of television, without ever going so far as to capitalise on her private life. Or do you think that Frau Hackenbusch is putting on an act for the nation here? A married woman with two children?"

"It's hard to imagine . . ."

"There you go."

"How important is Lionel to the success of the show?"

Sensenbrink can feel himself relaxing, sinking into the chair. If this interview were a cow that needed to be rescued from the ice, it would now be in safety. Yet he doesn't feel any better.

"Again your question hints at the answer. He's essential."

"Is it true you chose him yourself?"

"Yes, it is."

It takes him a moment to realise what this is leading to. Now comes all the trivia.

"And you've scripted nothing of what he says?"

"Nada."

"Not even phrases such as 'At night the sun shines elsewhere'? Or 'Nobody knows why the monkey scratches himself'?"

"Fabulous, isn't it? These words just tumble from the guy's mouth. Those clips are the most viewed on our website. The kids make memes out of them. Only yesterday I saw a young couple – he had a T-shirt that said: 'When the Lion yawns, the gnu goes to bed'. And hers: 'The heart beats in secret.'"

"'The heart beats in secret', 'At night the sun shines elsewhere' – have you got a clue what any of this means?"

"Not always. But it's a peculiar mixture of strength and thoughtfulness, which makes him the perfect foil for Nadeche Hackenbusch, who – and I'm certainly not saying anything new here – isn't particularly known for her thoughtfulness. You can try as hard as you like to deliberately cast someone like that, but ninety-nine times out of a hundred you'll get a turkey. Lionel is fabulous, a lucky find for any producer."

The niceties. Questions formulated in a way that allows Sensenbrink to place everything he wants to place. They signal that the climax of the interview is over. Sensenbrink feels something akin to the pain of separation. All the importance, all the attention is now dissipating. Yes, tomorrow it'll be printed and more people will see it. For most people – well, virtually everybody apart from Kasewalk and him – this whole conversation won't take place until tomorrow. They'll call or e-mail him: "Great interview in the *S.Z.*" All the same. It's like when the long summer holiday is coming to an end and you're thinking about the first day back at school.

"How's the programme going to end?" Kasewalk says. As if he could read people's minds. "Surely you can't wing it, you must have planned something."

Sensenbrink feels an absurd acrimony welling up inside him. Towards Kasewalk, strangely. It takes him a while to locate the cause, probably because it's so silly: he envies this man. It annoys him that Kasewalk will still be on holiday tomorrow. He'll interview someone else, and the day after that and so on. Kasewalk will always feature in the *Süddeutsche Zeitung*.

"That's one sunroof I can't open," Sensenbrink says. "Of course we're trying to tie up loose ends, but we're also aware that we have to make compromises. A refugee camp isn't a holiday home, you can't clean and tidy before you leave. That's what happens when you film real life. I fear the viewers might be left slightly unsatisfied. Unsatisfied or, to put it a better way, eager for the next series of 'Angel in Adversity'. We have new episodes planned for November."

"That's a nice way to conclude," Kasewalk says.

"Isn't it?"

They say goodbye and then it's over. Only for now, Sensenbrink consoles himself, only for now. If things keep going in the right direction, who knows where it might end?

# 13

The under-secretary parks the car in the basement garage. He knows that Tommy is waiting for him upstairs. He ought to be happy; they've got a three-day weekend ahead of them. And everything has worked out splendidly, even though they had a special meeting today in the ministry. He wasn't in the office any longer than usual. He should be happy, he should be leaping out of the car, full of joy and lust, he should already be removing his tie and chunky watch to save precious seconds. Instead he's still in the car, having switched the engine off, absentmindedly flicking the indicator. Left. Right. Left. Right.

He can't complain about the meeting. To the point and purposeful.

And he knows you can't take this for granted, having been to enough meetings in his life. Lohm is always telling him about endless meetings where the preparation's shocking and there's no outcome. One lot are worried about divulging information, another are worried about making decisions, and in between you've got those who haven't got a clue, nor are they worried about opening their mouths and spouting the most cretinous noise. Nothing like that happens in Leubl's ministry.

Left.

He called in pretty much every department connected with refugees and internal security, and relayed the minister's impatience. One could also say that he gave those assembled a rocket and made it plain that he, and nobody else, was Leubl's right hand.

Right.

"We need to keep an eye on this," he said. "Everyone here has to understand that it's serious."

"Possibly, but let's not blow it out of proportion. We've got enough problems as it is."

That was from Gödeke, of course. The roles assign themselves, and even if the anger in the room is so thick you can cut it with a knife, the police, protected by their limited powers, are always the first to break cover.

"If we remain vigilant, this might not turn into another one. I'm not even saying that anything's going to happen. But there are a number of possible scenarios and it could become the biggest problem of all. Let me reiterate: we have to remain vigilant. And I'm purposely not going to raise the issue of why nobody has brought this matter up for discussion till now."

"Because it's a shite programme. A shite T.V. programme on a shite T.V. channel."

There's always one who takes the bait. This time it was Dr Berthold, head of the department for public security. Sixty-four years old, normally unobtrusive and dependable, but noticeably reluctant, being on the verge of retirement, to be lectured by someone in their mid-thirties.

"Nicely put. It's a shite T.V. show on a shite channel. And so you imagine it's harmless?"

"I've no idea, for God's sake, but does that automatically make it dangerous? I can't speak for my colleagues, but I can't be the only one here who thinks we might benefit from being a bit more relaxed about this. What do you think's going to happen?"

"Well, the most trifling outcome would be them wanting to bring one of their refugee models to Germany."

This failed to ruffle Berthold. "You can forget that." And Dr Kalb from migration nodded sagely: "Asylum law applies to television too." Sometimes it's so simple, the under-secretary thinks – you just need to offer them up the knife.

Left. Right.

"Great," he said. "Then legally we're off the hook, aren't we? So what are we going to do if a million T.V. viewers sympathise with this model? For weeks on end? Is the minister going to stand up and say that legally this makes no difference?"

Berthold murmured something barely audible, which sounded like "But that's how it is." In truth, however, everyone around the table was suddenly struck by the magnitude of this affair.

"Gentlemen, this isn't a news team that's gone down to Africa," the under-secretary declared. "These aren't journalists who know how to report with a degree of neutrality and otherwise don't interfere. This is a bunch of idiots who spend the rest of their time making garbage like 'Wife Swap'."

It was at this point that he noticed a sense of unease creeping into people's faces. So he upped the ante.

"And they're not in some prefabricated T.V. jungle with plug sockets like on 'I'm a Celebrity'. They're in the real world now."

It was good to watch the pack gradually pick up the scent, Gödeke to the fore: "Are you worried that one of them's going to take her hostage?"

"You see? Doesn't sound so harmless now, does it? But this is only one possible scenario. The main problem is that nobody knows what's going to come out of it, not even the telly people. They think it's just like in the T.V. jungle, they think they've got it all under control. But they're not in control of anything, because in real life anything can happen. And as soon as the general public rewards this with high ratings—"

"—they'll have thirty models in tow, with families and friends too," Kaspers from crisis management interjected, leaping to his feet.

"And with two or three million viewers putting pressure behind it—"

"It's true, I know a few T.V. people too. And they really are like that, 'What's the problem?' they think. 'For any emergency we've got Medic Bob's safety goggles.'"

Now there was only one way the meeting could go. He just had to scoop them up, one by one.

"Welcome to the modern world. If all of you are now up to speed on the situation, we can move on to the positives. The good news is that it doesn't have to be a problem," the under-secretary placated them. "But it could turn into one very quickly."

Left.

He really can't complain. He didn't once have to refer to the minister; he didn't say something like, "Minister Leubl wishes . . ." He simply gave instructions.

"The most important thing now is to gather information. We need to know as much as possible about their team. So that at least we're prepared to some extent."

Right.

"Then we'll decide who to approach. We'll talk to their bosses. One of us and someone from the foreign ministry. All softly-softly, very restrained."

"We'll raise their awareness to prevent them from doing anything silly."

"We'll remind them of their civic responsibility, so they don't whinge about censorship."

"Right. I mean, it's in their interests too."

"The key thing is that they keep a close eye on Hackenbusch. She's as thick as two short planks," Berthold bitched.

"So our position is this: let them do their stuff, no problem. But they need to realise it's in their own interests to get out of there quickly."

Then he declared the meeting at an end and went to see Leubl in his office.

Left.

Right.

Left.

Leubl listened over the top of his spectacles as the under-secretary gave him a quick briefing.

"Good," Leubl said. "Good. Maybe we'll regain control of this." Then leaned back in his chair.

"Which brings us to the last point. How was this able to slip past you?"

Right.

"I . . . I . . . it just wasn't on my radar."

Leubl took off his glasses. "It *was* on your radar. You certainly didn't hear about the programme from me. You just didn't know what it might turn into. But why?"

"Why? I don't understand the question. I just missed it."

Left.

"Refugees. Television. Celebs. All the ingredients for a catastrophe. How come you didn't see the danger?"

Rightleftright.

Leubl was right. Why hadn't he seen it?

Leftrightleft.

"I might have been distracted."

"Exactly. You were distracted because you're gay."

"What?"

Now his fingers switch on the headlights. The wall of the underground garage glares brightly.

"Let me tell you what happened. Somebody told you about the programme. And you thought they were only mentioning it because Hackenbusch is a fag hag. So as far as you were concerned that was the end of the matter."

He flashes the headlights as if they could bore through the wall.

"But—"

"You know I don't hold your homosexuality against you. And just so you don't take it the wrong way, you don't have to be gay for this to happen. It could happen if you were a drinker, a gambler or because you're snorting coke or having an affair. It can happen whenever certain things are up closer than usual. As soon as these things blind you to what's really going on."

"I'll bear that in mind."

"Bearing it in mind isn't going to help. It's a sign that you have to make a decision."

The under-secretary raised his eyebrows at Leubl. Had this been anyone else, he might have expected to be told to turn straight or give up the job. But not Leubl, out of the question.

"You always pretend not to care whether someone's gay or not; in particular you pretend not to care that you're gay. But you do care!"

"Of course I care!"

Leubl nodded. "Which doesn't have to be a problem. It might even help you within the party. It certainly makes you a more human politician. But at the same time it makes you a poorer minister. Some ministers are always keeping an eye on their party, their constituency, or their anxieties and weaknesses and the manner in which they hide these or exploit them in public. They have their eye on so many things that they become a poor minister. A good minister is a minister and nothing besides."

Leubl reached for a file. The lecture was coming at an end.

"It's your decision as to what sort of minister you want to be."

The under-secretary takes his hand from the headlight lever and pushes the door open with his elbow. He gets out, lets the car door slam shut and goes to the lift that will take him up to his apartment. The apartment is in darkness apart from a tealight flickering on the floor.

He hangs his key on the hook and steps into the apartment. He spies a second tealight. And a third, and then a line of others showing the way to the bedroom.

He doesn't fancy it. He feels as if he's lost a match, a final. He hasn't played worse than anyone else, but it was his job to captain the team. He didn't act like a leader, merely like a hanger-on. And Leubl is right: he does care. Some people have to be better than others. If you're black or a woman or disabled or gay. And if you're not better than the others, can you afford to be gay?

As the under-secretary was leaving Leubl's office, his hand already on the doorknob, he turned around.

"Herr Leubl?"

Leubl looked at him and raised his eyebrows.

"Has it ever happened to you?"

Leubl calmly browsed his files.

"No. I'm not gay."

He took a moment before peering above his glasses, assuming a look of innocence.

"Let's say I decided my first priority was to be a good minister."

"It has happened to you."

"Yes. It happens to everyone. But my marriage came within a whisker of breaking down before I found the answer. So don't dawdle."

The under-secretary looks at the tealights leading to the bedroom.

He takes his key from the hook and leaves the apartment.

# 14

Something is happening. Or something is going to happen soon, either/or. She knew it from the first moment, she could tell by the look in Nadeche's eyes, and the look in his. They can't fool her. Some consolation, at least, for all she's had to put up with recently. Sometimes Astrid von Roëll has no idea how she's supposed to get it all done. Today, for example, they want her to write yet another piece. She wonders what on earth the editorial team back home are thinking.

"Hey, d'you fancy a green tea too?" she asks the intern. She's sitting at the screen beside Astrid, wearing earphones and scanning through the previous days' footage.

"Sorry?"

They're at the same desk inside a container. Three weak neon lights and one that flickers lend the room all the cosiness of an abandoned underpass. Two fans ensure the equal distribution of warmth and stale air; when you get close to them it's like being coughed at by a very old woman. Three people work at this desk and the moment someone leaves the room, another immediately claims the free chair.

"What I'd give for a green tea now!" Astrid says. She goes over to the small, calcified kettle and fills it with water from a vessel that she still can't look at with anything other than scepticism.

Water that doesn't come from a tap.

That sits around for days in the same tank.

Clean, of course, that's guaranteed. At least as clean as the official water points accessible to all refugees. And far cleaner than the unofficial ones – there's no comparison. Nobody would believe what she's seen here with her own eyes. One day it comes out cloudy, the next a rusty brown, and sometimes it's the colour of pee – she can't be doing with that. You can't drink the stuff and everything you wash with it just gets dirtier, both clothes and bodies. Even so, people queue for hours.

The water is lukewarm again. She lets it run. It doesn't look that bad. You just can't think too closely about how it sits all day in that gigantic metal container with all those particles floating about.

She shouldn't complain, but having to drink lukewarm water *all the time* is starting to piss her off. If you want something cold you have to get a Coke from the fridge, but it's not even Diet Coke, it's packed full of sugar and, besides, everyone looks at you. They watch to see whether you replace it with another one, whether you're drinking too quickly. And they wonder why you want a cold drink in the first place. Or why you're taking this perfectly good water . . .

"Hey! It's not going to get any colder!" Grande again. Miss Water Watcher, she really gets on her tits! Astrid turns

141

away, looks upwards and meekly turns off the tap.

"You could try to keep an eye on her!" Grande hisses at the intern.

"Sorry, mind was elsewhere."

"How many times? We pay to have this water delivered. I can't keep going over budget just because it's not cool enough for Frau von Roëll."

That's another thing. A couple of weeks ago Grande wouldn't have dared behave like this. They were delighted to have *Evangeline* on board as a partner. They'd have served her drinks at whatever temperature she desired. And nobody gave a damn when she used water from the plastic bottles, back when they still had green tea. But now the show's taken Germany by storm, it's being reported on everywhere, in all the magazines, newspapers, social media. Anybody who can afford it – and an astonishing number of media outlets still can – is sitting here in this container. Now Astrid has to fight tooth and nail to prove that she's not just one of many. *Stern* has sent someone, *Bild* too, of course, and now the *F.A.S.* as well, that Sunday version of the *Frankfurter Allgemeine Zeitung* that actually publishes articles about things that might interest a normal individual. And then some idiot back home comes up with the idea that she could write more, seeing as it's a daily programme. For their "online presence". Lou Grant, no doubt, that scheming fungus. She can just imagine him in the editorial meeting, saying in his nasal voice, "I want to read about this more often." But she bets he visits the *Evangeline* website as seldom as anyone.

The deputy editor relayed the happy message by phone.

To begin with she tried to be obliging: "I don't know whether they've got any more room here."

"What?" the deputy blockhead said.

"It's really cramped and that. And I presume we're talking about Sibylle or Sonja. They'd have to find somewhere to sleep too."

"Why would we be talking about Frau Bessemer or Frau Laienfeld?"

"Who do you think's going to write all that stuff?"

Initially he seemed at a loss. Then he said, in his really stupid way, "Hmm. Tricky. Let's see: what about . . . you?"

"Sorry? No offence, but I've got plenty on my plate already, what with the fashion shoots and all the research and—"

"Look, in a camp with more than two million people there must be something happening every day. Surely you'll be able to write a hundred lines or so about what's going on."

"I see. Well, O.K. then. I thought you meant on a daily basis."

It was probably only then that the lunacy of his demands occurred to him. Typical man: they never admit to their mistakes. They always have to stick to the wrong path, stubbornly and to the bitter end. It must have taken him at least a minute to come up with an answer, which turned out to be as idiotic as the first one. More idiotic, in fact.

"Yes, of *course* on a daily basis."

"I'm not a sodding typewriter."

"You're a journalist! Have you ever taken a look at a newspaper? There's stuff in there every day!"

This left her speechless. And then of course he turned the

143

screw – men are better at this than anything else; they can sniff out weakness at a distance of eight thousand kilometres and down a telephone line – by saying, "Do you seriously want me to go running around the office, saying that one of *Evangeline*'s best writers can't pull off what any hack for the *Nowheresville Arsevertiser* can?"

Insolent shithead! What cheek!

And the "one of *Evangeline*'s best writers" crap. Of course she's one of the best, that's beyond doubt. In fact *Evangeline*'s problem is that, apart from her, they employ losers. Sonja and Sibylle, they're nice girls and perfectly adequate for routine jobs. But on balance the entire company is nothing but a collection of overpaid dyslexics!

And even though Astrid isn't one of those perpetual whingers, even though Astrid isn't a clock-watcher, often staying longer than the others, even though Astrid's articles are among the most widely read in the entire magazine, even though she never makes a fuss about being the last to get a new work mobile, despite all this she demanded this be referred to the editor-in-chief. Because this was a matter of principle.

"And quality!"

"Sorry," the intern says. "I wasn't listening. What's that?"

"I said it's a question of quality too," Astrid says insistently.

"Is there something wrong with the coffee?"

"No! I'm talking about journalism! Quality journalism!"

The water is boiling and she makes a ghastly instant coffee. In the office back home they have a fantastic pod machine, so you can make whatever coffee you fancy: cappuccino, latte macchiato, everything. What a shame there's not one here, seeing as everything you need is right outside the door. The coffee grows in Africa, and someone told her that the aluminium for the pods comes from here too. You could save on all that transportation. But this is exactly what crisis areas are like, they have everything in abundance, yet can't do a thing with any of it, like that Ancient Greek man who stood under the fruit tree but couldn't get a bean. Syphonos.

"It's impossible for the same person to write one hundred lines every day. One *hundred*! Every day! How's that supposed to work?"

"I don't know," the intern says. "I'm subscribed to a couple of blogs on my mobile. They seem to manage it somehow."

"Sure. Blogs. Self-exploitation."

"And I've heard *Spiegel Online* are toying with the idea too. Normally they only do it for 'I'm a Celebrity'."

Cup in hand, Astrid plants herself firmly on the chair. *Spiegel Online*. Yeah. They sit there comfortably watching the show, then gossip about it afterwards.

"You've never written anything, have you?" she asks coldly.

"The odd essay, that sort of thing."

"That's quite different," Astrid explains, then adds in more friendly tone, "But you're still young. Good journalism takes time. That lot at Condé Nast laugh when they see our set-up. They know that good journalism has its price. They'd turn up with two photographers, four or five researchers and another two people to write the text. And what do we do?"

The editor-in-chief caved in immediately, of course.

Not directly to her, but to his deputy. That spineless character. They'd never have dared behave like that towards Nadeche. "There's no such thing as impossible!" Nadeche would say. They'd be a dream team: Nadeche Hackenbusch and Astrid von Roëll, the first joint female editors in upmarket tabloid journalism.

"They're lucky that I can do both: research *and* write!"

The intern nods and her eyes seem to twinkle with gratitude for this background knowledge about the particulars of the media world. But she's a bit too quick to turn back to her screen, at least for Astrid's taste. And has she actually got *two* earphones in?

She has. Bitch.

All because of that guy. She realised at once that there was something about him. How they found him in the first place is pretty incredible. He's not even that good looking, not at first glance anyway. But he has this astonishing way of saying things. And his way with women, well . . . even she finds it rather unusual. He's so respectful, but not submissive, not like those usual types who are "in touch with their feminine side".

She collared him on one occasion, for half an hour right at the start, before the telly people started shielding him. And what an impression he gave once she'd got used to his English, which took a little while because hers is a touch rusty too. She's never been particularly good at languages, but she understood everything all the same.

Anyway, you only hear properly with the heart, don't you?

He comes from a city – it doesn't really matter which one,

they can always check later – where his parents were English teachers, which was lucky for him, of course. Then civil war broke out, or it might have been a tribal conflict – again, this needs checking in the final edit – and his parents died, they weren't killed, or at least she doesn't think they were, more likely while fleeing or after their flight, exhaustion, homesickness, something like that can break you emotionally. Then he did something with cars and wanted to study, or even started a course (so there's actually a university?), something to do with cars or machinery, but then there was persistent unrest and he had to enlist in the army – the bottom line is that it's one of many refugee life stories, there's no need to drag it out. That's for the amateur bloggers. As a professional it's her job to focus on the key issue: what's it like working with Nadeche Hackenbusch?

"Oh," he said, beaming. "Malaika!"

Astrid takes a deep breath. She's going to get it over and done with now. One hundred lines. But they're going to notice how it affects the quality. She'll write about some crap like the weather, whatever. It mustn't be too good or they'll keep wanting more of the same. And the difference from the print edition must be evident straightaway. She's going to bang out such an amazing piece for the print edition they'll be worrying Condé Nast will be out to poach her.

# 15

"The material is ace," Sensenbrink says. "I wasn't expecting that. Were you?"

He's sitting in the cutting room, viewing yesterday's footage. In fact it's a compilation of yesterday's footage because crazy amounts of broadcast material are now coming back from Africa.

"No, I'm pleasantly surprised too," Beate Karstleiter says.

They're watching Nadeche and Lion Man cooking dinner with a family. It's quite banal actually, and yet fascinating, because there's practically nothing to see. There's no kitchen, only a fire outside of the house. There's no salad, no fruit, nothing. There's no real preparation either, because there's nothing to prepare. They have the ingredients you get as a refugee: beans, oil, sugar, salt and water. There are no spices in a camp where two million people abandoned their search for variety in their food years ago. The images are both dismal and intimate. Not even A.R.D.'s "Weltspiegel" programme would broadcast that, but Nadeche and Lion Man make the footage so effective.

Now, Lion Man translates into English, the refugee

woman of indeterminate age is about to disclose her secret. This is a good starting point because, with the best will in the world, Nadeche and the viewers wouldn't be able to make anything out of those ingredients apart from an insipid sludge. The scepticism in Nadeche's eyes is clear; it's the same look you see in those docusoaps, when the middle-class wife who's swapped house is trying to get the lower-class kids to eat fish. Unlike the lower-class kids, who are guided by a script, Nadeche is trying to be polite and her face beams with genuine hope, because like everyone else she believes in the dramatic art of television. The magic potion, the miracle in- gredient that bestows a happy ending on a looming tragedy, like in the normal episodes of "Angel in Adversity", where colouring pencils are produced for the children at the very last minute. The refugee woman says something. She closes her eyes, makes a few rhythmic hand movements, opens her eyes again and adds a little sugar to the pot with a meaning- ful look. Nadeche watches with interest. You can literally see her searching for the unique aspect of this process and failing to find it. She looks at Lion Man.

"What's she doing?"

If you focus on her lips you can see what Nadeche is actu- ally saying: "What do she?" But thank God they've already dubbed her in pre-production with the voice of the trans- lator. Initially they were going to use subtitles, but this was before they were fully aware of how absurd Nadeche's English is. By synchronising the translation with the original, they're ostensibly keeping the narrative up to speed, whereas what they're actually doing is fading out Nadeche's gobbledygook to the point where it's virtually inaudible.

"She's singing."

"A magic song?"

Lion Man laughs. So friendly, so amicable, so caring and yet so special that Sensenbrink can hear Karstleiter holding her breath beside him. This isn't just down to the dubbing; you can hear his real voice too. The original intention was to sync it, as with Nadeche, but Sensenbrink stuck his oar in.

"No, it's not a magic song, it's a children's song. She says you have to get to the end of the first verse."

"And then?"

"That's when to add the sugar."

"What about the recipe?"

"That *is* the recipe."

Nadeche Hackenbusch looks blank.

"But . . . that's not a recipe! When the water boils, put the pasta in – that's not a recipe either! Please ask her again." Sensenbrink thinks he hears, "Question her please again."

Lion Man asks the woman something. She replies with visible pride, and his face shows that he understood her correctly first time around.

"Malaika, look!" When he takes her by the hand, Sensenbrink can scarcely believe that Nadeche Hackenbusch, control freak of the small screen, is allowing him to do this, trusting him. Pulling her a little closer to the ingredients, he shows her in turn the plastic bottle with the indeterminate cooking oil and the carefully closed box of beans. "Malaika! That's all there is."

"I know. But the recipe?"

"What are you going to do with a recipe?"

He approaches the refugee woman, takes the wooden spoon apologetically from her hand and stirs the pot for a while before pausing.

"You want a new recipe? I'll show you a new recipe."

Then he stirs in the opposite direction.

"That guy is a guru," Sensenbrink mutters, then turns to Beate Karstleiter, who was putting her glasses back on. "I told you right at the start! Have you seen how he deals with her? She's putty in his hands."

Karstleiter clears her throat and nods.

"Do they always send so much material?" Sensenbrink says.

"Yes, but that's fine. We had a call from the boss's office just now. They're planning to extend the programme by fifteen minutes."

"Get in! Is this public education week?"

"No, they can't squeeze in the commercials otherwise. They don't want it to end up looking like an infomercial interspersed with a few clips of refugees. I'm flabbergasted, to be honest. They're not always as sensitive as this."

Sensenbrink folds his hands in his lap and taps his thumbs together thoughtfully. "It's astonishing, especially since nothing actually happens in the programme. Apart from that episode with the mass panic."

"Another reason I wouldn't tell them to be more sparing with the footage. You only capture stuff like that if the cameras are rolling all the time."

"And then we've got Lion Man having his merry way with

our star." Sensenbrink shakes his head. "If you were to write that in a script, nobody would believe you."

"We're already getting the first love letters."

"What?"

"O.K., not by the bucketload, but one or two a day."

"Proper letters?"

Karstleiter opens her eyes wide and nods. Sensenbrink glances approvingly at the screen. "I didn't know people still did that these days."

"We're surprised ourselves. Some are from young girls, and I wouldn't have thought they knew what a stamp even looks like. It's all down to Lionel."

"Lionel?"

"That's his name apparently."

"No," Sensenbrink corrects her. "That's what we called him. But it's not his real name."

"Are you sure? It's what Nadeche calls him too and he's never complained."

"A coincidence, maybe," Sensenbrink wonders.

"But it's not just love letters. Some people want to donate."

Sensenbrink is jolted from his contentment. "Wait. Let's not get our ducks out of line here. We're not Médecins Sans Frontières. A donation account and stuff, that's O.K., we'll get some organisation or other to piggyback on it. It'll go down well if someone like Bread for the World are behind it. But we're not going to start having Nadeche dole out money down there."

"That's precisely the problem," Karstleiter says, swivelling so pointedly in her chair towards Sensenbrink that he feels obliged to turn to her too. "If it goes on like this, these kinds of problems are only going to increase."

"Where's the problem? We send the donations to some aid organisation and that's that. Better still, we put its web address up on the screen and then the money won't pitch up here first.

"I'm not just talking about the public."

"What, then?"

"Haven't you been watching our angel? I'm not sure she's just making a television programme."

"Well of course she's doing more than that. But that's great! She's doing stuff I'd never have thought she was capable of."

"Yes, but . . ."

"What do you mean? You're looking at me as if it was a gorilla turd . . . This is T.V. gold! A presenter who believes in what she's doing!"

"So long as it doesn't turn into fanaticism, fine."

"Tell me, is this some kind of women's thing?"

He can say that to Beate Karstleiter, and sometimes she's allowed to call him "dick driven". Which of course he's not.

"Nonsense," she says dismissively. "All I'm saying is that a healthy, professional distance is no bad thing. If we suddenly find she's on a mission, she might end up more Schreinemakers-like than we'd find welcome."

Sensenbrink frowns. "I've never known you to talk like this. Schreinemakers is good. Schreinemakers is the jackpot. Or do you disagree?"

"No, no—"

"Or do you know something I don't?"

"There are just concerns—"

"But these concerns aren't actually yours, are they?"

Karstleiter briefly looks away, but she knows that this is confirmation in itself. "No, not mine. Not originally. But they shouldn't be dismissed so lightly."

"Alright. Where are they coming from? Legal? H.R.?"

"The ministry of the interior."

"*What*?"

"I was called by a member of staff from the ministry of the interior."

"Was this a prank call?"

"No, it really wasn't. It was the genuine number."

"Are you telling me they've got issues with our show? Are they *mad*?"

"No, no, he was very polite and said that we were in no way to regard this as a kind of intervention—"

"Well that's how I see it!"

"No, I think they're really concerned."

"About what?"

"As far as I understand it, they're worried that Nadeche or even the entire team down there will lose it and, with cameras rolling, drag back home a hundred refugees that the ministry of the interior can't support. And then the whole refugee thing will kick off again, now that they've only just got it under control."

"But those can't be our cats to herd. I don't give a toss if they're not doing their homework, or haven't been. I do, however, give a toss about television."

"All they're doing is trying to appeal to our sense of civic responsibility."

Pushing himself off in disgust, Sensenbrink rolls a couple of metres in his chair before the back of his head hits a shelf. He doesn't register the pain.

"This is censorship via the back door. But they've got me to deal with. They'll soon realise this isn't Bavarian state television!"

"All the same, I wouldn't dismiss what they're saying out of hand . . ." Karstleiter says.

"Are we on the same page?! I don't know these guys, and I've no idea what they're really planning or what motivates them. They call it responsibility, but they're playing party politics on the quiet because people who live in Leubl's village don't want any foreigners there. But there are a couple of other things I *do* know. First, I'm responsible for this department, these staff, these jobs and this firm. Second, we've got a licence to print money here! Not only that, but it's politically correct and irreproachable. Just for once, everyone wants a slice of it. Especially the refugees. We've also got a completely new, unique format. Infotainment with actual, real information. What's happening. Why is it happening. And I honestly believe that I'm fulfilling my civic responsibility in a far more substantial way by making ten million people watch *this* rather than a walking test card scoff oversized schnitzels."

"I just thought you should know—"

"So why didn't you tell me? Why do I have to find out via the bloody back door that my right hand is merely parroting back to me what the ministry of the interior told her? Assuming it *was* the ministry of the interior?"

"Because I don't disagree with what they're saying. And because I'd like you to listen, rather than ignoring them. Because I can imagine that a phone call like that would rub you up the wrong way."

Sensenbrink stands up, now furious. He refuses to be treated like one of those trainable howler monkeys – you only have to talk to at the right time and in the right way to make them do exactly what you want.

"Yes, and I can imagine that's just what they're thinking too," he says, his hand on the door handle. "That's why they go via my staff rather than calling me directly. If you conceal your sources, I don't call that more information, I call it manipulation. Assuming these people are from the ministry of the interior. It could be one of our secret services, or the Americans. I really don't care. If they call again, please pass on my best regards and tell them we're not relinquishing control over this."

Sensenbrink bursts into the corridor, slamming the door behind him.

Karstleiter sighs deeply and gets to her feet. She switches off the light, and just as she gently closes the door to leave the room, she says into the darkness, as if it were vital to get it off her chest, "If we still have control."

# 16

"Frau Hackenbusch! Frau Hackenbusch! You're cooking on gas! You're giving us pure gravy!" Sensenbrink sings into his telephone. "As you know yourself, specials are specials. But we've struck oil here! Our ratings have gone north even of the original series."

Nadeche is in her container. She's slipped off her shoes and is lying on the plastic sheet. The first thing she did after the day in the infirmary was to get rid of the Rolf Benz sofa. Five and a half million viewers watched her drag it to the infirmary because the people there needed it more than she did. Then, buoyed by determination, she lay down on the floor with a simple blanket, just like the refugees in their tents. Unfortunately there were too many creatures scurrying around. So now, besides the plastic sheet, she has half a box of insect spray. Although it's hot, she's turned off the air conditioning. For the people in their tents don't have air conditioning either.

Her back aches. Today she helped move sacks of beans from the lorry ramp. All day long she watched people waiting for something as dull as beans. For a moment the sight of this reminded her of girls queuing outside H.&M. for a limited-edition Lagerfeld collection. Even the anxiety in their eyes is similar, the anxiety that supplies might be limited. But because there are many more men here, the anxiety is underlaid with aggression. The organisations try, therefore, to restrict the numbers at the distribution point to ensure that there are enough beans for all. They say this is possible if they can control access. But once the refugees set their eyes on the beans, nothing can stop them. To begin with she tried to fetch some beans to bring to others too, but Lionel couldn't persuade a single family to rely on Malaika for their beans. So she had to be satisfied with distributing them. One sack weighs twenty-five kilos. Nadeche couldn't believe at first just how heavy twenty-five kilos is. But then a German aid worker told her that it was the same as two crates of beer.

She's absolutely shattered.

"All I can say, Frau Hackenbusch, is *chapeau*!" Sensenbrink sounds very jolly. "And I can, no, I *have* to say that the T.V. company is delighted and proud to be able to tell you – come home!" He finished off in English: "Mission accomplished!"

"Mischen what?"

"Mission acc— Job done! If I had my way, there would be a reception for your homecoming at the Römer."

"The what?"

"The Römer? In Frankfurt? You know, where they welcome back the national side, or the Olympic squad."

"Hmm? Oh, right," she says absentmindedly. "Well, we

can discuss that when we're back. But just now I don't know when that's going to be."

"That would be a bit late, but have a little think, I'm sure it can be done at short notice. In any event we'll be filming at the airport. Fans and fanfare, it'll be a great finale in a week's time. I can't tell you how thrilled everyone is here—"

"What do you mean, 'finale'?"

Now she's sitting bolt upright.

"Did you really think we'd let you go come home quietly? Oh no, this special's going to get the finale it deserves—"

"Yes, when it's done."

"Frau Hackenbusch . . . I appreciate you don't have a wall planner down there, but we . . . sorry, I mean you, of course, *you* will have been there for three weeks by then. The special is over."

Sensenbrink hears a noise on the line.

It's not a good noise.

It's an uncanny noise. Just as the entire programme has assumed an uncanny aspect. Yes, it's successful. It's unique, the ratings are going through the roof. But it's also become so peculiar. So . . . how can he put it?

So serious.

"Frau Hackenbusch?"

More silence.

That's the problem with programmes that get too serious. You can't just give them a shake-up like "Germany's got Whatever". That sort of show is a broadcaster's dream. You chuck out one juror and get the next one in, you change the mood, you change the opening titles, what was green yesterday is blue tomorrow, and nobody gets upset because it's all just entertainment. And you can pull the plug on entertainment any time it stops being entertaining. But what Nadeche Hackenbusch has launched down there isn't entertainment anymore. It's serious. And you can't just shunt it from the schedules if you don't like it, for that reason.

Oh, the relief when all this is sorted out, Sensenbrink thinks.

"Frau Hackenbusch? Hello?"

"This thing here," the voice from Africa says frostily. "This thing here isn't like, done till we're done."

Now she's standing up beside her thin woollen blanket. They could have given her a thicker one, they had a few of those, but Nadeche is not entirely convinced that the average refugee has access to decent blankets. Even the diamond pattern gives her doubts. Real blankets for refugees look different, surely. Dark grey. More like what you'd see in a prison film. "And if you were to take one step outside here, you'd see that nothing at all is done."

"Yes, well . . . nobody was expecting . . ." Sensenbrink reassures her. "The world's biggest problems, that's . . . that's . . . I mean, we're only a small outfit and we can all be more than proud that—"

"We can *what*?"

"*You*, of course! What am I thinking? *You* can rightly be proud . . . Have you read the *Spiegel* recently? Wait, let me read it to you, Frau Schreinemakers, if I may be so bold as to call you—"

"I don't give a fuck about the *Spiegel*! We've got work to do. *Here*!"

"Right . . . I mean . . . of course I hate to interrupt your work, but you must . . . you ought to perhaps consider that we can't broadcast the material!"

"That would be a first!" As a matter of routine Nadeche takes a can of insect spray out of its box and shakes it. She flicks off the top with her thumb, her index finger moves rapidly and surely to the button, and a millipede the size of a hand perishes in a cloud of poison.

"Frau Hackenbusch, take it from an old pro. The schedules are finalised, the advertising slots have been sold and next week sees the start of 'Ludmilla'—"

"What? That show about prostitutes? In *my* slot?"

"Come on, it's a serious but entertaining and touching docusoap, taking a critical, soup-to-nuts look at conditions in eastern European brothels—"

"It's utter toss. You just show bad Ukrainian boob jobs, that's what you show!"

"I admit that the format doesn't quite have the class of 'Angel in Adversity', but then again nobody could have imagined that the special—"

"The people here need us!"

"Frau Hackenbusch—"

"This is about people's lives!"

"Frau Hackenbusch!"

"People's lives are at stake. That's the difference. There's nothing scripted here, do you get me? It's like, happening live! People are starving here and the millipedes have no future!"

"Millipedes?"

"The milli ... the thousands of people! Tens of thousands! Hundreds of thousands!"

"I know, and let me tell you that nobody's more pained by this than me – but we've got a business to run here. I'm partly responsible for a T.V. company, for jobs! For my colleagues. Nobody is more convinced by what you're doing than me, Frau Hackenbusch, but you have to understand that my hands are tied!"

"How?"

Sensenbrink can't decide whether she simply doesn't get his arguments, or whether she doesn't know the idiom. It's happened before, and not only with Nadeche Hackenbusch. You explain the idiom and they just get angrier because they think you think they're stupid. Sensenbrink has learned his lesson.

"There's nothing I can do, Frau Hackenbusch. I can't broadcast programmes I haven't sold a minute of advertising for, and just chuck the advertising for 'Ludmilla' out of the window. It's already booked and paid for. That's impossible!"

"There's no such thing as impossible!"

"This time there is," Sensenbrink lies bravely. "However much I'd love to."

"What's that supposed to mean?"

The first stake is in the ground. Sensenbrink is careful not to sound too relieved as he exhales. Now he has to prevent her from holding this against him or the company. She has to believe that any other broadcaster would take a similar approach.

"This doesn't need to affect you in the slightest, of course.

I mean, I don't want to stop you from extending your stay down there—"

"'Down there'...It drives me nuts when people say that!" She picks up one of her sliders and flicks the corpse to the door.

"Er . . . sorry, that was a bit flippant. My apologies, but I've got to get my colleagues home in a week. The tickets are booked and there's really nothing I can do."

"And what am I supposed to tell the people here? Thanks a lot, it's been great, bye-bye and MyTV wishes you all the best for your future?"

Sensenbrink clears his throat. "Sorry to be blunt, Frau Hackenbusch, but with all respect for your incredible achievements, everything else is a political matter. We can draw people's attention to the world's ills, but we can't solve them. Surely this was perfectly clear to all of us at the outset!"

"You know what? Let's like, finish this conversation right here. Get Kärrner to ring me."

"Believe you me, we've discussed it in committee and Herr Kärrner is right behind me on this—"

"Get Kärrner to ring me."

She ends the call. And Kärrner does in fact ring her, less than half an hour later.

But Kärrner doesn't give in.

She tells him something about a long-term partnership and Kärrner doesn't give in. She switches to "longstanding friendship" and Kärrner doesn't give in. She says she recently met Whatsisname from ProSieben, and then something happens that's never happened to her before: Kärrner, who is in fact a charming softie at heart, doesn't give in. And after the two of them have said goodbye very amicably, after they've said how they really must see each other again soon, at Sergio's, which is now almost their "local", after they've hung up and Nadeche Hackenbusch has stared in disbelief as the screen of her mobile fades, she swings her leg back and kicks the cardboard box with such fury that the spray cans fly through the room like confetti.

# 17

"Malaika," Lionel the refugee wants to say, "we need to talk."

But before he's even begun to utter these words he realises it's probably not the best moment. He enters Malaika's container to find her pacing up and down like a sick giraffe. She spins around, makes a beeline for Lionel and literally hauls him in.

"Good that you come! Goodgoodgood. You believe not what for a shit they make."

It unsettles him every time they're alone together. This English is so different from the English all other Germans speak. Different from Marion's English and Grande's and Astrid the Writer's. Different from any English he's ever heard, in fact. He asked old lady Grande, who explained that it was a particularly good English, better than the English spoken by many in Britain. But Malaika had a particular dialect from a region of Germany where very few people live. Which is nonsense, of course. Everyone knows that there aren't any empty regions in Germany, everywhere is fully inhabited. In any case, it didn't sound as if old lady Grande was envious of this English, rather that Malaika had been handed a particularly harsh fate. As if she were some kind of linguistic orphan.

"Sit you down," Malaika rants. "That must you hear."

He sits. He tries to take her hands to calm her down. After all, he knows there's a lot about this camp she finds appalling and the people here love her for it. They've been living in these conditions for so long that they had come to believe that this life was their due. But from Malaika's reaction they can see that they too should be able to live differently, better even. And each time she's upset by what she sees, Malaika grabs his hand. Tightly. And if he gives a gentle squeeze in response she looks at him gratefully, her anger boils over and she tells the camera team exactly what they should be filming, and if they don't grasp what she's getting at quickly enough she'll seize hold of the cameraman and shove him where he'll get the best angle. She tends to forget to let go of Lionel's hand, pulling him behind her until eventually she realises, and then she strokes his arm apologetically. But today she doesn't want his hand; she is so worked up that she keeps her distance.

"Sensenbrink, this idiot!" she screams. "And the Kärrner is the same arsehole! As if all here shitequal is! All the humans! All the poor humans!"

He looks at her with eyebrows raised, helplessly holding up his palms because there's no point trying to interrupt her. All of a sudden she pauses to take a deep breath. She wipes the corners of her eyes with a sleeve.

"Yesyes," she says. "You can it *ja* not know."

Malaika squats beside Lionel and looks at him insistently. "They want to end the *sendung*." Unconsciously, she switches to German: "Oh, don't look at me like that!" But then she apologises right away: "Sorry, I forget always that your English not so special is. Finish, understand you? The German T.V. want make finish. A week have we only more. A week. I say to they: in three days can we not help people, unpossible. And they so: there can we nothing make!"

She leaps up. "I am so up one hundred eighty," she yells. "We have so much to do. We cannot simply homego!"

It's quite tricky to follow what she's saying, but the gist is that they're planning to terminate the programme. Even though everyone keeps saying how well it's going down. He curses silently. He's been relying on its success for far too long. This means he's got seven days' work left, seven days in which to persuade Malaika to take him with her. He's going to have to calm her down so that she listens to him. The way she is right now, nothing's going to go in. She needs to calm down, and when she's calm he can explain his problem. If she's at all interested. He gets up. He'd put his arms around any other woman at this moment, but perhaps it's not such a good idea with a German angel. Nadeche notices his intention all the same.

"You understand me," she says sadly. "That is nice. But one thing is safe, I swear you: not with us! Think only of all our work. It can not for nothing be! We can not come to all this humans here and make a T.V. sending and then go we simple again home. And here is all how it before was! Not now! Where the first time all Germans really look at all the shit of the world! This is stupid. This is so unhuman!"

He didn't put his arms around her. And yet suddenly she's in them. He can scarcely believe it: the gorgeous angel is actually in his arms, her head pressed against his chest, leaning on the one individual who has been at her side through the misery and adversity, and of course he responds by pressing her to him, carefully, very gingerly. Although it feels good to hold her, he must remain steadfast. Just bear in mind, he urges himself, bear in mind, bear in mind at all times: one false move of the hand and she'll never take you to Germany. Leave those hands of yours on her shoulders, leave those hands on her shoulders, and as he thinks "shoulders" for the second or third time he can already feel hands considerably lower, between the shoulder blades.

Not his hands, but hers.

This isn't good. This isn't good.

This.

Isn't.

Good, and he looks down and tries to loosen his grip around her shoulders, tries to tell her that everything will be fine with Kärrnerbrink, but he can't speak with her lips on his mouth, the lips of an angel, the lips of the most beautiful woman in the world, it's as if heaven itself were kissing him, nobody has ever kissed him like this before, so . . . so . . .

So German-like.

She kisses, not tentatively, but as German women probably do kiss: thoroughly. It feels unusual, different, but good, and when you're kissed by heaven you have to return the favour, anything else would be a sin, and he pulls her towards him, briefly enquires whether she likes feeling him close to her, but ... now she can feel him and she presses herself against him, this is no dream, it's not a comical misunderstanding between him and the woman from the distant foreign land, no, it's a great understanding, the very greatest understanding there can be between two people on this earth.

Those small, delicate hands that are forever energetically showing everyone what's what, they're everywhere, he's about to rip off his shirt, but like an army of ants her fingers have already unfastened all the buttons, even those on his epaulettes, he can't undo hers with the same speed, she's already slipped his trousers off, his shoes are removed from his feet so quickly that the word "pillage" darts through his mind, and at the same time the clothes fall from her like leaves from a tree, he sinks back, her ant-fingers all over him, caressing his face, guiding him unerringly between her thighs, then with a sigh she lowers herself onto him, all the way in, as deep as she can, and rather than wait she begins, in her German way, to move up and down, precisely and rhythmically until she breathes out quickly and slumps on top of him with a moan, released, her face resting on his, now allowing him to go about things more calmly, she feels good, he just prefers it *this* way, a little more *this* and a little less *that*, it seems to spark a response in her too, she comes back to life with little noises and, just as he's thinking he ought to be slowing it all down, really relishing it, like a moment designed for loving an angel, she sits up and beams at him, takes control and resumes her relentless rhythm. It's unfamiliar, but somehow good too, it reminds him of something, he can't grasp it straightaway, it's on the tip of his tongue, but then he's distracted by those very, very beautiful breasts, and for the first time with a woman he comes like a real German.

"That was so good," she whispers into his ear. "So good, so good, so good. You are so wonderful. You be my angel."

"Malaika," he says, "this is—"

"This is love," Malaika says, convinced. "But this is more. This must destiny be." Propping herself on her elbows she looks him seriously in the eye. "The same goals, the same love. I have *never* so what feeled. And I knowed that in the first moment where I you seen have. This is what comes only one time in hundert years."

He gazes at her, sweaty, stumped, spoiled. His thoughts trip over one another, he can't believe what's happening. Because if it's true, if Malaika, this wonderful angel, really does love him, then seven days will be plenty of time to convince her to take him with her. Can this be true? It sounds like one of Mahmoud's hoaxes, as if Mahmoud had tricked him, but the angel would never do what she's just done for a mere trick!

In the camp there are some girls who would do that for money, and some who would do it so they could tease him with Mahmoud afterwards. "Did you think this was love? Idiot!" But Malaika?

Besides, if it were a hoax it must surely be over by now. Mahmoud would have stormed in and laughed, and the angel would have sat up and laughed too. But the angel isn't laughing. The angel is lying by his side, her head on his chest and her ant-fingers are playing with his chest hair. This time, however, the ant-fingers are slow and tender, and she is breathing deeply and calmly. He kisses her forehead, she looks up with weary eyes and kisses him before snuggling up even more.

"I have noch never a man how you founded," she says softly into his chest hair. "A man and a human. I think all the time over that. This is the first time I do what real senseful. And it is the first time I love a real good man. I feel it. A better love for a better world."

Perhaps she's right, he thinks. He no longer believes it could be a hoax. She's so serious, there is such conviction in her voice. What is life actually all about? Is it just about working for an ever-better existence and getting your arse over to Europe? To earn money there? Is this Allah's plan? Is this the Christian god's plan? No, it's love. One should love a good person honestly, a good woman, and if she's an angel, well, it goes without saying. He's never thought of himself as anything special, but thinking about it now, he's never really been a bad person either. He's never been like Mojo the Blue, nor has he simply taken each day as it comes like Mahmoud, and if Allah or whoever else is looking for the right man for Malaika, a man for an angel, and he can't find anyone better anywhere in the world, well, who is he to argue with God? God is looking for the man who will make Malaika happy, and let nobody impede this love, he means to throw himself into this love with a pure heart, he means to give his best. And because God rewards the just and those in love, for those things alone, not out of greed or self-interest, the divine will is washing him into the heart of a beautiful woman.

And a ticket to Germany to boot.

"You're so right," he says, stroking her hair. "I love you. I love you so much. I love you so much that I'll come with you. You must finish your T.V. show, yes, but don't worry. I will come with you."

It's going to be marvellous. The angel will take him back to her angel house. He'll look after the house and garden and the goats. Yes, he knows more about cars, but Germans have their own cars. They don't have goats. They're going to get rich, or ever richer, because the angel will get richer through him and what he knows. And because he'll never forget where he comes from and the angel is an angel anyway, they'll continue helping the poor together, for television and on television. So the other poor people can come to Germany, full of love and pure of heart. The first person he'll get to join him is Mahmoud, who'll be deputy goat manager. The Germans will be amazed at how well it works, for Mahmoud is loyal and reliable, and together with those famous German engineers they'll turn Germany into the greatest goat nation on earth. They'll have a big car and lots of children and the peasants in their villages will say that the angel and the angel's angel are great and just and . . .

"What?"

She sits bolt upright like a meercat.

"What have you said?"

Has he done something wrong? Is there something he's misunderstood? How is it possible to misunderstand what has just brought them together. What they've just done together? What she said?

"I . . . I only said—"

"No!" she says, her voice strained, "Lionel! No!"

Seeing the confusion in his eyes she lays a hand on his chest, her small, delicate, warm hand. "You are so sweet. But you know self: we can not go. You can not go. The humans here need you. You have ever helped the humans here. You know all the humans here. All the humans love you. They trust you. And they need you. I can you not away taken. This is your life. This is your work. And that means that I auch not go away. For you. For ever."

She flings her arms around his neck and they pull him down like a millstone. His eyes roam the room. This can't be for real. What's happening right now can't actually be happening. Searching for hope, all he finds are cans of insect spray scattered everywhere. Only a few seconds ago she was the angel, his angel whose verve would carry him off to a better life. Now she's chaining him to this damn floor. It was his one great chance to escape and he's missed it. The television will leave, there won't be any money and nothing will change. Nothing, nothing, nothing. This angel isn't going to help him; on the contrary, he's going to have to keep on looking after the angel. It's not going to be him moving to a better country, but the angel moving to a worse one, to the most idiotic country a person can move to. His life will pass him by, not when he dies, but in here in this camp or in another one.

For if he wanted to leave now he'd have to take the angel with him.

And to be able to take the angel with him, this good

person, this unbearably good person, he'd have to take the
entire camp with him.

He leaps up.

# 18

"You're crazy, amigo," Mojo the Blue says, and he laughs.

He drops into his enormous desk chair and it tips backwards. It's not a natural laugh, but this is no natural desk either. It's as wide as a Mercedes is long and so deep that they'd both have to bend right across the top to be able to shake hands. The desk is immaculately lacquered all over in gleaming white apart from the inlay panelling. The gilding could look over the top, but in fact it goes rather well with the four golden lions' paws the desk rests on. On the desk sits a golden letter opener which could also be used as a bush knife. Or as a bridge across a small stream.

To Mojo's right is an iPad still in its box on another iPad still in its box, and beneath these a further three iPads still in their boxes. To Mojo's left is the golden remote control he uses for the large screen that covers the entire wall of the shack. And in between sits Mojo himself in a regal white leather desk chair.

Such an ensemble really deserves to be in a room with at least some rudimentary plastering and a nice paint job. But once you've sat at this gargantuan table for a few minutes, you realise there's no way it could have come through the window, let alone the door, which means that Mojo must have had the desk first and then built this office shack around it. And he must have been so desperate to sit on his white leather chair among all his iPads that he couldn't wait any longer, at least not for trivial matters like wall paint.

"Hahahahaha!" Mojo laughs. "Haaaaaaa hahahahaha!"

There's no amusement in this laugh. It doesn't sound as if he's found something funny, it sounds forceful, almost arduous, as if this noisy laughter were extremely hard work. It comes from Mojo having watched endless T.V. series on his office shack wall, series in which big-time gangsters laugh as he's trying to now. What detracts considerably from the bizarre impression he's trying to create is that Mojo doesn't have an especially unusual taste in films. He's seen pretty much the same T.V. series as everyone else, like "The Wire" or "Breaking Bad", which is why he sometimes speaks like a Mexican or Colombian. And he's forever practising gestures that he's invented himself. For a while he would leave a canister of compressed air lying around. And last year he had hamsters in the meeting room. He would take one out of its cage during a meeting and toss it up and down like a tennis ball, before strangling the creature. But nobody knew what this was supposed to mean because nobody knew what the hamster stood for. And being so easy to throttle, hamsters aren't much help with intimidation. Besides, the room stank of hamsters the whole time so he gave up on the idea. And it all sounds very funny when you tell it to Miki and Mahmoud at the bar.

But when you're sitting face to face in his meeting room, you're reminded that there are unpleasant things that no television gangster has ever done. But Mojo the Blue has.

"How does someone like you come up with a bullshit idea like that, amigo?"

"I didn't have much time. I still don't have much time."

"On foot?"

"On foot."

"You're batshit crazy. Hahahahaha."

He waits for Mojo the Blue to stop laughing. But Mojo the Blue adds an encore: "Bandele, take a look at this guy, our pedestrian. Hahahahahahah! Ha!"

Bandele dutifully joins in. His laugh sounds more natural; like any loyal employee he's had more practice. He laughs so loudly and heartily that Mojo the Blue waves his hand to shut him up. It's as if Bandele's been switched off.

"Any idea how far that is?" Mojo says.

"Do you know how long I've been here by now? If I'd just walked ten kilometres each day—"

"Sure, sure. If you fart once a day for a million years the wind's gonna carry you to Europe. But I don't care. 'Cause you ain't goin'."

"No?"

"No. Because you, amigo, are the angel's angel. Who owes me a few favours. How are you ever goin' to pay me back if you're not here?"

"First, I don't owe you any favours. And second, the time for favours is over because the television people are moving on out. Work's done. They're bringing the angel programme to an end."

"What bullshit is that? Everyone says the show's doin' really well. Bandele, is the show doin' really well?"

"Ratings are through the roof," Bandele says.

"Maybe," Lionel says with a shrug. "But now they're finishing up."

"When?"

"In five days. Like I said, I don't have much time."

"What about those favours you owe me?"

"I don't owe you any favours. But let me propose a deal."

"For your fart to Europe?"

He nods.

"I ain't sellin' no beans." Mojo roars with laughter, and Bandele follows suit.

"Very good . . . but I want to buy something else from you."

"And what would that be?"

"I need someone who knows the way. I need someone to bribe the border guards. I need someone to bribe the military."

"What you're lookin' for is a people smuggler. And I ain't no mutherfuckin' people smuggler."

"I need more than a smuggler. I need someone to provide food, to deliver water."

"But you can walk on your own?"

"I can."

"Still sounds like a mutherfuckin' people smuggler to me. Like a mutherfuckin' people smuggler with a restaurant car. Why don't you pay one of them?"

"Because I don't have enough money."

"And so you've come to me?"

Lionel nods slowly. This could get quite awkward.

"Hey, look at me! Did you see a sign out front of my house that said: 'Discounts for dumb niggers'? No? You know why you didn't see that sign?"

"Why?" Lionel asks, even though he knows what's coming. He's seen the film too.

"'Cause it ain't there!"

"This isn't about whether I've got enough money for a smuggler. It's about getting you a deal. Bigger than all the others. With an enormous profit."

"How come?"

"Because I'm on television."

"Why don't they pay for your smuggler?"

"It doesn't work like that. They won't take me with them and they won't pay for a smuggler either. And this isn't about you just turning up with a few bottles of water and some flour. I'm talking about planning here. A smuggler shoves you into a boat or lorry with a heap of other Africans. That's nonsense. I want your organisation and your contacts. I want your protection."

"What's in it for me?"

"More money than you've ever seen in your life."

"Listen, amigo, I've seen quite a lotta moolah," Mojo says, amused.

"I know," Lionel says seriously, looking Mojo in the eye. "I know. And because I know, I can say to you: I'll offer you . . . more."

Mojo leans forwards and stares at him. He's thinking. Then he flaps his hand at Bandele, who stands up and leaves the room.

"O.K., right now a journey to Europe costs fifteen thousand bucks. Or twelve thousand if you get a good deal. But you ain't got that kinda dough."

Lionel nods.

"I've seen twelve thousand bucks and it don't impress me."

Lionel nods again.

"But you can scrape together more from your television thing."

Lionel nods a third time.

"How much we talkin' 'bout here? Fifty grand? One hundred grand?"

"More."

Lionel leans back and casually rests his right foot in its canvas trainer on one of the desk's corners. He contemplates pushing off and balancing the chair on its back legs, but decides against it. He'll come across as more decisive if he's not wobbling.

"Five hundred grand?"

"One hundred million dollars."

Mojo shifts to the back of his chair.

"Get the fuck outta here!"

Lionel takes his foot off the desk and leans in towards Mojo. "Plus bonus."

"Get the fuck outta here!"

"I'll let you do the sums."

Lionel gives Mojo the details.

Mojo does the sums.

Then he agrees. Because it all adds up.

And because Lionel tells him that this is just the beginning.

# 19

He takes the AK-47 by the strap from one shoulder and hangs it over the other shoulder. Four kilos are four kilos. There are days when he doesn't feel it at all, and days when he thinks he's carrying a lead shotgun.

The simplest thing to do, of course, would be to put it down.

Nobody's going to come past anyhow, or at least nobody's going to creep up on him. The landscape's flat here, the view extends far into the distance and there's nothing to see. What could there be? To be honest, this border post exists for one reason only: five hundred metres away on the other side is an equally redundant border post. But since it *does* exist then he might as well carry the gun; at least it looks like something and feels like something. And he has to stand, because he can't hold it when he's sitting down.

Then he sees the cloud. A cloud of dust. In itself nothing unusual, but there's not really sufficient wind today for clouds like this. He screws up his eyes and blinks over at the other border post. He's not sure whether he can spot any trouble, but the guy on the other side seems to be on his feet as well.

A small cloud has detached from the large one. At first he wonders whether it might be a cloud of smoke, but there's no doubt that it's dust. The small cloud is approaching fast, it seems to be a vehicle, but he can't be sure because the border post is obscuring the view. Now the guard on the other side puts his hand to his head; he's making a telephone call. He probably doesn't recognise the vehicle either, he wants instructions, he's going to ask his boss what to do. A bit too late, in fact, for the small cloud is racing towards them, and even if he gets hold of his boss, there won't be enough time for instructions about the small cloud. Maybe he's ringing about the big one?

What could it be? In the end it shouldn't concern his counterpart on the other side of the border. Whatever's coming, it's leaving his country, so where's the problem?

Is it someone important?

Someone famous?

Here, of all places?

Can't be. If there was something special on its way the boss would be over there too, keeping an eye on it all. Because it's certainly worth seeing, what emerges from behind the border hut: an off-roader with zebra stripes.

In pink.

The car races unchallenged along the track towards him. About one hundred metres before the border, it stops. A small group of people get out, all of them white. They indicate various positions in the dust, which they take a closer look at, then point first at the other border hut, then at his. One of them raises his hands as if using magic powers on the other hut, then he twists slowly at the waist until the magic rays are aiming at his shed. Here. There. Here. There.

The hut conjuror returns to the car, opens the tailgate and now the magic hands make sense. When he sees the man take out a camera and tripod, it's his turn to take out his mobile and call the colonel.

"Something's going on here and I thought you ought to take a look. You see—"

"This is none of your business."

An unusual answer.

"Do you know about this?"

"I don't know anything."

"That's why I'm telling you. It's television. Television people. White television people. And a cloud."

"I've got other things to do. Just don't bother yourself about it."

"Do you know what's coming through?"

"Nothing that's anything of our business."

"As far as you're concerned, it's O.K. then?"

"As far as I'm concerned, nothing's O.K. I don't know anything because there isn't anything to know."

"I'm not sure we're talking about the same thing here. Because what's coming my way looks like a really huge amount of nothing."

"Now just you listen to me, you idiot. We're not at war. Unless you see an enemy army coming towards you I don't want to be disturbed again. I have work to be getting on with."

"I've no idea what's coming towards me!"

"What do you imagine? If an enemy were on its way,

the T.V. people wouldn't turn up beforehand, would they? And I'm not interested in anything else."

"I . . ."

"Your job is to spare me any aggro. I don't want any whining, any hassle, any dead bodies, do you understand? And I don't want to hear from you again unless there's a tank up your arse!"

The line goes dead. So nobody's going to come and see what there is to see. At a loss, he takes the rifle from his shoulder and looks over at the television people. As their camera slowly pans towards him, he feels extremely silly with his rifle in his hands, standing watch over the great big nothingness. He slings it back over his shoulder as phlegmatically as possible, as if it had simply become too heavy.

The cloud grows, it's coming nearer. Now the television people aim the camera at him and he tries to look as if he has everything under control. He peers over to the guy on the other side. What's he doing? He's taken his rifle off his shoulder and has his finger near the trigger. He's staring into the distance, but he doesn't move onto the road, he doesn't step in anybody's way, he remains in the shadows as if he's just as clueless.

The whites have enough pictures for the time being. They're no longer beside the camera, but they're not dismounting it either. They're in conversation, sitting in the shade of their vehicle. He has no idea what they're talking about, but they all keep shaking their heads in unison. If they weren't there he'd go over and ask the other guy if he knows what this is about. But he doesn't want to show weakness.

And he can hardly move position because the television people would notice and probably start filming him again. He doesn't want to make trouble.

The cloud grows. But another glance at his opposite number and he feels reassured. His counterpart is standing in the shade, smoking. Perhaps all of this is taking place only on his side and the television people are where they are because it affords them the best view. And his colleague is getting a walk-on part.

So why did they film him too?

Because he's watching, of course. They often do that, they show something and then splice it with the image of a bored lizard or a dog, watching what's going on and . . .

"This is none of your business." Strange answer.

The television people start to move. One makes a phone call, then looks over the top of the pink zebra car to the other border guard. The guy with the phone leans forwards and nudges the shoulder of a colleague, who nudges the next one and so on until they're all on their feet.

His opposite number gets moving. He wanders to the barrier and raises it. The television people peer into the distance and shake their heads. Then they look at him, as if it were his turn now to shake his head. But why, for God's sake? He almost wishes he could see a tank because then he'd be allowed to telephone for more instructions. Why does it have to be him on duty today?

His counterpart raises a hand to shield his eyes from the sun. The wind drives the dust in his direction, and the dust is quicker than what's churning it up. His head and the hand that looks like it's saluting are virtually still, but the guard is turning slowly as if trying to gauge a huge distance.

What on earth can it be coming towards them?

"This is none of your business."

What sort of an answer is that?

The colonel isn't here, and although he doesn't know why, he's beginning to suspect that the colonel knows precisely why. And if it's alright for the colonel not to be here now, can it be alright for him to be where the colonel doesn't want to be?

What could be coming towards them that he might be able to stop?

And if he does stop it, will anyone thank him?

Or will they say he ought to have let it pass?

Although he's got no solid proof of this, he's suddenly convinced that the only reason nobody's here apart from him is because nobody wants to be here.

Then he sees it. Emerging from the cloud.

Those are people.

A column of people. They're not armed. Just lots and lots of people, and behind them presumably lots more. Some have children, others are alone. They're carrying rolled-up blankets as if they're planning to spend the night somewhere. They're not running, they're strolling calmly as if they know they'll be allowed to keep going. In spite of the border. They don't engage in discussion with his counterpart, they simply wander through the open barrier. They look like people from the refugee camps. They *are* refugees, and now he realises what his opposite number was told by his superior:

"If they want to keep going, let them."

That's why his counterpart is standing there so casually, watching them all stream past. Through his binoculars he sees the other guard turn around, put his binoculars to his eyes and look in his direction. Their eyes meet. With a broad grin his opposite number waves at him without putting down his binoculars. He slightly fades into the cloud of dust thrown up by the enormous column of people now moving towards the television people and him. There is no end to the mass of people.

Still peering through binoculars, the other guard points at the people, makes exaggerated counting gestures, showing one finger, two fingers, three fingers, then tries to look puzzled: "How many of them *are* there?" He then laughs, throws his hands in the air, lifts them higher, then higher still. You might call the expression on his face one of disbelief, but this disbelief vanishes behind the overarching relief that these people are not his problem.

He realises that they would need a vast number of guards to stop these hundreds, if not thousands – a vast number of guards with truncheons or firearms. And he also realises it's no coincidence that he's here on his own. He doesn't have friends in high places to extricate him from this shit. He's the stupid arse nobody tells anything to.

He can no longer see the pink car or the camera. Too many people. None of them so much as glances at him as they approach. People usually respect a man in combat gear with a rifle, but these hundreds of individuals believe there's zero chance of him doing anything.

He hears curses he can't understand. Squinting through the dust and the people he sees the pink zebra car again, and a man cursing and shouting – he must have wanted to film the guard's reaction to all these people, but the camera can't pick up anything because of the dust. He himself can barely see the pink car.

What's going to happen tomorrow? Where are all these people going? Nobody's going to be happy to see them. Questions will be asked. And he can't conceive of any sequence of events that doesn't end with someone, at some point, wanting to know who was actually on border guard duty at the time.

It won't be a question of "who?", but "which idiot?".

Helplessly he gazes in the direction of where these people are coming from. He cannot see where the stream ends. It strikes him now that there are scarcely any old people among them, and everybody seems to be travelling fairly light, as if they'd had no time to pack.

Or they don't need much where they're heading.

With his rifle slung over his shoulder, he wanders casually to the road and tosses a question into the crowd: "Where are you all off to, then?"

He's answered by a woman holding two children by the hand.

"To Germany."

"You're walking there?"

"I'm not one of the organisers. If you've got any questions, ask the tall guy back there!"

He tries to spot a tall man in the chaos coming his way.

The woman moves on. The little girl holding her hand laughs and gives him a wave.

"Ottobafes!"

He reckons it'll be ten or twenty minutes before the pink zebra car has made its way through the crowd to his border post on the other side. So he's got between ten and twenty minutes until the cameras are here. He takes a deep breath, then realises what's going to happen.

The white people will come to his hut. They'll be ranting as they leap out of the car, scolding the driver for having taken so long. Then the television people will look for something or someone.

They won't find anybody. Someone will beckon the cameraman, who'll just have to film what's left: his uniform on a chair. And his abandoned rifle leaning against the hut.

And his cap, hanging from the muzzle.

# 20

Sensenbrink has had better days. He slept dreadfully last night, and the night before too. He's been shouting at his wife because she's getting on his nerves. She's noticed, of course, that he's not drinking, and she knows this is a bad sign; he stops drinking the moment he's got problems. It makes him feel he can really be in control of things. Sensenbrink knows this is nonsense; he doesn't drink that much as it is.

Then there's her bloody sympathy: "If there something bothering you?" Even the tone of voice is enough to drive him crackers. Normally he doesn't have anything against his wife, but that fucking tone of voice.

That sympathetic tone, that maternal tone.

That's probably it. It's the maternal tone of voice, which makes you react like you'd react to your mother. You stomp up to your room, slam the door then push the wardrobe in front of it. But to be fair, it's not the silly baggage's fault.

It's that stupid bloody cow's.

He can sense the rug being pulled out from under his feet. It's that feeling of risk, and Sensenbrink hates risk. He's a manager, for God's sake. If he loved taking risks he'd be an entrepreneur. But now this half-wit has practically tricked him into entrepreneurship.

This madwoman!

It was a brilliant programme, it just got more and more popular. Created out of nothing, nobody gave it the slightest chance, but that's precisely his strength – even if people have forgotten this of late. Sensenbrink has a sixth sense for the unconventional. He doesn't spend his time chasing after the mainstream because he's seen quite a lot in his time and he knows what works. But for this you've got to be a little older than all those bunnies in the office. If you ask Gretchen Daftbint and Co. which channel Loriot developed his material on they say, "YouTube!"

It was Radio Bremen!

Now *that* was television!

So can it be pure coincidence that it was him who turned A2 into a cash cow? The last series alone earned around 150 million euros, and that was just on advertising. Merchandising was on top. And what about the increase in the firm's share price – Kärrner made a tidy sum from his options. It could have gone on quite happily like that, and by next year they would have felt obliged to offer him a place on the board. A perfectly simple, bombproof idea. And what does that asinine bimbo turn it into? A kamikaze mission!

Nobody knows how this is going to end.

No, actually, it's quite clear where it's going to end: in a shitshow. It *can* only end in a shitshow. If you're at the roulette wheel and your number comes up, not once but twice, then you don't bet the whole lot again. You get up and say,

"Thanks, ladies and gentlemen, I'm done!" But that nutter put all the money back on the table so quickly they didn't even see it.

And before you've blinked she's marching across the border with one hundred and fifty thousand other nutters. What other choice was he left with than to sell this to Kärrner as the story of the century? What else could he have said? "Hackenbusch has got too much for me, I can't keep her under control. We need to abort A2 right now!"

They could have pulled out the camera team, of course they could have. You don't have to admit your star has lost the plot, you can just say people have had enough of poverty and misery, that sort of thing. But then Kärrner would say, "Are you telling me Nadeche Hackenbusch is walking to Europe with one hundred and fifty thousand refugees and we're not there?" Or, worse: "We were there, we had exclusive access and you pulled the plug? How stupid can you be? Go and see Frau Schaabe tomorrow, she's already prepared your termination contract."

And from then onwards Sensenbrink is known as the guy who tried to pull the plug on the biggest story of all time.

So you leave the cameras where they are. But no-one should get wind of the fact that you've no idea what's happening. The truth is there's a lunatic wandering around with one hundred and fifty thousand refugees and all you're doing is letting the cameras roll as you follow on behind. Sure, it's O.K. for a broadcaster to be like a lucky dip from time to time. But only for the viewers. The people filling the lucky dip obviously need to know what they're putting in there. And it's almost a miracle that by uttering the magic words "Hackenbusch" and "one hundred and fifty thousand" he was able to prevent Kärrner from asking the question he's bound to ask at the next meeting. By which time he needs to have an answer. Which is why Sensenbrink now raises the question himself:

"So, guys: what's our story?"

A room full of people without a clue. Some are scribbling on their pads. It's uncanny how much they're able to draw in such a short space of time. And yet they don't give the impression that they can think quickly. He can tell which are the new writers, because at least they find this uncomfortable.

"Wakey wakey! He*llo*? Input! What's our story?"

"Nadeche Hackenbusch," Olav says wearily.

"One hundred and fifty thousand refugees," Anke says. She's reliable, at least.

"And what then? A gangbang? What is this, some kind of word-prompt story? Hackenbusch and the refugees are our keywords, but where does the story go from here?"

"How are we supposed to know?" Olav asks, taking a chocolate peanut from the bowl on the table. "The story's only just unfolding."

"I see. So what are we going to do? Are we going to watch and write it down?"

"Well, that's journalism. Weren't we planning to go in a more journalistic direction?"

"I didn't say 'journalism'. I said 'Schreinemakers'."

"Is there a difference?"

This comment comes from a goatherd in a suit. Sensenbrink tries to make a mental note of his face, but he looks too much like ten other goatherds. Every day Sensenbrink hopes that beards will go out of fashion again, and you'll be able to tell people's ages once more.

"Schreinemakers knew exactly what she was broadcasting," Karstleiter says, coming to his assistance.

"I'm going lay the silver on the table here," Sensenbrink says sternly. "I don't expect you know how I begged that lot upstairs to go along with this. They've rearranged the entire schedule to keep us on air. They should be showing some shitty repeats, but they're not because the premise of this is cool. They're continuing to pay you, they're continuing to bankroll the entire department, even though repeats would be cheaper. How much longer do you think this is going to go on?"

"For as long as the ratings are good," a brother of the goatherd says cheekily.

"O.K., so let's ask whether the ratings are good. Silvie?"

"The ratings are certainly good. Right now I think we could even risk scheduling it against the news."

"But you told me this isn't always a positive sign," Sensenbrink says, keeping Silvie on track.

"Of course. The ratings merely tell us how many people are watching. It doesn't say whether they like it and how much they like it, and what motivates them. We're getting extremely mixed reactions from the viewing public. Hayat, would you like to come in here?"

Sensenbrink still doesn't know if the girl with the headscarf at the end of the table is a good addition or not. The more he sees her at meetings, the more he thinks that visually she's the perfect complement to all the goatherds. Strange, how some try to be über hip and others über conservative, yet they all look as if they could have stepped straight out of an Alpine village two hundred years ago. But Hayat has also been incredibly level-headed in her analysis of the figures so far.

"The response we're getting is that people think the show's cool," Hayat says. "So far. But it's an extremely volatile situation."

Sensenbrink grimaces as if he'd bitten on a cherry stone. "Who knows what volatile means?"

Nobody speaks up. "Volatile means crap," Sensenbrink translates, feeling stressed now. "It could flip tomorrow, which is precisely what we don't want. Now tell us more, but in lingo we can all understand!"

"The viewers started out as fans, but now they're not so sure. Because A2, including the special, has always had a very positive vibe. Nadeche Hackenbusch goes to the coalface. Nadeche helps out, eases suffering, comforts people. The viewers liked that, they enjoyed watching."

"But it's just like that now," Olav says.

"And with a love story to boot!" says Reliable Anke.

"No, there is a difference. With 'Angel in Adversity' you could count on everything turning out alright in the end. There were a few problems and the problems were solved. But people can't see any solutions here. There's no certainty about how it's all going to pan out."

"Doesn't that make it exciting?"

"In some ways, yes. But it detracts from the enjoyment."

"What, is it now our job to solve the refugee problem?"

"All I know is that the discussion is very animated," Hayat says. "There's no end of traffic. We're getting the standard questions too, of course. Plenty of people want to donate and don't know where to send money, or what for. But people are also confused. They don't know what sort of a story it is we're telling."

"That doesn't matter, so long as it's a good story," Olav says with a broad grin.

"For the moment that may be true. In the long term, however, it's a risk for the broadcaster. If A2 is to keep going, I'd suggest that we take a clear, unassailable position on this. If we don't, other people might stick us in a pigeonhole we can't wriggle out of."

Sensenbrink is amazed by everything coming from the headscarf. A headscarf that's sticking her neck out rather, but she's giving an accurate description of the situation.

"It would be a pigeonhole our advertisers wouldn't fancy sharing with us either," he says, to lend the comment a boss's weight.

"Surely that depends on the product," Olav says casually. "We just need to make it clear to people that we're telling a completely new type of story. A docusoap without a script."

"A bit like those celebrity chefs, but with a cause," a goatherd pipes up.

"A whole new dimension in reality T.V. A bit like 'Kardashian Marries!' – 'Nadeche Hackenbusch Migrates!'"

". . . and fucks a black man!"

"Ooooooh!"

Sensenbrink slaps the table several times. He can see the headscarf taking a deep breath. She doesn't dare speak without being invited, so he gives her a gesture of encouragement. Better than him actively getting involved. She seems to have an opinion on this and Sensenbrink would give anything to have one himself.

"A documentary is when you film whatever happens. But to put it bluntly, this time it's us who set all this in motion. You could even argue that the entire initiative only works because we're there with our cameras," Hayat says impatiently. When she gets no reaction she adds, "The viewers are thinking that people might die. Dead bodies! Because. We're. There. With. Our. Cameras."

"Well, I don't see it quite like that," Sensenbrink insists, "but Hayat is absolutely right – it's possible to twist it wilfully. Let me state again that, owing to a chain of quite extraordinary events, we find ourselves well behind the eight ball, but the great thing is that we're facing up to our responsibility 110 per cent. Which other broadcaster would do that? But . . . we also have a responsibility to the firm."

Sensenbrink is thinking hard. Now he needs a bridge, a convincing link to his plan or something along those lines. If only he had an idea.

"What do you mean by that?" Reliable Anke says.

"I mean," Sensenbrink lurches, "that I . . . I mean all of us knew this was a major experiment. That's why we asked Nadeche to stay on down there, right? My God, I really badgered that poor woman! But, as Olav quite rightly said, we don't know how this thing is going to pan out. It could even . . . how should I put it . . . not pan out particularly well. Some people might indeed die. Or lots of people, if it really goes tits up. And then we can't . . ." Sensenbrink stops mid-flow. He feels quite giddy at the thought of being summoned by Kärrner because the first corpses of children have appeared on screen.

"Then we can't be the broadcaster that exploits refugees to bump up our ratings," Karstleiter finishes his sentence. "You see, we need to be in a position where we can show what's going on, without being negatively associated with it."

"That's a rather business-like way of putting it," Sensenbrink says. "Let's just say it mustn't look like the MyTV Great Refugee Escape."

"Which means Nadeche is the problem here," Olav says calmly.

"How do you mean?"

"Well, if she weren't down there, we wouldn't be either. I mean, we'd planned to stop filming, hadn't we? If we'd just broadcast the finale and she'd come back home there wouldn't be a problem now."

"We've got to get her back, then," Karstleiter sighs. "It can't be that difficult. Let's face it, she wasn't that keen at the beginning."

This is going in the wrong direction, Sensenbrink thinks. "That . . . that shouldn't be our first option," he says. "We need to think of the company's figures, our advertisers. And the people."

"Advertisers *are* people," Olav needles him.

"I know you fought for this," Reliable Anke says. "But you said yourself that it's just too great a risk."

"But we can't pull out now," Sensenbrink says. There's determination in his voice, because he's just thought of a good argument. "If you see it as Hayat has outlined, if all this is only happening because our cameras are there, then conversely our viewers would complain if we took the cameras away. Not only the cameras" – here Sensenbrink introduces a pause – "but hope, too. It would look like we were abandoning them. We and, er, all the viewers."

"But the viewers could keep giving donations and all that," a goatherd says.

"We can't be the conduit for that," Beate Karstleiter says, shaking her head.

"That's what others do."

"Yes, for refugees in *camps*. That's fine. But we can't collect donations for refugees who are on their way to us. We'd almost be people smugglers."

"Hold on a moment," Reliable Anke protests. "People smugglers *take* money. We don't."

"That doesn't make it kosher," Sensenbrink says curtly. "Think about it! MyTV brings one hundred and fifty thousand refugees to Germany – that's completely illegal! Give me strength. We need realistic suggestions."

"Menschen für Menschen!" Hayat blurts out. "Remember?"

"What?"

"Menschen für Menschen," she says again. "Don't you remember?"

"Whatshisface?"

"That guy in the *Sissi* films?"

"He helped people in Africa too. It started out with a bet on 'You Bet!' He raised money then went to Africa to help people."

"Karlheinz Böhm," Olav says. "That was his name!"

"Great. But what good does it do us?"

"We can replicate the model," Hayat says. "Which means we wouldn't have to bring Frau Hackenbusch back." Sensenbrink can tell from the other faces that he's not the only one who can't see where the difference lies.

"And," Hayat says, a little less certain now, "it wouldn't be our campaign. We could just report on it in the normal way."

"If it's Nadeche Hackenbusch raising the money?" Karstleiter probes.

"Wow!" Olav says. "That's it. The story is that we've made a standard documentary, during which Nadeche got the idea—"

"She sets off with the refugees and if anyone wants to donate, the money goes via her," Reliable Anke says, finally twigging too.

"Obviously it would have to be organised so that nothing comes to us," Karstleiter says. "We're just the television crew reporting on the story, as any other broadcaster might—"

"With the difference that we've got access to the key figures at any time," Sensenbrink underlines.

"But we're totally committed. We're suffering too, we're hoping too, we're supporting too—"

"—we're not supporting their cause—"

"—never support their cause, that's what the right wingers said—"

"—never take the side of a cause—"

"—no, but the people—"

"Exactly, the people!"

"We're with them every day, we're behind Nadeche Hackenbusch's plan—"

"—It needs a cool name—"

"Na-dash to Europe!"

"I'm a Refugee, Get Me Out of Here!"

Sensenbrink leans back, feeling relaxed. He looks sympathetically at Hayat and gives her a smile. He knows what he's going to propose to Kärrner at their next meeting: "We've got Karlheinz Böhm with tits."

# 21

The under-secretary is poking around his salad without enthusiasm.

"Did you catch your girlfriend on telly yesterday?" Lohm says.

Lohm is sitting opposite and has almost finished his pasta.

"Don't!" Maybe he ought to have gone for a soup, but Carlo's soups are usually a bit dull. "She's finally lost it."

"I don't know. I mean, it's fun to have a laugh about, but if I'm being honest it's going down the Karlheinz Böhm route."

"Karlheinz *Böhm*?" The under-secretary utters the name as if it's an imposition. "Are you serious? A nutty Karlheinz Böhm, perhaps."

"Maybe, but the fact that it's someone like Hackenbusch doing this—"

"Well, it just goes to show how barmy the whole thing is."

"But exciting too. No normal individual would do it – you need idiots to pull something like this off."

"Not you too!"

"Who else?"

"I'll give you three guesses. The old man. It's sheer nonsense, just doom-mongering."

"But Leubl hasn't been completely wrong so far, has he?"

Now the under-secretary pushes his salad away definitively. Lohm raises his eyebrows and, when there's no reaction, he casually pulls the bowl towards him. "Your boss has a pretty good understanding that the situation is going to be hard to control."

The under-secretary watches Lohm fish out slices of carrot with his fork.

"Yes, yes, madness is always hard to control. But it's still madness."

"You took the words right out of my mouth," Lohm says, crunching into the carrots.

"It's going to end in a human catastrophe!"

"Is that any worse?" Lohm is now spearing cherry tomatoes by variety.

"What do you mean?"

"Well," Lohm says as a tomato rolls off his fork. He picks it up with his fingers and pops it contentedly in his mouth. "It started as a human catastrophe."

The under-secretary ponders this for a moment.

"It can get worse, and nobody wants that. Just imagine: one hundred and fifty thousand people running into the desert, without a plan!"

"Perhaps they have a plan."

"Are you actually trying to be a pain in the arse?"

"No, but why would one hundred and fifty thousand people go running off into the desert?"

"Am I Jesus Christ? Nobody knows why whales beach themselves either."

"But these aren't whales."

"It's mass hysteria, then, or whatever."

"Is it? These people are risking their lives. Sure, there are always some prepared to take more of a risk. But not one hundred and fifty thousand."

The under-secretary breathes in angrily and breathes out angrily. "O.K., fine. Let's assume you're right and this isn't a case of mass hysteria. So what does this plan look like?"

"No idea. Why are you asking me? All I know is that human beings aren't whales."

The under-secretary falls into a silent sulk. Catching the eye of a waiter, he orders two espressos while Lohm folds salad leaves into his mouth with astonishing dexterity. The coffee arrives. The under-secretary doesn't take sugar, but he stirs it with his spoon.

"O.K., then. Let's assume there is a plan. How's it going to work?"

Lohm chews thoughtfully. "One hundred and fifty thousand people. Maybe that just sounds like a lot, but in fact isn't."

"They might also be exaggerating," the under-secretary muses. "But let's leave it at one hundred and fifty thousand. Now get onto the civil defence organisation and ask them what you'd need to keep one hundred and fifty thousand people in supplies, at even the most rudimentary level. Find out the basic cost of a neighbourhood party."

"I expect these people can get by on less. From what I hear

they don't have so many neighbourhood parties down there, so they won't need any police officers."

"Still," the under-secretary interrupts him tetchily. "What's the minimum? What does each person need?"

"Water."

"Right. And we're not even talking about showers here, just water for drinking. Let's say each individual needs ten litres per day – that's one point five million litres."

"Is that a lot? How much can a tanker hold?"

"Half a million?"

"A bath takes 120 litres I think."

"How many bathtubs make up a tanker?"

Lohm puts down his fork and picks up his iPhone. He taps about on it for a moment, then reads out: "A tanker can hold between thirty and forty thousand litres."

"O.K., let's say thirty thousand. One point five million litres divided by thirty thousand . . . that makes fifty lorries."

"It's not impossible."

"Yes, but we're not just talking about once. This is every day. And you don't just need lorries, but the drivers too, and not just for a fortnight. If they're planning to walk the whole way, they'll need to be kept supplied for years."

"Well, well, now this madcap enterprise is even creating secure jobs."

The under-secretary shoots Lohm a fierce look.

"Don't look at me like that. I'm not saying it all works. We said there wasn't a plan, but in less than five minutes we've come up with a good reason why someone might be interested in ensuring that they don't all die of thirst. And we're not just talking about the drivers of the water tankers – these people have to eat too."

"Yes, but they can't cook. It has to stop somewhere. I mean, they don't have field kitchens to hand. And wood or camping gas for one hundred and fifty thousand people – that can't work."

"You mean it works for water, but not food?"

"This isn't the army we're talking about! These are muppets in flip-flops. I'm sorry, but that's the truth of the matter."

"So everything's tickety-boo."

"Exactly."

"They're going to die like beached whales."

"Exactly. And that's terrible."

"Of course. Really terrible."

"We're agreed, then."

By way of confirmation the under-secretary knocks back his espresso. Lohm sips his thoughtfully. The under-secretary once read that you shouldn't gulp an espresso like a schnapps. But he's seen Italians do it. Who to believe?

"The food thing is only one problem. The difference is that making the journey with a people smuggler is far quicker, and a lorry takes you through all those areas where there's nothing but a road and sand. I'm not saying the Africans aren't up to it, but they've got to go everywhere on foot," he says to Lohm. "There's no infrastructure – no villages, nothing. And they've got to transport all the gear too. Calling the undertaking into question doesn't make you a racist. I doubt even the Americans would be able to pull this off."

"Alright."

"Think about it! One hundred and fifty thousand – no way, José! That's the size of the U.S. invasion force in Iraq."

"Fine, I give up. You've won."

The under-secretary sinks back in his chair.

"Thank God. You were making me nervous for a moment."

"Good," Lohm says. "So we're just left with the images."

"Hmm?"

"The images! Don't forget this isn't just a question of logistics!"

The under-secretary flinches.

"This isn't just a mass of refugees perishing somewhere," Lohm says. "This is a mass of refugees with their own telly programme. Presented by Nadeche Hackenbusch. It's wiping the floor with the daily soaps."

"It'll tail off—"

"Yeah, right. People are starving, dying of thirst, the It-girl is flirting with a handsome, sensitive refugee and crying bitter tears – and all this is real, genuine. Go ahead and put your money on the likelihood of it tailing off, but I'll bet against you any time. Five to one."

The under-secretary doesn't move a muscle.

"I'm telling you, if they do it right, they won't just get enough viewers, they'll get *all* the viewers. Anyone who like a bit of sensationalism. The compassionate types. The Nazis, because it makes them furious. Because it's so different – not some star reporter being handed their water after filming—"

"If they do it right . . ."

"If I'm not mistaken, it's like 'I'm a Celebrity' but with real corpses and Nadeche Hackenbusch in mortal danger. With that they can't go wrong!"

"You're really enjoying this, aren't you?"

"What do you expect? I'm still with the Greens. And for all our fuck-ups, we never believed that sealing the country off was a solution."

"One hundred and fifty thousand people are marching to their deaths, and all you're thinking is: We told you so. Even the do-gooders used to be better."

For a moment they are silent. The under-secretary can see right through Lohm. He knows, of course, that hype doesn't last for years, but solid interest does. He knows what Nadeche Hackenbusch managed to achieve even in the first few episodes at the refugee hostel.

"She's giving the refugees a face."

"Hmm?"

"She's going to give them a face," the under-secretary says grimly. "And then it's all over. After that nobody's going to be able to look at the refugee problem objectively again."

"Has anyone ever been able to?"

"And we'll find ourselves squashed. Between refugee fans and real Nazis." The under-secretary shakes his head. "No, it all boils down to that daft cow. We have to pull her out of there."

"Oh, great plan. She doesn't exactly look like she wants to be pulled out."

"Have you got a better suggestion?"

"Sure. Make it look like an accident."

"This is no longer a joke!" He looks at Lohm in despair.

Lohm stops teasing him. "Shall I give you some consolation? It's not your decision. Ultimately it's the ministry of foreign affairs' business. Or your boss's. But not yours."

Sometimes he envies Lohm. His ability to push things to the back of his mind or postpone them. To retreat to the refuge of his job and pretend nothing else exists. Even when the Americans elected Trump. A question mark fell on N.A.T.O., on the entire world order, and Lohm simply attended to his environmental business as if it were just as important as before. As if it made a difference whether you saved or ran over a tortoise in a world where the U.S.A. no longer took part in environmental protection. But if needs be, Lohm can narrow his horizons to the ministry of the environment or the weekend barbecue. He doesn't make a secret out of this either. Lohm's philosophy goes something like: "This world produces more and more shit every day. And at some point it will have to surface. My job isn't to make the shit disappear. My job is to ensure that it doesn't surface here, but elsewhere. To ensure that it doesn't surface today, but at some other time. And that's what I do. I don't plant apple trees. I shovel shit from here to there and from today to tomorrow."

"What happens when you can no longer stop the shit from surfacing tomorrow?" the under-secretary once asked him.

"I'll be somewhere else."

The under-secretary can't be like that. He absolutely shares Lohm's basic pessimism, but he hates botched jobs and considers it a defeat if he has to resort to such measures. It's something else he admires about Leubl, this love of big, thorough, decisive solutions worth mustering a majority for. In this instance, however, he can't see a solution.

He doesn't have faith in his colleagues at the foreign ministry. Why should *they* solve the problem? Just to have more television idiots parachuting into crisis areas the very next day, confident that the foreign ministry will protect them if things look dodgy? Their only hope is the geographical distance. The difficulty of providing for and coordinating one hundred and fifty thousand people for months on end. Years. If the whole thing tails off then it's fine. But he hates this. Not being able to plan. Not being able to make decisions. Just having to wait. This is what he finds hardest. This and the knowledge that whoever does find the right solution will be guaranteed a ministerial post.

# 10,000 kilometres
# for love

**Nadeche Hackenbusch and Lionel: the megastar has let her heart decide – now the fate of 150,000 people hangs on the success of this love affair**

## By Astrid von Roëll

We all know the tale of the ugly duckling who turns into a dying swan. This time, however, it's different. The swan isn't dying and the duckling isn't ugly. Rather this is the story of a young, strong woman prepared to do anything and everything for love, thereby conquering the hearts of the entire world. It is the story of a woman radically reinventing herself, finally, finally living the dream that no woman has ever dreamed before. Now Nadeche Hackenbusch has made this dream come true: she has left her husband to accompany the great love you only meet once in life, on his way to Europe. On foot and alone. With 150,000 refugees.

Ten thousand kilometres. It will be a march for the right to life, a march for the right to a spark of hope – and a march for the right to a little happiness. A march full of danger, whose end nobody can predict. Such worry, such uncertainty, both are difficult to bear.

This isn't the same Nadeche Hackenbusch we knew only a few weeks ago. When I go to see her, her soft, long hair is tied up in a practical bun. Her long legs are in simple beige hiking trousers (Black Diamond), her Mammut softshell jacket is open, and a plain blue Merino T-Shirt underlines her modest appearance. She senses my astonishment when I look at her slender hands. "Yes, I know, no nail varnish – eight weeks ago that would have been unthinkable. But everything in life can change so quickly. I mean, can you believe it? I can scarcely believe it myself!"

The painfully fresh memories of the past few days flash

through her mind like the recap of a film. It hasn't even been forty-eight hours since she announced on her show her separation from Nicolai von Kraken, her husband of many years. Rumours circulate, thoughts are articulated that the programme might be extended for a few days because of the Hackenbusch crisis. But on the day for which the broadcaster had scheduled the grand finale, Nadeche Hackenbusch takes everyone by surprise with another announcement. Now, she reveals to a global audience breathless with excitement, she will return to Germany – but not alone.

"It was a spontaneous decision," the star presenter says. "A voice in my head told me that things just couldn't go on as they were." This voice, can it be any voice apart from the voice of the heart? For – as EVANGELINE readers have surmised sooner than anyone else – the reason for this separation is her amazing new companion, Lionel. The man they call "the soul of the refugee camp", the determined humanitarian, the young Gandhi of Africa, has taken Germany by storm with his tender honesty and refresh-ing truths. And what may look like an impulsive summer romance to those viewers who don't know Nadeche Hackenbusch, is in reality an encounter with an extraordinary man, and magical sparks are flying. An extraordinary man with an extraordinary life story that couldn't be more grim. He, the tireless helper of the helpless, is an alien from an alien world whose path to our country remains closed.

Just by looking at Nadeche Hackenbusch one can tell that this ruthlessness is working inside her, working at

## "It was a spontaneous decision"

her, doing something to her. A small wrinkle has appeared between her eyes, a wrinkle that lends her young face an unexpected maturity, a maturity forged by thoughtfulness and anger. It shows the fury of a woman who is not a government agency. A woman who always realises what people need, rather than what they ought to do. "I can't change the laws made by man," she says bravely, sweeping a stray strand of hair behind her ear, "but I can fight against their inhumane consequences. And I'm doing this side by side with Lionel. He is the man these people now need much more urgently than anything else."

She doesn't tell me outright, but her body language says it all: here the

## Lionel has stared hunger in the face

mills of fairness and justice are agglutinating the flour of a truly great love. For it's not only the people in the camp who need this slim, handsome bearer of hope with his mysterious yet endearing eyes. It is also the woman in Nadeche Hackenbusch who, like a delicate flower, is so desperate for his optimism right now. And how moving it is to see Nadeche Hackenbusch, a superstar across the continent of Europe, sacrificing her own needs as she denies the woman behind the angel. While the eyes of the world focus on the striking mass of people surrounding the young couple, newly in love, on their perilous journey, she puts her own requirements on the back burner. "We've got so much to do and see so little of each other," she says, and only those who've known her for longer

can hear the faint quiver in her voice that shows how much energy it takes to be Nadeche Hackenbusch in these days and months. For even if Lionel is the one the people trust, nothing happens without her vigour and drive.

In spite of the priority afforded to helping others, concern about the permanent strain on Nadeche Hackenbusch obliges us to venture a glimpse into her soul. At times of great stress it is dangerous to ignore strong emotions and profound feelings, and so now, in the dusty heat of Africa, the moment has come to ask the question on the minds of millions of Germans:

What's wrong with Nicolai von Kraken?

"I feel sorry for Nicolai," Nadeche says softly as she wipes sweat from her brow with her forearm. "But he knew that we were never meant to be together for ever. Nicolai needs someone else, he's still a child. Sure, the adoption, the acknowledgement of my children made him grow up a bit. But what I've gone through over the past few months has catapulted me a long way in my personal development and thus put an even greater distance between the two of us. Just compare the two. Lionel is a man who's stared hunger in the face, who has experience of this continent. Africa is beautiful and horrible, with tigers and poisonous snakes."

And what will become of her sons? Keel, for whom shoplifting is finally a thing of the past? And Bonno who's about to take the major step of starting at St Zwerenz private school? Don't her two children need her as well? Nadeche Hackenbusch gulps as only a mother can. She finds this hard to answer. It's one of those rare moments in life when a mother's duties and affection have to take a back seat too. For Nadeche Hackenbusch knows that without the power of love no angel can be of any help. And 150,000 people cannot choose the right path if she and Lionel don't manage to stay together for the duration.

This time it's not merely a love affair. It's probably the most important love affair in the world.

# 22

Mahmoud hasn't got a handle on anything, which means he has to see to it all himself. Mahmoud is assigned with supervising the food and water, and all he has to do is check that everyone pays and that the food and water are of good enough quality. And he's supposed to coordinate the people assisting him. It all happened so quickly. Sure, when Mahmoud asked, "Are you making me admiral for food and water?", he might have given the matter further thought. But he was happy to have washed his hands of it. And let's face it, who could he have brought along in Mahmoud's place? He mobilised all his contacts, only leaving out the complete idiots. And people can say what they like about Mahmoud, but he's not stupid. Still, you never know what might suddenly drive a man crazy. It could be a woman, or money, or in Mahmoud's case an official position. So he hasn't been able to wash his hands of this at all, because more and more of Mahmoud's time has been taken up deciding which badge to make for himself. He got hold of an old captain's hat, God knows where from, and you could ask the same about the epaulettes he sewed onto his T-shirt.

"Admiral for Food and Water"? How ludicrous is that? Why admiral? Mahmoud was never in the navy. And he'd only swim if you tossed him into the mouth of a crocodile.

So it's all down to him again. At least he can be happy that the hierarchy is functioning to some degree. Anyone who's worked as a people smuggler knows how to make quick checks or to deal with people who haven't paid. But beyond that you can't ask for much. He's only just managed to ensure that for each truck there are one or two people he knows and can to some extent rely on. They'll let him know if something's not working. Malaika lends him one of her pink angelmobiles, so he can rapidly access the section of the convoy in question. The thirty minutes it can take them to drive there, thirty minutes in which his mobile often has no reception – these are the times he can most easily fall asleep.

"We're there!"

"Hmm?"

"Truck 29!"

Lionel wipes his eyes with a damp hand. He feels slightly fresher afterwards, as if a dog had licked his face. He forces open his swollen eyelids and gets out.

People have surrounded his car and are beaming at him; children laugh and whoop as if he's about to pick them up and carry them around with him. At times like this he can understand where Malaika gets her energy from, this inexhaustible, terrifying energy. It's unbelievable how tirelessly she works. But then again it makes a difference whether you're dashing around the place as the good fairy the whole time, handing out water or medicine or those unusual things that European women evidently harness their breasts with like oxen before a plough – or whether you're responsible for all the other shit.

He slips a foot beneath the mudguard over the front tyre. Groaning like an old man, he heaves himself up to get a better view. Beyond all the children he sees Orma waving and making her way towards him through the crowd.

"They want to talk to you."

"Oh God! I told you to get rid of them! It's always the same thing."

"No, this time they say it's something different!"

"And you believed them? Really, Orma! It's the oldest trick in the book!"

Three figures approach him. A mountain of a man, in his late thirties perhaps, another man in glasses, and a woman he can tell has an excruciating voice just by looking at her. The mountain tries to say something, but the woman pushes him aside.

"What are we paying five dollars for?"

Of course. Always the same. Just the tone is different. This woman talks faster than other women. And her voice is higher. Much higher. Sometimes, when playing, children squeal as high as they can, but this woman trumps them all. He had no idea that people could talk at this pitch.

"There isn't enough water!"

"There has to be enough," Lionel sighs. "And there is enough!"

"Thirst isn't everything. We have to wash too, you know!"

The voice! Like bashing a long, rusty nail into your ear. And then twisting it. Lionel is delighted when his mobile rings.

"Yo, what's my favourite hiker up to? How's it goin'?"

It's astonishing that Mojo hasn't called until now.

"Not great."

"That's always the way, amigo! The legs feel at their heaviest just before the summit."

"We need to talk."

"You know what? I don't reckon we do. Hikin' tales are the most goddamn boring tales in the world. Either it's too steep uphill, too steep downhill or someone gets lost. The story's only excitin' if the hiker dies, but you've got a cell, you can call folk. And I've got all ten series of 'Baywatch' to get through. You know 'Baywatch'? It's a classic! O.K., let's cut the crap: where's my moolah?"

"I haven't got it."

The screeching woman looks at him expectantly. He looks past her at the dust, the sand and the wide, empty nothingness.

"Sorry, must have been some sort of interference on the line. It sounded like you said you hadn't got it."

"And I don't."

Mojo laughs.

"You're a scream. But you've been to my office. You've seen the T.V. set. Maybe you thought Mojo is one of those guys who buys big televisions to impress dumb niggers. But you'd be thinkin' wrong. I'm not like that."

"I—"

"Sorry, but I'm not finished yet. I buy big television sets because I like watching T.V. And I don't want no overbloated picture, I want H.D. I don't wanna see Pamela Anderson's nipples blur into little squares. I want those nipples so sharp that Pamela Anderson squeals if I touch the screen. I've got it all on Blu-Ray."

"But—"

"But it doesn't exist on Blu-Ray, is that what you're sayin'? Wait, can we be sure?"

"I don't know—"

"Me neither. Shall I ask Bandele?"

"The . . ."

"Bandele! Is 'Baywatch' out on Blu-Ray?" Mojo chortles. "Boy, am I excited!"

He laughs again.

"You should see this nigger rackin' his brains. You're O.K., Bandele. You might be a fool, but you're O.K. But this guy, our T.V. pussy magnet, he's no fool. He's one smart guy. Are you listenin'?"

"What?" Lionel tries not to sound stressed, but he's reached the point of sheer exhaustion.

"You listenin' to what I'm sayin'?"

"Yeah, sure."

"I'm sayin' you're one smart guy. You're thinkin' Mojo's tryin' to take me for a ride, I know 'Baywatch' only came out on D.V.D. And so I'm sayin' to you, you're right. And yet you're wrong. Right here in front of me I've got the entire edition of 'Baywatch' on Blu-Ray. Custom made. I know a guy who does this sort of thing for me. And this ain't some kind of computer freebie, he does it for me in a real American studio. You see, I'm an aficionado. Know what that means?"

"I can imagine."

Mojo pauses. "Really?"

"Well, what it means is that you don't just enhance the resolution of the scenes with tits in them, but everything, including the credits. It's much more expensive and you want me to feel afraid because you can afford to shell out a fortune for 'Baywatch'. But me being afraid isn't going to do you any good. I'm afraid all the time, see? The problem isn't that I'm not afraid enough. The problem is that we have a problem."

"Ooh! Customer not satisfied. May I register your complaint? Did you have different expectations of our product?"

He has to admit that to begin with he didn't have a clear notion of how it would work. And he's astonished that it's worked out till now. He can't say, of course, that he didn't believe it was possible, but then again he never posed the question. He just saw his great opportunity to get to Europe, to Germany, crumble before his eyes, and then seized the only contingency plan that could be cobbled together at short notice. Even if the chances of success had been twice as poor he would still have gone for it, because anything was better than the 100 per cent certainty of spending his life on this totally messed-up continent. Of course he was anxious from the very beginning. Most of all he was anxious about being disappointed.

On the first day his greatest fear was of turning up and finding that none of Mojo's promises had materialised. He'd already envisioned setting off, telling himself not to be impatient, that everything was very difficult to organise, then darkness would fall and he'd realise that Mojo's water wasn't coming, that Mojo had left him in the lurch, or conned him, or both.

And then the lorry appeared.

A dented ZiL from Russia, dating back to the fifties or sixties, but still roadworthy. And not just one; Mojo had got hold of them all. The next lorry was parked one kilometre further on. And one kilometre beyond that, a third.

"Aren't the trucks there?"

"They're here."

"Don't you like my trucks?" Mojo says sarcastically. "Would you rather Scania? Or M.A.N.?"

It's true, Mojo works with Russian, Indian and Chinese wrecks. But nobody expected anything different. Mojo has to take anything with wheels, even juggernauts or flatbed trucks if they're big enough. Those lorries that aren't tankers are loaded with plastic barrels, and you can tell how difficult it is to get hold of these by the fact that the water sometimes tastes of paint or diesel. But supplying the water is nowhere near as complicated as organising food.

How do you feed one hundred and fifty thousand people? Who have nothing but the odd earthenware pot? The usual camp provision of flour, sugar and oil is pointless because these people have neither the time nor equipment to bake or mix their porridge. Some of the white exercise junkies have got concentrates, which are very practical, but Mojo had to kick-start deliveries of these, and if he didn't steal them they would be unaffordable. What remained, to begin with at least, were carbohydrates and fats that are easy to portion up, such as bread, flatbread, nuts and dried fruits. In the first few days Mojo had to plunder a number of large bakeries. Well, not quite plunder, because he was reliant on them. So he gave them the money, but made it perfectly clear that virtually every other customer had to take a back seat. All the same it was hard to build up a continual supply. That's not the main problem, however.

"I don't care which lorries you use. The problem is you."

Silence on the other end of the line.

"Mojo?"

Not a sound.

"Mojo? Hello?"

"Say that again."

"I don't have the money. And you're the reason why not."

"What's goin' on here? Do I look like some kinda service hotline?"

"You're preventing us from being able to pay you. We can't give you anything from our coffers if you nail them shut! We need electricity."

"You've *got* electricity."

"Not enough. What use is it if only my smartphone works? Everyone has to pay their share, which means everyone needs a mobile!"

"There are one hundred and fifty thousand of you. Do you think everyone can have their own plug socket in the middle of the desert?"

"I don't know what else to say, but if you want your money you're going to have to sort that out. Not every phone needs to be charged every day, but every second day for sure. Maybe families can get by with one phone between them, maybe others can share sometimes, but the bottom line is that we need to be able to charge thirty thousand mobiles, at least. And we need generators that don't cut out. And a mobile network."

Silence.

"Hello? Do you get what I'm saying? If you don't secure the electricity supply, you won't get any money for 'Baywatch'. Because it won't work, no matter how afraid I am."

More silence.

"I not trying to get your back up. I know I'm empty-handed. I know you could say any time you're stopping deliveries because you're not getting any money. Then we'd die and that would be that. But you're in the best position to know what your daily cut of this can look like: ten thousand dollars, fifty thousand dollars. I'm not getting a cent of this money, but it's precisely the sum that's going to slip through your fingers every day if you don't sort out the electricity. Every single day."

Silence, but from the rustling he can hear that Mojo is still on the line.

"The same is true of food and water. If someone's got nothing to drink today, they can't pay tomorrow. The more that make it, the more money ends up in your lap."

"*If* you make it," Mojo says defiantly.

"If we don't, no-one will embark on this journey after us. And for every convoy that doesn't set off you'll lose the same amount. Every day. Man, you can bathe in money, but we need electricity."

"Hey, watch that tone of yours, amigo!"

"I don't think I'm your amigo," Lionel says, speaking as calmly and firmly as he can. "I'm your partner. I'm the guy who's going to make you rich. If you give us electricity!"

A short silence on the other end of the line, and the connection is cut.

Lionel slips his mobile into his pocket. At that very moment he realises he's made an unforgivable error. The woman plants herself in front of him. And while she squeals at him with every last breath of the air she's been inhaling for twenty minutes, Lionel hopes, like a lovestruck young man, that Mojo is going to call back.

# 23

It's completely unreasonable.

Astrid von Roëll has to admit it looks sensational. But still, it's completely unreasonable.

Video now too!

As if she were some kind of news manufacturer. Astrid is already writing this stupid blog until her fingers bleed. At least they *feel* like they're bleeding, and that's pretty much the same thing. One hundred lines a day, they said, and even that was madness. Ten weeks ago she had a week to produce one hundred lines, and what lines they were, bloody hell, it was verging on high literature. Her old head of copy would say, "Astrid, darling, I never have to make changes to your copy anymore. If everyone was like you I'd be able retire right now."

Now she's churning it out like the women in the factories in the Second World War. It's no surprise they fought to get the vote and Mothers' Day. And one hundred lines – what a joke! Of course it didn't stop at one hundred either: there had to be captions for the photos too, a line or two each. So that's about a hundred and twenty. Sometimes Astrid feels she's close to burnout. She needs to pace herself, so she doesn't even bother reading through the dross she regurgitates for the Internet. She bangs it out, then she's done with the shit. These people on their mobiles on the underground or the train or on the motorway don't read it properly anyway, so why should she bother writing it properly? She only makes a real effort for the print edition. It still has to be literary grade, and even though all this stress makes it hard for her, Astrid does have her pride. But she's beginning to wonder how on earth she's going to get on top of all the work. And for the last fortnight they've been demanding videos too.

"What more do you want from me?"

"This is just an experiment," the deputy blockhead said.

"What do you mean, 'experiment'?"

"We've got an advantage here, a priceless advantage, largely thanks to you. *Gala* magazine, *Bunte*, they're doing all they can to play catch-up—"

"Just let them try! Who they are going to get to do it? Seelow?"

"Yes, I know, they lack the quality, but they'll try to make up for that with volume. More photos, more copy—"

"And you're asking me to compete with that on my own?"

"Come on, a short video clip, it's not so much—"

"But I haven't a clue how to do it!"

This just slipped out. It's something women should never do – claim to be a dummy when it comes to technology. After all, there's nothing women can't do just as well as men. But it was the truth. And so immediately they sent Kay to help her out.

And Kay really is quite good. At what she does, in her own way. It's not journalism, of course, but still. Kay has had herself strapped to the roof of the S.U.V. – now *that's* pretty courageous. She's sitting on the roof in cargo pants and a sand-coloured military blouse, over that a sleeveless jacket like those ones men usually wear, with plenty of little pockets for tools and accessories. She holds the camera even when they're moving at top speed and zooms in on the pink zebra pick-up hurtling through the dusty desert beside them. Astrid can follow the footage on a monitor – that, at least, was a concession she wrested from the deputy blockhead.

Kay has Nadeche Hackenbusch in full focus. Nadeche is standing in the cargo area at the back of the pick-up, holding on tight to the driver's cab. Her long hair is fluttering in the wind and she's wearing a checked shirt tied in a knot at the waist. Nadeche flies past the endless stream of refugees, some of whom wave at her, and she waves back with a broad smile.

"Go!" she shouts, clenching her astonishingly strong-looking fist. "Go, go!"

Her eyes are hidden behind an unbelievably cool pair of desert sunglasses, while her face, neck and bare arms are a deep brown. Nadeche looks so confident, so infectiously full of enthusiasm, as if the German border were already in sight. To glimpse her, you couldn't imagine that this march might end badly. Astrid hears Kay knock once on the roof; the S.U.V. accelerates and overtakes the pick-up. Now Kay is filming Nadeche from the front. The screen shows Nadeche in the wind, behind her a cloud of dust rises, a picture of freedom and courage. Joan of Arc can't have looked any more captivating. Priceless, Astrid thinks, simply priceless. What a shame millions of people will only see this on their smartphones. This kind of thing's made for the big screen.

Now Nadeche has spotted something. She hammers on the driver's cab with a small clenched fist. Crazy. And not at all ladylike. Nadeche bends forwards, steadying herself on the wing mirror. Kay is filming all this. Nadeche yells something to the driver and it looks fantastic, like a captain in a storm with the water slapping his face, wind roaring, but it doesn't bother him and he shouts to his helmsman . . . well, whatever they'd shout to each other in storms, because they're real men. And this is exactly how Nadeche Hackenbusch looks just now. Then she straightens up, the pick-up slows down, veers off towards the convoy of refugees, and Kay captures the entire manoeuvre on film: Nadeche Hackenbusch to the rescue. The pick-up races at top speed towards the shoal of refugees like a helpful shark.

She stops beside a family, a couple with three children. Their large plastic bottle has a leak. Nadeche leaps from the cargo area, a construction worker, firefighter and top model all in one. She casually pushes her sunglasses onto her forehead, her warm-hearted eyes shine from her dust-covered face. She grabs two plastic water bottles from the cargo area and hands them to the family. This is where you notice the difference: a guy would have tossed the bottles at them while driving past.

"That reaches for today," she says in her English. "Go, go!" She is about to climb back onto the pick-up when her mobile rings. She glances at the screen and gestures to Kay to press pause. Turning slightly to the side, she says, "Yes? . . . I can hear you fine . . . But I'm quite close to the T.V. car, so that may change if we drive off. How far away are you?"

When Astrid gets out the heat hits her like a hammer, but anything's better than sitting inside. She circles the car to find some shade.

"Yes," Nadeche says, "Yes. Aha. Yes, yes. Yes, yes, yes, you're doing that already. But the question is: what's the thing called!"

Kay clambers down from the roof and comes round to where Astrid is standing. She sits on the ground, but leaps up because the sand is so hot. She fetches a small mat from the car and sits on that instead. She taps Astrid's leg, but Astrid wants to stay on her feet.

"Listen, don't get angry with me, but like, what kind of a shit name is that?"

Astrid peers over the roof at Nadeche, Nadeche looks at her and rolls her eyes. Astrid makes a "what to do?" gesture. She doesn't know what it's about, but it's clear Nadeche needs her support.

"You might be able to use it for a cancer story, but just listen: The Hackenbusch Foundation. It sounds like it's for ill people."

Nadeche grasps her head and looks at Astrid.

"I know it's all about suffering and that, but it shouldn't sound ill and miserable. The people here might be poor, but they're not sick. Or at least not so sick that it's contagious. You can absolutely touch them, it's not like cancer at all."

Now Nadeche makes an "I'm right, aren't I?" face, and Astrid's expression suggests she is right, but she makes a mental note to google it later.

"No, it can sound serious without sounding shit. End of discussion. What else have you got? Children for the Future. Hmm. Hang on. Children for the Future?"

Astrid is unsure. Should she say something or not? Children for the Future doesn't sound wrong, but who knows if she . . .

"Oh, right. Interesting. But now you see the mistake straightaway. You always have to say who's behind it. I wouldn't have known that about Steffi Graf either if you hadn't told me . . . You see?"

It's crazy, all the things you have to take into consideration, Astrid thinks. She probably allowed herself to be fobbed off far too quickly when it came to the video thing. Yes, it's great that her name will be in the credits. But she could have got more out of it.

"Yes, yes, I know, Menschen für Menschen, but that's logical. That Böhm guy, if I were in his shoes I wouldn't give a toss. Nobody knows who he is these days. I mean, when did he last make a film, anyway?"

Astrid rapidly waves her fingers back and forth across her throat – she knows the *Sissi* films very well – but Nadeche puts her hand over the phone and hisses. "Are you mad, Assi? This is like, important. It's gonna take time."

Astrid tries other hand gestures to calm her down, but Nadeche has turned away in disgust. It's hard to tell who's pissing her off most at the moment.

Kay takes two bottles of water and hands one to Astrid. She guzzles half of hers and pours the rest over her head. Astrid is just about to take a sip when she hears the frantic snapping of fingers.

"Ah, that sounds quite different. Do you know what that reminds me of? It sounds like the Bill Gates thing."

Nadeche holds out her free hand and frantically grabs at nothing. Astrid hastily passes her the bottle of water.

"Thanks. No. Why Hackenbusch Foundation? That could be anybody . . . Anybody called Hackenbusch . . . *Nadeche* Hackenbusch Foundation. Write it down! Got it? Now, what else? . . . Wait, did you think that was it? It needs something else!"

She holds her hand over the phone again. "Now I'm going to get the less-is-more spiel again," she says with a smile. Astrid smiles back.

"Well of course there's something missing. I don't want to have to stand there next time I'm in New York with everyone saying, 'Aha, interesting, Nadeche Hackenbusch Foundation,' but in fact everyone's totally like, 'A Foundation, but what's it for?' Do I really have to think of everything myself?"

Nadeche takes a sip, then drips some water over her wrists and into the crooks of her arms.

"And don't give me that 'Menschen' stuff again, it sounds too much like 'Problem Child' – all 1960s lentils and kaftans, ugh! No, we need that thing, what's it called? . . . Astrid, what's that thing called when everyone chips in?"

"Crowdfunding?" Astrid guesses.

"That's it, krautfunding. But we've got to make it clear that it's not any old kraut funding it, but me . . . People? Dunno. Nadeche Hackenbusch Foundation for People . . . sounds O.K., but something's not quite right. Shouldn't it be 'for the people'? . . . What do you mean, North Korea?"

This time Astrid holds her tongue. Nadeche takes a large slug of water then nonchalantly hands the bottle to Astrid so she can put the top back on.

"Humanity? No, not that. Why do you lot always have to go one step too far, always another thing and then something else until it sounds really shit? Humanity is too much. I mean, who do you think I am? Yes, I'm Nadeche Hackenbusch, but the whole of humanity? . . . I can only help individuals . . . Yes, humans. Well, sometimes a few more, but the whole of humanity is five billion people! No, we're going to stick with the Nadeche Hackenbusch Foundation for the Humans. That's what's going out – end of. Tell Madeleine to get going with it this afternoon. Strahlemann & Bullwinkel can design another pretty logo, by tomorrow, and then it'll be up and running. We haven't got for ever. And I want offices in Berlin, Hamburg and Düsseldorf. No skimping, either. You have to spend money if you want it to come in. Over and out!"

She slips the mobile into the back pocket of her trousers and smiles broadly. Astrid raises her eyebrows.

"I've decided to set up this foundation after all. For donations. So people see that it's serious and that. We'll have them like, howling at their telly screens! You heard our conversation. Now we've got the name at least – and it's great, isn't it? What about you? Have you got your footage? Because now I've got to go and save a few people!"

Nadeche climbs back onto the pick-up with astonishing agility. She pulls down her dusty shades, bends round to the driver, raps twice on the metal and says, "Let's roll."

# 24

Mojo the Blue strokes the underside of his nose with his right index finger, to the tip and back again. He repeats the movement, this time with less pressure. The nose shouldn't be pushed in. And it's got to be slower. Not like lighting a match. Or is it?

Mojo picks up the remote control. He rewinds the video and plays it again. He was wrong, in fact it's just like lighting a match, but without any pressure. And you don't stroke all the way, it's a combination of stroking and tapping. Too long for just tapping, too short for just stroking. The index finger isn't rigid, it's relaxed. And you shouldn't glance at your finger, not ever; your eyes must be fixed on the person opposite the whole time. Mojo presses pause. He picks up his mobile, taps the camera function and switches to selfie mode. He films all the variations, then checks them.

"Bandele!"

Bandele turns round in the passenger seat.

"I need a bigger screen. Sort it!" He gently caresses the side of his nose, then the tip of his index finger springs forwards like in a ski jump, pointing at Bandele for a fraction of a second. Bandele nods and faces forwards again. Mojo sinks back in his seat, satisfied. A good gesture. Better than the rest of the film. The boss who makes the gesture has funny hair and he dances too much, but it's a good gesture. He probably has to dance so much because he's a white man ordering a whole load of blacks and latinos around. He needs to show them he's black enough to be their boss, that he can move, and he does move well for a white guy. But Mojo doesn't have to dance. A boss needs to stand out from his employees. They have to admire him. They have to aspire to be like him. And what's going to happen if they find out that he's no different from them? If you want to be a leader, you have to keep giving your people goals, rather than the message that they've already arrived.

And you mustn't get shot.

Mojo snaps open a water bottle and takes a sip. He's not going to die among tomato plants like the Godfather. He's not going to get shot either. He's going to see what comes, that's all. Just because everyone makes mistakes at some time or other, it doesn't mean he has to. And the jury's still out on whether everyone actually has to grow old.

He senses the car slowing. They drive past a long column of lorries before coming to a stop. Bandele gets out and opens the door for him. Mojo puts on his sunglasses and climbs out of the car. The boys have already leaped out of their S.U.V. Two secure the area, but there's nothing out of the ordinary so they sling their AK-47s casually over their shoulders. A small lorry has stopped behind Mojo's car. The doors open and five men get out.

"Vamos," Mojo says.

Bandele gives the five men a signal. Two of them put on the baseball caps they're holding. Mojo starts walking, Bandele joins him and the five others follow. It's a good feeling, walking past these tankers. He wasn't sure to begin with, but this armada of lorries has been worth all the effort alone. *His* armada. It's one thing to know it's possible, but to see it actually happening is something else. He strolls along as if inspecting a parade. But he shows no pride – that would be silly. He just takes it all in his stride.

His trucks.

His armada.

They make for truck number 34 where a large group of men are assembled. They shrink back a little when they see the boys and Mojo. Mojo looks at them silently. At some point Bandele says, "O.K., listen in. Here are five new drivers. One of you needs to explain to them how all this works. Any volunteers? Forget it. Who does this truck belong to? Who has truck 34?"

A hand is raised. A beanpole with a Brazilian football shirt.

"O.K., Pelé," Bandele says, "tell them."

"I dunno . . ." Pelé looks embarrassed. "Where . . . where should I begin?"

"Who gives a fuck? Just begin!"

"O.K., then. It's no great shakes, really—"

"Did you hear that?" Bandele roars at the five men. "No great shakes. So keep your ears open!"

"You . . . you basically fill the lorry with water. You get

237

told where the water point is, because it's not always the same one. Then you drive there. But you don't have to find it yourself, the other drivers know where they're going and you just follow them. And it's the same on the way back. Then you get told your location and what number to mark on your lorry."

"And? What else?" Bandele reminds him.

"Oh yes. You're responsible for the generators and charging stations. The generator must be full of fuel. When you arrive at your location you set up your charging station. It's a bit of a faff to get all the cables and plugs out."

"Is that a complaint?" Bandele says.

"No, no," Pelé replies hastily. "No complaint at all, it's fine, and you can always rope in the odd child. It's simple enough if you've got three or four helpers. And you don't start up the generator until all the cables are laid out?"

"Mobile network?"

"I don't know about that. My lorry's only got water and electricity. Only every fifth or sixth needs to know about the mobile network and how to work it."

"What about the rules?"

"Oh yes, the rules. You don't just fill the lorry, you have to clean the tank too. Electricity is as important as water."

"Distribution?"

"Nobody gets anything from us directly. They distribute everything themselves."

"Exceptions?"

"No exceptions."

Bandele steps to the side; he has no more questions.

"You see?" Mojo says. "Well done. No great shakes. Any fool can do it." He nods at Pelé, and Pelé, visibly relieved, rejoins the others.

"Any fool," Mojo repeats. "But no-one here's being paid like a fool, are they?" He steps up to them as they start grinning broadly. "You there, Ghostbuster, what do you earn?"

"Two hundred and fifty dollars a week," a strong-looking man in a Ghostbusters T-shirt says.

"And you?"

"Two hundred and fifty dollars a week." A boy, not even twenty, with a bare torso.

"Two hundred and fifty bucks a week. Any of you know anyone else who earns that?"

A shaking of heads.

"Two hundred and fifty bucks a week. For a fool's job. If you're pocketing two hundred and fifty bucks, what do you think the guy's gettin' who pays you so much?"

Silence, but Mojo's not having that. "C'mon, gimme a figure!"

"Five hundred?"

"A thousand?"

Mojo laughs. "I pay two hundred and fifty bucks a week. To a guy who thinks I do this shit here for a thousand."

"A day?" says the driver sheepishly. Mojo laughs even louder, then turns to the boy with no shirt.

"Xbox or Playstation?"

"Xbox . . ."

"Xbox? O.K. Xbox. 2010. The Xbox 360 has Kinect. The thing that registers your movements. And it can monitor

239

you too. Why? Because behind the Xbox is Microsoft. They collect your data, the Americans collect your data, it goes straight to them via the Internet. So, you're workin' in our business and want an Xbox? It's a good thing you don't have one. Right then, Ghostbuster: Xbox or Playstation?

"Playstation, Mojo!"

"You think the Japanese aren't watchin' you?"

"I don't know—"

"Think about it, bozo. The Japs are watchin' you just the same. Hey, shirtless, here's your second chance: Xbox or Playstation?"

"Neither!"

"Why's that?"

"So nobody's watching me."

"Keep up, man. Who's going to keep tabs on a dumb ass-hole like you? Who gives a fuck what you're up to? You're just a nigger on some unimportant continent and you want to go without cool games because someone makes you believe you're being watched? Come on, now, Playstation or Xbox?"

"I . . . I don't know, Mojo."

"Yes," Mojo smiles, clapping him reassuringly on the shoulder. "It's fine. You're all dumbasses. You know nothin' and still I pay you two hundred and fifty bucks a week. Why? Because I earn so much from this thing that I couldn't give a fuck how dumb you are. Because dough rains down on me every day like it's monsoon season. I've never made so much dough for such little effort in such a short time. I have hookers who earn in an hour what you lot earn in a week. I order them by the dozen and send half of them back again, unfucked.

And it goes on like this, day in, day out. Until these refugees get to where they want to go. What then, Pelé?"

"I . . . dunno . . . ?"

"Then come the next lot. From that camp or some other one. I don't give a fuck. They've heard how it works, you see, and so they come to me and say: Do something like that for us too. And so I do. And it's monsoon season all over again. I can't shut my door because there are so many bucks flyin' in. What then?"

"I . . ."

"Then I pay you three hundred bucks a week just to get rid of the money!"

They're all whooping by now.

"And my hookers? I have to pay them five hundred bucks. Just to get shot of enough greenbacks that I can at least see outta my window."

Now he's got them.

"That's what the future looks like, folks. There's just one thing could get in my way. What's that again, Bandele?"

"An asshole," Bandele says impassively.

"That's right: an asshole. An asshole who stops these happy walkers gettin' to their destination. How might an asshole stop them, Bandele?"

"No electricity."

"Right again! No electricity. Every last buck, all the organisation goes via their cell phones. No electricity, no moolah. No moolah, no hookers. Anything else, Bandele?"

"No water."

"Right. No water. Why's that so important, Ghostbuster?"

"Because . . . because of the hookers?"

"Exactly! If there's no water when the walkers arrive in the evenin', they start to panic. The shit starts flyin' around, and when that happens we've got dead walkers. Every walker who dies on me costs me dough today. And tomorrow they'll cost me more dough. 'Cause every walker who makes it will make sure ten more sign up tomorrow. Now I ask myself: How can it be that there's no water? We've got one hundred trucks. And there are two in reserve every day. How can anything go wrong?"

The men say nothing.

"Any ideas? Suggestions?"

Mojo looks around.

"What would an asshole do? He might think, 'I'll sell off a few bits of my truck. Spare tyres. Spark plugs. I mean, we've got trucks in reserve.' Could that happen?"

Now they avoid his gaze.

"Or does he start cuttin' a few little deals? There's always something the walkers need, not just water. He can sort them out. But then the water truck doesn't get on its way because someone's waitin' for their goods. Know anyone like that, Pelé?"

All of a sudden it's as if Pelé has a highly infectious disease. One moment he's in the middle of the crowd, the next he's repelling the others, at least that's what it looks like.

"Mojo, that was just . . . I didn't wait. Not one second!"

"Five-hundred-dollar hookers. I know you guys ain't had none, but I swear they're worth every last dime. You can't imagine it, but these five-hundred-dollar hookers don't want to get it over with fast. Once you've had one you won't go takin' a cheaper broad no more. And now here's a price question for you, Pelé. How do you think it feels, havin' your dick in a five-dollar hooker after a five-hundred-dollar one?"

"Mojo, that's . . . I don't know . . ."

Incredibly fast. Incredibly loud. All they can see is Mojo putting something back in his trouser pocket, but now Pelé's sitting on the ground holding his belly, from which blood is spurting.

"Tell us, Pelé."

Pelé opens his mouth and groans. There's fear in his eyes.

"Mojo," he says.

Mojo squats beside him.

"Tell us. It interests me. It interests me far more than who helped you. You see, that don't interest me one bit."

Mojo takes Pelé's hand and pushes it carefully to the side. He gently lifts the football shirt to examine the wound.

"It don't interest me because I already know."

It's a remarkably slick movement. Two bangs and two more men are sitting on the ground, desperately trying to stop the blood with their hands. It looks as if they're trying to squeeze the blood out of their bellies. A third man has broken away from the crowd and is sprinting away. Mojo casually drapes the bloody Brazil shirt over Pelé's wound. Without a word, Bandele has one of the boys toss him his rifle. He takes rapid and accurate aim, the rifle coughs, then Bandele returns it to its owner without even a glance at the target. The two men moan, Pelé begins to scream.

"Get a grip!" Mojo says. "It's important you listen to me.

I need you alive! And you over there, come back here. I don't wanna have to keep yellin' no more."

Pelé's face has turned a greeny-beige colour and is bathed in cold sweat. The group turns towards the escapee. They can hear a whimpering, which must be significantly louder fifty metres further on, and they see him convulse with pain and turn over awkwardly. First he tries to crawl forwards, but abandons the attempt so abruptly that they can imagine the pain he's in. In tears, he hauls himself onto his side and starts wriggling back to the others.

"Imagine you're in a Western here," Mojo says impassively. "You know what a Western is, don't you? John Wayne! There we go! Only one thing ever matters in a Western: that the herd makes it. The *entire* herd. I can't replace any of the cattle. But I can replace the cowboys. Which is why I only go for cowboys I trust. Where are the keys to your truck?"

Pelé pushes a quivering finger into his trouser pocket. The beads of sweat shine on his green face like morning dew on a leaf. It takes him several attempts to fish the bulky keys from his trousers. He holds them out to Mojo. The blood drips into the sand a few millimetres from Mojo's shoes. Mojo beckons the new boys over and points to the keys. The bleeding men are having such difficulty fishing them out of their pockets that it's hard to watch. Then he stands up.

"Pelé here says that nothin' happened. But I don't wait for things to happen. I spy the source of trouble and eliminate it. I don't train folk, I don't have to educate nobody. Any jerk can do this job."

The group makes room, a hunk of flesh scrambles into

the circle, collapses and rolls onto his back, shattered. Mojo bends over him and says gently, "Keys, please." He gestures to one of the new boys.

"Any jerk," Mojo repeats. "That's why I don't give a fuck if someone screws me, or someone just knows about it, or someone else has forgotten to ask. I'll just give his job to some other dumbass. He'll do it better. Pelé and his pals here will take care of that from now on, won't you Pelé?"

Pelé nods fervently.

"Can I rely on you, Pelé? Will you do your job? Will you protect the herd with your life?"

Pelé nods again. He tries to get up. One hand grabs onto the front tyre of the truck whose keys he's just handed to one of the new guys.

"Stay as you are," Mojo says soothingly. "Stay just as you are. You're all to stay just as you are. You're gonna stay here till the trucks are gone. When Bandele comes tomorrow I want him to see you. And if you're still alive, then anyone who helped you is gonna die."

Pelé begins rolling to the side. Mojo puts a hand into his trouser pocket.

"This is modern management, you know? You give everyone the task you're confident they can do."

Mojo counts banknotes. He goes over to Pelé and kicks him in the shoulder until slowly he opens his eyes.

"It's an important job and that's why it's well paid. Three thousand bucks for each of you." Mojo pushes the notes between Pelé's bloody fingers. "This'll allow you to buy some help."

Mojo bends down and hands over the next wad of cash.

"I expect Bandele to find you here tomorrow. He's gonna tell me that he saw you lyin' there with your dough. Then I'll know that all these cowboys here have learned that I'm the only one who pays them."

Nobody speaks. Mojo takes the next two bundles and tosses them at the men who are panting, sweating, and gurgling softly.

"Questions?"

Mojo looks at each of them in turn. Bandele puts up his hand.

"What about him?" He points at the fifth new man.

On this occasion someone might have been able to detect the movement, but now Mojo uses the other hand. There's no discernible difference, although it almost looks as if he's a touch quicker with this hand. A fat man collapses, his eyes full of such complete astonishment that one might almost think him innocent. If something like innocence existed in this life.

"Did you check out your colleagues?" Mojo asks.

The corners of the man's mouth edge outwards and he shakes his head barely discernably. It looks as if he's about to cry. Mojo puts his hand over his mouth. He takes another bundle of cash from his pocket and puts it in the fat guy's lap. Then he points to the other drivers one by one.

"You're gonna teach them by tomorrow morning."

# 25

"O.K.," the under-secretary says. "Can someone please tell me, in plain language, why this nightmare's not over yet?"

It's six o'clock in the morning and with him around the table are men who'd rather be in bed. Schneider's there, Dr Berthold, the B. (police), E. (Europe and international) and M. (migration) departments, and two gentlemen whose faces are new to him. One is from the foreign ministry and he gives the impression that it's a particular imposition to be here, probably because the foreign ministry – so they say – regards Nadeche Hackenbusch as an internal matter.

"Are they off their heads? Could you get *more* foreign than this?"

"That shouldn't bother us," Leubl told him. "Just let me know if you think they're actively putting the brakes on. We'd be better off taking charge of this business ourselves, before they come on board as reluctant partners."

"You've got a point."

"Of course, it mustn't look as if we're trying to shut the ministry of foreign affairs out. Just keep inviting them to take work off our hands whenever they fancy and they'll leave the whole thing to us."

The expression on the face of the man from the foreign ministry is just what the doctor ordered. The man next to him, on the other hand, appears overwrought and tense. His suit is crumpled, he probably hasn't been home in a while. His hands tremble as they reach for the coffee thermos, and he downs the first cup like others might a cold beer on a summer's evening. He even puts the cup down on the saucer as if it's a beermat. When the saucer shatters, he shakes his head, sweeps the shards to one side and looks for a replacement. Unable to find one he puts the cup on a napkin and helps himself to more coffee. He might be exhausted and his movements jittery, but he doesn't look listless. He wants to explain why he's had so little sleep. He's from the intelligence service.

"Where shall I begin?" he says, rubbing his eyes.

"How about with your name, if it's not a secret?" Dr Berthold says crabbily.

The under-secretary shoots Berthold a withering look, then tries to relieve the tension. "We're all tired, so let me just make some brief introductions. The not-particularly-friendly gentleman is Dr Berthold, public security. Herr Gödeke, federal police; Herr Kaspers, crisis management; Dr Kalb, migration; Herr Gondorff, international affairs. From the foreign ministry we have Herr . . ."

The under-secretary leafs through a slim pile of printed e-mails, but can't find what he's looking for. He rustles the papers ill-temperedly, but he lacks the nerve to try to weasel his way out of this one. "Sorry, I can't . . . would you mind awfully . . . ?"

"Zeitz."

"O.K., Herr Seitz, and . . ."

"With a Z! Zeitz."

"My apologies, Zeitz from the foreign ministry. And you are Herr . . . ?"

"Echler, foreign intelligence. Regional analysis and procurement."

"Excellent. It's good to have you here. God knows we could do with some regional analysis right now. So tell us, what's going on down there? I mean, how on earth are they still on the move?"

"I don't understand either," Gondorff adds unnecessarily. "If it's that simple, why hasn't everyone set off on foot before?"

"To put it bluntly: why aren't they all popping their clogs?" This is Berthold. If the under-secretary were asked whether Berthold means to be quite so callous, he'd say he's about 75 per cent sure the answer's yes. Rapping on the table several times, the under-secretary gets the attention of those present, then motions to Echler to speak. Echler sits up in his chair and smooths his tie, only to realise he's not wearing one.

"The answer is . . . well, there are a number of reasons. But basically the explanation is simpler than you'd think. Do forgive me, I've only just been briefed, it's been quite a long night and I'm afraid I don't have a fancy presentation for you, so I'll just begin wherever . . ."

The under-secretary gives him a nod of encouragement.

"Right, we don't know who's the brains behind it all. But the question raised by Herr . . . Gandorf? . . . the question isn't an unreasonable one. We're also surprised nobody's done it before. I mean, you don't have to be Einstein to come up with a plan like that."

Echler switches on the overhead projector beside him. "Like I said, I don't have a fancy presentation. And rather than have all the image files arranged in the wrong order, I'm going to do it the old-fashioned way, by hand. So, here are two aerial shots of the trek. What you're seeing here is a never-ending column of people. But this is only the first step."

"What? Them walking in a column?"

"Yes, I mean, they wouldn't necessarily have to do it that way. But when you compare the two images, you see the really clever thing. The dark worm is the column itself, and I'm sure that's obvious to everyone here. On the left you've got a picture from the middle of the column, while on the right is a picture of the front. Any of you notice anything?"

"There are big dark maggots in the column."

"Exactly, those are tankers carrying water. You can see . . ."

". . . that the gaps between them are identical," the under-secretary prompts.

"Right. This isn't a coincidence."

"Because the lorries are driving alongside the procession," Zeitz assumes.

"Actually, no," Echler says. "You can't see it but these lorries aren't moving. They're stationary. The people are walking past them. Now please look at the photo of the front."

The under-secretary screws up his eyes. He'd love to be

the first to solve the puzzle, but he's too shattered. He sees the dark worm with the tankers at regular intervals. It makes him think of beans in a pod. Only that here some of the beans are outside the pod.

"They've obviously got too many lorries," Dr Kalb concludes.

"You mean the right amount. These lorries don't just supply the trek, they also give it its structure. The lorries park up ahead, at regular intervals. This means the people can't get lost because they walk past the trucks as if they were markers. Do you understand? The lorries provide water, and they also show the way." Echler almost looks excited now, and he's talking quickly. He's clearly impressed by what he's discovered.

"It's an astonishing logistical achievement. Provision for one hundred and fifty thousand inside a camp is a manageable undertaking. People live in their areas, you give them a toilet, a water point, you organise the whole thing as you would a campsite and it's job done. But one hundred and fifty thousand people on the move? You're staring at chaos. But they've got it under control."

"Do they have help? Military? Do they have any governmental support?"

"Not so far as we know. It's just all been thought through systematically. They must have worked out how many people can be supplied by one water tanker, how much space they need, then they calculated the distances between lorries. The result: one tanker supplies three thousand people, so they need to be one thousand metres apart."

"Are you trying to tell us that one of those refugees figured this all out?" Dr Berthold scoffs. The under-secretary adjusts his estimate to 85 per cent.

"Why not?" Echler retorts. "You could do it with a slide rule. You'd need a certain degree of efficiency too, of course. You need every lorry in duplicate."

"As reserves," Gödeke says.

"No. Because you can't drive away, fetch the water and get back all in a day. So two lorries take it in turns. One stays where it is while the other fetches water for the next day. But what's really smart is that they don't just swap places. Every day, the replacement lorries wait along the stretch yet to be walked. Those are the lorries that are ahead of the column. And now look at this!"

He swaps the pictures for two close-ups that have presumably been taken by a drone. On two trucks are marked large numbers: "3" on one, "16" on another.

"They've numbered the trucks. Are they worried one's going to go missing?"

"Oh, it's better than that," Echler beams, as if he'd dreamed up the idea himself. "They're a bit like house numbers. Think about it, these people come from a camp. They're used to having their individual areas or zones numbered. The lorries work in precisely the same way. Those who spent last night at truck 16 will spend tonight at truck 16 too. They live permanently at truck 16, so to speak."

"What's so clever about that?"

"It prevents chaos. Just imagine. It's early in the morning, you're right at the front and want to get moving. Now, the situation could easily be that you've no idea where you're going, nor how far you have to walk. And whatever you decide, you have to let the other one hundred and fifty thousand people know. But no. The guys at the front wake up beside lorry number one. Up ahead of them lorries are already parked at intervals of one kilometre. These lorries are numbered 15, 14, all the way down to one. And so those at the front keep going until they're back at lorry 1, when they're done for the day. Everyone knows that when they arrive at the number they were beside the previous day, their leg is over for the day."

The under-secretary is unsure how to interpret this admiration, but it doesn't appear to be a good sign, and the rest of them around the table seem to be of a similar opinion. But Echler won't slow down. "It's foolproof," he says with relish, "and it also gives them a uniform daily march. They don't walk seven kilometres today and twenty tomorrow. They walk fifteen kilometres every day, no more, no less."

"I'm impressed," the under-secretary says. "But there are borders."

"There aren't, actually," Echler says with confidence.

"Country borders," the under-secretary specifies crossly.

"Sorry, I misunderstood. The border thing is quite simple: bribery. They must have someone who knows who to bribe."

"Hold on a moment," Gödeke protests, "nobody just lets one hundred and fifty thousand people into their country."

"Well, first that depends on the sum of money you're talking about, of course," Echler says calmly, "but also on the people. I agree with you: nobody would let one hundred and fifty thousand soldiers into their country, or one hundred and fifty thousand armed people. But these guys are not making that error, at most they're carrying a penknife. The next point is that the person taking the bribe doesn't want any trouble. So you've got to be able to reassure them of a few things."

"That you're only passing through," the under-secretary suggests with a sigh.

"That sort of thing." Echler smiles at him like a teacher happy to see the class joining in. "And that you're not going to starve in their country, that they're not going to have to feed you. And if all this is understood, if these people come and then leave again, if these people bring their own food, water and accommodation, why wouldn't you allow them passage in return for a heap of money?"

"Because it's illegal?" Zeitz says. "Has that crossed your mind?" They haven't exactly sent their brightest spark, the under-secretary thinks.

"Let's get this straight. One hundred and fifty thousand defenceless people are on the march through regions full of terrorists, Islamists, criminals. Those very same regions they're all clearing out of. Am I completely wrong, or could this go tits up?" Dr Berthold says, as if nobody need worry.

"Who says they're defenceless?" Echler beams, as if he'd organised the trek himself.

"You were the one who said they were unarmed. You said they had to be unarmed or no-one would let them into their country."

"But not defenceless. They're being protected. They're paying one of the local criminal gangs. Where the state isn't reliable, organised crime is all the more so. The advantage is obvious. The military don't have to get involved because these are the very homegrown criminals they lack the means to combat on a day-to-day basis. So the threat is no greater than usual.

"It might work right now," Dr Kalb says, "but this is just a snapshot in time, isn't it? For how much longer will it all be tickety-boo? Four weeks? I mean, they're approaching another border, aren't they?"

"If you want my honest opinion, so long as they can find the right people to bribe, I can't see how the strategy is going to fail any time soon given how ramshackle these countries are," Echler purrs. "I imagine in the next country that border official is eagerly awaiting their arrival so he can hold out his hand."

"And if they've got two different countries to choose from, they can pick the cheaper one." Kaspers is furious.

"Anything else?" Gödeke huffs. "A free-market competition for the cheapest route?"

"I suspect so," Echler says soberly. "Not that they need it."

"O.K., hopefully this means we can now move onto the key question," Dr Berthold says. "Who's paying for all this crap?"

"Oh, yes," Echler says, hyped now. "You're going to love this. At least the socialists among you will – are there any here, in fact?"

"We're still a people's party," Dr Kalb says, slightly miffed. "But I can't for the life of me imagine what I should love about this arrangement."

"It's a bit like the cooperative model," Echler grins.

"It's *what*?"

"Our colleagues from the N.S.A. gave us a bit of help here. Everyone on the march pays five dollars per day. It works via their smartphones, there's no particular software. People get a confirmation on their mobiles and they can show the trucks they've paid for the day, so they're given water and something to eat. You can do the sum in your heads. They've got 750,000 dollars at their disposal. Per day. At least."

"At least?"

"I wouldn't be surprised if they're not making far more for extras. You've got to bear in mind that everything's dirt cheap for them."

"Five dollars a day adds up."

"Say they walk for two years – that means they've spent roughly 3,500 dollars. Back in 2016 a study showed that the average cost for a migrant trying to get to Europe was seven thousand euros. They had to spend years saving for that. But now they're able to pay in instalments. If they make it as far as here, they'll be bringing money with them, I tell you!"

"It's just a question of time, then," Dr Berthold says, leaning back. "If there's so much money flying around they'll soon be killing each other."

"Is that true?" Zeitz asks cheerfully.

Echler shakes his head. "There's no money flying around. The money is transferred via smartphone. No-one's got any cash on them. The largest amount is on this Mr Lionel's device around lunchtime. From there, tranches go to various accounts, presumably the suppliers . . . protection money, bribes . . ."

"Seven hundred and fifty thousand dollars," Kasper muses. "That's a hell of a lot of money down there."

"Per day," Echler adds cheerily.

"And this Lionel," the under-secretary chimes in. "What sort of a chap is he?"

"We've got very little on him," Echler says, pulling out a piece of paper. "We don't know his real name yet. He probably lied about his date of birth, and it's also possible that the camp's records were incomplete or there was a faulty entry. But two sources say that for a time he did small jobs for people smugglers."

"Aha!" Gödeke says, "He *is* a smuggler then."

"Not in any serious sense. He was a sidekick. And when people smugglers got so expensive that nobody could afford them anymore, he was no longer needed. But he's still got his contacts and that's how the organisation works when they're on the move. Checking whether everyone's paid, distributing food and water – of course you can't organise that with all those kids from the camp. He's got mates to do it, mates from his time as a smuggler."

"Who's paying for that, then?"

"Seven hundred and fifty thousand dollars," the under-secretary hisses.

"You might think so," Echler concedes, "but apparently they're doing it for free food and board. They're refugees too, don't forget. That Lionel pays his five dollars per day too, by the way."

"I'm touched," the under-secretary says through clenched teeth. "I suppose Hackenbusch does too?"

"No," Echler says dryly. "She pays ten."

"So, in the eyes of the foreign intelligence service we have an admirable model here."

"It's not our job to give an opinion," Echler states. All of a sudden he looks grey and exhausted, as if the life had been sucked out of him. "You may detect a certain respect in my voice, but it's relative. In truth these people have made use of the little they have in an unexpectedly efficient way. And what must worry you most about this is that the model is transferable. No doubt weaknesses will come to light in specific situations, but the model can be developed, it's got plenty in reserve and it's adaptable."

The under-secretary has heard enough. He pushes his chair from the table. "Thank you. I will inform the ministers. So, your conclusion is that the undertaking is unlikely to collapse any time soon?"

Tiredness has now crumpled Echler like a stubbed-out cigarette. But the question allows him to blaze one final time.

"Who's talking of collapse? It's working!"

# A woman shows
# her greatness

A cruel scandal haunts Nadeche Hackenbusch.
While the star's husband reveals his true face,
she is helping young female entrepreneurs
keep their chins up.

By Astrid von Roëll

How astonishing are the twists and turns life's path sometimes takes as it leads us to our destiny. Life, it seems, never takes the direct route, and we're often prompted to ask why. But deep down life knows that speed is of no use if it merely takes us to the destination too early. And seldom has this been so evident than with Nadeche Hackenbusch during these past few days under the scorching African sun. "Twenty years ago I would never have coped with any of this," she says thoughtfully as the desert wind plays her dark hair like a harp. "I didn't appreciate it back then, but now I'm hugely grateful for everything I learned. Because now it's standing me in good stead. Me and them."

By "them" Nadeche Hacken- busch means the hundreds of thousands she is navigating through the dangers of the Dark Continent before the breathless eyes of the world, with Lionel, her new man, at her side. It is no coincidence that Nadeche Hackenbusch should choose this moment to bare her soul more honestly than ever before, and exclusively to EVAN-GELINE. For while this still astonishingly young woman is confronting what may prove to be the most dangerous adventure she will ever undertake, in her private life she is also experiencing the most severe crisis that fate can have in store for any individual. It is scarcely imaginable. A woman, who is currently responsible for hundreds of thousands of people, who is in the throes of a young, sensational love affair, which contrasts so palpably and refreshingly with what is often paraded as a "relationship" today; this same woman is now peering into the abyss of unconscionable recklessness.

Nicolai von Kraken. The man with whom she renewed her marriage vows only last summer on the snow-white beaches of St Barts, where they were toasted by the foaming, champagne-coloured sea. How bitter must it be that this very man, who swore to love her in bad times as well as good, is now standing in the way of her true love. That this man, to whom she entrusted her sons Keel and Bonno, has sent via a heartless lawyer the bizarre message that, if they separate, he will advance a claim for half of her fortune. Nadeche courageously turns her head to look outside – the limitless expanse of infinity does her good.

"It grounds me," she smiles bravely. "All this here grounds me. This land, these people, Lionel. There's so much in life that is more important." She doesn't want to talk about Nicolai at the moment, nor can she – her lawyer will not let her. "But even if there's a lot going on that seems unfair, if certain people start behaving in a way that a woman never would – here, in this land, I learn day by day that nothing happens in vain."

We are on the way to an assignment that is particularly close to Nadeche Hackenbusch's heart. Because once again we're talking about women who are making a greater effort than others and who are obliged to overcome ever greater hurdles than other people: young female entrepreneurs. Having pinpointed an opportunity in the extremely difficult conditions of this endless trek, having realised that in the middle of nowhere the essentials are often lacking, they are offering their services. And in such a situation it is like a gift from heaven to have Nadeche Hackenbusch on hand. She knows better than anyone the hardships facing young female entrepreneurs.

Few people have had to fight so hard for the recognition that men simply gather up as if it were lying around on the floor. In early

**Once again women are making a greater effort than everyone else**

1999 she took her first tentative steps, because even then she knew that "a woman can't rely on her looks. This is true for all women, me included. But you can't imagine the resistance I came up against. I mean, this was just about still in the nineties!" She began sensationally with her line of cosmetics, *Smell d'Elle by Nadeche*. In spite of a pioneering concept, however, in spite of clever ideas, the highly promising product line had to be taken off the market after only four weeks.

The speed at which she learned was clearly demonstrated by the success of the HackenPush-ups, which held up remarkably well in an unfavourable environment. "Unfortunately the market then let us down, which can happen any time, of course," she laughs, even though she's

## "A woman can't rely on her looks"

perfectly aware that here too the industry put a spoke in her wheel. In the same year the HackenPush-ups were introduced, there was a trend for smaller bras – off the record, renowned market analysts do not regard this as a coincidence. Of course, Nadeche Hackenbusch refuses to let this discourage her. Anyone who knows her is aware that she already has another project in her shrewd pipeline, even though it has to take a backseat for now. "I can make use of my experience here just as meaningfully as back home," she says with determination. "Maybe even more meaningfully. After all, I know the difficulties."

What she has to witness here in Africa is scandalous. "The young female entrepreneurs are being exploited." Their trade is small-scale handiwork often much in demand en route, especially given the large number of single men who are inexperienced in many ways. "And so day by day these women work hard to allow them to continue on the trek," Nadeche Hackenbusch explains. "Being paid by the day gives a chance to those who haven't saved up enough." This very fact is frequently exploited, however.

Every one of these migrants must pay by midday. "And the closer the midday deadline looms, the greater the pressure some of these women are under." What Nadeche Hackenbusch then sees makes her livid.

"The clients try to beat the price down, they try to wangle extra work out of the women." Particularly infuriating is the fact that these customers are always men. "It's quite clearly a question of education," Nadeche Hackenbusch says critically. "Women are more skilful at handiwork, they're trained in it, whereas men aren't. But the fact that men don't want to pay an appropriate price for these services . . . I'm sorry, that's just typical."

There's no sense of guilt here, however. We accompany Nadeche Hackenbusch exclusively as she seeks out one of the defaulting customers and takes him to task. The young man finds the encounter uncomfortable, but he won't shoulder his responsibility. "I can't help it that I'm not married," he says, and when Nadeche energetically asks him what marriage has to do with it, he replies, "If I were married my wife would do it for free." The determination with which the presenter and show icon intervenes here is astonishing. And afterwards she stands there watching the sheepish customer transfer the money he owes via his smartphone to the happily beaming small entrepreneur, barely sixteen years of age. The two are reconciled, he offers an apology and shows contrition. "With a little luck," Nadeche Hackenbusch says hopefully, "he'll become one of her regular customers. Long-term business relationships can break down the gender barrier and contribute to understanding between people."

A woman who prefers to work with people rather than against them. Who, despite the problems in her private life, believes in the future of men and women. I ask her whether that would have been possible twenty years ago. "Twenty years ago I wouldn't have been able to help these young women," Nadeche Hackenbusch insists. "I'm sure that destiny arranged it for me to be here at this time. It's not about getting to your goal as quickly as possible. You've got to be there when you're needed."

# 26

Sensenbrink closes the door behind him. He wanders around the desk and slumps slowly into his chair. He stares apathetically at the wall opposite. There hangs the poster of "You're Not My Mother", the first show he was solely responsible for. And one for "Extremely German", which sadly never went further than the pilot. It was very funny. In four weeks, three asylum seekers had to adapt to the host country as well as possible, and the winner came away with a marriage of convenience. That was just an in-house joke; the only prize was money, obviously. But still, one of the three did actually manage to postpone his deportation for half a year by pointing out all his efforts on the show. Life doesn't write the best stories, television does.

Sensenbrink gets up and goes over to the small fridge. He takes out a juice and removes the cap with a bottle opener. He goes back to the desk and sets the bottle down beside the telephone. A year or eighteen months ago the broadcaster axed juice for the staff. And mineral water. Instead they attached a carbonator to the water supply and put a sign beside it explaining why tap water is excellent and the carbonator as good as mineral water, if not better. Ever since the "Angel in Adversity" ratings skyrocketed, Sensenbrink has again had his own fridge with bottles of juice and mineral water. Funny how nobody found it necessary to give him a sign explaining why bottled water isn't so bad after all. People are stupid, but not that stupid. Sensenbrink looks at his juice and realises he doesn't want it. If he were a smoker he'd probably light up now. He leans back, an uneasy feeling in his stomach.

An empty feeling.

Maybe it all happened too quickly.

Sensenbrink isn't a fan of hasty decision-making. There are many people whose best reactions are spontaneous, who come up with the funniest ideas on the spot and under pressure. But it's not Sensenbrink's cup of tea. You can be spontaneous when it's not important, at the holiday house on Mallorca, for example – then you can be spontaneous all day long. But he isn't, not even there. Because being spontaneous is exhausting, and the results are mostly rubbish. You end up somewhere and it's raining, or you don't have any swimming trunks or any condoms, because you had no idea just *how* spontaneous you were going to be. Spontaneity is like sex on the beach: it sounds great in theory, but in the end it's just sand in your bits and you're so sunburned your skin peels off your shoulders in huge strips.

At any rate Sensenbrink sets great store by planning. He wants to know what to do in the worst-case scenario, and if he doesn't know, then nine times out of ten he manages to postpone the decision. He would even go so far as to say that postponement is the recipe for success in modern management. Very few decisions need to be taken on the spot, and you can prepare yourself even for these. Today ought to have been one of those days.

He waited as long as he could. He devised two plans. And he even got some wonderful reading material when Olav, who was the last to arrive at the meeting, sauntered into the room like some kind of artist with an advance copy of *Evangeline* under his arm. Flopping into a chair, he spun the magazine onto the table with an elegant flick of the wrist, where it came to rest in exactly the right position. Though on a round table it's always going to be exactly right for somebody. "Tell me," he said. "Is there something wrong with my eyes or did I just read in *Evangeline* that our star's collecting money for prostitutes?"

There was a kerfuffle, of course, as everyone pounced on the magazine. Everyone, that is, apart from Sensenbrink – this was Beate's job. And there it was, a six-page report on the Hackenbusch–von Kraken divorce story, and reading the end of it anyone would have to agree that Olav was right, unless they were as thick as a post and as blind as a bat.

"I really don't know why we're fretting over every story here," Olav said. "I mean, all these discussions, twice a week, about exactly what's happening and how explicitly we should be showing it. In the concept phase and at the final approval stage, our legal advisor looks at all the hoo-ha and gets on everybody's nerves – so why are we going on about it all if our little sunshine is doing whatever she likes down there? One day she's the angel in adversity, the next she's the lover of the super refugee, and today? Surprise: the mother of the nomadic prozzers."

There was quite a commotion around the table, something Sensenbrink is usually pleased to see. Commotion is good so long as you assume the role of peacekeeper before anyone else gets there. And what's so lovely about Beate Karstleiter is that, with all her insecurities, she gets too caught up in the heat of the moment to beat him to it. So this time he just waited calmly until she said it was serious and obviously needed checking out right away. At this point he was able to say, totally relaxed, "Just chill, all of you. You're behaving as if 1968 never happened."

In retrospect, Sensenbrink has to admit that he couldn't say with any precision what became permissible in 1968. Quite a lot in any case, and afterwards women were allowed to wear miniskirts, although . . . there had never actually been a law against miniskirts. Fortunately, nobody had asked.

"As far as I know, pimping is still illegal," Reliable Anke said.

"Pimping is illegal if you take money for it," Sensenbrink said, leaning back coolly. "At most, at the very most one could say that Nadeche Hackenbusch is working as a volunteer pimp."

"Are you saying that volunteer pimping isn't promoting prostitution?" This comment was from Hayat. He originally wanted her as a regular in meetings because she seemed fairly bright, but now he doubts whether that was such a good idea.

"I don't have a clue about jurisdiction in other countries."

"*Evangeline* is published *here*," Olaf said bluntly.

"And it's their problem," Sensenbrink countered. "More importantly, did we know this sort of thing was going on down there?"

"I didn't."

"Me neither."

"But why not? It's quite a story! Whores shagging their way across the desert to Europe. We could even film it. Either Nadeche will burst into tears or do her human touch thing, but she won't walk straight into a trap." A short pause to build up momentum, then, "If our top star is heading for Shit Valley, it's because we haven't done our job. Because we haven't been vigilant enough."

A longer pause. An awkward silence is fine, but you have to give it time. A really good awkward silence, an effective one, is like pancake batter: it lands in the middle with a loud hiss, and then you watch it slowly spread.

The silence was, in fact, the ideal platform for the next point: "Good, well, this allows us to zip straight on to . . . to the elephant in the room."

It was surprising that nobody had raised it before, but there are some issues everyone shies away from. That's when you need proper decision-makers who don't flinch at putting the unpleasant stuff on the agenda too. A general can't just award promotions; sometimes he has to send soldiers into the fire as well.

"So far we've been lucky that nobody has sent up a balloon on this one, but in our position we can't afford to be blasé. I'd rather only show the good sides too, I admit, but we can't. We have to defend our newly gained journalistic expertise. A2 can't just become some sort of picnic . . ."

Those clueless faces. As if he were talking utter shite. He assumed it showed just how far ahead he was of his troops. On and on he went in that imperious tone. He doesn't want to know what they thought.

". . . the next few days and weeks might not be pretty, but we mustn't in any circumstances allow any other medium to force our hand with the story. We determine the topics, we determine the tone, we determine the race from pole position. We're the ones checking those boxes . . ." It was roughly at that point that people stopped nodding their agreement.

". . . but most important of all is the data. We need to know what's going on and what isn't. Unsanitised. And none of the figures leave this room, O.K.? But we mustn't kid ourselves. I want conservative estimates, you can even err on the pessimistic side, I won't hold it against anyone. This is so we can sketch a credible worst-case scenario."

Sensenbrink was perfectly aware that the next few weeks would be decisive for his career. He realised that he was pumping with adrenaline, now that everything was at stake:

"Right, numbers on the table. How many dead?"

The entire room was as silent as a mouse.

"It's O.K. We'll cope. How many?"

Then someone said, "None."

"Ooh, that's big. But it was to be expected. What we need now is a crisis strategy and—"

"Sorry, but I don't think you understood. There have been no deaths."

This moment is playing as an endless loop inside Sensenbrink's head: his face, the interruption, the ten heart-wrenching seconds it takes him to say, "What do you mean, no deaths?"

"Well, there haven't been any."

"There are one hundred and fifty thousand people marching across the desert, across *the desert!* We all knew that people could die."

"*Could*, yes. But none actually have."

It's not a pleasant memory. Him sitting there, mumbling some nonsense: "But there have to be *some*! Are they burying their bodies at night?"

"It's possible," Karstleiter said. "But unlikely."

"But this completely flies in the face of common sense! The whole operation is shot through with danger. What happens, for instance, if someone can't pay?"

"It's a question I've been asking Grande for some time now," said Reliable Anke, who might have mentioned this a bit earlier. "It seems this hardly ever happens."

"But where are they getting the money from?"

"You have to realise that these people do *have* money."

"Where from?"

"Some have saved up – they just don't want to invest it in a country fraught with crisis. Others are financed by their families. And now, with these daily instalments, they've got more time to cobble the money together."

"It might be different for the women," Olav said. "Nobody invests in them. But, thanks to *Evangeline*, we now know how gaps in funding can be bridged."

"What about the elderly? The sick?" Another stupid question. In retrospect Sensenbrink feels like a total arse. Somehow everyone else in the room seemed to have a better grasp of the situation than him.

"What makes you think there are elderly or sick people on the trek?" Olav said. "Surely they wouldn't bring them along in the first place?"

"I can't recall ever having seen anyone elderly or sick in one of our programmes," Reliable Anke added.

Sensenbrink still doesn't fancy the juice. With a shake of the head he pushes the bottle around on his desk like a lonely chess piece. He then dished out praise at random, he seized on the nomadic prostitutes thing and ordered a special "special", without Nadeche Hackenbusch – if there are a few tits on show they can for once do without their star. He managed get himself back on track, but now . . . this emptiness.

He wasn't happy, but he was facing the biggest gamble of his life. He had everything on the same horse, make or break, Sensenbrink, the man who'd handled the tricky story with the hundreds of deaths. Ice-cold, professional, assured. This is the wood they cut board members from.

And now this.

He ought to be relieved. He had been scared stiff, after all. But Sensenbrink only feels disappointment. He feels cheated of a once-in-a-lifetime opportunity. Of a grand finale: you don't know if you're going to win, but you're impeccably prepared. And then it's cancelled.

Because nobody's dying on Nadeche Hackenbusch's fucking trek.

# 27

Leubl feels old. He knows, of course, that he is kind of old. He also knows that his job allows him to pretend he's middle-aged. But in all honesty, when you hit your mid-sixties you're not young at all anymore, even if John Travolta has a different take on this. And it doesn't make you any younger if John Travolta is one of the few faces you recognise on television. Especially when Binny's in charge of the remote.

Leubl eyes the fridge longingly. A second beer would be nice. But his wife doesn't like it. Not when Binny's there. "It's bad enough you drinking and ignoring me," she said. "But you're not going to do that with your granddaughter. You're going to talk to her!" Leubl squints at the television and sees that Nadeche Hackenbusch is up to mischief again. She's not in the studio, but she's hooked up to a mic and in an embrace with lover-boy. With a curious combination of brazenness and subtlety, he's the one who's got Germany and the television industry into this pickle. And all Binny can do is delight in it: "Aww! Look, Grandma, look how he's staring at her. He's so cute. So kind!"

"Binny," Leubl says sternly, "just because he's cute, that doesn't mean he's kind."

"Yeah, I know he wants to f—" Binny slaps a hand over her mouth and puts on her sweetest face. Leubl pretends not to have heard. "But that's O.K. That's love, and if love didn't exist, then Mama wouldn't be here and nor would I."

"Hmm. That's not just love," Leubl says firmly. "It's something else too. He realises that he has better options with that Hackenbusch woman than without her."

"Wait, are you saying that's why it can't be love?"

"Yes. Yes, it can," Leubl's wife says, coming to his assistance. "But what Grandad means is that you have to watch out with men."

"Wait, did you watch out with Grandad?"

Leubl's wife laughs. "Probably not enough."

Binny mutes the volume. Ad break.

"Why would Grandma have had to watch out with me?"

"In case it wasn't just love."

"Oh, it was easier to tell back in those days," Leubl's wife says. "The boys all told the girls they had to go to bed with them or they were square."

"Wait, that means it was easier? Is that what you did?"

Leubl looks at his wife. Do children always have to know everything? His wife looks back. Sometime you have to come clean. Sitting up in her chair, she says, "I did some things. But there was plenty I didn't think was good."

"Like what?"

"Hmm." Leubl can see his wife assessing how much she ought to reveal. He shoots her a glance.

"I hated the way they insisted that either you go with them or you're a nerd. Who wants to be thought of as a silly, old-fashioned cow?"

"So . . . ?" Binny says, glancing at Leubl. "What about Grandad?"

"Grandad was different. I was sitting in the park with my friends and a few boys, we were smoking, and then Grandad came up to us. Quite briskly, like a child marching up to a diving board because he's worried he'll chicken out if he spends any time thinking about it."

"I know the feeling. What happened then?"

"Well, he said some very lovely things. I could tell he wasn't finding it easy . . ."

Leubl clears his throat as a warning.

". . . because Grandad's face was redder—"

"—than a socialist's flag, yesyesyes, we've heard it all before."

Binny giggles. "Wait, you believed those lovely things?"

"I liked it that he said them in front of everyone. That was brave. The cool boys in their flares, so laid back, big sideburns, then Grandad comes along in his suit with his C.S.U. badge and says—"

"That's enough!"

"—that he thinks I'm the most beautiful girl in the world, and if I go with him now . . ."

Leubl turns away in discomfort.

". . . he'll make me happy for the rest of my life. This at a time when all the boys ever said was how great it would be if you let them bonk you."

"Bonk!" Binny chortles.

"Exactly," Grandad smirks. "So making me happy was a totally novel approach."

"And? Did he make you happy?"

"Well," Leubl's wife says generously, "he tried and . . ."

Binny's fascination with the past doesn't prevent her from turning up the volume when the ad break is finished. The young presenter has just welcomed someone new into the studio. "Campino!"

"Woah!" Binny says. "Who is *that*?"

"Please," Grandma says. "*Campino*! Even *we* know him."

"Well, that's fine then."

"Old-school," Leubl says, standing up. It's worrying that a do-gooder like Campino has put his weight behind the project. In fact it's not good at all. There must be some of that pear schnapps left in the cupboard. Leubl can sense his wife watching him, but he doesn't care.

"No, Grandad, it's not old-school anymore."

"What is it then?"

"Jurassic."

Shaking his head, Leubl pours some honey-yellow schnapps into a glass. The soothing aroma of pears tickles his nostrils as Campino says he finds something "über-cool, even though it's showing on a crappy private T.V. station."

"Watch it!" the presenter says, laughing. "They're paying my mortgage!"

"Well done, mate!" Campino says, slapping him on the shoulder. "'Cause people like you normally end up on 'Germany's Top Welfare Cases'."

They switch to Nadeche Hackenbusch and she squawks excitedly about how pleased she is to see Campino there. Campino crows back that he thinks what she's doing is "über-cool", "wicked" and reveals that his band, "Die Toten Hosen", are going to play a benefit gig in Berlin. "Listen to who's going to be there: Lindenberg, Niedecken, Grönemeyer – and all proceeds go to the Nadeche Hackenbusch Foundation for the Humans." Nadeche bursts into tears and says how lovely he is, so wonderful of him, etc.

Wackersdorf, Leubl thinks. He can't hear the name Niedecken without thinking of Wackersdorf nuclear repro-cessing plant and the music festivals that helped thwart its completion. If the world of pop music throws its weight behind the refugees, the government's going to have to redouble its efforts to counteract Hackenbusch's project.

"Moist!" Binny says, "A bunch of old songs."

Perhaps it'll only be a mini Wackersdorf.

"Why on earth are we watching this?" Leubl says, return-ing to the armchair with his glass.

"Because Schminki's on now!"

"Who?"

"Schminki Pengster!"

Leubl discovers nothing about Campino's other plans because Binny's busy telling him who Schminki Pengster is: *the* YouTube sensation. She shows him some clips on her mobile, but Leubl remains in the dark about Schminki Pengster's magic. He knows, of course, that there are plenty of people who have what amounts to their own personal channel on YouTube, but he'd always assumed that they did things which would be too bold for television. But all this Schminki Pengster does is showcase products or play tricks on people. It's unclear what expertise Schminki Pengster has as a product tester, but expertise isn't the appeal. It's the sheer professionalism with which Schminki plays the role of best friend, sharing her life with five million best friends. And the inconsistency is so glaring that Leubl can scarcely believe his smart little Binny has fallen for it.

"But I know that, Grandad!"

"Then I really don't understand."

"Ask Grandma. She understands – look, there's Schminki!"

Leubl looks at his wife. With a shrug of the shoulders, Frau Leubl opens her eyes wide and says with conviction, "Grandma understands everything." Leubl takes a generous sip of his schnapps and sees a pretty brunette flinging her arms around the young presenter as if he were a soldier returning from war. She holds out her hand respectfully to Campino and then sits between him and the presenter on a preposterous T.V. sofa, which looks like a cross between buffers and asymmetrical bars. Then she says that what Nadeche Hackenbusch is doing is "über-cool" and "lit", and suddenly Leubl feels endless gratitude towards Campino because at least he made that comment about the crappy T.V. station.

"So you went down there and brought us back a film?" the clone says, beaming.

"That's exactly what I did," a rapturous Schminki replies. "I thought, you know, why not go and pop in on Nadeche?"

"And we'll be seeing that right after the break!"

Leubl downs his schnapps and mutes the sound.

"You watch her videos even though you know she's not your friend?"

"Of course!"

"But—"

"Of course it's not all genuine. But you get loads of great ideas. Because she's got such an exciting life! She doesn't have to go on holiday to the arse end of the world. She stays in a hotel on Mallorca. With her boyfriend."

"Or someone playing the part of her boyfriend."

"Huh?"

"Well, you don't have a clue what happens when the camera's switched off. They just show you what they *want* to show you."

"I don't believe that. Schminki made a video of them breaking up and that was really sad. She was serious. That was definitely genuine."

Schminki's film is now playing. Schminki throws her arms around Nadeche too – Binny's big sister meeting her own big sister. But clearly this is more than a courtesy visit. There are a few images of excited children running after Schminki's car and crunching on so many sweets it gives you tooth decay just listening to it. Afterwards Schminki says she wants to use the opportunity to get to know this beautiful country and showcase it for others.

"This can't be real, can it?" Leubl's wife says.

And now comes a clip which is much grimmer, both visually and in its content. Schminki travels through another part of the country where she meets a man who organises desert safaris. Tent, mattress, a nice dinner – like camping on the beach, but without the sea. The obligatory camels, a bit of shopping at some market. Schminki's filming switches between images of herself, exotic fruits and cute animals, because "we shouldn't forget that this is actually a very beautiful country – and not at all expensive." Then she buys a T-shirt for three dollars and makes a call to Nadeche Hackenbusch, so the film at least ties in somehow. In its unscrupulousness the link is quite skilful, Leubl thinks, certainly more sophisticated than the stuff in Schminki's own videos. The phone call must have been written into the script by the programme editors. Schminki thanks Nadeche for the chat, hopes that all the refugees arrive safely in Germany one day, and maybe they'll be able to return to their former homeland on holiday one day.

"Absolutely," Leubl's wife says, "Ideally on a T.U.I. package tour. I think I'm going to be sick." She gets up, walks briskly to the television and switches it off.

"Grandma!"

"Binny, we need to have a chat."

"Wait, what? Now? Turn it back on, Grandma!"

"Never in my life have I seen such cynicism."

Leubl fancies another schnapps. He can see his wife steeling herself for a fight and he senses the battle is already lost. He's seen it before, like when Binny's mother was determined to be together with that dreadful man. George or Paul – it was a Beatles-like name. There was nothing they could do to stop her, she would have to experience herself, even though both Leubl and his wife made it clear from the outset that the guy was a bastard. But at least the Beatles arsehole was an amateur. Binny is entering a world of professional bastards.

He watches as his wife sits beside Binny and explains what is so terribly obvious to her and to any halfway normal adult. Binny protests and says her grandmother's got it all wrong, she's perfectly capable of telling the difference, and she'd love to spend the night in the desert, eating fruit. She says she'd like to live in a world where everyone could go on holiday. The battle is lost, Leubl thinks wearily, we don't have a snow-ball's chance against this Schminki, who lives the sort of life every fourteen-year-old dreams of. No meddling parents, only smart hotels, acres of clothes and cosmetics, and a boy-friend – all proof of success and the right way to live. She's got talent too. This Schminki moves as if she were born for television. She's in a state of happy excitement, but not nervous; she comes across as confident, but not arrogant; she's got everything most people would have to spend years practising. There's only one thing she's lacking: a stance.

And whereas George or Paul, the bastard, had been perfectly satisfied with a bit of sex, this Schminki will well and truly exploit his granddaughter by hoovering up her attention.

Something's got to be done, Leubl thinks as he dozes off. It's a job for the minister of the interior.

# 28

He told everybody that they were walking at their own risk. There could be no guarantee of success, only a better chance of succeeding. Yes, they said. Great that you even got it off the ground.

"I can't promise you anything," he told them all, "except that you won't drown." A great joke, it goes down well every time, he must have told it at least a hundred times by now and everyone always laughs. On a few occasions he followed it up with "and you won't need a life vest either", but it detracted from the joke, so he dropped it.

He also told his guys, "Don't make any promises!" And they certainly won't have; after all, they're not getting kick-backs, at least none worth mentioning compared to before. All he said was that he was the one organising it all because somebody had to. But that didn't mean he was the tour guide or mayor or whatever.

So why has he now become just that?

He never wanted to be mayor. He's the one who came up with the idea, and maybe a couple of helpful solutions, but that's all. The whole organisation with the lorries, for example, that wasn't him; it was Mojo's idea. Or the contact with the regional warlords: you pay one and he keeps the others at bay. You just need to know which of them stands by his word, but the system of regular payments is amazingly effective at keeping them in line. Everything comes from Mojo, who obviously gets his cut, but that was precisely the plan. Sometimes one person has an idea, then another, and sometimes Malaika can help out or U.N.H.C.R. or the T.V. people. He is not personally responsible, so nobody needs to thank him, he doesn't want anyone singing his praises if things go well, but nobody should level complaints at him either. He's just the guy leading the march.

He sees a cloud of dust on the horizon. A pick-up with mounted machine guns on patrol. There have been one or two attempted ambushes, traffickers in girls perhaps, maybe just competitors trying to show that those now acting as guards can't guarantee protection. But they can – as soon as they came within range the pick-ups raced towards them. And that's been the sum of it, up till now at least. It helps that there isn't much to steal. The lorries, food, water – none of it is really worth the bother. Water, food, electricity, it's all so well organised now that there's just the odd tweak needed here and there. And otherwise he just walks. Fifteen kilometres per day isn't much. In the evenings the odd shag with the angel, and dreams of the future.

But they won't let him.

She won't let him.

Because she's an angel, and angels understand nothing of life.

First she pestered him to protect the little whores. It had

nothing to do with protection, of course; she wanted him to see to it that they didn't have to sell their bodies anymore. As if he – or anyone else in the world, for that matter – could put a stop to that. Besides, they have to earn money to pay for food and water and protection.

"No! I pay for they."

A true angel. If a little unworldly. He told her what he predicted would happen then, when word got around that the angel was paying for the little whores. Very soon everyone would stop paying in the hope that the angel would come to their help. He calculated the revenues for her. In fact the angel's arithmetic isn't that bad. She realised that she'd never be able to stem the tide. Then he told her that after she ran out of money, she'd have to get people used to paying again. Which wouldn't work. She wouldn't be helping the whores, she'd be leading everyone to their deaths.

"But we must something do!"

"No. We must bring them to Germany."

Then came the first sick people. He aimed for young people and didn't have any difficulty finding candidates; he could take his pick. He also made it clear to his guys that they should only take young people who could nurse their own minor ailments. Children weren't a problem, nor young families. He wanted to regulate the uptake via the circulation of the app. But because it could be copied, of course, some elderly people did come along at first. They soon realised that they weren't up to it, so they turned and headed back to the camp. Does he care if they made it? Probably not. He isn't the tour guide, for God's sake.

He's just the guy with the idea, nothing more. Just the guy with the idea.

Then she came with all the sick people.

When you've got one hundred and fifty thousand people, some will get ill, it's obvious. So what? He didn't guarantee to anyone that they'd stay healthy. Somebody catches something and can't keep going. Which means they've got to find someone to carry them or drag them or whatever. And if they can't find anyone, they have to drop out. Which doesn't mean they're going to be driven in a pink zebra car. Because if that happened, all of a sudden there'd be lots of very sick people. So they have to drop out. Some are lucky: being at the front they can rest for a day before rejoining at another point. But when the column of migrants has passed, that's that. They can hope that someone will come by and help, but that might take time because the group has been avoiding the main routes. They have the water they've got with them and perhaps a few morsels of food, but perhaps not. Maybe they'll die, maybe not – he'll never know because he's not going to drive back to check. Lots of people die in Africa.

So far, apart from the elderly, they've all kept up, but it's only a matter of time before someone just can't keep going. A broken bone. An appendix. These things happen. Then there really will be dead bodies on television. There haven't been any so far only because it's so difficult to film at sea.

"No! We need a doctor."

And so they agreed on a doctor.

Or someone doctor-ish: Pakka once helped out as a hospital orderly. Malaika has made one of her zebra cars available to him. Now Pakka drives up and down the column and treats people. He gets medicines through Malaika's connections. Painkillers, plasters, bandages. He doesn't give anyone a ride; he tries to ensure that people can keep going on their own. When there's nothing more he can do he says, "Sorry." That's it.

"That is it? But that is impossible!"

He tried a joke, "Nothing's impossible", like she always says when she won't take no for an answer. But this is all about the mechanism of the column, which mustn't be broken. Everyone must be aware of the risks, everyone must keep paying, everyone must keep walking. The procession cannot stop, because the moment it stops the locals will worry it's here to stay. The supreme advantage of this procession is that it passes. A column that stops is a camp, and nobody wants a camp. When people stop, you can't be sure they'll ever get moving again.

Malaika wants a doctor. The money in her foundation, she says, will pay for a proper doctor. Alright, a doctor, another car and more equipment, her foundation will surely be able to cover all that. But no transport.

Then there were the pregnant woman.

It doesn't stop. He specifically said at the beginning, no pregnant women. But some didn't look pregnant. And others have become pregnant en route. So many young people, a few prostitutes. With some it's pretty obvious now. He's been told that walking is fine, even late in the pregnancy, but it gets difficult close to the birth. And then there are the newborns.

"You know that not! You have no childs! I have!"

She sits up on the flatbed of their pick-up. It's the only luxury they have: a flatbed for two, with half-metre metal sides for privacy. He sits up too and puts his arms around her.

He read on the Internet that one hundred and fifty thousand young people would produce between one hundred and fifty to two hundred children a year. There's no way they'll be able to support them all. The tougher mothers may manage, but what else can he do? Wave a magic wand?

"Another truck. I pay. Another truck. And a sister for babies!"

She kisses him.

He's getting used to her idiosyncratic English. She wants another lorry for newborns. And when it's full, the oldest baby will be returned to its mother, and so on. For newborns only. No patient transport.

It doesn't sound that bad. Better than dead children. A small bus full of babies. The pictures would be good. Babies aren't threatening. But it won't prevent hardship. People might still die. Children might die.

She nods.

He agrees to it, and it feels as if a heavy weight has fallen from his shoulders. There are enough heavy weights, but now there's one fewer, and Malaika has this tireless confidence. She embraces him and gives him the sense that he doesn't have to do everything, everything on his own.

It's because she's an angel, he keeps telling himself.

# 29

"Hey, that's not shit on the ground there, is it?"

"What?"

Sensenbrink leaps up. He's in editing suite 3, currently *the* editing suite of the entire firm. Up till now he's been sitting there fairly quietly, sending messages via his smartphone, while Karstleiter and a technician check the new material. But now he's on his feet pointing at a small, curly shape on the screen.

"Can't you see that? Freeze the picture, I'll show you. Back ten seconds . . . that's it! There and there! And there!"

"Hmm," the technician says. "I don't know. I mean, they could be stones."

"Stones? What sort of stones do they have down there?"

"Lava's often dark—"

"We're not on fucking Lanzarote! There! Again. Rewind again. Stop! There! Those things!"

"Sleeping animals, perhaps," Karstleiter says.

"O.K., Charles Darwin, what kind of animal sleeps in the shape of a sausage? Have you lost it? That's shit! Period. Zoom in."

The sleeping sausage gets bigger, but not sharper. Nevertheless, it's now almost impossible to construe it as anything else. Since there's another sleeping animal not far away, and this one's trodden flat in the middle.

"There we go!" Sensenbrink says. "There *are* no animals that soft. Who commissioned this?"

Beate looks at the list. "Korbinian, from Anke's team."

"I want Anke here. Now!"

Karstleiter makes a call. Sensenbrink tells the technician to start the film again. The refugees have been on the march for ten weeks; the stories are getting pretty thin. They can't keep constructing everything around the unconventional lovebirds with their outlandish mission. As with any successful format, they're facing the challenge of fragmentation. He put more writers onto the story, ten to begin with, then another ten, and anybody who was a writer at the start is now a chief writer.

"It's the same every time," Sensenbrink sighs to Karstleiter. "None of these creatives are leaders. Anke is good, but only with words. People like her shouldn't be promoted. Take away their keyboard and replace it with people, and they just want to be nice, and all of a sudden . . . Yes?"

"What's up?" says Anke, who's actually reliable otherwise.

"Come in, take a pew. We're just viewing the material. Did your department script this? What's it called, again?"

"The working title is 'The Rearguard'," Karstleiter butts in.

"'The Stragglers', actually," Anke says. "Yes, that's ours."

"You see, Anke, we're dialoguing here about what we're seeing on that screen. He says he sees animals. I say shit."

"You're right."

Karstleiter and Sensenbrink exchange glances, then their heads turn to the young woman as if to order.

"What do you mean, 'You're right'?"

"You're right. Those are heaps of shit."

"Human shit?"

"Well, we haven't analysed them individually, but—"

"Hey, don't get all sarky on me!"

"—but if my eyes don't deceive me, then yes."

"What were you stir-frying in your think-wok when you put this together?"

"Don't you like the topic anymore?"

"Did I ask for heaps of shit? Why would I do that?"

"Herr Sensenbrink, we were all in that meeting. We discussed the possible topics we could focus on. There were the standard ones, like oldest refugee, the youngest, the most beautiful, those furthest at the front, those furthest at the back. Someone even said, 'Awesome, right at the back, it must be really grim there'—"

"That's fine," Karstleiter says, "but I don't understand these pictures! How can they have gone unnoticed? I'd go fifteen metres further on and film there. Don't any of you have eyes in your head?"

"Yes, and I said exactly the same as you! But everywhere looks the same. When I rang the civil defence people they just laughed. 'What did you imagine?' they said."

"But up till now we haven't—"

"Because we've been filming almost everything up near the front. In fact it's just a simple arithmetical problem.

I'd happily talk you through it, but it's a little . . . unappetising."

Sensenbrink groans and slumps in his chair. A meek wave of the hand gives Anke the floor.

"It's like this," Reliable Anke says. "Those right at the front look for a secluded spot to do their business. Anybody who's been on a hiking trip knows the procedure. But being a hiker doesn't make you any more imaginative than anyone else. So you've chosen your spot, and when you get there—"

"—there's already tissue paper lying around," Karstleiter says.

"Exactly. The spot you thought was suitable has been earmarked as suitable by someone else before you. And the more people that pass, the fuller these suitable spots become. So then people start looking for less suitable spots, which are a little further away. Or they go for more obvious places. Children, for example, will just do it by the side of the road, though they'll aim for somewhere that hasn't been used before. But take a section where fifty thousand people are walking, and by the evening you'll be hard pushed to find an unused spot."

"Yuck!" Karstleiter says.

"What then?" Sensenbrink says.

"Then people camp there. To begin with the most popular sleeping area was the road itself, where there weren't any little heaps. But when night fell people kept getting run into. They soon learned to keep the middle of the road empty. But then this free space became the first choice for people to do their business—"

"But why?"

"Well, I'd be the same. The first place you go at night is somewhere you're guaranteed not to bump into someone. Anyway, it's dark at night so people can barely see you in the middle of the road."

"And it's close," Reliable Anke says. "Your alternative is to head off somewhere far away. But you don't want to do that: it's dark, it's not safe, you want to stay with your herd, you're afraid you might not find your way back—"

"Fine," Sensenbrink says, "But does it have to look like that?"

"Yes," Anke says soberly. "It does. What we've just been talking about is only the first day. And this column is fifty or so kilometres long. Which means that the second tranche of people, those who are fifteen kilometres behind the front, are walking through a section that fifty thousand people have already used. And the following day, the third lot of fifty thousand—"

"Spare me the rest!" Sensenbrink closes his eyes and turns away.

"Each person produces 300 grams of shit per day," Karstleiter reads from her smartphone.

"You can work it out yourself," Anke says. "This means that, every day, those at the very back have to walk through an area in which around forty-five tonnes of shit have been deposited over the previous three days. That's a quarter of a million heaps, depending on the size—"

"Enough!"

"Drone images even show patterns."

"What?"

"O.K., you've got a column in which a constant number of people always group themselves in a similar way, that's to say around the water tanker." Reliable Anke takes a sheet of paper and starts to sketch circles and lines. "The following morning it always looks the same. Here's the water tanker, there's the road and the shit is dispersed roughly like this." She makes lots of dots on the paper.

"Enough, enough!" Sensenbrink pleads.

"The further back you go, the more you see people with plastic tarpaulins. So they can sleep on a halfway clean surface. Now there are even specialists, earning a bit on the side by folding the tarps in such a way that the outer and inner sides don't come into contact."

"Mary, mother of Jesus! We can't show *any* of this."

"Even though it's almost another good story."

"No, it's not! We can't use it. We're broadcasting the greatest live drama in the history of German television. Of *any* television. This is bigger than 9/11. We've got exclusive access to the lead figure. The two lead figures in the drama. It's the most important show we're putting out there right now. We stand here, aware of our responsibility towards history. Everyone on the board agrees that we bear a responsibility towards humanity. Towards journalism. Towards democracy! But not by showing pictures of shitheaps."

"It may sound cynical," Anke says, "but when the provisioning wasn't so great, the problem wasn't quite so ... spectacular."

"The cement mixers?"

Anke nods.

It was some viewer. One of these globetrotters. But also a truck manufacturer or engineer. He'd seen the episode about the dreadful quality of the food, endless howling and tears. The N.H.F.H. pulled in donations amounting to tens of millions. And then this globetrotting engineer rang up and said you could run the whole thing much more efficiently, especially in Africa where people mainly eat porridge. Of course they couldn't all stir their porridge while on the march, but it could be done centrally. And the porridge could be delivered in cement mixers. It would be stirred en route, and with a few modifications it might even come out in a better state than it had been when it was poured in. This was a huge initiative: two lorries were donated and more were purchased. And because this was a humanitarian crisis, normal construction firms dropped down the distribution list, which made no sense, because dubious local gangsters latched onto the idea enthusiastically and organised some old cement mixers from China, which worked just as well. Ever since, serving each refugee a portion of porridge on a bit of cardboard has been a doddle.

Karstleiter pushes her mouse around. The screen is bright again, and the problem is clearly visible. "Everything is interconnected," she says.

"But it's got to stop, it's mission critical." Sensenbrink says. "To be blunt: this is no longer advertiser-friendly space."

"But it's the authenticity that marks us out," Reliable Anke says, confused. "The journalistic quality. The fact that we don't prettify anything."

"Try telling that to the folks at Salomon or Adidas," Sensenbrink says.

"Tsk, tsk," Karstleiter says. "Or Meindl, for that matter. Viewers aren't going to buy 300-euro hiking boots when they're watching people standing up to their ankles in shit."

"I get that you don't like it, but I can't work magic. All I can suggest is that we start filming from the front again."

"That's not going to help. Someone else will film it. It's amazing that nobody else has picked up on it. The turds have to go."

"But what do you think's going to happen? Are you going to ban people from pooing?"

"Maybe we don't have to," Karstleiter suggests. "Maybe nobody will notice."

"The longer it goes on, the more likely someone else is going to pick up on it. We can't risk it any longer."

"Why not?"

"Why not 'any longer'?"

"Because," Sensenbrink sighs, "because we've just started sales talks."

"Is the company being sold?"

"No – the show."

"We can sell a licence?"

"Licences."

The two women and the technician exchange glances. Three approving faces: raised eyebrows, an understanding nod and pursed lips. The pursed lips belong to Reliable Anke, who asks, "Do we have to licence it? I mean, it's news. An event. It's not something we've organised."

"We've argued about this already," Karstleiter reminds them. "It's quite clear that, without us, none of this would be happening."

"Exactly. It's all about legal security. People broadcasting this don't want to find themselves facing injunctions. So they buy the rights in advance – cheaper than a trial."

"Who are we talking about here?"

"O.K., but this is really top secret. The Dutch are on the verge of getting a licence."

"And then they'll start their own refugee trek?"

"Are they going to send Lara Stone down there?"

"No, no, they'll broadcast ours. And it's not just the Dutch."

"Who else? The French?"

"Them anyway. The Italians have been enquiring too."

"Haven't they got enough refugees of their own?"

"They're just thrilled that these refugees aren't heading for Italy. Just like the Brits. They can watch the show, stick their tongues out and say nyah-nyah."

"But 'Angel in Adversity' quite clearly follows the educational format – it's pro-refugee."

"Depends on the voice-over."

"Surely they can't run a different commentary over the top?"

"If they pay enough, they can do what they like," the technician says.

"The turds won't bother them, then."

"They won't bother the Brits or the Italians. But they will the Americans."

"The U.S. market?"

"Yup. They first toyed with the idea of organising the same set-up with Salma Hayek, then Angelina Jolie, but ultimately they gave up."

"Because Nadeche Hackenbusch is better than Angelina Jolie?" The technician screams with laughter. "They can't think that, surely not!"

"No, because the situation is different."

"How so? They've got a border too. Who else if not the Yanks?"

"Yes, but nobody has to walk for so long. In Mexico they can take the bus."

Everyone nods; it makes sense.

"So they need our Nadeche. Who'd have thought it?"

"But not if she's standing in shit. That's the last taboo. Not even 'I'm a Celebrity' has shit. Sperm: yes. Genitals: yes. Shit: no. They'll serve you up a pair of boiled monkey's nuts, but not boiled monkey's arsehole."

"The turds will just have to be cleared away, then."

"But how?"

"Doggy poo bags?"

"Very amusing."

"Why not?" Karstleiter muses. "That would be the cheapest solution. There has to be a central distribution system for the bags, though."

"I can see the headline now: MyTV treats refugees like dogs."

"But we're using cement mixers to help them."

"Being treated like a house isn't as bad as being treated like a dog. At least not in headline terms."

"Take a reality pill, all this is nonsense. Look at those people. Do they look like the sort of people who always clear up their mess? Here in Germany the take-up is marginal, and even then people just tend to leave the bags wherever they like. So we don't just have shit everywhere, but shit wrapped in plastic."

"Children will throw them at each other . . ."

"Or someone will sell the bags on. No, there has to be a different way."

"We'll get some diggers along to plough it all into the ground."

"Too expensive. You'd need so many diggers and if the turds really are dispersed as you say, you'd have to plough hundred-metre-wide strips through the landscape."

"One hundred metres won't be enough," Reliable Anke insists. "I can do you another rough sketch."

"Please don't. Let's say five hundred metres, then. But that won't work either. Let's face it, our concern isn't environmental protection here!"

"What's that supposed to mean?"

"It means that we can't start clearing turds with a digger until everyone has passed through. But why would we bother clearing up behind the column? I mean, we're not filming there. We want the front, middle and end of the procession to be clean. But we can't go digging around among the trekkers on a daily basis."

"The only other option is Portaloos," Reliable Anke asserts. "Like at a rock concert."

"But for a moving column of people?" Karstleiter says.

Sensenbrink shoots her an angry glance. Scepticism isn't helpful here.

"Portaloos don't weigh much," he says encouragingly. "And they're easy to assemble."

"Most people do it around the water tankers," Reliable Anke says helpfully. "So let's set them up there."

"Have you any idea how many you'd need?" the technician says. "Thousands!"

"At least they'd use them," Reliable Anke continues. "You can close the door behind you."

"And every day they'd be driven to the next stop?"

"That's another whole load of lorries," Karstleiter warns. "Just saying."

Sensenbrink tries to calculate how many would be needed to transport thousands of Portaloos. Once again he feels as if he's back at school, struggling with a complicated maths problem involving little heaps of shit, Portaloos, lorries and refugees. You always have to start by formulating the question. So: how many lorries . . .

"Actually we're not talking about that many," the technician says. "You only have to transport them every three days. I mean, the water trucks stay in the same place for three days. So you can leave the loos where they are too, and use them again."

"That's right!" Reliable Anke says. "It's only the Portaloos at the back that need to be transported to the front. You empty them, then bury all the mess with a digger behind the column of people."

"Far fewer trucks, then." Nice to see Karstleiter making a

sensible suggestion too. "But that's still ten or fifteen juggernauts with Portaloos. Drivers. Helpers."

"Which they've got already. You just need a few more of
them."

"O.K., so the problem is solvable. But who's going to pay.
The refugees?"

"Chance would be a fine thing!" Sensenbrink rubs his
eyes. "They don't seem too bothered by the piles of turds."

"But they're benefiting from the coverage. The trek is
gaining acceptance, and if the Yanks buy the rights they'll get
even greater exposure."

"Let's focus instead on where we can save. The firm could
give us the loos at a discount. Or even donate them. It's for a
good cause and we'll mention them during the programme."

"An airline could sponsor the transport to Africa,"
Reliable Anke suggests. "Then all that's left is money for running and maintenance. I don't know how much the licences
will bring in, but—"

"No way!" Sensenbrink shakes his head emphatically.
"The broadcaster can earn something from all this, but we
can't organise it."

"O.K. But who, then? The Foundation?"

"That's more like it. The refugees have to sort it out themselves," Karstleiter says, "and the Foundation can look after
the costs. That might even appeal to Nadeche. Because of Bill
Gates. He arranges for the provision of clean water and the
sanitary facilities are pretty similar."

Sensenbrink's gaze wanders to the video on the screen,
which plays silently. He sees Lionel hugging Nadeche

Hackenbusch, checking the water quality with the truck drivers, counting the packages with those golden isolation blankets.

"And while we're about it," Sensenbrink says, now back in his role of leader and decision-maker, "Lionel needs new shoes. They can't be falling off his feet. They make him look pathetic rather than enterprising. Find him a sponsor. From now on he gets new shoes every four weeks."

# 30

Twenty minutes. That should do it. A bit of canoodling and then chop-chop! The under-secretary doesn't fancy the full monty tonight. Nobody's going to get his brains fucked out this evening, that's for sure, no matter how long Tommy stands there panting. The under-secretary gives Tommy a kiss and feels himself being nudged in the direction of the bedroom. This must be brought to a swift conclusion. Once they're in the bedroom the lighting will have to be adjusted and then the box of toys will come out. Not that the under-secretary has anything against toys, but recently it's all been taking too long. Yes, he used to like it, but that was then and this is now. By the same token the future will be the future, but he's going through a bad phase right now and frittering away hours in the bedroom isn't going to make anything any better. The under-secretary kisses valiantly and tries to nudge Tommy away with his hips. The intended destination is the sofa, where there are no toys and where the business will be carried out rapidly and unbureaucratically.

"Mmm, I've glot thumethling nlew you've weally glot to thlee," Tommy slathers into his mouth. His fingers work their way inside the under-secretary's shirt. Now this: new acquisitions for the toy box. It's never ever enough. Nineteen minutes, probably more like eighteen. It helps that he's somewhat taller and considerably heavier; it means Tommy can't dictate the action so easily. He tries to make it look playful, but it backfires.

"Oooh!" Tommy groans. "Someone's playing hard to get!"

Trousers down, both of them, or nothing's going to happen, then he has to jockey Tommy into the right position, but not too quickly because Tommy likes it when you coerce him a bit, ten minutes at least, it's going to be bloody tight. And this calculation doesn't even take into consideration that he has to get a hard-on . . .

"Are you looking at the clock, or what?"

"No, I'm just—"

"Are we in a hurry again?"

"Not at all, come on, I love you, let's stay here and—"

"On the quickie sofa?"

"Mmm?"

"You heard me. I'm not stupid. Bedroom: Emmanuelle in the Garden of Earthly Desires. Sofa: wham, bam, thank you, Ma'am. You want the sofa. I get it. I can't remember the last time you watered the Garden of Earthly Desires. No surprise nothing's growing there anymore."

"If we go on arguing there won't be any time left at all!"

The under-secretary doesn't say this, of course, even though it's the only logical response when there are sixteen minutes remaining. But strictly speaking the calculation isn't right anyway. Even with the quickest quickie Tommy wants to lie in his arms for a bit of a cuddle afterwards . . . and when is the right time to switch on the television? After five minutes? Ten? He shouldn't have got into this in the first place.

"Sorry, Tommy," the under-secretary says. "I have to watch the programme. I *have* to."

"You *are*, you're looking at the clock!"

"I'm sorry, really. I can't help it. Leubl's on."

"Because of the refugee nonsense?"

The under-secretary nods. Tommy takes a deep breath. He does his best to give the under-secretary a kiss. "Fine," Tommy says. "Fine. I'm not going to whinge. You're my under-secretary, you are the cock of my life." He turns and bends down to the shelf below the countertop. They went for Corian in the end, and it's not as low-maintenance as everyone makes out.

"I'm not going to have a hissy fit and I'm not going to make your oh-so-difficult life any more difficult."

He takes out a bottle. Red. The under-secretary can't see which one, but it's probably the rich Barolo. Tommy holds the neck of the bottle in his right hand. He swings back and aims at the wall they were going to buy art for a couple of weeks ago. Then he tosses the bottle very gently onto a sofa cushion.

"Catch!"

The corkscrew sails through the air, the under-secretary just manages to catch it.

"I'm not going to make a scene because I'm grown-up and mature. I'm going to sit myself down on the quickie sofa like a good boy and support my man. I won't tell him I don't want to watch his fucking stupid show, I'm above all that. But he ought to know that my resilience has its limits. And that I need a little support too. Open the wine, you frosty cow!"

The under-secretary looks gratefully at Tommy. Tommy looks back at him with surprising affection and buttons up his trousers. The under-secretary pours wine into two glasses while Tommy switches on the television. The weather forecast. Tommy shuffles along the sofa and cuddles up to him. "Refugee shit," he mumbles. "Why do they have to make yet another programme?"

"Do you ever listen when I tell you something?"

"Always. Wait, how does it go again? Oh yes. Refugee-refugeerefugee. Herr Leubl. Refugeerefugeerefugee. Herr Leubl. Refugeerefugeerefugee. Hackenbitch. Have I left anything out?"

"No," the under-secretary says, forming a circle with his thumb and index finger. "Perfect!"

"Tell me."

"If you ever picked up a newspaper . . ."

Tommy digs the under-secretary in the ribs.

"*I'm* not being difficult. So it would be very, very nice if *you*—"

"O.K. The media have got wind of the fact that there's not going to be a catastrophe. At least not anytime soon."

"So?"

"Well, it means that one hundred and fifty thousand people are marching in our direction. And people are beginning to think they could actually make it."

"Could they?"

"Shhh," the under-secretary says. "Let's see who they've got on the programme."

"What do you mean, 'Shhh'? You can see!"

"Just shut your trap!"

The under-secretary doesn't say this, of course. He lets Tommy talk and hopes that at some point the verbal diarrhoea will stop of its own accord. Leubl appears on screen. He's wearing his Lino Ventura face: the strict father, but deep down a good man. This face has won him the last eight elections; he's perfected it over the past few decades as his forehead has become more furrowed. Nobody in politics uses wrinkles to such good effect. But his high forehead is ideal for it. Unfortunately, nobody in the under-secretary's family has lost a single hair. He ought to start wearing glasses – that can be effective too.

"O.K., Mitzi Wallenstein-Abbraciavento, no surprise there," the under-secretary comments.

"Oh really, is that so?" Tommy tickles the under-secretary, who tries to push away the intrusive fingers with a movement that could just about be described as "affectionate".

"They've got to wheel in some human rights fusspot. Oh look, Schwägerle. I hope they give him subtitles." Schwägerle is harmless. Once a week he writes a decent op-ed, but he's nowhere near as assertive on television. That's down to his gruesome Swabian dialect. When the under-secretary was party chairman, the first thing he did was to ban Swabians from radio and T.V. interviews, except for with regional broadcasters. It doesn't hurt anyone if they clog up the peasants' airwaves with their farinaceous babble. But not nationally.

Dialects in politics are like four-wheel drive: you have to be able to switch them on and off, or they end up doing more harm than good. He still thinks it's a miracle the C.D.U. put up with Wolfgang Schäuble for decades. "But now they need a right-winger," the under-secretary says.

"I used to have something going with a Hamburger S.V. fan," Tommy says. "Whenever they showed the team line-up before the game he would talk just like you're doing."

"Didn't I tell you: Blechdecker."

"And van der Vaart in midfield again, of course," Tommy mimics gently. "Can't someone get rid of him and his druggy blondes?"

"If Blechdecker didn't exist they'd have to invent him. You need a Nazi for the programme, but can't invite one on. Great that the socialists have one of their own."

"Talking of reds, top me up, would you?"

The under-secretary pours wine into Tommy's glass, spilling a bit when he sees what's playing out on the screen beside Blechdecker. An image of Nadeche Hackenbusch fades into recorded footage that shows the trek setting off, and the first interviews in which refugees talk enthusiastically about Germany, their planned destination. Of course there's that cute little girl again; by now she's become a YouTube hit in her own right. In one video she's dancing, and another she holds up empty bottles to people and says, "T'posit, please!" Then the mood changes and the real reason behind the disquiet becomes apparent: the popularity of Pegida is once again on the rise. And just as the presenter asks Nadeche Hackenbusch how things are going, Tommy says, "Oooh, look how brown Nadeche is! She looks great. I do think, though, that if—"

Watching television with Tommy is a nightmare. The under-secretary bends to kiss him on the lips. Some quiet, at least.

". . . coming to you," Frau Hackenbusch crows. "It's going to be quite a while yet, of course. But if we all help each other we'll get there! I'm so proud of Germany!" Tommy's tongue insinuates its way into the under-secretary's mouth – excellent, now he can hear the presenter ask about the mechanics of the operation and how she's managing it. She replies that she's not managing anything, just offering humanitarian assistance. Either she's smart or someone's got her a lawyer.

"Is your boss going to say something to take the heat off?"

"Not quite yet. First we need a journalist to say the refugees could make it as far as here." And here we go. Schwägerle butts in, waffling away as if he were walking alongside the refugees himself. In truth, Schwägerle hasn't done any proper reporting for at least fifteen years. Feeling tense, the under-secretary reaches inside his flies and pulls out Tommy's hand. He tries to push it away somehow, but unfortunately Tommy has two hands. Some things would be simpler with Captain Hook.

Now Schwägerle is talking about the infographic that recently appeared in *Focus*, the development and structure of the column, and explains that there must be an extremely sophisticated organisation *in his trousers*.

"Please, Tommy, it won't be long."

"But I just felt something that *is* quite long."

"*Please!* I need to concentrate!"

*Behind the trek*, the sophisticated organisation is *behind the trek*. It's all going to get quite dangerous, Blechdecker says, before issuing some sort of warning about Islamic State. This man has had one of the most astonishing careers in recent years. He started out as a bog-standard cabaret artist, appearing on a few comedy shows and taking a pop at the C.D.U. and S.P.D. like any other whingebag. And at some point people noticed that he never distanced himself from the A.f.D. in any of his routines. Then he wrote a rather ugly book that sold like hotcakes, and ever since the S.P.D. has been trying to get rid of him, in vain. Now Blechdecker says something about being a minority in his own country and terrorism, and that the Germans have a migrant blindspot.

"What's a migrant blindspot?" Tommy asks with astonishing attentiveness.

Leubl shakes his head. Now it's his turn, and after just a few words the under-secretary's thinking how he'd love to set up a fan club for him. Leubl thanks Nadeche Hackenbusch for her efforts. He says how much he admires her work, but advises her to be careful she doesn't become liable for prosecution for people smuggling. It's the most polite, friendly and charming warning ever issued on television. Then he insists that people shouldn't be worried. This is a rather vague assertion and thus rather daring too, because you can never know what the viewers' worries are: is it whether the refugees come or not, or is it whether or not Nadeche Hackenbusch and Lionel are going to find somewhere nice to live? That, at least, was the last *Evangeline* exclusive: NADECHE AND LIONEL: DREAM APARTMENT IN MUNICH? But Leubl covers all bases by referring to an array of well-functioning agreements; to the legal situation, which is clear, and to the E.U.'s binding accords. He refers to Frontex and the massively reinforced defence of the external borders. And to the fact that, technically, there are obstacles to surmount which are a touch more complicated than a border in Africa.

"I admire your optimism, Frau Hackenbusch," Leubl says. "The effort and confidence you display is something I encounter far too seldom in Germany. Don't get me wrong, I have great sympathy for the people you're marching with, for their impatience and their hopes. I find it perfectly understandable that in such circumstances people don't think purely in terms of the existing legal framework. They have to look out for number one. But if you continue like this, you're heading for disaster. I doubt you'll get that far, but when you hit the Suez Canal or the Bosphorus at the latest, you can go no further. Those are eyes of the needle and no sovereign government in the world is simply going to let you through."

It's not the law, it's not the government and it's not the Germans – it's the Suez Canal and the Bosphorus. Nobody can criticise a canal and a strait. The under-secretary leans back in the sofa in admiration. He becomes aware that Tommy's hand is no longer down by his crotch, but his mouth is. He tries to push him away, but then Tommy flicks his tongue in a particular way, and it's . . . soooooo good.

Wallenstein-Abbraciavento is just as surprised. By Leubl, that is. She was prepared to take potshots at the government, at the C.S.U., at the E.U., but not at the Bosphorus. It takes her so much by surprise that the only thing she can hold against

Leubl is that he's fondling his balls . . . no, that's Tommy. The only thing she can hold against Leubl is that he's not giving more support to the refugees, seeing as his trousers are off. And this is child's play for Leubl, of course, because all he has to say is that it can't be the federal government's handjob to get refugees . . . oh my God, who'd have thought you could get refugees so deeply into this country and this country is so warm and wet!

Thank God it's Schwägerle talking again now. If there's one thing that makes it impossible for a normal man to maintain an erection it's Swabian, this dialect-cum-contraceptive. Schwägerle elaborately explains that for an accurate assessment of the situation you need to have a good knowledge of African history. One can comfortably ignore what he's saying because no amount of African history is going to help refugees across the Suez Canal or the Bosphorus. Leubl has set down two large full stops, and viewers can now visualise one hundred and fifty thousand refugees standing on the banks of the Suez Canal, unable to swim across. Blechdecker can lash out all he likes, but the comforting image of the hundred and fifty thousand, which the Suez Canal separates from the Promised Land like the deep water of the folk song that keeps the two royal children apart, is cemented in people's minds. Relaxed now, Leubl can turn to Nadeche Hackenbusch and praise her in such a way that you can literally see the Green voters migrating to the C.S.U.; this Lino Ventura exudes a feeling of warmth and objectivity that makes you feel warm and cosy and wet and you stretch out and grow and if possible keep your hands off Tommy's head because you could never move him as perfectly as he moves himself, instead you could deal with this briefest pair of briefs if your head weren't spinning.

And when Schwägerle appears menacingly on the screen again, the under-secretary, as quick as a flash, grabs the remote and switches off the television. He gets up slowly so as not to interrupt Tommy; now he does fancy the bedroom after all, and the toybox, and then his mobile buzzes three times.

Tommy glances up.

But three buzzes means Leubl.

Tommy swallows the under-secretary like a hoover.

The under-secretary feels soft and warm and unsteady. He moans something incomprehensible, and with a sound that is something between a victory cry and leaky bicycle tyres, he collapses onto the sofa. He needs to summon every iota of his strength to pick up the phone. And as he reads the text from Leubl, he hears the spanking-new living-room door slam with such ferocity that the spanking-new handle falls off.

"9.00," the text reads. "Theresia."

# 31

Leubl is in his usual seat in Café Theresia, waiting for a coffee and a croissant. The seat is concealed by the loaded coat rack, in the spot where waiters used to sneak a quick smoke when it was still allowed in cafés and restaurants. Even now this table isn't really for guests; the waiting staff still have a coffee here, perhaps a little cognac or a digestive bitters. An exception is always made for the minister of the interior, however, for old times' sake. When Leubl first ordered a tea in the Theresia, the Beatles were still playing concerts.

Leubl opens the daily paper. He already knows most of the national news, but sometimes he likes to read the local section. Old Rebach's columns, though they're getting worse and worse. But when you're as old as Leubl you're grateful for anyone who doesn't consider "the past" to be just the last twenty-five years. He could do with a coffee now. A coffee and a croissant. But it's slow in coming. The under-secretary will be here in a quarter of an hour, and by then he'd like to have eaten his croissant in peace and brushed all the crumbs off. Leubl doesn't like people watching him eat, telling him "It looks delicious!" Leubl has learned to come to terms with much in life, but not with people who talk at him while he's eating.

Not to mention those who want a taste.

Leubl checks the time and feels himself becoming irritated. In the mirror he catches sight of the under-secretary approaching his table. He sits down just as Anna serves the coffee and croissant.

"Punctual to the minute," Leubl says with a certain degree of regret.

"But I thought . . ."

"It's fine." Leubl pushes the croissant to one side.

"Don't you want it? It looks delicious."

Leubl takes a deep breath. "I'll have it as a take-away." The under-secretary waves subtly and gestures to Anna that he'd like the same order. She confirms this with a nod.

"You were great yesterday," the under-secretary then says.

"Do you think so?"

"Very convincing."

"Did you see the viewing figures?"

"No, why?"

"I had them sent to me: 65 per cent higher than normal," Leubl says.

The under-secretary whistles through his teeth.

"Let's tot up the Pegida figures too, and I don't just mean the loonies in Dresden. It's happening all over Germany. They're making a comeback. Big time."

"But like you said, the refugees won't actually be able to get here."

"I'm afraid that's irrelevant."

"What do you mean?"

"Ever seen *Jaws*?"

"Spielberg? Yes, but years ago."

"Dun-dun-dun-dun-dun-dun-dun-dun-dun-dun," Leubl hums. "Remember the music?"

"I think so. Creepy."

"Before the viewers see the shark, before they see its fin, they hear the strings: dun-dun-dun-dun-dun-dun-dun-dun-dun-dun. Softly at first, then increasingly louder as the shark gets closer. Why does the director do this?"

"Because it's scary," the under-secretary says.

"Precisely! Because it's scary when something unstoppable approaches slowly."

The under-secretary considers this briefly. "One hundred and fifty thousand refugees on prime-time telly every evening."

"Dun-dun-dun-dun-dun-dun," Leubl hums, twisting his hand to imitate a shark. The hand twists its way back to Leubl, then slaps the back of his other hand on the table in front of him. "Dead certain. It always works."

"But how many people think they're a threat? I mean, the refugees have got plenty of fans too."

"Those fans are just as much of a problem. The refugees have popstars behind them, and that Internet saleswoman. And the more momentum that's built up, the greater the number of people who begin to worry."

"But what I thought was absolutely superb was that thing about the Bosphorus. The Suez Canal," the under-secretary says.

"But it's not going to help us."

"What? All of them coming to a standstill at the Suez Canal? How much more clearly can you say it? It's obvious. Theirs is a hopeless cause."

"Yes, but it'll be another year at least before they even *get* to the Suez Canal." And what do you imagine this country is going to look like after a year of watching the shark get closer and closer?"

The under-secretary tries to imagine. He nods and kneads his cheeks. "And it won't stop there. They're not stupid, are they?"

"Not at all." Leubl refills his cup.

Anna arrives with the under-secretary's order. "Well, then. We need a quick solution," he says. "But we can't drive one hundred and fifty thousand people to the Suez Canal just so that they can see what would happen."

"Thank God, that's the last thing we'd want," Leubl insists. "It's not a good image: one hundred and fifty thousand at the Suez Canal, one hundred and fifty thousand at some mountain pass. Those kinds of pictures would just escalate the situation. We can do without escalation. Escalation requires decisions to be taken. And we've nothing to gain from taking decisions. What we need is well-cultivated boredom."

By now the under-secretary has scoffed his croissant. He dunked it in his coffee and polished it off without dropping a single crumb. There aren't even any floating in his cup. Leubel wonders whether these homosexuals might not possess special abilities after all.

"Isn't this going to become the foreign ministry's business?" the under-secretary suggests. "Surely they can't just keep walking through all these countries?"

Leubl shrugs. "What do you intend to do? These countries are trying to play for time. They fob us off for as long as it takes the procession to pass through. They've no interest in fast solutions."

"Which means we're running out of possible solutions."

Leubl doesn't respond.

"Or have I missed something?"

Leubl sips his coffee.

"O.K., let's put it another way: what do we need? We need a fast, boring solution. For example, the refugees all turn around one by one and . . . No, they can't be that daft. But . . . they get lost in the desert . . ."

Leubl holds his lower lip between his thumb and index finger and listens.

". . . they disperse," the under-secretary adds, still thinking aloud. "O.K., that sounds really boring. They disperse because . . . because nothing's working anymore."

"Why not?"

"Back luck. Fate."

Leubl scowls. "That would be a tragedy."

"O.K., sure," the under-secretary ponders. "We don't want tragedies. Not bad luck, not fate, but—"

"—their own stupidity," Leubl says.

"Their own stupidity," the under-secretary repeats thoughtfully. "That's it! They have only themselves to blame. They botch it. Sounds good." With the tip of his index finger he picks up a flake of croissant from his plate and pushes it between his lips. "Let's see . . . they can't get lost. And most of them can't do much wrong overall. If something is susceptible, then perhaps it's the organisation."

Leubl looks out over the room. More or less incidentally he says, "We'll just have to see what sort of people that lot have got themselves involved with."

"Well, they're criminals . . . businesspeople . . . Mafiosi . . ."

"That's who they get their food and directions from," Leubl says from the corner of his mouth. He leans forwards, picks up his cup and empties it. "And water."

"And water." The under-secretary allows the thought to take effect. "But that would escalate pretty quickly too. The cameras are a permanent fixture there . . . People dying of thirst in the desert is just as potent an image as a great white shark . . ."

"That depends. My favourite film goes like this: somewhere, in the vague vicinity of a largish settlement, the water runs out."

"They stay in the settlement, of course, without any water they have to stay there," the under-secretary keeps the thread going. "One week, two weeks, three—"

"But they don't get any further," Leubl says. "So what do the people living there say?"

"The inhabitants become anxious, the government has to do something about it . . ."

Leubl looks at him over the top of his glasses.

"The government has to . . . do something about it," the under-secretary repeats, and then it clicks. "All of a sudden they *have* to do something about it."

Leubl gestures to Anna for the bill.

". . . and the hitherto smooth passage of people, which has been a profitable enterprise, becomes a problem case they're left with."

Anna arrives. Leubl glances at the bill. It's unbelievable what you can charge for two coffees and two croissants these days. He'll pay for it, without getting a receipt. He can't bring himself to foist these prices onto the taxpayer.

"And if that's the scenario, would they let people like that into the country again?" he asks the under-secretary as he puts the change into his wallet.

"I would see to it that whoever's responsible for having dumped these people in my country has the smile wiped off their face," the under-secretary says, getting up. "But first of all I'd seize the money they've earned for it. And anything else they've got. They won't do it again."

"Let's hope so," Leubl says, putting on his overcoat. They wait for Anna to bring the take-away croissant to the table in a paper bag. Leubl takes it, now with a certain relish after all. He'll have it in the office, on the sofa. On his own.

# 32

Nadeche Hackenbusch couldn't say precisely when the thought occurred to her. Certainly not in the first week. Probably not in the second, either. But certainly not just now, a quarter of an hour ago. The thought goes: it really is quite a long way away.

She has to admit it wasn't that clear to her. She *does* know that it's a long way; she realised that on the flight out. There are some flights where you can see two films in succession, or even three films plus an episode of "The Big Bang Theory". There are some flights where you don't want to watch anymore films and you think, "I'd love to have a book now." But it's in the suitcase. Then there are flights where you get pyjamas and a sleeping mask once they've cleared away dinner, and when that happens even Nadeche Hackenbusch realises you're so far away from home that you'd definitely have to change if you were taking the train. Or have a few stopovers. That's really far away.

But not as far away as this.

She wakes up and crawls out of the car. Lionel is already up and about, and the first thing she sees is that . . . this morning looks just like yesterday morning. It's as if they haven't moved at all. The main difference between days is that the broadcasting van might be three metres further to the left or four metres further ahead. Every day the sky is the same shade of blue; there are no clouds here. And the best thing you can say is that it's not as hot as it's going to get. But there's hardly anyone you can say that to. If you even hint at it in an e-mail, they'll write back straightaway, saying, It's always hot down there. But this country is too inventive for that. This country get can really cold at night as well. "This country" is definitely the right name, because you never know if you're in one or the other. It's not like in Europe where you'll find a baguette in one country, but not in the next one. They may well have differences here too, of course, African differences, but to find that out you'd have to get to a town. A real town, not just something around a watering hole.

A town. What she would give for a town right now. With one shop. Selling shoes.

No . . . handbags. A town with one shop that only sells handbags.

Nadeche rummages around for her boots and knocks them together. Not that she's ever found a scorpion inside. It's probably a myth that scorpions hang around in shoes. A myth dreamed up by those tropical researchers, because nobody here ever wears boots. Even Lionel's trainers are exotic. This sliders culture is something she can't get her head around. But maybe it's to do with one's homeland. This African soil will never be as familiar as a German meadow.

Nadeche Hackenbusch hops out of the car. She usually

feels stiff for the first few steps, but all in all she's astounded by how easy she finds this simple existence, physically at least. The television van is opposite, with its pink zebra stripes. There's a pretty little fleet of cars now, if you include the doctor's car and the midwife's car, which will be here soon for the newborns. It makes her feel proud. Many people have their own companies, but this here, this is ... more. It's like the Red Cross, or a bit like the pope, this new reasonable pope who likes gay people too. The HackenPush-Up was hers, and it was something she could be proud of, but it wasn't the same, it lacked this ... higher purpose. This here is something only she is capable of, only Nadeche Hackenbusch, no-one else. In the entire world.

A handbag shop and an iced mocha cappuccino.

She stuffs a handful of nuts into her mouth – a mini breakfast. Nuts can get you a long way, she'd never known that. Bimsheimer Müsli has become one of the show's main sponsors, and their ads always go on about "Germany's nuttiest muesli". Nutella has got involved in a big way too, even though that really stretches the definition of nuts. They asked whether they could supply Nadeche. She's got nothing against Nutella, but it would send out a ludicrous message. The average refugee crunches their way through the day on nuts, while every morning Nadeche Hackenbusch spreads her bread with Nutella from her fridge. Because without a fridge it would turn into drinking chocolate in the heat. It's better if she sticks to normal nuts. You get used to them anyway. But it helps that food has never been that important to her. Nicolai was the gourmet: the basil would be from here, the steak from there, and then he always pretended to be able to tell the difference. Foodies love identifying differences. The moment you tell them where something's from they say, "Ah, yes, you can taste it!" Once she said to Nicolai, "That's bullshit. If the bread came from somewhere else it would taste exactly the same." And he had to agree with her.

It really is a hell of a long way. Not just because of the flight and all that. She found out when she asked Nicolai on the phone why the kids weren't in bed yet. "Why should they be in bed already?" he replied.

"Already? But it's got to be like, much later your end!"

"Huh? What's the time there?"

"Half past four."

"Same here."

Only then did she realise how far away home she really was: she's twenty-four hours ahead! And they've got to cover every minute of that on foot. Crazy. And no chance of any holiday.

Now she had to admit that some things were impossible after all. She talked about it with Lionel, before the television discussion. If she abandoned the trek now, if she went home, they probably wouldn't allow her to fly out again. They couldn't prohibit it outright, but they could make it difficult and drag the whole process out, and in the meantime there are no Hackenbusch images to broadcast. Viewers bail out. And all of a sudden one hundred and fifty thousand refugees are one hundred and fifty thousand nobodies in the middle of nowhere. It doesn't have to be like that, but she can't risk it. She can't leave here.

Although the flight alone is tempting: a bed, coffee, champagne.

So chilled that the glass mists up on the outside.

No. Impossible. It's too high a risk. That's why it has to be a live link-up too. It's not a problem technologically. And if they want Nadeche Hackenbusch *in natura*, then let them come to Africa. After all, they go the whole hog for those summer interviews with politicians.

Still, she can't promise there won't be occasions where she'd try to take off. She loves Lionel, no question. And these people are important too, of course they are. Increasingly important even, because there are more of them now. Four or five more lorry stations have joined the trek, another reason why Lionel is often out and about in the mornings. His people can decide most of the cases, but some are touch and go. To begin with Lionel wanted to shirk responsibility, but he realised that by engaging with the newcomers himself he was able to avoid problem cases. The supply of medicines is working well now, but there's only one pink doctor's car and it has to stay that way. She spent a day with it for a programme. There isn't so much to do, but there are lots of decisions to make. If the patient is fit in two days, they can be treated. If it's quicker than that, they just need a few pills. People can't get really ill, it's as simple as that. She was glad they didn't come across any seriously ill people during their day of filming. It happens very seldom, thank God. Because Lionel only takes the right people.

That being the case, she could comfortably go shopping for a couple of days.

But there's a reason why she'll never, ever run the risk of this initiative failing. And that reason is now knocking on the side of the car.

"Morning, Nadeche!"

Virtually without an accent – it's astonishing. She knows so much already. Nadeche helps her and she seems incredibly gifted. She can work hard for hours on end, and yet she's always happy. She picks up on things so quickly that you can barely keep up. And four weeks ago she knew only two words.

One was "t'posit", the other "Ottobafes".

# 33

"Now what's the matter with the air-conditioning? Are we all supposed to freeze our arses off, or what?"

Astrid von Roëll sits in the motorhome that *Evangeline* has finally hired, and shudders as she zips up her outdoor jacket. She's working intently on a piece about Airbnb apartments in Paris. Astrid is a little shocked by how people furnish their apartments in a capital city. In a world city of such cultural repute!

"Look at that. Look. At. That!"

"I can't just now," Kay says from somewhere.

"I mean, they can live however they want," Astrid says in disbelief, "but I'm not going to *rent* something like that!" She nudges the mouse. "I wouldn't pay 117 euros a night for that!"

"Could you switch the aircon off and on again?" Kay shouts.

"Hmm?"

"The aircon! Off and on again!"

"How does that work?"

She hears a muffled thump, like someone hurling a heavy

tool on the ground, and the door is flung open. Kay comes in and stomps pointedly over to the aircon controls, which are beside the door. "Look. Here: off. Here: on. Oh, wonder of wonders, it's the same button!"

"Sorry!" Astrid smiles her third favourite smile. "Now I know for next time."

"Why are you going to Paris? I thought you had to write."

"They've asked me over for an interview."

"Who? France Télévisions?"

"I've forgotten. Something with Tee Vee. Or Tay Vay."

"Can you speak French?"

"May wee!"

"Wee lala!"

"The point is, they speak English."

"What do they want from you exactly?"

"Silly question. They need an expert."

"The apogee of serious journalism: journalists interviewing other journalists."

Kay goes back out, slamming the door behind her. Astrid gives her the finger. She shouldn't get so big-headed just because she knows how to hold a screwdriver. The aircon isn't going to be broken for ever, and then she'll be back to being a mere cameramouse.

Her footage isn't even that good. Astrid has seen better, like those wildlife documentaries on Arte. Although the drone idea was a nice one, and Kay was the first to do it. As it flies along the procession you're thinking it's just a normal hand-held camera, but then slowly it pulls away and up. Or that shot of the entire column. All in one go, fifty kilometres

325

without a cut. People are still baffled by how she did it, because not even those expensive camera drones can fly that far. And you have to stay within range for the drone to pick up the signal. Despite its length the clip is the biggest hit on the website. On the back of it the deputy blockhead gave Kay a permanent job – reacting quickly for once. But it's a long way from being art. There's something engineery about it, anyone could learn it if they had the time and the inkling. And there are things Kay can't do. Astrid once watched her paint her toenails – what a sorry business that was!

"Is that supposed to be a kitchen! Where's the micro-wave?"

Kay would film everything, whether people or guinea pigs. In fact this is the real difference between Kay and Astrid: Kay hasn't grasped that she's part of something massively important here, something unique. This is world history. This is politics, foreign affairs even. And domestic ones too. And the deputy blockhead can count his blessings that Astrid von Roëll understands the significance of all this. Because there's nothing about it in her contract. But why did they make Lou Grant Fake News Director?

"*Creative* News Director," the deputy blockhead corrected her.

"Whatever. If anyone's making news here, it's me!"

"Yes, but—"

"Even creative news! Well, I'm not reporting to him, no way!"

"No, no—"

"Others can report to him if they want!"

"No, of course you'll still be reporting to the editor-in-chief—"

"Directly. I will report *directly* to the editor-in-chief!"

"Yes, sure. But look, someone's got to do the work here. You're just a bit prejudiced. You don't have to love all your colleagues, but even if *you* don't rate Herr Grant, he's good."

"If you're satisfied with 'good' . . ."

"Frau von Roëll, how about leaving the quality control to me?"

Creative News Director. A position that never existed before. If anyone deserves it, it's her. Because political journalists are ten a penny. Anyone can do it. These *Süddeutsche* and *F.A.Z.* lot think they're the cat's meow, but basically all they print is news. And if you've got the right phone numbers for those presidents and press officers then it's no big deal, it's exactly the same as what she does, just with other people. But the point is: political journalists are limited. They have no human understanding. Especially the men. All they ever think is politics.

"I just want to say," Astrid asserted, "that we mustn't forget who's behind all this."

"And?"

"Well, we ought to give that person some official status too."

"A job title you mean?"

"Exactly. Job title, whatever. In the masthead."

Just then she pictured the expression on his face.

"And what did you have in mind?"

"Creative News Director."

"Hmm, I thought you'd suggest something like that."

"At Large."

"I'll have to discuss this with the boss, but the most I can offer is a job share. So you'd do it together with Herr Grant from now on."

Was that brazen of her? A man would never ask himself the question. She discussed it with Nadeche too, and Nadeche encouraged her, saying how important it was that she, Astrid, refused to budge even one millimetre. She mustn't slip back behind Lou Grant. You see, Nadeche went on, it's only when you look at it from the outside that it seems to be about power and positions and whose name is biggest in the masthead. "But behind all that," she said, appealing to Astrid's conscience, "behind all at it's always about men."

That's Nadeche in a nutshell: clever in her own way, but uneducated. She didn't mean men, of course – she meant women. And that's why Astrid has to be Lou Grant's equal, at least in the masthead, so that content by women gets the appropriate weighting.

"And like, the appropriate pay," Nadeche emphasised.

"Actually, they've already bumped up my salary."

"All the same, they've got to up the ante." As far as Nadeche was concerned it was quite clear. "Every euro you *don't* get goes to some guy. The more expensive you are, the more normal it becomes for other women to be more expensive too. That's the only way it can work."

Astrid hadn't looked at it this way before, but Nadeche is right, of course.

"And what can Lou Grant do that you can't?"

"Nothing. Nada. On the contrary, I'm learning something every day here!"

"Exactly, and he's just getting like, *even* stupider every day."

They laughed so much, and it struck Astrid how little time they'd spent in each other's company recently. The months here in Africa have changed them both. More obviously Nadeche, who's never been so thoughtful. But Astrid has changed on a human level too, for even though empathy and sensitivity have always been her strengths, she's now made another big leap forwards. It would be impossible to experience the things she's seen here without gaining in maturity. Here you learn how fragile life is, and yet how strong people can be. You realise that profound emotions are felt amidst extreme poverty too. Health, food, water – these are the truly important things in life. And her copy reflects this.

Astrid re-read her reports of the last few weeks recently, and the writing really is different. It has depth, it's reflective – she doesn't want to say it's philosophical, but actually, why not? Other people have picked up on it. Christine, Uschi, the woman from the deputy mayor's office and Regine – all of them have e-mailed, asking whether she was going to make it to the Oktoberfest. Unfortunately it's not going to work out this year. And all of them said, or hinted, that her writing had developed a new, more profound tone, and her stories were raising *Evangeline* to a new level. They don't even bother to read *Gala* anymore, they just chuck it straight in the bin.

A new level. The whole magazine!

She really does need to up the ante as far as her salary is concerned.

"Better now?" the pushy plumber/competent camerawoman asks. Pushy plumber, competent camerawoman – two "P"s and two "C"s. This kind of repetition has come to her so easily of late, it's been tripping off the tongue. When was the last time something entered Lou Grant's head, apart from a cotton bud?

"No."

"Are you sure? Switch it on and off again!"

"I'm in the middle of a sentence, Kay! Sorry, but this is really important!"

She hears that thump again. The door is flung open and Kay stomps over to the controls, while four fingers carefully type:

"By Astrid von Roëll (Creative News Director at Large)".

# Dream couple
# seeking security

Nadeche Hackenbusch and Lionel: in the most unfavourable circumstances the German superstar is creating a modest home for her love. The man of her heart gives his thanks – in the language of her home country

### By Astrid von Roëll

One is instinctively reminded of *War and Peace*, that wonderfully profound novel by Leonardo Tolstoy: a young noblewoman, played by the unforgettable Audrey Hepburn, finds her great love, and this in the midst of hardship and in Russia. But when one points out this striking comparison to Nadeche Hackenbusch, and tells her that over the past days and months she has truly become an Audrey Hepburn of hearts, she just laughs modestly and reaches for the hand of Lionel, her new Bolkonsky, a man as good-looking as he is mysterious. They gaze into each other's eyes, then Nadeche says, "With all of this going on we mustn't forget how privileged we are.

We're able to shut ourselves away in the little free time available to us." For there is one place where these two people, who do so much for hundreds of thousands of others, can be themselves for a while. Exclusively for EVANGELINE, they have left the door to this paradise ajar.

When we visit the two of them early in the evening, they're a little coy, like a young couple in their first home. They emerge hand in hand from behind the pink car, looking dreamy and – there's no other way to describe it – in love. "We washed the car especially for you," Nadeche Hackenbusch laughs. "Well, it was me actually."

Could we be hearing the first hint of discord in this blissful young love affair? But when Nadeche gives her Lionel an affectionate kiss, our concerns dissipate like a colourful swarm of happy butterflies. "Yes, he was against the idea," she admits, chuckling. "Because of the water – and of course he's right. Men are often more sensible about these things. But a woman will always be a woman!"

It is hard not to agree with Nadeche Hackenbusch. This warmth, this inimitable naturalness, this deeply felt humanity. Who wouldn't feel sympathy for this special woman, especially now, in these days, weeks and months? Incomprehensible criticism still rains down from her embittered-and-soon-to-be-ex-husband Nicolai von Kraken in Germany. I ask whether she's any the wiser as to why the less-than-successful producer is so indifferent towards the welfare of his children. She just looks away and wipes a tear from her eye. She is still distressed by how von Kraken forced her sons Keel and Bonno into the spotlight. That appalling appearance on a much-watched television programme, when they begged their mother to come home. Many experts have since condemned this stunt, most recently Germany's most famous family lawyer, Karl-Theoderich zu Boten-Fürstett, who did not mince his words: "This is a real case of abuse of two innocent children." Alone, a mother remains powerless if the rule of law has no feelings.

Nadeche Hackenbusch changes the subject, and who can blame her? She takes us around the car, an ISUZU D-MAX Single Cab (from 22,500 euros). Attached to a frame mounted on the flatbed is a tarpaulin that covers the back of the vehicle like on a real lorry. "It's a weatherproof tarpaulin," Nadeche says tenderly. A simple fabric covering – is this the Nadeche Hackenbusch of old? "Yes, of course," she laughs with a wink of the eye. "Look, they've dyed it specially so it matches the rest of the car. I mean, it's got to look right too. A leopard can't change her spots, can she?"

And yet this top presenter hasn't lost her practical nous. The tarpaulin can be rolled up on all three sides. "We could have got a matching hard top instead," Nadeche says (available in all colours, price on application). "But the people on the march with us don't have hard tops."

It's astonishing what the deft hand of a woman can conjure in a simple cargo space of 2,305 mm × 1,570 mm. She's got two pink cushions (Morphea, covers by Katinka Svensson), and she's styled the floor surface into a cosy dream with two exclusive insulated sleeping mats (EnForcer DreamHill, www.summitz.com). An inviting haven that tempts one to spend time there. Photographs of her sons are fixed to her side of the flatbed. "Lionel did that for me. I'm not so handy with a screwdriver," she says. "Now every night before I go to sleep I can think of my two boys."

Two L.E.D. lanterns stand tall in the cargo area, one on either side, with drinks holders humorously attached. They (LightUp, various, inc. www.handwerk.de) also match the colour of the car. This is nothing like camping in the 1970s. Which is no coincidence as Nadeche Hackenbusch has experienced these grim aspects of the past too: "Sweaty times in polyester, I really don't need that anymore," she grins. "But with modern, functional clothing, who does? These days we don't do that Adidas tracksuit look." We have to agree with her. Even though Nadeche Hackenbusch doesn't look quite smart enough for the Salzburg Festival, her plain merino shirt from Mufflon would be fine for any day in the office.

But the question must be asked: can they, in the midst of such persistent suffering and struggle, allow themselves such an oasis of peace? "Lionel always tells me we can sleep when we're in Germany," Nadeche says. "But my response is that if you don't get enough rest, you'll arrive there dead." And there's another reason the dream couple need to spend time alone: Nadeche Hackenbusch reveals exclusively to Evangeline that she's teaching Lionel German. For the German media, but also for the future he dreams of in the Federal Republic. "I don't want to be lazy," he

> "Now every night before I go to sleep I can think of my two boys"

says with astounding fluency. "I'm thinking of working as a chief executive."

This sounds amazingly ambitious, but every day he shows astonishing management capabilities. "Lionel thinks of things I'd never come up with," Nadeche marvels. "While I prefer to take each day as it comes, half the time it's like he's already got as far as Uruguay or whatever." Nadeches serves up the customary porridge plus a few nuts. "In Germany I'd start by drinking a prosecco," she says. "So cold it makes your teeth fall out. Lionel doesn't know prosecco yet, but I'll teach him about that too." Then she laughs out loud and says, "I'll sort that out before you become a chief executive." She harbours no doubts: "I spent enough time with a man who called himself a producer without producing anything worthwhile. Lionel produces more here every day and he risks his life for the hundreds of thousands who need help."

The sun sinks over the endless horizon of Africa. We take our leave as the two of them retire to their tiny nest (maximum load: 1,225kg). As we walk away, we can see the little lamps light up inside the ISUZU D-MAX. It's a light of hope in a land that can turn darker than any other place on earth.

**"The first altercation in this young blissful love affair?"**

# 34

"Performance reviews," Mojo says with a sigh. "Know what they are?"

The sun is going down and the temperature is becoming bearable, even here where there's nothing. Or less than nothing, to be precise. The column has already moved on and behind it the entire stretch of desert doesn't just look desolate and empty, but desolate, empty and bulldozed.

Echler nods. He looks around and considers fetching binoculars from the Humvee.

"There's nobody here," Mojo assures him. "Anyone wantin' to use a directional mic here would need a range of 50K, Mr Jones."

Echler is giving him a searching look, probably. You can't see his eyes behind the sunglasses, but the corners of his mouth are extended slightly outwards. Mojo points at Echler's broad-brimmed hat. Echler's head nods, the corners of his mouth turn upwards. He looks at the sky.

"Drones? You're drivin' without a licence plate, so even if they *are* watchin' us, nobody's gonna be able to prove it's you. At most they know that somebody's meetin' me."

Mojo throws out his arms and smiles broadly. "And I meet a whole lotta people."

"Well, then..." Echler gives his driver a signal. The Humvee's engine starts up and it drives off. Echler peers over his shoulder at Mojo. Mojo smiles, then nods at his car. The car comes to life and drives away too.

"What about him?"

"Bandele? Bandele ain't here. Don't look at him. Bandele is air. Ain't you, Bandele?"

No reaction from Bandele.

"How dumb of me." Mojo shakes his head. "I've just been speakin' to thin air. Come on, let's take a little walk."

The vehicles have left tyre tracks in the reddish-brown dust. Echler can see other tracks beneath these, probably from the lorries. Larger tyres have been here too, from a tractor perhaps. Echler walks beside Mojo and he can feel the heat of the ground through his boots. Mojo smells faintly of eau de cologne. Taking a sniff, Echler asks, "Calvin Klein?"

"Hey, not bad," Mojo laughs approvingly. "Calvin Klein! You hear that, Air-Bandele? This guy's a real sniffer dog! Calvin Klein. A present from my kids. D'you have kids?"

"No," says Echler.

"Kids," Mojo continues. "A blessing and a curse. So young, so clueless. D'you know what my kids like most of all? Barney, the dinosaur."

Echler looks at him, eyebrows raised.

"It's a terrible show. A fluffy pink dinosaur who's always singin' goddam awful songs." In a squawking voice Mojo starts warbling something that sounds very like Yankee

Doodle. "Yadda yadda yadda, And so it goes on. They'd already binned the show, but then they bought it back to life. It's horrible. Any sane guy watching it feels an immediate, uncontrollable urge to throttle that dinosaur."

"In a children's programme?"

Mojo shakes his head. "Not in the show – in his head. I wanna kill Barney. You'd wanna kill Barney too. But of course we don't. Of course I don't. My kids love Barney. But . . ." he says, raising his hand in warning, ". . . they gotta watch it on their small T.V. Barney ain't comin' nowhere near my big screen. If I catch even a glimpse of Barney on my big screen then it's contaminated and I gotta destroy it."

Echler looks quizzically at Mojo. Mojo winks and slaps him on the shoulder.

"Just kiddin'," he laughs. "My kids' T.V. ain't small."

"Well . . ."

"But that show is dire. And not just dire. It's dangerous too."

"Is it?"

"Yup. That's what the experts are sayin'."

"Because men are starting to kill dinosaurs."

"Don't joke. I'm bein' serious. Really dangerous. For the kids!"

"I see."

Echler would quite like to get down to business now. It may have turned cooler, but here cooler basically means less hot. Besides, he's got a stone in his shoe. But friendliness and small talk are part of the way of life here. It would be impolite to launch straight into the matter at hand.

"Barney tells the kids a whole pack of lies," Mojo insists.

"Well, at least people don't generally sing in daily life."

"It's not just the singin'. He tells them that everythin' in this world is beautiful an' good an' nice."

"That's not so bad," Echler says. "They learn the rest soon enough."

"No, they don't," Mojo groans. "They grow up with their heads full of Barney. And then I have to do performance reviews."

Echler shrugs. "What can you do?"

"I could do with guys like you," Mojo says ruefully. "You ain't seen Barney. You know what life is like. But too many of my guys are just dumb niggers."

Echler doesn't respond.

"They come to me and complain. Always complainin'. Now they're complainin' because of the cabanas."

"The cabanas?"

"You know: the plastic cabanas. They come from Germany, don't they? Cabanas for shitting in."

"You're doing that too?"

"I'm a businessman. If someone needs little shithouses drivin' around then I get someone to drive little shithouses around. Of course I could say, I don't drive shithouses around, but then what? Then some other dude comes along. And if some other dude drives shithouses around for a while, who knows, he might get silly ideas."

"Like he could drive water around too?"

Mojo lands a very gentle punch on Echler's upper arm.

"You're a smart guy. Did you hear that, Bandele? He ain't

just got a good instinct, he's got a good head too." He taps his nose with the tip of his index finger; Echler's sure he's seen this gesture somewhere before.

"But the dumb niggers come to me and say, I ain't gonna drive no shithouse. I say, you'll get a stack of cash. A stack. Ain't that fair enough. An' they say, sure, but you never said I'd have to drive shithouses. I say, it don't matter what you drive. Porridge, water. It don't matter. And they say, but no shithouses. I say, sometimes in life you just gotta drive shithouses around. They say, not me, no way."

"Because of Barney?" Echler suggests, glad to have something to say.

"Because of Barney," Mojo confirms. "Because in Barney-world there ain't no cabanas for shittin' in. An' so they believe there ain't no shithouses for them either." He stops, his shoe has got stuck. Something is sticking out of the ground. Mojo bends down and pulls on it. It's some kind of cord, or a hose. Mojo gives an almighty tug. The hose is evidently long, two or three metres of it come out of the ground. Mojo rolls it up, just as Echler's grandmother used to do with packing string. Then he tosses the bundle to Bandele who stuffs it in the pocket of his cargo trousers.

"So I say, what's wrong with shithouses? They say, shithouses stink. They say it like kids do. And I say, they're German shithouses. They don't leak. They don't stink. They say, sure they do. And I say, No way, José." Mojo rolls his eyes, then spies another hose on the ground. He seizes it and begins to pull. Echler thinks about his grandmother again; this time she's weeding. Two or three metres. Mojo rolls it up.

339

Echler looks at his watch. He's got time, but not so much.

"What then?"

"What am I to do? I get new guys to drive around an' try to convince the old ones. It's a process," he says, circling his hands around each other. "I think we're headin' the right way."

"Marvellous," Echler says. "That brings us to another process. We had a deal."

"I figured you'd ask about that."

"Did you think we'd pay you and that would be that?"

"I see the whole thing more as an exercise in trust-buildin'."

"As *what*?"

"I know now that you're an honourable guy. If you say you'll pay, then you pay."

Echler stares at him. His sunglasses prevent him from looking as angry as he'd like to.

"That's good," Mojo says. "I don't trust many folk. But I trust you now. I don't know who you work for, but you can go to them and say, 'Mojo trusts me.'" He bends down again and pulls a hose from the ground. "Help me, would you?" he says, pointing at another.

"What is that?" Echler asks.

"Bad for the environment. Plastic. Plasticiser."

Echler cautiously pulls on a hose.

"Sure," Mojo says, "there ain't no fields here, no agriculture, but . . . somehow it all ends up with the dolphins. It doesn't have to be that way."

Echler pulls. "We paid you a seven-figure sum. Why haven't you delivered?"

"I have delivered," Mojo says. He rolls up another hose and tosses it to Bandele.

"You know what I mean. Why have you kept on delivering? The deal was, no more water after that dump of a place."

"Harder than you think, ain't it?" Mojo jiggles his head at the hose Echler is tugging on. "This goddam plastic shit!" Echler nods. You'd think the thing had roots.

"Your dough – let me be frank about this. I thought it was just a deposit." Mojo checks the ground to see if he's missed a hose. "You buy into a business by acquirin' stocks."

"Stocks?"

"Speakin' figuratively, of course," Mojo adds jovially. "You don't actually have no real stocks."

"We paid you a seven-figure sum—"

"Yeah, yeah, I got you. You thought you could buy me out with that? Another one." Mojo bends and pulls up a hose. "And one by your foot too."

"Seven-figure!"

Mojo vigorously plucks the hose from the ground, then stands up straight. "Hey, I know you're disappointed. That happens in business. But be honest: did you *really* think those few bucks would be enough? You're a nice guy, and smart too. I like you. But what do you imagine I earn? I'm responsible for a shitload of jobs here. An' this model can run an' run, for a very long time. To put it plainly: if we're goin' to do business, you're goin' to have to replace these costs. Give it a hard tug, then it'll come."

Echler pulls harder, then straightens up too.

"O.K. How much?"

"I can't disclose my calculations to you right now, understand? But I've got one thousand drivers workin' for me. An' the way things are lookin', I can keep' em busy for ten years minimum. So your seven-figure sum would have to come rollin' in every week."

"Are you saying you want to be on our payroll?"

"Kind of, yeah."

"For doing nothing at all?"

"It's a paradox, ain't it? But how else is it gonna work? The business partners I've had up till now have ample financial resources."

"But we can't do that! There's no way I can pay you millions on a weekly basis!"

"You can pay it in one lump sum too, but that'll be more expensive. To adjust for inflation. And those are amounts that I don't imagine your government can send over unnoticed."

Echler puts his hands on his hips. He wonders whether to demand back the money they've paid Mojo, but this doesn't seem a particularly good idea. "I can ask again," he says, pulling his hose from the ground. Something really stinks. He checks the soles of his shoes.

"Smell anythin'?"

"Actually, no," Echler says. "I just thought I did."

"If so, it's the hose."

Echler checks the end of the hose. Indeed. It is pretty pongy.

"But apart from that you don't smell nothin' do you?" Mojo says, sniffing. "That's the standard procedure. Every day we dig a pit behind the last people. The cabanas are emptied into the pit an' then driven to the front. The excavator then fills in the pit. Six feet of sand, you don't smell nothin' no more. The excavator is great. German firm: Lieber? Liebare?"

"Liebherr."

"That's the one. This entire procession is cleaner than any refugee camp."

"What about the hoses? Are they for the anaerobic digestion?"

"What's that?"

"No idea, I'm no sewage expert. In Germany we collect sludge in septic tanks. I imagine it's the same principle."

"I don't understand nothin' 'bout that. But the people gotta breathe."

"Which people?"

"People who've seen too much Barney. Dumbass niggers. I'm goin' to ask you again, an' please give me an honest reply. Be as rude as you like. D'you smell anythin'? D'you smell shit?"

Echler takes a big sniff, then shakes his head.

Mojo bends down. He's found another hose. He squats and pulls the hose to his mouth. "Like I say," he bellows into the narrow opening, "we can smell *nothin'* at all. I hope you guys understand that now."

He stands up. "I think we're done talkin' here. Get in touch again if you wanna get involved properly. And thanks for your help. Bandele, call the cars back." Mojo pulls hard on the last hose, which tautens and then keeps stretching, as if someone were holding onto the other end.

Finally, it jerks out.

# "We're sticking with the programme!"

SPIEGEL interview   MyTV head of entertainment, Joachim Sensenbrink, on the success of An Angel in Adversity, social responsibility and making money out of refugees

**SPIEGEL:** Congratulations, Herr Sensenbrink!

**Sensenbrink:** What for, exactly.

**SPIEGEL:** Well, what would you like to be congratulated for? You can take your pick. MyTV's turnover is skyrocketing, as is Angel in Adversity's advertising revenue. And we hear you're going on the board of directors.

**Sensenbrink:** I can confirm the first two here, but not the last. It's a matter for the supervisory committee and nobody else.

**SPIEGEL:** Can the supervisory committee overlook the man behind this upturn?

**Sensenbrink:** You tell me. As far as I know the supervisory committee can do anything.

**SPIEGEL:** Now, we've heard a funny story that says Angel in Adversity in its current format wasn't developed by you, it was a spontaneous decision by your star presenter.

**Sensenbrink:** Yes, I've heard that too. But I can assure you that at MyTV it's still the broadcaster who decides what's going to be shown. Of course we discuss it with our stars, but the final decision is ours.

**SPIEGEL:** Which means we must be talking to the right person. What's it like making money out of refugees?

**Sensenbrink:** It's always nice to earn money, but you're implying that we're doing it unjustly. I see it differently. I'm very happy to thrash/this out with SPIEGEL if you tell us what we're doing wrong.

**SPIEGEL:** Let's put it this way: each episode of Angel in Adversity carries more than 60 minutes of advertising.

**Sensenbrink:** How much

advertising do you consider permissible?

**SPIEGEL:** That's not the question.

**Sensenbrink:** If I follow you, you're saying that every cent we take from advertising is somehow immoral.

**SPIEGEL:** Isn't that the case?

**Sensenbrink:** It can't be. We're a private T.V. channel. The alternative would be to make programmes about refugees for nothing. Which means we wouldn't make them at all.

---

## "The refugees aren't as naïve as you would have them be"

---

**SPIEGEL:** Or, like other broadcasters, you'd report on it in your news bulletins. They could certainly do with improvement.

**Sensenbrink:** Obviously we're not going to let other people prescribe the weighting we give to different issues. Others have tried and as we've already said: we're sticking with the programme.

**SPIEGEL:** Critics say it's gone past that point, and argue that without your company's involvement this wouldn't be an issue at all.

**Sensenbrink:** The refugee issue has been on the agenda since 2015. Even Donald Trump couldn't dislodge it.

**SPIEGEL:** It was topical, but not in this form. Without Nadeche Hackenbusch, without your star and your cameras, the trek would never have got off the ground. Your entire programme would never have happened.

**Sensenbrink:** I dispute that.

**SPIEGEL:** You may not have invented the issue, but you escalated it.

**Sensenbrink:** That's a matter of opinion. Let's take the example of an earthquake in South America. You write an article about it. You broadcast a radio report. You give it television coverage. You make a documentary. In the end it's the same earthquake. Cameras, images in general, don't make an event bigger – only more visible.

**SPIEGEL:** And yet you lend it social significance.

**Sensenbrink:** It's still the viewers who decide how important it is, by letting their remote controls do the talking. We're just giving them the choice. And we've got it wrong before. We've had the odd reality show go south straightaway and haven't had to do a SPIEGEL interview about it. But a broadcaster like MyTV can't survive on that.

**SPIEGEL:** Now your company is flourishing. At the same time, so is the A.f.D., which is getting close to 20 per cent in the polls – in some parts of Germany it's much higher. Pegida too: they're having no problem getting tens of thousands of people out onto

## "The viewers let their remote controls do the talking"

the streets. It was only bad weather that prevented one hundred thousand people from demonstrating in Berlin last weekend.

**Sensenbrink:** There's no connection. If we report on wintry weather, people go out and buy jumpers. But we haven't invented the winter.

**SPIEGEL:** Sometimes you broadcast twice a day. You're making more out of it than there actually is.

**Sensenbrink:** 150,000 people are on the march to Europe with Germany's top presenter right in the thick of it – I don't know how this can be exaggerated.

**SPIEGEL:** So you don't care about the social consequences?

**Sensenbrink:** You make it sound as if we're encouraging the far right.

**SPIEGEL:** Aren't you?

**Sensenbrink:** Let's get one thing straight: Nadeche Hackenbusch is not on the far right.

**SPIEGEL:** That's not what we said.

**Sensenbrink:** Nadeche Hackenbusch is helping refugees, tirelessly. The programme is . . . I wouldn't go so far as to call it pro-refugee, but it's pro-people. I can well imagine the far right not liking this, but that doesn't mean I'm going to pull the plug on our reportage.

**SPIEGEL:** What you're doing is no longer reportage.

**Sensenbrink:** It may not be the traditional, dusty old format SPIEGEL T.V. serves up, but it *is* reportage.

**SPIEGEL:** Is it true that the times when the refugees walk have been organised to fit the T.V. schedules? In every film about the desert you learn that people are supposed to walk in the evenings and at night.

**Sensenbrink:** There are better kick-off times for footballers too, but the question is: does the club want the game to be broadcast?

**SPIEGEL:** Are you comparing a march for survival with a football match?

**Sensenbrink:** All I'm saying is that most refugees have seen a football match on television. They're not as naïve as you

---

## "The programme encourages discussion. That's democracy"

---

would have them be. They also know that things like ad pop-ups exist.

**SPIEGEL:** For Portaloos.

**Sensenbrink:** I haven't received any complaints so far. The product has to prove itself over and over again on primetime television, and it comes through with flying colours. The customer is satisfied, and the refugees are too.

**SPIEGEL:** And you're already planning part two.

**Sensenbrink:** So what? You're talking as if the refugee issue has been solved. But it hasn't.

**SPIEGEL:** Well, the Mediterranean was so impassable that even the C.D.U. stopped moaning temporarily. And all of a sudden there was room for the F.D.P. in politics again.

**Sensenbrink:** Temporarily. We're giving the refugee issue the space it actually warrants.

**SPIEGEL:** Or the broadcasting slots you need.

**Sensenbrink:** If 150,000 people embark on a march because our cameras just happen to be down there, you might assume these people would have embarked on the same march at some point whether cameras were there or not. Maybe they would have waited until there were 300,000 of them, but they would have set off all the same.

**SPIEGEL:** Now you're speculating.

**Sensenbrink:** But we're talking about MyTV here! The channel for lightweight films and dumbing down. But now it's about the refugee crisis, which has become an international issue, by the way. Almost all E.U. countries have bought rights to the show, as has the U.S. Even SPIEGEL can't think that's bad.

**SPIEGEL:** In Hungary and Poland they're watching with a certain degree of schadenfreude.

**Sensenbrink:** Our market research has come up with different findings. Attitudes towards refugees have become more positive among regular viewers.

**SPIEGEL:** Among those who support refugees. Among those who oppose them, rejection is ever stronger.

**Sensenbrink:** In any event it encourages discussion of the issue, and that's called democracy.

**SPIEGEL:** How will the programme continue in future?

**Sensenbrink:** I don't know. But I'm not going to deny the fact that it could end tragically.

**SPIEGEL:** So you'll broadcast the great catastrophe as a Saturday night finale?

**Sensenbrink:** Whatever happens, our reportage will be appropriate. But given the magnitude of events, any other broadcaster would do the same. Do you seriously believe that neither A.R.D. or Z.D.F. have anyone down there? If the refugees do make it to Europe and fail, the public channels will report on events just as we are.

**SPIEGEL:** The presentation might be slightly different, though.

**Sensenbrink:** That's true, you won't get any smug commentary on our channel. That remains the privilege of licence-fee payers.

# 35

One thing you can really learn from Malaika is how to work the journalists. Malaika always knows what she wants to get out of them, like a real dealer. She's like Mojo, or better. If a journalist says they want to write about this or that, Malaika tells them they ought to write about something else, like the medicine crisis, for example. And in return she'll put her shorts on. Or they'll get him, Lionel, in the shot too. Now there's a second truck for looking after newborns. And some firm is donating health-boosting supplements that get poured into the tankers carrying drinking water.

Still, it's exhausting. Especially since the programme has been airing in other countries. Now they could be giving interviews all day long. But most astonishing is that all these dozens of journalists ask the same three questions:

How did you come up with the idea?

Where are you hoping to get to?

Will you make it?

They could look at all the old interviews to find out what Malaika and he have already said, but they don't. Sometimes two come at the same time and realise they're asking the same thing. Even then they don't come up with any other questions. Nor do they mind that the answer is always the same; they just want to have it repeated, especially for them.

He can tell the story in his sleep, of how he came up with the idea at Miki's bar. It's a memory he's cherished, but recently it's felt like a well-squeezed piece of fruit that everyone keeps putting back. Malaika doesn't appear to mind one bit. She blossoms when reporters arrive on the scene, and cheerfully regurgitates all her set phrases. Sometimes he gets the impression she thinks she's giving the answer afresh each time, but is that possible? It feels more and more artificial. Please say that again, Lionel. Please make it shorter, Lionel. Please speak a little slower, Lionel, and as you say it could you look out over the plain and hold that expression for ten seconds?

He's reached the point where he almost believes his name *is* Lionel.

His phone rings. Perhaps he should make Mahmoud newspaper admiral. But then that idiot will put on his daft captain's hat again. Better if he does it himself. Taking a deep breath, he answers.

"Ciao! How's my favourite hiker?"

"How's it going with 'Baywatch'?"

Lionel sounds as relieved as he actually is.

"Who's gives a fuck about 'Baywatch', amigo? Ever seen 'Friends'? You should take a look sometime! You'll get a boner just watching the intro. It's the best porn show in the world. They're all bouncin' around in this fountain. Jennifer Aniston, check out her ass. Her tits. She's wearing this tight sweater which they make nice and wet for us. Aaaah. That face! An' nobody's fuckin' her. Nobody! Or at least nobody who counts."

"Maybe that's not what the programme's about."

"Get the fuck outta here! There are two other broads in it, an' they're not gettin' it either. A blonde horse an' some dull brunette. Let me tell you, amigo, it's deliberate. It's what's called dramatic technique! Jennifer Aniston doesn't get fucked because she's always hangin' round with these dreary donkeys. The whole show is literally screaming: Mojo! Come to the U.S. an' save Jennifer Aniston from her god-awful life."

"Well? Are you going?"

"Too right I am! I can't go into more detail or my pants will burst. There's more important stuff. I've been hearin' a few funny stories. Stories about you."

"There are no funny stories here."

"So, you goin' to Morocco?"

"No."

"Libya?"

"No."

"Tunisia? Algeria?"

"Nope."

With his silence, Mojo adds an unpleasant spice to the conversation. Lionel doesn't quite know what's expected of him, so he keeps quiet too. He wins.

"So it *is* true!"

"What's true? I never said I wanted to go to Libya or Morocco."

"Ah, but you never said you didn't want to, either."

"But it doesn't matter. I mean, it's good for you. You're being paid by the day."

"It's not about days here! You're an investment for the future, amigo. You've gotta get your ass to whoreland. Only then will the roubles start rollin' in. I don't get nothin' outta you shufflin' through the desert for years."

"Then we're agreed."

"No, we ain't. You're gonna get yourself to Morocco or Libya an' find yourself a boat like any normal person."

"I can't."

"You tryin' to tell me what to do?"

"I can't say to people that they've wandered through the desert for months, only to drown like thousands before them."

"They'll get their chance, they're not askin' for no more."

"But they don't want just any old chance."

"Morocco's a golden opportunity, amigo!"

"No! Boats are shit!"

"Boats have been around for thousands of years. Nobody's complained."

"You can't control the sea. You can't control the quality of the boats."

"Nor the desert neither."

"You can't get drier than the desert. And our strength is in our numbers. The people smugglers want lots of money, they'll divide us up into small groups and let us drown one by one. And those that make it are just a bunch of Africans. The Europeans will just send a bunch of Africans straight back, or worse. We'll have no T.V. crew with us, and we're in their hands in the middle of the sea."

"But supernigger here has a better plan."

"At least it's a plan that doesn't rely on others. It just relies on ourselves. Our feet. Our money."

Mojo listens in silence.

"That's good news for you too. More success, more money, more vehicles, more Jennifer Aniston."

"How far you gonna go, then? Egypt?"

"Further."

"Further?"

"If we only walk as far as the sea, all this would be in vain. We're not going to the sea. We're going the whole way."

"Through Egypt?"

"Through Egypt."

Mojo pauses.

"That's our—"

"Shut it. I'm thinkin'."

Lionel keeps his mouth shut.

"Now listen up, dumbass. Listen carefully, O.K.?"

"I'm listening."

"I'm feelin' very patient at the moment, dumbass, and I'm not usually so patient. You've told me a load of crap in the past, but it was true crap. You promised me moolah, and I got lots of moolah. I respect you, amigo. You're a bro. A crazy bro, but a bro. And I like you and your crap. You listenin'? I'm even prepared to admit you're right sometimes. Boats are shit, the sea is shit. Smugglers take your bucks an' let you drown. It's a smart idea of yours to pay by the day. I'd rather have your money up front, but I can see it's better for you, amigo. You're not so crazy, crazy bro'. But the model has its limits. I can't go further than Egypt."

"You'll keep getting your percentage."

"Damn right, but this isn't about my percentage."

"What then?"

"Ever looked at a map, dumbass? I'm not talkin' 'bout Syria here, or Jordan. Sure, there might be folk there who'll let you through, but for every one of those, there'll be at least three who won't. Forget it! The Turks – nobody knows what they want except respect. It's everything. An', hey, you'll also get by minor obstacles like the Suez Canal. All that seems kinda possible. But there's one thing that's absolutely unthinkable."

"Israel?"

"Israel."

"Ten kilometres as the crow flies. Fourteen by road. A joke."

"No, a joke is what it ain't. Ten kilometres across a country that's a bigass paranoid military power and deploys its weapons against anythin' that seems suspicious or it don't like the look of. The Jews shoot first an' ask questions later. They might let one or two of you through if they're in a good mood or wasted. But not three, no way. Let alone my trucks. So that's the end of the food and water. Not to mention shithouse paradise."

"What about Jordan?"

Mojo takes a deep breath, then yells, "Jordan, waddya want with Jordan? O.K., with some dough you might be able to arrange a few things. But don't imagine you'll ever be gettin' *into* Jordan."

"Ten kilometres as the crow flies," Lionel says obstinately.

"A clear line of fire, you mean! The Jews will blow that pretty black head of yours clean off. An' for sure that's adios, amigo. From what I hear you still need a head in life. Even in whoreland."

"We'll find a way," Lionel says. "And your lorries are coming with us. If we don't make it, at least you'll have had six more months of earnings off us. And now I have to go, I've got an interview."

He presses the red button and puts his phone away. Of course he knew about Israel. He'd been hoping Mojo would come up with something. Mojo, the cornucopia of ideas. Suddenly Lionel is overcome by despondency. When it comes to Israel, Malaika is going to be about as helpful as the admiral for food and drink. Yes, he's got time – they need to get there first – but he's got even fewer ideas for Israel than he had for all the other borders.

His phone rings. An American number. He's about to take the call when a text arrives. From Mojo.

"Watch your ass, crazy bro."

# 36

It's dark. Most of the offices are empty, even emptier than at the weekend. Many doors along the corridor are locked. Chairs are pushed in, neatly parked as if the desk were a mini garage. It's strange, but you can see straightaway whether a desk has been cleared for the weekend or for the Christmas holidays. Weekend desks are tidy; holiday desks look as if their occupants aren't coming back. Leubl likes that. It's how his own desk looks just now.

He lays his coat over the railing and peers down. They've put up a Christmas tree in the foyer. Without any presents. This is what differentiates Christmas trees in shops from those in offices. Shop trees have presents beneath them. Frau Krassnitzer at reception looks up at him and waves. She's packing away her things. Leubl waves back and mouths a silent, "Happy Christmas!" She blows him a kiss, and Leubl feels a pleasant peacefulness spread through his body.

Taking his coat, Leubl continues on his way, along the corridor to the corner office at the end. The door is open and he knocks.

"May I come in?"

"Who else if not you?"

The under-secretary is still at his desk.

"Time to knock off! Not even an under-secretary can make the world a better place on the evening of December 23rd." Leubl hangs his coat on the stand.

"It's not work-related," the under-secretary says.

"So, what have we got, then?"

"You have a choice, as ever." The under-secretary reaches down and sets a bottle on the table. "Firstly, Glühwein. From Bavaria. I looked out for it especially."

Leubl eyes the bottle. "Franconia isn't Bavaria, believe you me. Not that we haven't tried."

"Is that a no, then?"

"It wouldn't be my first choice."

"I even brought in a mini gas cooker. So we wouldn't have to make it on the unromantic hotplate."

"What else have you got?"

"A cuvée from Apulia."

"Sold!"

"As if by magic it's already been decanted."

Leubl looks as if he'd expected no less from the under-secretary and he goes over to the comfy chairs, where a short, thick candle is alight. Its flame is reflected in the dark windowpanes. From the corner of his eye Leubl notices the under-secretary covering his screen to eliminate the blue glare. He brings over two glasses and a decanter, then sits opposite Leubl and swirls a little wine around the glasses.

"Does that really make a difference?"

"Not with wheat beer."

He pours each of them some wine and respectfully pushes the glass towards Leubl. Leubl picks it up and takes a sniff. He closes his eyes; the under-secretary has made a good choice, as ever. He holds out his glass and the two men toast with a faint clink. The wine rolls around his mouth, nestling against Leubl's gums like a cat in a blanket. "Now," Leubl says, leaning back, "this is when Christmas begins."

The under-secretary puts down his glass and leans back too. Both of them look out at the illuminated city.

"So, what are you giving Tommy?"

"The Prince of Namibia, 22 × 5 cm, veined, with suction pad and scrotum."

"You can do better than that," Leubl says, unmoved. "You wouldn't even fool your mother with that one."

"He's getting art. I'm going to try something new. What about your wife?"

"The same as in 1969. Actually, we don't give each other anything."

"Since 1969?"

"Since 1969."

"You were early to the party. Anti-consumerism and all that. Not even the S.D.P. was as far advanced back then."

"Well, two thousand years before the Left even thought about the planned economy a certain Jesus Christ was already expelling merchants from the temple."

The under-secretary takes a sip of wine. "Do you do everything Jesus says?"

"Who knows what Jesus says." Leubl gazes with relish at the glass in his hand. "Believe you me, if God wants to say something, he'll say it so that everybody can hear. And if someone claims to know better, it's safe to assume they don't."

The under-secretary takes a sip. "I like it."

"My daughter hated us for it."

"What? The God thing?"

"No, for the abolition of presents. With her own children she did it very differently from the word go. But ten years later she'd come round to our way of thinking."

For a while they sit there in silence. Leubl thinks how lovely it would be if it started to snow.

"What are we going to do now?" the under-secretary asks.

"We're going to wait."

"That's all?"

"It was worth a try. But it was clear it would only work if we were dealing with someone who couldn't count. Someone who'd prefer one million euros today rather than ten million tomorrow."

"And now?"

"Now nothing. What were you thinking?"

"That we might reach further into our box of tricks."

Leubl looks at him over the rim of his glass. "By our standards we're already up to our necks in the box of tricks."

"But . . ."

"Any other suggestions?"

"I don't know . . ."

"Out with it!"

The under-secretary pauses for a moment, then says, "The Americans would be doing more. Or the Brits."

"Such as?"

"Without going into detail, they'd play dirtier."

"Go into as much detail as you like. But we can't ban the television cameras. We're not the Russians."

"No, but . . ."

"What other dirty stuff do we have? Should we start bombing the lorries?"

"Not exactly bombing . . ."

"Fine. We'll get elite police commandos to go along and slash all the tyres."

"If you put it like that, of course it sounds silly . . ."

"Put it differently, then. If it's effective, it's an attempt by the German government to have one hundred and fifty thousand people die of thirst. And if it's ineffective they'll all have new tyres within three days."

"Perhaps we ought to . . . the brains behind this venture . . ."

"Poison him with polonium?"

The under-secretary rolls his eyes.

"The whole thing isn't dependent on this Lionel chap. The organisation isn't so complicated that someone else couldn't take over. And then they'd have a saint to embalm and carry at the front of their procession as one big accusatory finger pointing at us. Does that make things any better?"

"Are you saying there's nothing we can do?"

"Nothing," Leubl says, "apart from drink this excellent wine."

He takes a sip. Feeling the eyes of the under-secretary on him, he returns his gaze.

"What? What were you expecting?"

"I don't know. It seems strange. Uncomfortable."

"Because it's a feeling people are unfamiliar with these days."

"What feeling?"

"The feeling that something's going very badly wrong."

"Are you saying you think they're really—?"

"I'm saying we've got a poor hand. And we're not playing poker. We can't take three new cards. It would be useless in Skat too. We've got a poor hand and we have to live with it."

"Meaning?"

"Don't you play cards? It means that you lose, and then you pay."

"Who said we were going to play in the first place?"

"We did. Because we didn't stop when we had a much better hand."

The under-secretary rests his elbows on his knees and thoughtfully swirls the wine around his glass.

"People aren't going to like this," he says.

"Politicians can't only bring good news."

"But then they don't get re-elected."

"Maybe, but voters have to come to terms with the fact that sometimes they're living in an economic miracle, and sometimes in an oil crisis. Never in history has there been a country where things just kept getting better and better. Conversely, there hasn't been a country where the lights suddenly went out. Usually it gets darker bit by bit."

The under-secretary pours more wine.

"There are alternatives, of course. Other countries can lead the way."

"You know what I think of that."

"But we've got to do something!"

"Because we're German?"

"What's that got to do with it?"

"Because we have to have a plan for everything. There are plenty of countries who view it differently. They're saying to themselves: let's wait and see whether this really happens."

"Didn't we just—"

"We've established that we've got a shitty hand. But that doesn't mean others won't make mistakes. They might overthink, or not think enough. They might play the wrong card. New, unexpected players could come to the table. The situation is not altogether hopeless just because we can't shoot anyone."

Leubl cheerfully raises his glass. The under-secretary hesitantly follows his example.

"It's Christmas. Nothing can be done at Christmas. I'm going home to my wife and I'll give her nothing. And you're going home to Tommy with the Prince of Namibia."

The glasses clink softly. Leubl looks out of the window. It's beginning to snow. He puts his glass to his lips and once again treats his gums to this fantastic wine. When he hears the under-secretary sigh, he gives him an encouraging clap on the shoulder. "Maybe we'll get lucky and the Russians will attack us. We'll be East Germany all over again, and then we'll see how many refugees actually want to come."

# Part Two

# 37

Whenever he can, Lionel takes one of Malaika's cars. He doesn't drive far, just to the nearest hill or mountain. There aren't many of these in northern Iraq; the real mountains don't begin until the border. Lionel drives up as high as he can and gets out.

He views the column of refugees through his binoculars. It's now almost twice as long as when they set off. It's hard to believe you'd be able to tell the difference between fifty and a hundred kilometres. It helps if you've got used to fifty over the course of a year, and ultimately it boils down to whether you can see the end of it or not. Or, to put it another way: how high does the hill have to be for you to be able to see the end? In this part of the country, at any rate, they're not high enough.

He didn't think he'd feel this way, but things were some-how more relaxed before Jordan. Simpler. Nobody believed they'd make it that far. That's why the crowds didn't get any worse, even though north Africa is full of people desper-ate to get to Europe. It's competing madness. Some try to cross the desert alone, and compared to this the idea of the column doesn't seem quite so crazy, even if it wasn't as tried and tested as the good old cross-the-sea-from-north-Africa-by-boat routine. So the column was mildly attractive to those who fancied risking a little more. They could adjust to the vast numbers of people.

Roughly every four to six weeks he would tell Mojo to add another lorry. At some point the burden on Lionel stopped growing. The refugees no longer expected miracles and seemed content with what they'd got the day before. Even the most persistent whingers couldn't dispute the fact that they'd come fifteen kilometres further by the end of each day. When they reached Jordan, everything changed apart from the magic function of money.

Mojo had established the contact, and he still gets his commission, of course, because the money goes via him. Lionel learned from Mojo that Jordan isn't just full of Jordanians, but full of Palestinians too. And these Palestinians are fairly well organised, and no less keen on earning money than anyone else. If only because they've got bigger projects planned in Israel.

The Palestinians did in fact set up the same infrastructure as Mojo's contacts had previously. Even the shithouses were back; Malaika and her foundation had organised them via Mojo. This was the funniest thing about the whole business, because Malaika and the television people always acted as if the foundation's money was nice and clean, and had to be spent carefully and somehow more sparingly than other money. He kept out of it, but unlike him Malaika could have dealt with the Palestinians directly. She nonetheless kept going to Mojo, as if he were the only person in the world who knew how to find shithouse drivers. Mojo reliably took the money and sent a good three-quarters of it to Palestine, or wherever. How long did it take him to earn his 25 per cent commission? Fifteen seconds. In fact, probably more like five, because he's bound to have the Palestinians on speed dial.

Visibility is excellent. The water tankers and concrete mixers float on a sea of sun, stones and dust. Every so often an unfamiliar vehicle pushes its way through the apathetic crowd, which gives way slowly, then closes the gap again behind the car. To the people in the car it must seem as if they're driving through highly viscous oil.

Once the car has passed, the people move so uniformly that they appear to be stationary. It was a while before they got this right. It was the most difficult thing they were asked to do – moving to avoid a jam. The trick is that all those camped around a lorry have to be up and gone by the time the people from the lorry behind arrive. It's no simple feat, and if new trucks join the convoy you can't wait for the new-comers to figure this out for themselves; you have ensure that at least 10 per cent – and preferably a third – of the group are experienced walkers.

Following the track, the procession gradually fades from view and into the expanse of the plain. He can't see Malaika's cars; today she's filming much further back. But given the length of this column no-one would be surprised if they didn't see a pink zebra car for days. This does her image no harm at all; in fact it only enhances her popularity, especially with the children. His mobile rings, but Lionel doesn't answer. You don't always have to answer the phone. In fact sometimes you shouldn't, to stop yourself from going mad.

There are so many people – it's insane.

They'd barely been in Jordan for five days when Admiral Mahmoud told him about the flood of newcomers. These were people who had watched on television and on their phones the pictures broadcast around the world. All those rubber dinghies, the constant ferry traffic. A paltry fifteen kilometres across the tiny, glassy Red Sea, a crossing so harmless that even the toddlers were looking forward to it. Israel ignored them. The pink zebra cars were already waiting on the shore – these, the medical vehicles and the infant transporters were in the end the only vehicles that had to drive through Israel, and they were given free passage. Malaika had sorted it out with a Jewish-friendly magazine publisher, Astrid's ultimate boss. When people got out of the dinghies and started walking again, the trucks were already in position. Everything went smoothly, but the inflow of additional migrants was so enormous that extra trucks had to be added after only five days. Mojo could barely contain his laughter.

"Say, why d'you think it's been goin' so slickly?"

"Because we're paying you."

"You guys don't pay that well. Just remember: the military, the coastguards. You yourself know what you're shellin' out. Didn't you think it was cheap?"

"No, it's more expensive than Egypt."

"Yeah, but not much more. Even though there's no civil war in Jordan and it's a relatively solid country."

"So what does that mean?"

"Do you have any idea what's cookin' there?"

"There's no war – we're not interested in anything else."

"There's no war, but there *are* refugees. Hundreds of thousands of them."

"And?"

Mojo sighed.

"Right. We've gotta country full of refugees. Millions of refugees. You're there because you can't go nowhere else, but the bottom line is: nobody likes you. Sound familiar?"

"Look, I'm not stupid."

"An' along comes the super-refugee who's managed to bring one hundred and fifty thousand of the world's biggest losers ten thousand kilometres. A distance so great that they ain't never goin' back. Have you got it yet?"

Lionel didn't say anything. He couldn't, because his head, stomach and everything else was now churning.

"They're goin' to send you on through, keepin' you well away from their cities an' as close to their refugee camps as possible. An' the more of those refugees you take with you, the less they're gonna hold you up."

"But Mojo, how am I going to organise that?"

"Don't be like that, you'll manage. Just keep rememberin' that this is your ticket, amigo. Not only through Jordan, but through Iraq too. So stop your grizzlin' an' get some towel-heads on board."

Since then Lionel and his people *have* been getting

towelheads on board. Eighty thousand joined in Jordan alone. He even managed to negotiate a few little concessions, just in time. Extra lorries weren't a problem, and water was provided for nothing anyway. When they crossed the border and the Peshmerga took over the transport, trucks and supply business from the Palestinians, there were two hundred and thirty thousand of them in total. Almost eighty truck stations. Eighty kilometres.

They integrated the newcomers into the column and kept hold of the reins. As much as he is terrified by the magnitude of this operation, he is comforted by the fact that it's mainly Africans calling the shots. There are remarkably few arguments, because it's unequivocal that this is a black set-up. The Syrians, Tunisians, Egyptians, Lebanese, Afghans, Palestinians and Iraqis can be glad that someone's bringing them along. It's the first time Lionel or anyone has seen black people so clearly in charge of such a massive initiative. And without debate, for it's clear the others have never pulled off anything like this.

Now there are three infant transporters in the convoy. As well as the food and water, the lorries also carry a supply of donated blankets organised by Malaika's foundation. But even at night the temperatures are bearable now. It's summer, not entirely coincidentally, for MyTV calculated the best time to arrive: before the summer holidays and after the end of the football season. The T.V. executives have been popping corks to celebrate the fact that the refugees' trek is taking place in a year without the European Championship or World Cup.

They were joined by a further seventy thousand in Iraq. Lionel lowers his binoculars and looks down at the endless worm of people. The head of the procession has now passed his observation point, heading for truck 7, six more kilometres. Truck 5 would be four kilometres; he no longer has to work this out by counting on his fingers. At some point the number could reach three hundred and fifty thousand. Lionel takes a deep breath. It unsettles him still, but he's less panicky than he used to be. Three hundred and fifty thousand – sometimes it even sounds good.

Two more weeks.

Then they'll be at the Turkish border.

# 38

The under-secretary pushes his way through the crowds on Marienplatz. He could take a driver – the ministry, the government, someone would organise it and pay – but the under-secretary likes to follow Leubl's example: a politician must take every opportunity to see what's happening on the streets. And there's so much happening that the under-secretary doubts he would have made swifter progress in a car. Marienplatz is as full as during a Christmas market, as it is every Monday. It wasn't always like this.

He remembers the loonies in the past – Pegida in Munich. Demonstrating every Monday against Muslims or the call to prayer. A handful of idiots, literally: if there were six of them it was a crowd. Nowadays it's different. Police vans are lined up on the other side of Viktualienmarkt.

Edging his way through the mass of people, the under-secretary sees the huge digital screens above heads and shoulders. The organisers have hired three of them. The first shows drone footage of the procession on a loop: the legendary drone video, forty-five minutes in one take of never-ending refugees. The second, also on a loop, meticulously shows the procession day by day, like footage from a front line in war-time. In between are the most menacing images: the endless snake on the footpath in the Suez tunnel, the dinghies on the Red Sea with their provocative hint of invasion. Beside these, a count-down of the number of kilometres – the distance to the German border. Clever and effective, because at the start of the video twelve thousand plus kilometres looks reassuring, whereas at the end there are only three thousand to go. The under-secretary can count too, of course, but it's only just struck him on this Monday in Munich that the refugees have completed three-quarters of their trek.

The third screen shows the procession growing bigger: a simple graphic which stays at a constant figure of around one hundred and fifty thousand for ages, before rising steeply in a hair-raising finale and more than doubling by the end. The under-secretary gets caught up in a group of concerned citizens engaged in a lively discussion with an overweight bald man, about some mid-twentieth-century annihilation methods he has tattooed on his arms. Although these were highly effective measures, they say, you couldn't repeat them in the same way in the twenty-first century. The overweight bald man listens sympathetically to their arguments, then insists that you could. It's only temporary, after all, and once the problem is solved such measures can always be discontinued. One of the citizens says that if it's only temporary, then of course you can consider anything.

The under-secretary is stuck. He fights his way back towards Viktualienmarkt and enters the subway to cross Marienplatz. His party colleagues from city hall have on several occasions given him a lively account of how desperate the municipal government has become. Liberal Munich, a city that feels left-wing, where a red–green electorate exploits the advantages and money of conservative Bavaria, has now become as radicalised as Dresden. Every week tens of thousands of people gather here, and it's only stayed at that number because there's a second demonstration every fortnight on Odeonsplatz. The city tried to ban the protests, citing historical reasons, but the case was rejected in court. The tally of those now attending regularly hits six figures. And it's only peaceful because the enormous police presence diverts counter-demonstrations into other parts of the city.

When the under-secretary emerges on the other side of Marienplatz, he hears it again. "We want our country back!" The country has almost become used to this. All restraint has long since disappeared, which is why this other, appalling slogan has caught on. It came from the east, of course; nobody else could have given these words legitimacy. And they chant it relentlessly, which in Munich normally only happens with beer-hall ditties:

"Don't give them money and soya flour – we need a wall and firepower!"

The under-secretary is elbowed in the ribs. It's not deliberate and he doesn't react. Violence hangs in the air, and thanks to the police checks you can still assume, but only just, that nobody is armed. The crush eases slightly, he slips into a narrow stream of pedestrians walking in the opposite direction to the main flow, and allows himself to be carried past Marienhof. When he arrives at the hotel he's a quarter of an hour late. He walks up the steps to the bar. Lohm, sitting comfortably in a corner, waves to him.

"The capital of the far right," he says as the under-secretary sits down beside him. "Haven't you lot got anything under control anymore?" It still sounds like mockery, but these days not even Lohm can hide the fact he'd like the old C.S.U. back, the one that used to enjoy big majorities.

"Don't ask," the under-secretary groans. "A new study came in yesterday."

"And? As bad as the surveys?"

"Worse. They analysed our support base and it turns out that . . . we don't have one. And apparently we never have."

Lohm looks at him. "In figures?"

"Still just over 23 per cent." The under-secretary tries not to hang his head.

"Oh shit," Lohm says, turning to the waiter. "Half a litre of wheat beer, please."

The under-secretary orders a gin and tonic with the second-most-expensive gin.

The waiter brings the drinks. The under-secretary takes his first sip. Nowhere near enough gin for his liking.

"I hardly ever see you anymore," Lohm says with concern. "And whenever I do it's not worth it. You look like crap."

"Thanks a lot."

"You ought to take a week's sick leave and let Tommy spoil you." Lohm pokes the inside of his cheek rhythmically with his tongue.

"Tommy's moved out," the under-secretary says absent-mindedly.

"Really?" Lohm abruptly puts down his beer glass. "That's . . . a pity."

"It's for the best." The under-secretary knocks back his drink and waves to the waiter. With his fingers he demonstrates that he needs another gin, gin on its own – there's plenty of tonic left in the little bottle. It's getting loud outside the hotel. A new group of demonstrators has arrived, they can hear them through the soundproofed window. A squawking police loudhailer, the firepower slogan, but then another one the under-secretary has never heard before:

"Helmets on, get 'em in your sights – the German police need more rights!"

He looks at Lohm. Lohm raises his eyebrows and throws wides his arms with a shake of the head.

"Do you know that one?"

"I've heard it in Berlin and in . . . oh yes, Erfurt. I still don't know what they mean."

"They're just sucking up to the police. Something the far-left have never grasped."

"No, I mean, is it a play on words? As far as I'm concerned there are enough far-right in the police already."

"Who knows," the under-secretary says. "They're not known for sophisticated wordplay. I suspect they mean both."

"So what's the ministry of the interior doing?"

"Too little, if you ask me." The under-secretary listlessly jiggles the ice cubes around in his glass.

"Do I hear something approaching criticism of St Leubl there?"

"Just look at those arseholes outside. We can't let it go on like that. We have to defuse the situation."

"And I suppose you'd know how to do that."

"Oh yes. Ohhh yes."

"I'm listening."

"It's not witchcraft. The first thing is to erect border fences. Every kilometre of fence means one hundred fewer demonstrators."

"Interesting equation."

"One hundred and fifty if it's a good fence. Razor wire. Watchtowers. Floodlights."

"Spring-guns?"

"If you aim them outwards, let me tell you: two hundred fewer demonstrators. Per rifle."

"And Leubl's not keen? Funny that."

The under-secretary ignores the sarcasm, partly because he doesn't want to hear it. "I've given him a whole heap of suggestions, but he's not going for them. He's not rejecting them, but he's not going for them either."

"Perhaps because it's not legal."

"We have an upper limit on migrants, that's all the law you need."

"But that was wishy-washy from the outset."

"Oh no. It's only wishy-washy if you don't have the bottle. I admit, it is an elastic clause, but if you're careful to harden the elastic in it, the thing is an absolute Enabling Act. You've got to keep your nerve. O.K., the federal chancellor's office, the ministry of defence – none of them is keen to break cover, but that doesn't surprise me either."

"You're surprised at Leubl."

"Because he's not afraid, he's a man of conviction. Because he knows what the C.S.U. is really made of, not just how best to sell them. And that's why I can't work him out. If he's not going to do anything now, when will he? It's only another three hundred kilometres before they hit Turkey."

"The Turks are a different kettle of fish, don't you think?"

"Exactly. We've got just enough time to do something. If we began *now*."

The under-secretary orders another gin.

"Maybe he's still deliberating," Lohm surmises, handing the waiter his half-full glass of beer. "I need a grappa."

"One thing's for certain," the under-secretary says sombrely. "Leubl has long known what he intends to do."

"You could just ask him?"

"Our department isn't like yours. We don't have jolly discussions after which everyone talks about their feelings. The ministry of the interior is a place for real men."

"Real men running around like the Village People."

"Ha bloody ha."

"Where's the problem? Your boss knows the solution, so lean back and enjoy the journey. O.K., presumably none of the others see it like this. If I spread this around, they'll say old Leubl's gone gaga and they'll start panicking. But you still trust him, clearly."

"He's not gaga. But it doesn't make any sense. Waiting doesn't get us anywhere. Waiting just makes everything worse. There are no countermeasures that become more effective the later you implement them."

"Let's go and grab a bite to eat before I get completely plastered," Lohm suggests. "On the other hand we could just get arseholed right away. I didn't know the situation was so desperate. I thought you still had a trump or two up your sleeve."

The under-secretary stands up. "We do have one," he says, but doesn't sound confident.

"Sounds more like the seven of diamonds than the jack of clubs."

"Hmm? Is that sheepshead?"

"It's Skat, you pantomime Bavarian. So, have you got a good trump or a shitty little one?"

The under-secretary waggles his right hand, then raises it with a flourish. The waiter comes with the card machine. The under-secretary pays and picks up his coat.

"Tomorrow we'll know if it takes the trick. The day after at the latest."

"And if not?"

"Then the boss will tell me I was right and I should get cracking."

"And you'll say: you could have told me that in the first place."

"Exactly," the under-secretary agrees, and the two of them go down the steps.

*You could have told me that in the first place.*

# 39

"Refugeesrefugeesrefugeesrefugees," Astrid von Roëll types into her laptop. Then she carefully types in capital letters: "PUKE!!!" With three exclamation marks. She highlights everything and enlarges the text to 132 pt. She tries to find a particularly severe font, then changes her mind and plumps for a particularly cutsie one: first "Gigi" then "Palace Script".

What a fuck-awful job!

Admittedly she felt like this as long as six months ago, and was in a similar state quite recently too, but now the moment really has come. The moment where she's written everything, well and truly everything there is to write about refugees. O.K., everything interesting about them in connection with Nadeche Hackenbusch, but here almost everything is connected to her. Including what all these people used to do. That material was actually quite readable, because many of these refugees weren't refugees at all before. And that's not obvious to people who don't know any better. Some even had proper jobs, not just what they call "farming", which usually means they own a goat or two. No, proper jobs. One repaired cars, another was a teacher, and one woman even had a really exciting job, running a boutique for shoes and T-shirts and stuff.

Astrid stares reproachfully at her keyboard. She raises her hands like a concert pianist and then slams them down and hammers away at it angrily. "Lalalalalala," she says out loud. "Shitshitshit."

Career stories get tiresome too after a while. You can describe a person's life, but the lives of one hundred people? Give it a rest! Especially when you consider that real life goes on for the reader. Real life goes on for the reader *especially*, and for all normal people who aren't stuck in this strange refugee world. Maybe after a while everything begins to seem normal here, but it's not! You mustn't let yourself get carried away. Most of humanity owns more than one pair of shoes. As well as a second and – God forbid! – a third T-shirt. Just because the people here aren't so fortunate, just because lots of people spend the night wrapped in gold foil, it doesn't mean it's the same everywhere else. Thank God!

That fucking gold foil gets on her tits too.

No sooner do you step outside the camper than you hear this rustling everywhere. Someone once told her that there's no more beautiful view on earth than the sky above the desert, but that someone certainly never gazed at the sky surrounded by rustling enamelled larvae. Who cough. And snore.

A starry sky.

That's another thing: a starry sky.

Nobody here even bothers looking at it. Quite right too. Once you've seen one, you've seen them all. And even the most persistent environmental bore would have to concede that you don't have this problem with a neon sign.

She wonders whether there are neon signs in Silopi.

She googled and found out that when they get to Turkey, the nearest place of any size is called Silopi. With one hundred thousand inhabitants you could call it a town. She'll pay Silopi a visit. She gave Cairo a miss; she didn't want to risk being separated from the column. In Jordan and Iraq they were led through the bleakest of areas and only ever past refugee camps. But when they're in Turkey they're practically in a proper country. She's been twice on holiday, once to Antalya and once for a long weekend in Istanbul. They've even got trams there. Strange, how as a western European you automatically add the word "even" – "even trams" – but Turkey, well, Turkey and Germany are both members of something, not the E.U., the other one, the U.N. She'll leave Kay alone for the day, take the car and drive to this Silopi place. One hundred thousand inhabitants, surely they do the odd bit of shopping. There'll be bars and shops and boutiques and restaurants, and she'll shop like there's no tomorrow. Whammy bammy wowie zowie!

My God, how she misses all that. And the worst is that you can't cross off the days, because nobody knows how much longer it's going to take. Probably less than six months, possibly quite a lot less than that, but it's still too vague to start counting. Sometimes she dreams that the German government will simply say, "That's enough, come in the lot of you, we'll work it out somehow." Why not? At least the whole thing would be over with. And she'd stroll nonchalantly into the editorial office as if nothing had happened, and Sibylle is the first to throw her arms around her, then Sonja. A bit like when those young mothers come into the office and show everyone their identical babies, but far more heartfelt, of course. And far more interesting, because she really will have something to talk about. Then the deputy blockhead comes in. "Oh, what's this gathering all about?" And probably Sibylle would say, "Just look who's here!" And then the deputy blockhead, deeply moved, says, "Frau von Roëll! I don't say things like this often, but I'm delighted to see you back safe and sound. You've rendered such invaluable service for this firm." And he really *doesn't* say these sorts of things often, in fact she's only heard him like this once before, when the great Birgit Schetzing-Frank, who was anything but great, left the magazine. But then she, Astrid, says:

"Herr deputy blockhead, all I've done is what any woman would have done in my position."

Or maybe just a plain "Thank you, thanks . . . please, have a glass of Sekt."

The deputy blockhead then says, "Sekt? No, no, for an occasion like this the company will splash out – champagne!" And everyone cheers and Sonja says, "Tell us all about it." Not out of politeness, like when someone comes back from a tedious holiday to the Maldives, no, everyone is genuinely eager to hear what she has to say. They gather around her like the Lost Boys around Wendy, and she takes a sip of champagne and starts off with just a short tale, a tale which seems quite ordinary to her, but everyone's gobsmacked, and only then does she realise that Lou Grant has been standing in the doorway the whole time, getting more and more annoyed. Exactly. And because he wants to appear polite he can't leave – what a shame, oh, what a shame! – he has to stay there watching everyone gush with admiration, and he grinds his teeth with fury, because all this time nobody has paid him the slightest attention. She can picture the grinding, chips from his teeth dropping out from the corners of his mouth, but she can't worry about this because at that very moment the publisher walks in. "Hello" and "Frau von Roëll" and "Please call me Hartmut" and "We must sit down for a chat, I've got great plans for you." When he hears the words "great plans" Lou Grant shrivels, because Hartmut has no plans for him, apart from redundancy, ha! And that's why, regrettably, he doesn't hear her tell Hartmut, "That really is incredibly kind of you . . ." Hartmut: "No, it's kind of *you*, I insist!" Her: "No, of you, but . . . I'm moving to New York at the end of the year, a new job with *Vogue*: Creative Premium Executive Director at Large." And everyone cheers, and Sonja and Sibylle squeal – how delighted they are for her! Because they imagine that at some point in the foreseeable future they too will be working in New York – but they definitely won't be with *Vogue*.

That's for sure!

Then again, she might show some magnanimity and briefly wander over to Lou Grant, to show him that you don't always have to behave like an arse, and maybe she'll tells him that in a funny way she'll miss him too. She'll give him the sweetest of smiles and offer to meet up for a coffee if he's ever lucky enough to secure a job in New York.

Ha!

Until then, however, she's got to fabricate more of this stuff. As if it were easy. It might be for those who just churn out garbage, but she has a reputation to lose. Astrid von Roëll will not submit garbage, and that's the problem. Even if you were to tot up the total amount of quality journalism in the whole world, it wouldn't amount to the volume they're asking of her. And she's tried everything, absolutely everything – she learned how to do this job, after all. She realised pretty quickly that there was a lack of personnel here, not just assistants for her, but people doing things. Celebs.

"If you don't have any celebs, make some!"

These were the words of her old editor-in-chief, and before long there was a celebrity butcher, a celebrity baker and a celebrity hairdresser. The T.V. formula: someone becomes famous because they've spent enough time on screen. But what happens if you try that here? These people don't have jobs or anything – they're just poor. With Nadeche she comes across a load of these characters, and they all make an effort, but to tell the truth she hasn't yet met a single one she'd see a second time. Even the models from the first shooting have got nowhere. On the contrary, at least two of them – she won't swear her life on it, mind – are virtually tarts now. Not that she's judgmental, but anyone who hooks up with lorry drivers has no place in *Evangeline*.

International sports stars would be good.

The only one left is that pal of Lionel's, the admiral, but he's good for a photograph at most. He's definitely not worth an entire story, though during Advent, Astrid wrote an article on him out of sheer necessity. The sad soul behind the funny face – what a load of crap. The saddest thing that happened to him was that business with the little dog, and even then she almost had to put every word in his mouth so her piece had a hint of spice.

"You must have had a dog when you were a child, did you?"

"What?"

"A dog. I mean, it doesn't have to have been yours. A neighbour's sweet little dog?"

"A neighbour's dog?"

"Bow-wow. Dog. Was there one? Not now, when you were younger. There were dogs when you were small, weren't there?"

"Dogs? Sure, there are dogs everywhere."

"There you go. Lots of dogs. So there must have been one dog that died, yes? The poor dog. And you were very sad."

"I don't know. I'm not too bothered about dogs. Dogs run around, dogs die . . ."

The blockhead! How is she supposed to produce quality journalism with an idiot like that? And he's the most interesting of them all, although of course no-one believed her.

Not even the deputy blockhead: "Frau von Roëll, you're exaggerating. You have more than one hundred thousand people there. There must be something you can find to excite *Evangeline* readers!"

"What do you imagine it's like here? For God's sake, these people get up in the morning, walk for bloody miles, then lie down again at night. And the same the next day. And the next day. And the day after that. It's like a factory where everyone just wanders around. The only thing that changes is the weather. They even eat the same thing every day."

Astrid checks the time. She needs an idea in the next twenty minutes, half an hour at most. Preferably an idea that could be spun out for a video tomorrow too. It used to be easier; she always came up with something to do with Nadeche, but that was when they spent more time together. Nadeche doesn't seem at all pissed off by this whole thing. Then again, she knows she's going to get a nice fat book contract out of it.

The last time Nadeche really made time for her as a friend was over a week ago. She can't remember what they talked about. Probably Nicolai von Kraken and all the stuff he's coming out with. That business is still going on, but she's already spent the week mining everything from their conversation. This shitty blog really sucks you dry. She can't write anything about Keel sniffing glue – she promised not to – and nobody wants the refugee fashion project. The editorial team doesn't reject it out of hand, of course, they act interested, but they know their readers. No-one wants to look like a refugee, least of all the refugees themselves. As soon as they get to Germany they're bound to buy themselves something decent to wear.

Astrid closes her eyes and tries to remember everything Nadeche Hackenbusch has ever told her. She concentrates, she pictures Nadeche sitting in the pink car, her desert sunglasses pushed up. She's drumming something on the steering wheel, her other hand fiddles with her hair . . .

Then it comes to her.

## 40

She's never seen Lionel so irate. Never – she'd remember if she had. Lionel very rarely gets angry. Sure, it must be exhausting for him, but still. There's so much he seems unsatisfied with. For the first few months he gave the impression of being happy enough with her and the pink zebra pick-up. And that may have been the case – it was definitely an improvement on the camp. Besides, Lionel's still got a job with the T.V. company. He gets a salary for his work on "Angel in Adversity". She helped out a bit too, but he's been directing the entire operation, and eventually it became clear that they couldn't fob him off with the paltry sum they offered at the beginning. They still don't pay him that much, even though she told them to splash out. Five thousand euros a month – what a joke! It's tax free though, at least for the time being.

It's not that Nadeche can't understand Lionel's fury. He was expecting something bigger when that Echler guy came. He'd been after an appointment for weeks, without saying why. They told him just to turn up, but he insisted the meeting had to be in private. Strictly confidential. No cameras. So they had to agree on a meeting place. Echler suggested somewhere, but Lionel immediately panicked: "They'll kidnap you, they'll take you away and never let you go."

At first she thought he was crazy to live in such permanent fear: "We're talking about Germany here, and not Nazi Germany: it's the Federal Republic!" But no matter who she talks to, no-one thinks it's an absurd idea, and she no longer finds it so odd herself. So they reconnoitred the meeting point themselves, then notified Echler at the last minute before driving out to meet him.

A half-dilapidated hut in the middle of a dusty nowhere. Why on earth someone would build a hut here was as difficult to fathom as why they didn't build it properly. None of them build German houses. It's just about O.K. when someone's living in these shacks, but the moment they stand empty they crumble like a dried-up cake. They sat in the shade of the only intact wall. Nadeche insisted on laying out a blanket, to make it a bit cosier and more official. They sat down and waited.

"They're going to come and take you all to Germany, you'll see."

"Germany's good, but not *that* good," Lionel says.

"What else do you think they want?"

"We'll soon see."

A cloud of dust appeared on the horizon. Lionel got to his feet and went to the car. He put the key in the ignition and started the engine, so they could drive off at once if necessary. But it was just one vehicle, a battered white Toyota pick-up. Through the binoculars they couldn't make out anyone on the cargo bed, just two people inside the car. It stopped a fair distance away and one man got out. He said something to the driver before shutting the door. The pick-up then drove off again slowly. The man was wearing a polo shirt, beige cargo pants and hiking boots. Unless he'd hidden it very well, he wasn't carrying a weapon. He put on his sunglasses and started walking towards them. He waved.

Lionel switched off the engine but left the key in. He walked around the car and waved back, then stood beside Nadeche and waited. The man took off his sunglasses and offered his strong hand first to Nadeche.

"Hello, and thanks for coming. My name's Echler."

They sat in the shade and offered Echler water, but he took his own bottle from a trouser pocket.

"Are you like, from the government?" Nadeche was far too curious to formulate her question with greater subtlety.

"For obvious reasons I can't tell you who's sent me here," Echler said politely. "But I come with a considerable level of authority. And on the basis of this authority—"

"What does . . . authority mean?" Lionel said.

"Right, O.K. It means there are rather a lot of things I'm able to discuss with you . . . do you understand? Good, and once you've seen what I'm allowed to discuss with you, you'll realise there aren't so many people who could have sent me."

"The German government has sent you?"

At this point Echler held out his hands apologetically. His expression remained so unmoved that any change had to be imaginary.

"O.K., so what do you want to talk about?" Lionel said.

"You like getting straight down to business – you'll go far in Germany."

The conversation was going well. Nadeche beamed and said, "I taught him that."

"What do you want to talk about?"

"Well, first up let me offer you my congratulations. What you're doing is an astonishing achievement, really astonishing. It's impressive, I don't mind saying."

"You weren't expecting this, were you?" Nadeche teased him.

"You work for television, you know yourself just how unique this whole thing is. Not just in terms of a programme, but as an achievement. But we also view it with a certain degree of concern."

Lionel laughed at this point, not a pretend laugh but a real one, so the mood must still have been good.

"You're concerned? You don't need to be concerned. We're making good progress."

"Yes, but now a completely different game is about to begin."

"That's right. It will be simpler."

Here Echler assumed an emphatically anxious expression and leaned forwards. "I admit that none of us have much experience of an undertaking like yours. Nor do I dispute that you've been making use of your opportunities creatively. None of us would have thought that you'd make it to Jordan, or that you'd get further in Iraq than in Syria. And yet all of this was relatively simple. Egypt, Jordan and Iraq are chaotic countries where money always gets you places."

"Money always gets you places."

"But now you're entering the civilised world. You're

entering Turkey, and countries that have a proper structure. You won't be able to bribe your way past the Turkish president. These are crisis areas, heavily patrolled. There are lots of soldiers, not just a single guard in whose hand you can stuff a wad of notes. They've got tanks."

"Then we'll give them two wads of notes," Lionel said calmly. "We know where we're going. We know what we're doing. We're always living in fear. Turkey doesn't make us more fearful. It's just a different fear."

"Less fear, actually," she said to emphasise and reinforce his point. "If you knew how frightened people are of those dinghies, you'd realise that this is nothing by comparison."

"We didn't see any of that on the Red Sea," Echler remarked.

"Fifteen kilometres across a sea that's as calm as a swimming pool," Nadeche said. "We were able to control the entire process from start to finish. And the people we were paying were well aware that if a single refugee drowned, no others would get in the boats and the deal would be like, over. They kept such careful watch over the operation, it was like a ferry service run by the vehicle inspectorate. Getting everyone under the Suez Canal was far trickier."

"Still, Turkey is a different ball game altogether. And you know it."

"Is that why you're here? To tell us that we'll be in Turkey soon?"

Echler leaned back again. "Perhaps I'm not expressing myself very well. Ultimately you're the ones who can best assess your situation. You know where your strengths lie.

All I can do is presume that the situation is difficult or might become so. And I'd like to assure you – both of you! – that you're not alone. There are authorities ready to offer you a helping hand if you so wish. That there are . . . alternatives."

Echler looked at the two of them and when neither said a word he must have thought he hadn't been clear enough. "I want both of you to know," he said more slowly, "that you have alternatives."

This wasn't especially clear either; in essence it was same as what he'd just said. And while Nadeche was wondering whether she was just too inexperienced to tell the difference, or whether there was some trick behind it, Lionel said, "So what does that mean?"

"You're going to bring everyone to Germany?"

"Frau Hackenbusch," Echler said, somewhat irritated now, as if she'd asked a really stupid question, "how could that work? We can't possibly bring two hundred thousand—"

"Three hundred thousand."

"O.K., three hundred thousand people to Germany. I mean, it's not even legal. How do you think that could work?"

"So what did you mean?"

Nadeche's voice may have been slightly shrill because Echler immediately made pacifying hand gestures at her. "Let's discuss this calmly. You don't have to go along with it, of course. And let me say in all honesty that it's not just charity I'm offering here, because that also requires a certain degree of cooperation, I'm not going to pretend otherwise. I just want to tell you what the people who sent me here have been thinking."

"And what's that?"

"As I said, from our perspective it looks as though you're heading for a dead end here. Unfortunately. You know it and you can't prevent it. But these people can also see the enthusiasm with which you personally have made your way to Europe, to Germany. We're following very closely your preparations for our country, such as learning the language. You're showing initiative, decisiveness, ingenuity and persistence. These, as Frau Hackenbusch will surely confirm, are qualities we need in Germany. I don't wish to resort to clichés, but if there are such things as German qualities, then they would be precisely the ones you're demonstrating on a daily basis. What you're doing here is, in truth, nothing other than making an incredibly passionate case for Germany. In recognition of this potential – and of course in view of the human consequences – it's possible that we will be more accommodating towards you than you might have been expecting." Echler paused, then added. "Within an appropriate time frame, obviously."

"So are you going to like, bring these people to Germany or not?" Nadeche said.

"I don't understand you. What are you saying?" Lionel said.

"It's difficult because none of what I'm offering you here is official. If someone asks me, then I know nothing. If the press gets wind of any of this, the deal's off the table."

"What deal?" Lionel said.

"Yes, what deal?" Nadeche said.

"I can – under certain conditions – make it possible for you, Herr Lionel, to come to Germany."

"Come?"

"Permanently. You'd be naturalised. Under certain conditions."

"How? When? Immediately?"

"Please don't pin me down on this, but we're certainly not talking about weeks or months. By the end of next week. No bureaucracy. Frau Hackenbusch can tell you, I'm sure, what a special opportunity it is to live in a civilised country like Germany."

"What about the others?"

Echler sighed ruefully. "As I said, nobody can bring three hundred thousand people to Germany. But in this instance, in view of the particular grit you've shown and because you haven't managed this all alone, in this instance we assure you that our offer also extends to . . . thirty of your colleagues."

"Which thirty?"

"You can choose. They'll have to pass a security check, of course, but that will be it. You can bring thirty colleagues of your choice to Germany."

This wasn't the point at which Lionel went ballistic. On the contrary, what really impressed Nadeche at that moment was his composure.

"Can you write that down for me? On a piece of paper?"

"Only if you agree. As I said, only a couple of people know I'm here. If you reject my offer, it'll be as if our meeting had never taken place. But if you agree I'll bring you confirmation within twenty-four hours."

"From whom?"

"From the very top. I can't name names, but it will be a

guarantee that puts your mind at rest too. You'll be picked up by German helicopters and flown away. Let me reassure you: we understand your situation, we understand that you need guarantees. And you will get those guarantees."

"If we cooperate?"

"Yes, but within reason. We're not going to make huge demands of you."

"What, then?"

"Nothing outlandish. We're assuming that Frau Hackenbusch will be accompanying you to Germany, so there'll no longer be any need for the camera teams to stay here. This would actually be an essential condition too, but it's no great shakes. I don't know how you call this in the media, but we consider the story closed. We've come to the end."

"Why?"

"Because they want to like, terminate the project," Nadeche said.

"Oh no, no, no, you've got it all wrong. This might be the case from your perspective, but the people I work for are still counting on this thing failing, irrespective of what you decide here. No, so far as I've understood, this is all about vested interests. Your potential has been recognised and they don't want this potential – I'll put it bluntly – to go to waste in some suicidal enterprise."

"So what interest is there in his . . . potential?" Nadeche said.

"This isn't just about naturalising you as a German citizen. It's about wanting to employ you because of your special, proven abilities. Basically, this is a job offer. You speak a number of languages, you're a great organiser, you, Herr Lionel, are definitely a leader, 100 per cent. The way I see it, this here isn't an act of clemency. You've been headhunted, so to speak. They want you for German Refugee Aid. As the chief executive."

"Chief executive?" Lionel said.

"Yes, so far as I understand."

What Lionel did then was something Nadeche would never have managed. Lionel smiled, turned to Echler without any discernible sarcasm and said with a broad smile, "One hundred colleagues."

"What?"

"I need one hundred colleagues."

He saw Echler squirm, heard him say how difficult it all was, before going to fifty, to seventy, as if you could bid for people's lives like at an auction, it was unbelievable, it was intolerable, and Lionel kept bargaining the whole time to rip the mask from the face of this unscrupulous country, this unscrupulous people trafficker, to expose them in all their wretchedness, laying bare their own dishonesty. What a pity no camera was on hand to capture the scene! She was so full of admiration for Lionel, for the elegance and calmness of his performance. There was no way she could have managed it, it was stressful enough having to watch him quiver with rage. Then she brought the farce to an end.

Nadeche leaped up and told Echler that this was out of the question. That Lionel wasn't the person Echler was portraying him as and that, unlike Echler, Lionel was a decent man, a man with a heart, a conscience, who would never, under any circumstances, abandon those people who had placed their trust in him. She wouldn't either, she and her cameras were staying with these people for as long as it took to get them to Germany. He should take his cheap little attempts at bribery elsewhere, because that's exactly what this was, a cheap little attempt at bribery. He was trying to corrupt thirty or one hundred people with a German passport, his filthy loose change and some crappy chief executive post.

Of course she saw the look in Lionel's eyes. She'd completely ruined his moment. He'd wanted to play it cool, he'd wanted to elegantly walk away from this sleazy guy and all his stupid offers, like great politicians do. He'd probably wanted to casually bargain Echler up to one thousand colleagues, and then send him packing with a smile so that this man from Germany felt his own meanness in his bones, so that the lesson made an impression on his dull, mediocre brain. But sometimes there's no time or scope for education. And by now they'd made their point perfectly clear. All the same, Lionel was mightily pissed off when Echler went away with his tail between his legs. For a brief second it even looked as if Lionel were weeping with anger, and he actually sent her away because he was ashamed. But those are the very tears for which she loves him.

But the strangest thing of all was that if she didn't know him better, she could almost have believed that Lionel was furious with *her*.

# 41

Try as he might, Leubl can't place this man's face. Leubl has unbuttoned his suit jacket, the man is about to attach his mic, then Leubl will fasten his jacket again, concealing the wire that runs to the battery. Leubl will place the battery where it least bothers him. Like the inside pocket of his jacket.

"You can put the battery where it least bothers you," the man says. "Like the inside pocket of your jacket."

Leubl scrutinises the man as the tiny microphone is clipped to his lapel. It's just good manners as far as Leubl's concerned. It's a fact that if you travel a lot and appear often in the media you can't remember everybody you meet, but Leubl tries his best. He doesn't want the microphone man merely to be a microphone man. And this doesn't just go for microphone men; when he's been to a hotel he'll still have a good idea of what the chambermaid looked like a couple of days later, as well as the waitress who requested his room number at breakfast and asked whether he'd like tea or coffee. He doesn't just know the journalists, he has a sharp memory for the different photographers too, even those who work on smaller regional newspapers. But it simply doesn't work with television staff.

The microphone man says something Leubl's heard a hundred times before and forgets again immediately. Today heralds the beginning of his goodbyes, of that there is no doubt. And he won't miss the T.V. studios.

How long has he been in politics? Fifty-one years? Fifty-three? It depends on where you start counting. The only thing that's certain is that he was motivated by sheer disgust to begin with, rather than an active interest in politics. He had an aversion to the thing that called itself the student movement, and which kept sucking up people who weren't students at all. His friends, apprentices, artisans, members of the chess club (obviously), even some from the football club! Leubl still gets angry thinking about it. He feels as if the '68ers stole his youth.

He remembers his disbelief at the success of this fad. Because – and this needs spelling out clearly – it was nothing but a bloody fad. But the '68ers' secret was to act as if they were far more than this, as if they had an entitlement that was far more important than just a desire to do things differently from their parents. Leubl takes a deep breath.

"Is something wrong?" the man without qualities says.

When Leubl makes a few practice movements the microphone cable doesn't tauten or bother him. He glances at the man, they agree that the work is done and they part company. Leubl wouldn't be able to give an adequate description of him later. He returns to his dressing room and waits for his cue.

A few magazines lie around on the table. Including *Evangeline*. There's a small article about Uschi Glas.

Uschi Glas. One of the few who didn't lose their head back then, even though the pressure was great. People can't imagine this today. Nowadays everyone pretends these were just harmless people who stuck tulips in soldiers' rifles. And what could be wrong with that? Aren't flowers the best things that can come out of the barrel of a rifle?

But these weren't dreamers or idealists, at least most of them weren't. They were just irritating windbags who spotted their chance. Oh, the self-righteousness with which they disparaged most people as bourgeois and extolled themselves as shining revolutionaries! And the dictatorial attitudes. They replaced the mustiness of the crusty academics in their gowns with their own mustiness: the endless discussion, the frightful hair and the dreadful rhetoric where you had to be careful to avoid mentioning certain things, and instead say "relations of production" as often as possible, or "critical" or "counter-revolutionary". And the only reason this stale worship of Marxist texts worked was because they'd discovered the pill and the cheap revolutionaries had secured the most desirable girls. Which was why any bright lad jumped on the bandwagon sooner or later. And then the less desirable girls. And the not so bright boys. It was all so transparent, but nobody minded. Apart from him. He had no desire to spout phrases about the proletariat and the equal cooperation of all forces of production just so he could be with Elisabeth Förtsch, and join her in idolising Rudi Dutschke.

And so he joined the C.S.U.

So that was that as far as Elisabeth was concerned. And for what? Three years later she was pregnant like every other country girl, the difference being that her revolutionary father wouldn't pay a penny for his child. She accepted this, even thought of it as emancipation.

Leubl picks up the magazine and leafs though it absent-mindedly. A veritable journey through time. Not everyone ages as elegantly as Senta Berger. And here's Uschi Glas again, who's transformed herself into a mother of the nation.

There's a knock at the door. A young assistant peers in and says, "Are you ready, Herr Leubl?" Leubl gets up and follows her.

"You know the routine?" she says.

He nods. "I've been on Klobinger twice already." But he knows the explanation is going to follow.

"Sure, but just to be on the safe side and because we've got a new production manager. I'd like you just to sit down for me so we can get the lighting right. I'm not gonna to lie, we could use someone else for this, but like I said we've got a new production manager and he doesn't believe in lighting doubles."

"The whole world is full of questions of belief," Leubl says patiently. He gives the assistant another glance: she's got brown hair. He could have sworn it was black or dark-red earlier.

She takes Leubl into the studio and over to his chair. On the way he shakes hands with all the cameramen, lighting assistants and runners, partly to be friendly, but also out of habit. These people are voters too, after all. Robert Klobinger isn't there yet. Leubl sits down, swivels in his chair, sinks into it. There was a time when he used to be nervous, but then he gave his first interviews when there were only three channels, and each television appearance got as many viewers as an international football match. Today he knows that most mistakes are forgotten, despite YouTube. Klobinger arrives on set, they shake hands and a brief announcement comes over the studio loudspeaker. Leubl gets up and goes off set, where he stands between two walls of compressed wood like a customer in a joinery. An assistant goes up to the table in front of Klobinger, puts a hand to his earphone, raises the other hand and counts down with his fingers: five, four, three, two, one. The last finger points at Klobinger and with a sleek movement the assistant vanishes like a magician in a stage show.

Klobinger greets the audience. A short introductory film shows Nadeche Hackenbusch and that idiotic but ingenious Lionel, their march with the hundreds of thousands, at once simple and colourful, like Xenophon's March of the Ten Thousand, Mao's Long March, Gandhi's Salt March, Mussolini's March on Rome and hundreds of other marches throughout history. Nothing needs reinventing, Leubl thinks. Basically everything's always the same.

The film shows the severity of the early days, their passage through the desert, beneath the Suez Canal. The presentation is gratifyingly sober; on R.T.L. they would have probably coated these images – powerful enough in themselves – with some bittersweet music. Then come the mass demonstrations which grow larger week by week, the election results, the survey findings. The film shows the general feeling of unease and those that feed off it.

When the film ends, Klobinger introduces today's studio guest and Leubl strides over to his seat. He strides well; over the years he must have walked an entire Camino de Santiago for all the news features he's done. Leubl in the corridors of parliament, Leubl on his way down the stairs. Don't look into the lens, keep relaxed, walk past the camera. It's always the same.

". . . Federal Minister of the Interior, Joseph Leubl, C.S.U. Delighted to have you on the programme. You've seen the film and on several occasions you've highlighted the obstacles awaiting this procession of people. How surprised are you that the refugees have made it this far?"

Leubl shakes his head. "Not particularly. What is surprising is that nobody came up with this idea before. I mean, it was only a matter of time. The truth is, you can only lose your life once. If these people are prepared to put their lives on the line for a perilous sea crossing, then why not undertake a perilous march instead?"

Klobinger looks at him in amazement. Leubl savours the moment. He's spent long enough reciting the usual formulas into a microphone. He knows what's going to happen. The weakness he's showing is too enticing, and now Klobinger's going to have to ignore his pre-prepared list of questions. Leubl sees Klobinger absentmindedly twiddle the card in his hands. Then, as if he had written it down for him in advance, Klobinger obediently asks:

"Why isn't Germany better prepared? Have you failed?"

"I think you know as well as I do where the responsibility for this lies. The voters didn't want to see any more refugees, so we politicians built them a privacy screen. We closed the borders in Africa and dammed up the flow of refugees. Everyone knows what happens when you construct a dam without allowing for any outlet – the dam overflows or bursts."

"I don't know whether flooding is the right analogy here—"

"Take it as you wish."

"—but to stick to your metaphor, perhaps your dams aren't good enough."

"You may complain, but people were perfectly aware of what we were doing. We signed agreements with Morocco, Egypt, Turkey and Tunisia – and these are the most stable of the lot. You wouldn't buy a second-hand car in any of these countries, nor would I, and nor would the voters out there. And if you concentrate millions of people who might not have sufficient money to pay people smugglers today, but enough for the 2015 prices, then all in all there's enough money for them to go where they like on foot if they're clever about it."

"But the agreements—"

"You can stop ten refugees, fifty, one hundred, but not a quarter of a million of them, particularly not if you've got T.V. cameras marching alongside. And if these people can persuade you that they don't intend to stay in your country, then what happens is exactly what we've seen: rather than stopping the refugees, the military guides them through. At most the army will check to see no-one gets up to anything they shouldn't."

Klobinger is visibly reeling. He puts his pile of cards down, because the next question is his own.

"Are you saying that these people are going to continue with their trek?"

"Yes, of course."

"And who's going to stop them?"

"I don't know," Leubl says. "Maybe I.S.I.S. could have done."

"Are you being serious?"

"You, like anyone else, can look at the map. They've got to Turkey. Are the Turks going to stop them? Not with force."

"How do you know that?"

"Because I've spoken to my Turkish colleagues."

"But don't the Turks have to—"

"Let me tell you what's going to happen. The refugees will arrive at the Turkish border. And then they'll keep going. Very slowly. They'll press against the border fence or whatever it is in their path. Put yourself in the shoes of a Turkish border guard. You've got a choice: either you commit a mass slaughter of defenceless people before the eyes of the world on prime-time television, or you watch these people crush themselves to death against your fence."

"Did you come up with that?"

"No, I'm just relaying what that Lionel fellow has told his Turkish contacts."

"That they'll march to their deaths?"

"No, that they'll risk their lives just as they have before. But far more efficiently than in the rubber dinghy lottery."

"What about the Turks?"

"So what do we think the Turks will do? If the refugees follow through with this, the Turks will open their gates. Why should the Turks slaughter people on our behalf?"

"Because ... because maybe they'll hold on to the refugees?"

"You know as well as I do that Turkey isn't exactly a dream destination. These people want to come *here*. And now guess what Lionel said he'd do at the next border? He doesn't need to come up with a new idea every time. One will do."

"Are you telling me you think they'll make it all the way to the external border of the European Union?"

"No."

"But who's going to stop them?"

"You've misunderstood me, Herr Klobinger," Leubl says calmly. "They're not coming to the external border of the European Union, they're coming to Germany."

"But what about the Hungarians, the Austrians ... ?"

"We've had enough experience of the solidarity of our eastern partners. I'm not counting on their help. They'll let the refugees through just like they did last time."

"Yes, but ... but that means you'll have to be prepared to ... to defend the German border by force of arms."

Leubl takes a deep breath. He's seldom been as relaxed as now. He leans forwards, but only slightly; he doesn't want to overemphasise his response. "Against the refugees? No."

Klobinger was counting on a longer answer. An evasive answer. A different answer. Leubl can tell this because first Klobinger grabs his pile of questions in confusion, then puts them down again.

"Have I understood you clearly?"

"I think so."

"You wouldn't give an order to that effect?"

"I *won't*."

"Has this . . . erm . . . has this been agreed with the federal government?"

"I've agreed it with myself."

"Er . . . I'm, er . . . so that falls within your remit. As . . . as minister of the interior."

"That's correct."

"So then – and do forgive me for putting it like this – but then that probably spells the end of your tenure as minister of the interior."

"Possibly. The government is welcome to look for someone else who has a different take on the situation. But I doubt they'll find anyone prepared to break their oath of office."

"What do you mean 'break'? The oath of office demands the protection of our borders."

"The oath of office demands we promote the welfare of the people and protect them from harm."

"Isn't that the same thing?"

"Only if you consider refugees to be harmful."

Momentarily Klobinger looks as though he'd like to call for a commercial break.

"Do you view it differently?"

"Viewed objectively, refugees are a sure indication that the quality of life is better here than say in Russia."

"Allow me to recap. The federal minister of the interior is saying on German television that he's refusing to prevent hundreds of thousands of illegal border crossings? Because in his opinion such a large number of refugees is a seal of approval for Germany?"

"If you're going to recap, please do it correctly. I'm refusing because thousands of dead refugees would constitute the greater harm," Leubl says, before adding, "For the time being." Klobinger is obliged to follow this up.

"For the time being?"

Leubl leans back, and there is a composure and calmness to his voice. "Take the analogy of the lifeboat. When it's full, letting anyone else in will endanger the lives of those in the boat. And so they have to shoot to save lives. But everyone knows what the lifeboats on the Titanic looked like: they were half-empty. Anyone shooting now would be a murderer."

"Are you now telling me that the boat is half-empty?"

"It's getting emptier as we speak. Because this is no ordinary boat, this boat isn't made of wood, it's made of an economy that functions incredibly smoothly. And the more people there are working in this economic system, the more room there is inside the boat. So if you do it properly, this boat grows while you're sitting in it."

"Are you saying, then, that we should take in refugees so we can take in even more refugees?"

Leubl nods.

"And when will that become fewer again?" Klobinger asks smugly before taking a sip of water.

"It won't."

Klobinger chokes; Leubl passes him a handkerchief.

"But this will allow us to salvage some of our prosperity," he says.

"But from a purely technical point of view," Klobinger says, coughing and thumping his chest, "from a purely technical point of view, this prosperity can also be salvaged by comfortably sailing around in a half-empty boat, can it not?"

Leubl shakes his head.

"Because sitting in the half-empty boat you've got people who've killed other people just to ensure they're nice and comfy. They're murderers and their killings will catch up with them. First they'll try to play down the murders. Then they'll try to excuse them. But that won't work because everyone can see that the boat is half-empty. And so they'll try to silence their critics. Do you understand?"

"Is this inevitable?"

"Absolutely. When bodies were floating in the Mediterranean in 2013, already then we were guilty of failing to help. But who would admit to that? People who'd never set eyes on a refugee in their lives began to paint themselves as victims. This initial lurch to the right was our reaction to corpses that were still two thousand kilometres away. What kind of lurch to the right would you expect if mass murder takes place outside our front door?"

Klobinger ponders this. "Is this a warning about the end of democracy?"

"No: the end of prosperity. Many believe you don't need democracy in order to have prosperity. But the truth is: smartphones, Coca-Cola, the Internet, Porsche – whether or not you can develop these products decides whether you're a

Champions League country or a Division Two nation. Ideas like these don't originate in Russia, Turkey or China, which is why refugees come to us rather than them."

"The Nazis came up with some very advanced inventions," Klobinger needles him, "like the V2, for example."

"War is the father of all things, not the Nazis." Leubl retorts. "But you're right: a society of murderers needs enemies to keep the pace going. And this is why I won't let the refugees be shot at."

Klobinger pauses, then says, "So what will you do?"

"We'll do what we ought to have done years ago. We'll prepare ourselves and the German people for their arrival."

"For their arrival? Or for their staying here?"

"Especially for their staying."

"And how do you intend to prepare the German people?"

"We'll tell them what's coming: several hundred thousand people. The majority of these people will stay. More will come, and—"

"But—"

"—more will come and because we know and accept this we'll be able to anticipate and process it in an orderly way. In the future we'll have to train these people in their home countries. Those that apply themselves the most will be brought to Germany sooner. We'll construct training centres, both in Africa and in eastern Germany, so that Helmut Kohl's 'blooming landscapes' become a reality. We'll spend billions, and by that I mean more like fifty than five. Every year. This will ensure that the people who come to our country are fit for purpose. And those critics in Germany who voice the loudest complaints – we'll grab them by the scruff of the neck and see just how willing they are to pull their finger out for their country—"

"Excuse me—"

"—and I'll enjoy watching those whingers refuse a decently paid job just so they can keep on being Nazis."

Leubl slaps his palm on the table and sinks back into his chair. Not in exhaustion, but more like a boxer waiting for his opponent to respond after landing some heavy blows.

"Excuse me," Klobinger says. "Herr Leubl, has any of this been agreed with the government?"

"No," Leubl says soberly.

"But then . . . then all I see here is a minister venting his spleen. What you're saying may be understandable and humane, but on a practical level it's not going to change anything."

"You're mistaken," Leubl says slowly. "Some things in life are not about justice, the law or authority, but about reality. Look, there's nobody jumping at the task. Nobody wants to shoot defenceless people. I'm the one shouldering the responsibility here. You won't hear anyone in the chancellery saying, 'Leubl's wrong, *we'll* open fire instead of him.' If anyone has a different solution to the problem, I'll be out of office an hour after this programme's finished. But tomorrow morning you'll see I'll still be in my job. There is, however, some good news too."

"Which is?" Klobinger sounds floored.

"First, there's an excellent chance that we'll be able to maintain our level of prosperity in the future. Second, we'll have better-trained immigrants than any other country in the world. For we'll be able to train them according to our needs. The deal is: we offer them protection and an income, and they help us out in return. Third, with a little luck, other affluent nations will be able to copy our model."

Klobinger says nothing; Leubl smiles at him. "Have some water." Klobinger obeys, flabbergasted. Then he says, "And this from a C.S.U. man . . ." Leubl shrugs. He picks up the carafe of water and refills Klobinger's glass.

"You know, in the C.S.U. you sometimes have to adopt ruthless standpoints so people don't go running off to Nazi parties. Because it's the C.S.U.'s job to dilute Nazi thinking with conservative positions in a way that's compatible with democracy. But at some point I realised that the opposite was happening: our Christian core was being swamped by Nazi sauce."

"Well, er . . . that's a nice note to finish on," Klobinger says to the camera in dismay. "Thank you so much for joining us tonight. Next time we have . . . er . . . er."

Leubl picks up the cards and helpfully hands them to Klobinger, who hurriedly scans the last one until he finds what he's looking for: ". . . yes, er . . ."

Klobinger falters, then says with a croaky laugh, "No, I'm sorry, I really don't think that's going to happen now."

# 42

That shitgibbon!

Sensenbrink is sitting in his chair, one fist clenched. He doesn't know what to do with this fist. He could slam it down on the armrest, but that wouldn't be enough. The table won't do it either. So he keeps it raised and clenches it even tighter, like a hedgehog when it's been prodded.

"Now he thinks of it. *Now!*"

Beate Karstleiter assumes a contrite expression. It is deathly quiet around the table. Sensenbrink is shaking his head, pale with rage. His other hand shoves a large pile of papers in disgust, then grabs them and sends them sailing across the room with a scream of anger.

"It's totally fucked!"

"Hold on a sec," Karstleiter says cautiously. "Maybe we won't have to bin everything quite yet—"

"Oh, really?" Sensenbrink sneers. "The minister of the interior has just given the entire nation spoilers about how our show's going to end. On primetime telly."

"*Probably* going to end." Karstleiter makes a flappy

gesture with her hands, something between appeasement and deference. "Probably. *Maybe*."

"Maybe? Right, here's a simple question. Do you think A.R.D. is going to shove another edition of 'Focus' before 'Tatort' on Sunday night? Tell you what, let's do a little poll here so we can include the others too. Hands up those who think that in a fortnight's time, we'll get to watch 'Tatort' at the normal time on Sunday!"

Sensenbrink doesn't wait for the result. He doesn't say it, but everyone knows what he means. The broadcaster has pretty much freed up the whole schedule for him that day. The Grand Prix has been booted off and they've given him the evening slot, 8.15 p.m., when they usually put on a Hollywood blockbuster. To transmit the showdown. Hundreds of thousands of migrants marching live to the Turkish border, with nobody knowing how the guards are going to react. The most appealing refugees at the front, women and children, with no certainty they'll survive the evening. It'll be the most exciting news broadcast since the fall of the Berlin Wall, with one of Germany's most beautiful women as its star. A dozen teams of drones, pictures from every angle, a hundred refugees wired up to cameras and transmitters, images from right next to the fence, even if shots are fired.

"Just picture it," Sensenbrink said to the small gathering of top executives. "The Turks shoot, we check the images in the production control room and you get it all: the flinching, the fear, the panic. These brave people can't go away and don't want to, we see it, we hear the original sound, then camera 52 wobbles, the director notices and immediately switches, but camera 52 goes down, two more shots and there's slight movement to begin with. And then" – Sensenbrink paused briefly – "then ... *nada*. And we see an unchanging picture from ground level. A little crooked, a final movement ... then ... it remains static."

Nobody stirred. Fifteen or twenty seconds of silence before Kärrner said, half in jest, "Maybe it just fell over."

To which Sensenbrink calmly replied, "Yes, maybe."

At that moment he had Sunday in the bag. Five hours of live broadcasting. And open-ended, too.

Now they're going to have his balls for breakfast. What are we going to broadcast on Sunday now, Herr Sensenbrink? The same people as ever, but this time with cameras in their buttonholes? May we remind you that "refugeecam" was introduced after the first three months? People even cracked jokes about it, remember? You can go now, Herr Sensenbrink. Thanks for nothing.

"Maybe they won't do it . . ." Reliable Anke offers.

"*What*??"

"Well, perhaps they'll have a rethink . . ."

"Without telling us?" Sensenbrink waves his hand in resignation. "No, one thing's for certain: if the Turks were going to be kind enough to act as a buffer for us, someone would have given us the heads-up already."

"But the others don't want to ruin their story either," Karstleiter says. "If the Turks helped us, the A.f.D. and all those who feed off panic would try to play it down. I mean, the social networks absolutely thrive on panic."

"But then the government would say so. And the Turks

would hold a press conference on the inviolability of their borders, national sovereignty, state monopoly on violence, blah blah blah . . ."

"All the same, you never know what the Turks will come up with. It may be that negotiations are going on," Olav says serenely.

"It's politics, and in politics everything is still a question of price," Karstleiter agrees.

"O.K., smart-arses. It's cost Germany three billion just to get them to keep an occasional eye on their coastline. How much do you think we'd have shell out to have them open fire on defenceless people on live, primetime television? Calculators out – if it's south of fifty million then I'll pay it out of the advertising revenue."

"Fifty billion?" someone suggests.

"Don't bother trying to figure it out," Sensenbrink barks. "They wouldn't do it for all the money in the world."

"Come on, let's all try to be level-headed about this," Karstleiter says, playing matron. "What has changed? The Turks won't open fire. Fine. But listening to all of this, it doesn't sound like they would ever have opened fire anyway. So in the end nothing has changed."

"Our pain point isn't that the film would have changed," Sensenbrink sighs. "Our pain point is that the old fool has told everyone how it's going to end."

"And it's true the other channels have the better story," Reliable Anke says. "The grassroots of the C.S.U. are in uproar, everyone's debating whether Leubl's right, the far right are gaining supporters by the million—"

"That spontaneous demo in Berlin straight after the pro-gramme – the police counted one hundred thousand people. In the middle of the night!"

"If the police say it was a hundred thousand, you can be sure it was double that."

"And again this evening!"

"A.R.D. and Z.D.F. are covering all of this. And what are we doing? Scratching our arses. We might as well forget the 'refugees prepare for the border' routine. Two weeks of pre-liminary reporting down the pan."

"How about we opt for the wedding?" Karstleiter says.

This is Karstleiter's one drawback, Sensenbrink thinks. She's not a writer. At least he can rely on Olav to put her right here. Or Reliable Anke, because Olav is glancing at his mobile and is about to leave the room with an "I've got to take this" gesture.

"Didn't we say we were going to be off-grid?" Sensenbrink says poisonously.

"Yes," Olav says, almost out of the door, "but only if it's not important." Sensenbrink throws a pen across the room in resignation.

"Well, what about the wedding?" Karstleiter persists. "That would be a great story, wouldn't it?"

"We could do the wedding, but only if Herr Sensenbrink expressly wishes it," Reliable Anke says. "To be honest we wouldn't recommend it. On the contrary."

"Who's 'we'?"

"Well, the writers."

"Why not? A wedding would be fantastic!"

"But only if the rest of the story is right," Reliable Anke says. She sighs because she's having to explain something that everyone in the room already knows, with the exception of Karstleiter and perhaps the Hayat girl: "'Nadeche and Lionel marry after their happy arrival' – what a lovely story. 'Nadeche and Lionel marry because they don't know if they'll still be alive tomorrow' – an even lovelier story."

"Like Hitler and Eva Braun," Sensenbrink adds generously.

"But 'Nadeche and Lionel marry because there's nothing else going on'," Reliable Anke says, her hands mimicking a small explosion, "that'll go phut. It'll be like those people who feel they have to renew their vows to save their marriage."

"O.K., O.K., it was just a suggestion."

"Quite apart from the fact that our lovely lady isn't even divorced yet," Sensenbrink says. "By the way, is that in the pipeline now? Has von Kraken agreed? Who's seeing to this?"

A hand in the second row goes up and an older woman says, "We're onto it. Together with *Evangeline*. It's probably just a question of money."

"Meaning?"

"Meaning that Nicolai von Kraken wants money from Nadeche. He seems like a most unpleasant type, really sleazy—"

"What do you mean 'sleazy'?" Sensenbrink says, irritated. "Does he deserve the money or not?"

"It's a matter of perspective . . ."

Sensenbrink's jaw stiffens.

". . . but from a purely legal standpoint, probably."

"But not morally, or what?"

"Well, there are complications there."

"Like what?"

"It's not as if Nadeche is short of money," Karstleiter says.

"Short of money? No. But from what I hear the problem is that there have been a lot of divorces among Frau Hackenbusch's circle of friends. And Frau Hackenbusch clearly hasn't yet heard of one where the wife pays money to the husband."

"Because usually it's the guy who's got the money," one of the goatherds says. Sensenbrink gives a nod of agreement in his direction. "Exactly. But where would he get his money from? She only needs to take a look at what the so-called producer has produced in the last few years. It falls into two categories: flop and hot air."

"Yes, but I bet Frau Hackenbusch still thinks a case in which the woman ends up paying can only be the result of adultery. Which means she'll insist it goes to court and we can forget a quick divorce altogether."

"No," Sensenbrink says. "If push comes to shove we'll pay off the jizztrumpet ourselves. She doesn't give a shit about justice so long as she doesn't have to fork out. We'll sort it. Then they can get married the day after tomorrow. But it's true the wedding will be crap if it goes ahead just for the sake of it. Shower me with some more ideas."

"We could complain to the government and urge them to do something . . ." Hayat suggests.

"Yes, of course. 'Dear constitutional court, please save my television programme,'" Sensenbrink scoffs.

"We could show the other side," Karstleiter suggests.

"What do you mean?"

"Well, after every episode of 'A2' we could have a quarter of an hour on Pegida."

"Like that weird postscript to 'Germany's Next Top-model'? The programme after the programme?

"That sort of thing."

"Right, and then we could have the programme after the programme after the programme, where the chief of police voices his concerns and then the caretaker's brother-in-law . . . no, that's too cheap. We're doing a show about angels and heroes, not Nazis."

"They're not all Nazis . . ."

Although the spontaneous laughter that erupts in the room doesn't get them any further, at least it relieves the tension. Karstleiter is just trying to get people to shut up again when the door opens and Olav comes in.

"Look who's back!" Sensenbrink says, with more than a hint of reproach. The criticism merely bounces off Olav, though not on account of his usual complacency. Olav is tense to the core. He bends to Sensenbrink and Karstleiter, after which Karstleiter says pretty quickly, "O.K., let's take a break and reconvene at five. Until then I'd like all of you to try and come up with a contingency plan."

There is frowning all around and chairs are shifted. Everyone goes back to their office, and only Reliable Anke hears Olav say to Sensenbrink as she goes out:

"If that's really true, they won't schedule 'Tatort' for later on Sunday. They'll drop it altogether."

# 43

She should put the joint in the deep freeze. Definitely, in fact: there's far too much meat for just her, even if Binny has some too.

If Joseph doesn't come home tonight the joint will be too much. So she'll have to freeze it.

It's fine.

It's quite simple, actually.

She stands up.

She sits down.

She doesn't know anyone who enjoys roast meat as much as he does. All kinds of meat. Even pickled pot roast, but only when she makes it. "I've had far too many disappointments in restaurants," he always says. "Most places can do a fried schnitzel, but a roast, I mean a decent roast, even a really good roast . . . oh my. And the dumplings."

He loves her dumplings. But if he's not coming home, it's certainly not worth the effort to make the dough. It doesn't keep for ever, does it? So now she doesn't have to boil any potatoes.

She gets up.

Oh yes, *no* potatoes.

She sits down.

It's nothing new. He called her just before the event and said he'd have to stay in Berlin for the weekend.

"Have you got another woman on the go?" she asked, and he said, "Chance would be a fine thing!" They both laughed. Like everyone else she's well aware of what's been happening since his appearance on Klobinger's show. That was something really new, a completely different dimension from the usual media scandal, the ranting newspapers. Three hundred thousand people in Dresden, one hundred and fifty thousand in Dortmund.

"Leubl's wiping out the Germans."

"Eastern Germany isn't your refugee dump!"

"Our hatred! Our marches! You can wipe those refugees' arses!"

People panic-buying, even where they live.

Talking of which: she really ought to go out before the shops close. She stands up.

She sits.

Maybe the government could have calmed the situation by disclaiming what Leubl had said. He could have tendered his resignation and someone else could have looked after it. Then he'd be getting his roast tomorrow. His roast veal. The government didn't disown what he had said, however. But nor did they get behind him and say, The man's right. We'll sort out fifty billion for that. It would have taken some wind out of the protesters sails. But not even his own party had risked putting their head above the parapet.

The parliamentary party leader: "These matters are up for discussion."

The secretary general: "Herr Leubl is a man of experience, but fifty billion euros – that figure's just been plucked straight out of the air."

The chancellery: "We haven't received any such information from Turkey. It's conceivable that this represents individual opinion."

Since the programme he has been on duty 24/7. He's visited locations for his plans. Arranged emergency accommodation, as if the refugees were already there. And to anyone doubting him, he's said, "A minister of the interior who unilaterally talks crap is out of a job the following day. So you don't need to believe me, you just have to look to see whether I'm still minister of the interior." And indeed, as each day passed, he was still minister of the interior.

"Is this by any chance the minister of the interior wagging the federal government's tail?" Klobinger said in a teleconference. Joseph remained loyal, but Klobinger was right. What Joseph was doing ought to have been the chancellor's job.

What should she cook if Joseph isn't here tomorrow? She can discuss it with Binny, who'll be here soon. She'll let Binny choose and she'll cook it. And the day afterwards, and the day after that too. For one thing is certain: Joseph won't be back tomorrow or the day after that.

She'll cope; he's often been away for several days at time.

He always says you should look at things objectively, and yet the only objective difference is that in the past he's always been able to say precisely how long he was going to be away.

He always said what lay ahead for both of them, and when he would be where. And he always called her in the evenings. Even when telephoning used to be a tricky business, or in the Eastern Bloc when their calls would be tapped. But not this time.

She stands up and goes to the sink. She turns on the tap and watches the water gush down the plughole. She holds her hand in the jet of water; it's cold. She tries to remember whether she wanted hot or cold water, until it dawns on her that she doesn't need any water at all. No dumplings, no potatoes, no water. How silly of her. She shakes her head and turns the tap off. Then she goes and sits down on the sofa.

What is she going to cook now?

She'll think of something when she gets to the supermarket. It's incredibly well organised; she often gets ideas when she's there. The last few days haven't been so nice, though. The looks she's been getting by the fruit, people staring at her over the racks. She's even been screamed at a few times. People have been friendly too, of course; some neighbours came to help her immediately when that madman tipped over her trolley. In the car park in broad daylight!

"Your husband better not show his face here again, the foreigner faggot!"

What nonsense. What's a foreigner faggot, anyway?"

Maybe she shouldn't go to the supermarket. She gets up and walks over to the remote control, which is lying on the tiled floor. The back has come off and the batteries have fallen out. She can only find one and puts it back in. The other one must have rolled under the sofa. She puts the remote control on the coffee table. She hopes it still works. She thinks about trying it, but then looks at the television and leaves the remote where it is.

She sits down.

Her solution for the joint is a good one, the deep freeze is a good solution. You never know quite what to do, and then you just put the problem into cold storage. People should freeze much more. Why isn't there a gadget that lets you freeze everything? Freezing isn't always the solution, obviously. It wouldn't help with the television, even she can see that.

She doesn't understand much about television sets, but a television needs a screen, of course and a box that isn't broken. These are things that Joseph deals with; he loves electrical shops, but Joseph isn't here. He's not here now, he won't be here tomorrow, nor the day after that, so he can't go to the electrical shop. But she can get by without a television. There's seldom anything good on T.V., and often it's appalling.

Do they really have to show everything?

Like those people shouting Joseph down. With no sense of propriety. That hatred, those faces. The police officers could barely keep the podium clear for him. And it was impossible to understand a single word, all you could hear was that crowd baying, shouting so loudly. Screaming that they didn't want any of this; they wanted things to stay as they were. It didn't occur to them for a second that in that completely neglected area they have an unemployment rate which beggars belief. Then the eggs were thrown. When they chucked eggs at Helmut Kohl, in fact when anyone chucked eggs anywhere, Joseph would say with a shrug, "The egg is the classic means by which the proletariat expresses its opinion." This time too, no doubt.

In spite of this he tried talking to them. Then the bodyguards started putting up the stupid umbrellas again. Still the eggs came.

And then the tomatoes.

A few eggs and a tomato salad, she thought, something light and summery – that's actually O.K.

Bright red on his white shirt, overripe, an intense red, he cracks another joke then staggers – as he always does when she bumps into him by mistake – as if the tomatoes weighed a tonne. She loves how he always tries to defuse tension with humour. But then she noticed he wasn't making his funny face. He was opening and closing his mouth, like someone saying the word "roast". Or rather two words: "roast veal".

Then the right-hand side of his face exploded.

She didn't want to see it, but the remote control had already crashed to the floor and broken, and what can you do when the man you've been happily married to for forty-nine years explodes on television and you can't find the button on the sodding television set and the images keep coming, the tomatoes, "roast veal", the head.

The tomatoes, "roast veal", the head.

Objectively.

Objectively.

He said he wouldn't be there that weekend. It happens regularly, it's quite normal. He won't be there at the weekend. She gets up.

She sits down.

The tomatoes.

Roast veal.

He won't be there.

Joseph.

# 44

Nothing is different. It's the same city, the same building, the same room, even the same people. Gödeke, Kaspers, Kalb – they're all here, and this time they all look exhausted, not just Echler. It's 7.00 a.m. Einsteiger, the new under-secretary, summoned them at short notice yesterday evening; the first they heard of the meeting was at 11.00 p.m. The man who used to be under-secretary and who's been minister of the interior for not even ten hours appointed Einsteiger himself shortly before 11.00 p.m. He hasn't slept either. Since he was sworn in he's spent the whole time studying aerial photographs and comparing maps. He called some old friends in the army. He took a shower, put on a fresh shirt and grabbed something from the fridge without thinking – for the first time in ages – how full the fridge used to be when Tommy lived at the flat.

Tommy.

That seems like years ago.

The new minister of the interior hangs up his coat with the others and goes over to the drinks table. Yes, he was the last to arrive, but he's only five minutes late. Still, there's barely any coffee left in the thermos. He picks up the telephone and orders more, then goes with his half-empty cup to his chair.

"I do apologise – this isn't the greatest start, I know," he says, "but I had yet another telephone call. I imagine all of you here have had plenty of calls. Talking of which."

He switches off his smartphone. Gondorff follows his example.

The minister of the interior briefly stares at the middle of the conference table. Then he sits up and takes a deep breath.

"There are no words to describe a situation like this. But as grim as it is, for the time being we're going to have to let others do the grieving. Herr Leubl's death doesn't alter the fact that time is slipping away from us. On the contrary, it merely intensifies the pressure."

The minister of the interior looks at each person around the table. The faces are virtually expressionless, they reveal neither criticism nor agreement. They can anticipate what's coming, but they can't believe he's actually going to say it. He doesn't know what their reaction will be. He suspects, however, that there will be general agreement; government authorities are usually fairly conservative.

"It's no secret that I wasn't entirely in agreement with Dr Leubl's strategy. But nor do I wish to criticise it here and now. First, because he's no longer around to defend himself. And second, because I never doubted for one moment that if anyone could pull that off in Germany, if anyone could have successfully convinced the Germans – me included – that the concept of an 'integration industry' was viable, then that person was Joseph Leubl."

Nods of agreement around the table.

"I have to say, however, that this also means I no longer share this belief. In fact, I'm now convinced that such a path is fraught with risk and, without the highly respected and unifying figure of Dr Leubl, would certainly lead this country to disaster."

"Finally, someone's said it," Dr Berthold mutters smugly.

The minister of the interior briefly considers whether to let this comment pass. But Kalb beats him to it: "Oh, please."

"I'm just telling it how it is."

"Be that as it may," says the minister of the interior, taking charge again, "I am not Joseph Leubl. But I am now the minister of the interior. And it is my belief that Germany cannot cope with a level of immigration – and this includes asylum seekers – that would exceed the upper limit. Likewise, any imposed immigration or asylum is unacceptable to the German people and they will not stand for it. It is our job, therefore, to put a check on this flow of people with all the means at our disposal. The legal situation is clear, and it affords us all manner of options."

"Except the army," Dr Berthold says drily.

"That's not at all clear," Kaspers says.

"What do you mean? Look it up! The constitution allows for a state of emergency to be declared only in the event of an armed attack. And from what I've seen on T.V., not one of them's even got a musket."

"What about sticks? Penknives?" Gödeke suggests.

"So you launch an armed attack on Germany with walking sticks and penknives? Have fun in court," Berthold scoffs.

"All you need is a judge with a bit of imagination," Gödeke says with a shrug. "We wangled all sorts of stuff in Hamburg."

"Thank you, gentlemen," the minister of the interior says. "I fully support ideas along these lines. The refugees are creative, so we have to be too, even though I suspect they won't do us the favour of storming the border brandishing sticks. If indeed they get that far."

"There is every possibility," Gondorff insists. "The scenario painted by Dr Leubl is most credible."

"But it will become ever more credible if we signal in advance that we intend to do nothing to stop it," the minister of the interior says. "As far as the solidarity of our European partners is concerned," he says, eliciting snorts from around the table, "we mustn't be under any illusions. But this doesn't mean that everything is lost. We have two key allies. First, the unequivocal legal situation: Dublin is still in force. And second, the fear of other countries of being stuck with the refugees when they get there. Bulgaria, Serbia, Hungary – take your pick – they're all terrified, and we need to exploit this fear. The same is true of Turkey by the way, especially Turkey. So I don't see it as a given that these refugees will be able to simply walk across the borders, not at all."

"What are you thinking, then?" Kalb asks.

"I'm thinking that the tighter we make our borders, the tighter other countries will make theirs. If we close them convincingly, the Austrians will follow suit, as will others further down the line. It's like dominoes, but in reverse. They pull each other up rather than knock each other down."

"It's a bluff, though, ultimately," Kalb says. It's not clear whether he means this as a question or statement, but now there's silence around the table.

"I'm not bluffing," the minister says coldly. "And anyone who's half-hearted about this can apply for a transfer now. Which is why I'll happily take up Herr Kalb's point. The danger is that other countries doubt our determination. So our measures must leave absolutely no room for any doubt. Not merely as far as the refugees are concerned, but also the Austrians and whoever else. Are we agreed?"

Nobody says a word. The minister turns to Echler and says, "Could we have a brief résumé of the situation, please?" He leans back and grabs his cup. The coffee isn't very strong, but it's certainly cold.

"O.K.," Echler says. "We've got six more days, seven at most, before the refugees reach the Turkish border."

"What's going to happen from there?"

"I can't tell you exactly, but the structure of the refugee column allows us to make some assumptions with a fair degree of certainty." He switches on a projector and beams a graphic onto the wall. "The marching speed cannot be changed at will, but if the column moves fifteen kilometres per day, this means fifteen trucks will arrive at the border every day. Each truck supplies three thousand people, which gives us a total of forty-five thousand per day. The problem is: if the people at the front stop, if they set up camp, this destroys the structure of the column. Because on day one you've got a chaotic camp of forty-five thousand people, ninety thousand on day two and so on. It's unmanageable."

"The military can do it."

"Yes, but these aren't soldiers and they don't have any generals either. The trucks just make it look more organised than it actually is."

"O.K.," the minister says. "Their goal cannot be to amass three hundred thousand people in one place."

"Not if their heads are even half screwed on, no. It wouldn't be possible to supply or direct them any longer. They won't risk it. So they'll wait until there's a critical mass – I don't know, twenty, thirty thousand of them – and then they'll march on the border."

"What about the Turks? How accurate are Leubl's assumptions?"

"Hard to say," Echler says. "I mean, Herr Leubl knew what he was talking about."

"Having said that, his information was very much in line with his political convictions," the minister says. "So I'm asking you again, how reliable are his assumptions?"

"Well, what militates against them is that our relations with Turkey aren't exactly at their best, so the Turks are less predictable. It's possible that there will be considerations in our favour we're not actually aware of yet. But they might take a leaf out of Jordan's book."

"Why Jordan . . . oh, shit!" Kalb exclaims.

"Exactly. Jordan managed to offload around eighty thousand of their own refugees as the procession passed through. Iraq almost the same number. And Turkey, of course, has refugees to dispense with too. More than enough. So it would be an option for them to follow suit."

"Which is why our declaration must be absolutely

clear. The Turks have to understand that they won't be getting rid of a hundred thousand refugees, they'll be saddled with another three hundred thousand. To put it bluntly, we need a wall. It doesn't have to be pretty or environmentally friendly, it just needs to be tall and solid. I don't care whether it looks like Berlin or Israel afterwards. And another thing: I don't want any innovation. We're going to use technology that already works elsewhere. We're talking about a wall that nobody can climb over or steamroller – it must be able to withstand a mass stampede. One hundred kilometres in each direction at least."

"But where? We've got around four thousand kilometres of border."

"Do I have to work everything out for you?" the minister asks. "We don't really have to worry about the French or the Danes. I'm talking about all the borders along their route—"

"What about the Poles?"

The minister hesitates. It sounds like a stupid question at first, but it's possible, of course. Poland and the Czech Republic make up a good third of Germany's border. And anyone who's already walked ten thousand kilometres isn't going to be bothered by a minor detour.

"Maybe we don't have be quite as thorough as you suggest." Kaspers says, raising his hand. "Fifteen kilometres a day isn't that quick. Besides, we know what their plan is. They're not looking for the easiest way in. They want to get to our border and do their victim thing there. So we can wait to see which route they take and only then reinforce whichever border as we see fit."

The minister nods. "All the same, we do have to send the Turks a signal as quickly as possible. So let's take one of the potential borders and show them what we intend to do if the refugees proceed according to plan."

"The federal police will prepare and train for scenarios along the border with immediate effect," Gödeke assures him. "Including the use of firearms. And with the press in situ. The media will get special treatment. And even though the army can't lend us its soldiers, it might be able to help out with some heavy machinery? Heavy weaponry too? Who'll look into this?"

"I'll deal with it," Dr Berthold volunteers.

"Thanks," the minister says. "In the meantime I'll see to it that the necessary finances are in place."

"All that remains is plan B," Kaspers says, leaning forwards.

"What plan B?" the minister says.

"Actually, it's plan A. What Herr Leubl was getting off the ground. Given the current state of affairs, it has to be our plan B in case—"

"No plan B," the minister says. "That has to be kiboshed at once. It has to be clear to everyone that we don't have a plan B. It has to be clear to the Austrians that the refugees will put us in a catastrophic situation. That we cannot afford to open our borders."

"You want press coverage of this too?"

"Full on," the minister says. "The more, the merrier."

# Major concern for Nadeche Hackenbusch

**Experts fear that the star presenter is on the verge of collapse at the most difficult time of her life. The bitter truth is that while she's helping thousands, her ex-husband is leaving her in the lurch**

By Astrid von Roëll

It can be likened to the most impossible task ever faced by a woman in a fairy tale: spinning gold out of straw. But this time it seems the unbelievable can be achieved; it looks as if the German presenter, superstar Nadeche Hackenbusch, will pull off the miracle. Albeit a miracle with the sad aftertaste of a weeping eye: this straw isn't straw and the gold is silver, spilling down in a curl from the sky like a small trickle of twisted time.

Nadeche Hackenbusch, who in May was crowned Woman of the Year by the renowned media group PRINTERNET (which includes *Grandezza*, EVAN-GELINE and *Hengst*), gazes thoughtfully at this trickle that fizzes from her scalp like foam on the (dark) beer of her end-lessly long, dark-brown mane. "My first grey hair," she says, winding the strand carefully around her slim index finger. She says it lightly, but can it be as easy to accept as her unmis-takeably confident eyes wish us to believe? For this woman, especially?

It is now well over a year since Nadeche Hackenbusch decided to take on probably the great-est challenge of all time. And even though it is often said that love heals all wounds, these few undeniably silver hairs tell a dif-ferent story. They tell of a pain that Nadeche Hackenbusch would never wish to show.

In all this time it has only been possi-ble for her sons Keel and Bonno **Behind this Moses lies an unhappy marriage**

437

to visit their mother twice (reported exclusively in EVANGELINE). And Nadeche Hackenbusch makes no secret of the fact that it's better this way. "This is no place for children," says the woman whose Nadeche Hackenbusch Foundation for the Humans, with its three infant transporters now famous around the globe, makes it possible for young women to enjoy the blessing of motherhood. But each day of this march, which has stirred the hearts of the world, is also robbing Keel and Bonno of the one person a youngster should really be able to count on in life. It's depriving them of the closeness, the warm and tender caresses that no telephone calls or e-mails can substitute for. Particularly harsh is the fact that the woman who is helping so many others is being left in the lurch at a time when she has the least opportunity to fight back.

Of course Nadeche Hackenbusch will not say a bad word about Nicolai von Kraken. Keel's alcopop scandal, Bonno's transgender plans – it would never occur to this woman to lay the blame for her children's crises on the poor parenting skills of Nicolai von Kraken.

But she is also weary of defending her ungrateful ex-partner time and again. She was even generously accepting of his bizarre affair with Internet sensation Schminki Pengster, twenty-three years his junior, which met with all-round disbelief, disgust and hostility. But worried friends are noticing that she falls silent when conversation turns to her family, a family who for so long now have had to forgo Nadeche's much-needed help. When the adoptive father of her own children makes more absurd financial demands by the day via an armada of unscrupulous star lawyers. Not to mention the custody issue. "Of course," Nadeche Hackenbusch says indulgently, "Keel and Bonno are in good hands for the time being. But there's no denying that in the long-term women make better mothers."

These burdens continue to intensify, while day by day the greatest rescue operation ever led by a woman shows no sign of abating. The fact that they are approaching Turkey can only be small consolation. "Sure, I'll be delighted if we make it there," the successful presenter says with confidence.

"They have streetlamps, it's a completely different kind of country. You can see this in places like Antalya. They've got trams there."

But it is this very proximity to their goal that lends this hopeful march its inexorable drama. While hundreds of thousands of people, thanks to the sacrificial devotion of Nadeche Hackenbusch, are on the threshold of a happier life, her few really close friends able to peek behind the scenes are asking: How much longer can this woman cope with the relentless strain? How long can the portentous love of young Lionel relieve the inhuman pain inflicted by this unusual life?

"Modern women such as Nadeche Hackenbusch are particularly at risk," Professor Gabriel Schaffhausen warns. All this time the assistant professor of cosmetic psychology has been observing the unsettling course of events from his position at the renowned Heribert Sinsheimer Institute in Munich. "These women constantly achieve and expect more from themselves than most men, even top executives," the expert says. "The symptoms can be complex and bewildering, but the isolated appearance of grey hair is not untypical and could be a warning signal. That is distressing in itself. If the strain goes on for longer, there's the danger of burnout." Or something even worse? "It cannot be ruled out," the 77-year-old says, deeply concerned.

But Nadeche Hackenbusch doesn't have time to react to risks like this. Thousands have their hopes tied up in her, especially thousands of women.

## How much longer can this woman cope with the relentless strain?

She is both role model and pilot at a disorienting time of high emotion. And these people are happy that they can rely on a woman like Nadeche Hackenbusch. This story is a story of a modern, female Moses. But this Moses is looking back on more than a long march through the desert. Behind this Moses lies an unhappy marriage which has failed because the love died.

# 45

The minister of the interior feels uncomfortable. It's not the first time he's worn a bullet-proof vest, but even during his spell in the army he always felt awkward in one.

"Where's your bloody vest?" the corporal would scream at him. "What do you think's going to happen to you if you don't wear a vest?"

"Nothing," was his standard answer, "so long as I shoot first."

The corporal: "Are you alright?"

He feels a nudge in his ribs. "I asked if you were alright." Beside him is Cilic, the minder and liaison officer the Turks have assigned him. The minister gives a start. He nods and adjusts his vest. They're in the monitoring centre at the Habur border crossing point. A medium-sized room of the sort you only find in this part of the world: a concrete box chilled to ice-age temperatures, four walls painted in an indeterminate colour, slight cracks in the plaster, tiled floor and all the monitors somehow bare, despite the mass of technological equipment, as if the building were about to be torn down. Hanging on the wall is a solitary portrait of Atatürk, still, it seems.

Men sit at tables and screens, someone pops in occasionally, but not often, as if reality outside could upset the images on the monitors. Three screens show the security cameras at the border crossing, two others show the C.N.N. pictures and – no doubt as a concession to their German guest – those from MyTV. One monitor is in reserve, and the two remaining ones are relaying the slightly shaky footage from the helicopters. Some of these are clearly violating prohibited airspace on the other side of the border – they're a good way into Iraq. The pictures do not fill the minister with confidence.

Six thousand transporters are processed here every day. But on this day hundreds, maybe thousands of lorries are backed up along the road to the border. The Iraqis have closed it to trucks as well as private cars. They're keeping the way free for the refugee column, which is marching past the queueing lorries. An endless train of people, with the occasional small gap, but endless nonetheless. The lorry drivers wave, some hoot their horns angrily because the refugees are preventing them from crossing the border. The cameras capture the water tankers far in the distance. They have stayed at the back, presumably so the refugees can make a more impressive display of their numbers later on. The minister sighs and glances at the ugly digital clock on the wall.

Four in the afternoon. Back home it's an hour earlier. Lunch is over, families are bored, young people are bored. Everyone's so bored that even the Grand Prix is worth watching. But not today. Today everyone's watching this mass of people conquering the most important stage of their infinitely long journey. And everybody wants to see if Leubl was right. As far as Iraq is concerned it seems he was. The minister shrugs.

"But that was to be expected." Cilic must have read his thoughts.

"Of course," the minister says, irritated. He wishes he were less transparent. And then he feels cross straightaway, because his anger must be audible. And silly. Did anyone seriously think the Iraqis would hold them up? How childish, the minister thinks, like when he was younger on his way to school and hoped until the very last corner that the building had burned down. But assistance from Iraq had been conceivable at least. Until now.

The lorry drivers are out of their trucks, making tea, eating, chatting. The behaviour of car drivers is more ominous. Many are turning around and driving back the way they've come, as if the border will not be passable in the foreseeable future. Several days, probably the exact time needed to allow a few hundred thousand refugees to walk across it.

"What's in it for them?" Cilic says, taking up the thread of the minister's thoughts. The minister closes his eyes so nobody can see him rolling them. He'd like nothing better than to go outside and have a cigarette. But he doesn't smoke.

"Can I bring you a tea?"

"That would be very kind."

Cilic makes a sign and somebody leaves the room. On the screens they now see the first refugees leaving Iraq and entering that strange no-man's-land between two border crossings, which has never belonged to either side. They don't appear to be in any hurry. They could take a short cut by going cross-country, the option's there, but instead they follow the road with its sharp bend. It is almost as if they're determined to stick to the official route. Taking the more westerly of the two roads, they approach the Turkish border as per the regulations. Their lorries are still out of sight; perhaps the concern is that all that steel looks too powerful, too aggressive, not vulnerable enough. As if this advancing column weren't aggressive in itself. Coercion, the minister thinks. Ultimately this is coercion pure and simple. He wonders whether Turkish law currently recognises something like coercion.

Or something like law.

He looks at the map on the wall, comparing it again with Google Maps which has a zoom function. In the next few minutes they'll probably cross the Habur, which forms the border with Iraq here. They're walking more slowly now, using the bridge to make the human column denser. Women, children. Nadeche Hackenbusch is clearly visible on the screens, the beaming Joan of Arc of commercial television. She's holding the hand of a little girl, and even the minister can see she's cute.

The minister peers outside, through the Venetian blinds that keep the room dark. "Let me tell you what I think," Cilic says. "If I were in your position I'd have bombed the bridge. Or blown it up." He takes one of the glasses of hot tea from the copper tray a young boy has just brought in, and hands it to the minister.

"Thank you. The Federal Republic of Germany doesn't just blow up other countries' bridges."

"In the past you weren't so . . . finckty? Finckity?"

"Finickity. In the past we weren't the Federal Republic."

The tea boy is definitely not with the army, so how come he can just walk in here? He could have been bringing in half a kilo of T.N.T. Why bother with the bulletproof vest?

"Sorry, I didn't intend to be impolite," Cilic says, "but without that bridge they wouldn't find it so easy. In matters like this I'm a military man through and through. This isn't an invitation, of course. I mean, the bridge belongs to us."

"If it reassures the soldier in you, we would have considered it if this were a river like the Rhine or Danube. We would even have paid to have the bridge torn down and rebuilt. But the Habur . . . I mean, on a good day you can get across it with your trousers rolled up."

"The Habur looks different in the spring," Cilic says.

"Tell them that. Maybe they'll wait."

The minister abruptly puts down his tea glass. Through a window he can now see them coming, the first refugees he's seen in real life rather than on television. They're walking across the bridge, a dense column of people, an endless, dense column. And it looks much bigger than on T.V. His eyes dart from the window to the screens and back again, he sees Lionel in close-up on MyTV, dismantling his phone – he pointedly removes the battery, killing the connection, making further communication impossible.

The minister steps outside. He stands on the metal grate of the top step and leans forwards slightly. The procession is not moving particularly fast, a bit like human lava, and there is no end in sight. From here you can see for miles, you ought to be able to see where it ends. The reality of this mass of people in motion catches him unprepared. He's watched the television footage, like everyone else, but he suddenly feels as if he's underestimated the whole enterprise. Hurriedly recapping the last few days, he really can't find fault with himself. He set in motion what needed to be set in motion, he pulled out all the stops. Construction of the wall began four days ago. They chose Passau because the confluence of the Danube and the Inn allow them to achieve maximum visual impact at minimal cost. The border bridges alone make a striking impression. Eight-metre-high concrete walls crowned with razor wire, which is nonsense, but on balance it doesn't cost any more than not having the razor wire, and it looks more menacing. The wall doesn't extend for ever of course – they didn't factor in especially good swimmers among the refugees – but at least people can see how seriously Germany is taking the matter. The Austrians and the E.U. didn't hesitate to lodge protests because of Schengen, but a minister of the interior can delegate that to his colleagues. And he's been proved right by the success of this measure. There was no immediate let up in the protests, but nor have they got any bigger. It's clear that his actions have been welcomed, the population is reassured. And yet right at this moment he feels as if he hasn't done his homework, he hasn't revised the material, not enough at any rate, now, minutes before the big test.

By contrast, the Turks have definitely done theirs.

They gave him a promise and they've kept their word. They won't give the refugees the slightest encouragement.

Even the helicopters delivering the video footage are armed. The border is blocked with heavy steel barriers and lined with infantry with MPT-76 assault rifles. Up until a few years ago they still bore the German G3, Heckler & Koch. Some are still in use, but the Turks have responded to German sensitivities. There are no Leopard tanks keeping watch over the valley from the hillsides either; the Turks have drafted in U.S. equivalents. These tanks are on standby, loaded with live ammunition, and if deployed, nobody can argue they were German weapons. The Turks have brought along water cannon too. Every option must be kept open to avoid them being compelled to fire live ammunition from the outset.

Only now does he realise that the ancient loudspeakers have been croaking away continually in Turkish and something you could, with a great deal of imagination, take to be English: "This is the Turkish army speaking. You are illegally approaching the Turkish border," Cilic translates for him. "Stop where you are and turn around. Or we will open fire." Again and again. The words have no effect. Then he hears a roar and Cilic claps him on the shoulder. He hands him ear protectors.

The minister looks up to see several fighter planes circling in the air, F-16s probably. Two of them now approach at low altitude. Although he puts on the protectors, the noise is still unbearable. As the jets thunder so low that the refugees can practically count the rivets on the undercarriage, children burst into tears and scream. The minister watches women try to shield the children's heads with their hands. Many look for things to stuff in their ears. But what he doesn't see is anybody stopping. He looks back through the open door into the control centre. MyTV is cutting between different shots of the mass of refugees, occasionally inserting images of Nadeche Hackenbusch striding forwards in that idiosyncratic, semi-religious combination suitable both for a school outing and for national mourning. And now the lens is pointing at him. Weeping women and children, and in between the minister with his well-protected ears. An idiotic image.

He looks up and sees the drone hovering barely ten metres above. Staring straight at the camera with a deadly serious expression, he raises both hands and removes his ear protectors so he can toss them into the crowd. Live. Let them try editing that out. Nadeche Hackenbusch isn't the only one who knows how to play to the camera.

The jets return, this time flying even lower, slowly, scarcely faster than a car in city traffic. He knew this was possible, but he's never seen it. The noise is painful; he opens his mouth and screams to create some counter-pressure on his ear drums. He could swear he can feel the heat of the engines – certainly those in the column must be able to. Some people clench their fists, women raise their hands in supplication. Now MyTV shows Nadeche with her hair swirling about like a backcombed flaming thorn bush, shooting accusatory looks at the jets, as if the pilots were able to see her – in fact they probably can. It may be coincidence, but when the aircraft now fly off it's as if Nadeche has personally shooed them away with her angry stares.

Now the water cannon commence operations. A few jets of water splutter over the masses. It's strangely futile, and in this heat probably even pleasant. It soon becomes clear that the cannon will achieve nothing, especially if they're not aimed directly at the people. The minister raises his eyebrows at Cilic, who points at the column with an awkward gesture. Of course the Turks aren't going to shoot twenty bars at infants and small children. As a compromise the mass of people gets a generous soaking. What are they trying to achieve? The problem is obvious: there's no way the refugees could turn around now. Even stopping would be difficult. It occurs to the minister that the entire border could have been constructed differently. It's almost as if people are being squeezed through a large funnel towards the crossing point here, whereas it ought to be the other way around: the crossing point should jut out into the crowd like a wedge, to divert the pressure to either side. He makes a mental note of this.

The refugees at the very front have now arrived at the metal barriers. They stop. These are women with children in their arms. The people begin to concentrate, it's getting cramped, and then the metal barriers open. Rejoicing all around.

The minister looks at Cilic in disbelief. "Already? You didn't fire a shot! Not even a warning shot."

"Who are we supposed to be warning? And where are these people supposed to go?"

"You're literally inviting them in!" This is all the minister says because he's not sure whether a drone is listening in.

"You know as well as I do. If we don't open the gates until everyone's squashed in, dozens of people will die. We might as well shoot into the crowd at random. And we're not going to do that. Certainly not for a country which is only too ready to level accusations of genocide. Do you expect us to do your dirty work, just so people can then say, 'Again? You're doing the same as you did to the Armenians?'"

"It's your decision," the minister says. Leubl knew, it could have been anticipated, but still it makes him feel queasy. "I mean, look at it from this perspective: they're going to be blocking your roads for months. Have fun with that."

"I don't think it'll take that long," Cilic says.

Deflated, the minister leans over the railings and watches the soldiers move out of the way. They form a sort of cordon wherever they can, and many receive kisses from the women and grateful hugs from the men. He can no longer hear the fighter jets. Soldiers are pointing in the same direction, as if the refugees can't find the road by themselves. All they have to do is go with the flow. It reminds him of images of Bornholmer Strasse in Berlin, 1989. Would a wedge-shaped border have helped the G.D.R.?

Cilic has gone back inside. Perhaps he feels offended, but the minister doesn't really care. He was here, he assumed his responsibility and took the last possible opportunity to avert the conflict in advance. It didn't work, but nobody could have expected that. Now they have three, maybe four months to prepare. Not much time, too little time in fact, but there's nothing they can do to change it.

The soldiers wave and keep pointing. They must feel like they're working at an information desk, the same stupid questions. These poor guys must be saying over and over again, "This way for Germany. This way for Germany."

"I don't think it'll take that long."

It sounded odd, the way he said it. Perhaps it was his accent.

The minister has seen enough. He's going to get the helicopter to fly him back. He looks inside the control centre one last time, at the screens, the images from the helicopters. C.N.N. footage on a loop – they repeat the same pictures as if new ones would be too expensive. And at the MyTV screen. He freezes, then rushes out the door.

He can't see it, but he has an idea where it is. It's where the soldiers are pointing.

"Where are you going?" Cilic calls after him. "You can't just . . ."

The minister leaps down the steps. He pushes his way past a number of soldiers and follows the refugees. Cilic hurries after him. The minister passes the water cannon and personnel carriers. They'd set up a machine-gun position – what a joke! He can see three armoured combat vehicles and two heavy-duty M6os on the mound. None of this was for the refugees, it was all for him, the gormless German.

"Minister!" Cilic shouts. "You can't just—"

"On the contrary," the minister shouts back. "I most certainly can!"

Now that he's running he realises how cumbersome the bulletproof vest is. He tears open the zip and tosses it aside. It might be almost a kilometre away; he follows the road, plunging through the loose chain of soldiers waving the refugees on, now making faster progress on the tarmac. And then he sees it. It's far bigger than it looked on the screen, an enormous car park which must have been enlarged only recently, using heavy machinery. He sees the refugees heading towards it, some are already boarding a bus. And behind this bus the next one is waiting.

"I don't think it'll take that long." The duplicitous fucker.

There must be dozens of buses. Hundreds. From every year of manufacture, every size, every make, even buses from municipal corporations. The minister can feel his heart hammering, and not just because of the short sprint.

He turns around. Cilic catches him up, exhausted.

"Minister—"

"What *is* this?" the minister bellows. "What the hell do you think you're doing?"

"You have to understand . . ." Cilic pants.

"What do I have to understand? What the hell do you think you're doing? WHAT DO YOU THINK YOU'RE DOING?"

"You'd do the same!"

"What would I do the same?"

"Did you seriously think we could allow half a million people to make their way through densely populated area. This isn't some banana republic, this is the Republic of Turkey! Somehow we have to keep these people under control. And if they have to pass through our country, then at least they can be quick about it!"

The minister looks helplessly at the car park. Cilic is right, of course. It's obvious. If someone's on a bus they stay on the road. They've got emergency accommodation they can put up with for a while. Maybe not half a year, maybe not even two months, but definitely for the time needed for the remainder of the route. It needs to be fast for the Turks. Perhaps, the minister thinks, his fence-building has even accelerated all this.

The time needed for the remainder of the route.

The minister does some frantic calculations. Turkey's road system is not particularly extensive; it's unlikely they could keep their larger two-lane roads free all day just for the buses. So the buses will be diverted onto side roads. But the moment they get near a motorway, things will move much more quickly. So it's patently clear he doesn't have another four months. Turkey is almost two thousand kilometres long. Ten days by bus at the most.

He's got another two weeks if he's lucky.

# 46

They're flying.

Lionel's up at the front of the bus beside Mahmoud, who's doing the driving. One hand is holding onto Mahmoud's seat and the other onto a pole. He looks through the window in front of him and sees the bus suck up the dusty track beneath. He glances at the speedometer. The needle isn't working, but it could be forty kilometres. Per hour.

They're flying.

This is without question the ugliest bus Lionel has ever seen. It might be the oldest bus he's ever seen too, but he can't be sure because it's so ugly it defies all other classification. At the front it's curved and notched, like a carrot. Its windscreen is made of two panes of glass, divided down the middle, so it must be older, from the sixties or maybe even the fifties. Beneath this, and just above the bumper, is a radiator grille so unusually small and narrow that the round headlights are perfect as the corners of a mouth. The undersized grille lends the vehicle the features of a surly caterpillar.

A violent judder shakes the bus. Whatever suspension it

once had must have given up the ghost long ago. The judder is followed by a short, unpleasant crunching as parts of the undercarriage plane the tarmac, and the engine grumbles when Mahmoud shifts up a gear. As the bus pulls itself together and accelerates, Mahmoud adjusts his captain's hat.

"Sorry about your job," Lionel says to Mahmoud.

"What?"

The bus may be old, but it's louder than it is old.

"I said, I'm sorry about your job," Lionel shouts.

"Why?" Mahmoud shouts back.

"Well, you used to be an admiral."

"I'm still an admiral," Mahmoud shouts, pointing enthusiastically at his hat. The bus jolts and the hat slips down over his face.

Lionel looks through the side windows. They were kept small, as if glass were more expensive than metal. You wouldn't need to do much to turn this into a prisoner transport vehicle. The Turkish countryside drifts past. It's not so different from other landscapes they've passed through: hot and vast, rocky and dusty. There are more buildings here and the roads are better. They just seem shockingly bad when you're in an ancient bus.

But at least they're in a bus. They're flying towards their destination. Who'd have believed it?

It was the Turks' idea. They called him and asked whether he was the guy off the telly. Yes, he replied, he was the guy off the telly.

"Is it true what they're saying?" A voice, neither young

nor old, calm, composed, energetic. A man. He spoke the sort of English Lionel knew from British people.

"What are they saying?"

"They're saying you're planning on coming into Turkey with a mass of people."

"We're planning on passing through."

"I'm sorry?"

"We're planning on passing through. That is correct."

"Then I'm afraid I have to inform you that we cannot allow this."

"I know."

"You know?"

"I do."

"What does that mean?"

"I know that you can't allow us to do it."

"So what?"

"I've no experience in these matters. But we've been on the move for a long time now. We've crossed many countries. And nobody has actually given us permission to pass through, but then again nobody has really troubled us either. The same thing could happen with Turkey."

"I don't think so."

"I'm sorry, I might not have expressed myself very well. We know, of course, that we're making a huge wish come true here, so it's only fair if we make other people's wishes come true in return. Just tell us what we can do for you, and what we can do for whoever else—"

"I don't think you understand. This is the Republic of Turkey. What you're talking about might work for planning consent. But not for hundreds of thousands of people. Let me spell it out: if you try to cross our border, no matter where, we will stop you. With all the means at the disposal of a sovereign state."

"Yes," he said, "then I suppose that's what you'll have to do." He remembers how his temples were throbbing. Because he had always known this moment would come. The moment when money no longer helped. The moment for talking. "Then we will use our lives."

"What's that supposed to mean?"

"We'll keep marching. You see, for us it makes no difference. It's the same as stepping into a tiny rubber dinghy. Putting one's life at risk. For us your country is like the sea. We don't expect the sea to let us pass either. We just keep going and see whether we die." At this point he took an especially deep breath, even though he didn't need to; it was merely for emphasis. "You would have to kill us."

"Then we will kill you. Do you understand?"

"Then you will kill us. I do understand."

The line went silent for a while.

"Then you will kill us like the sea kills us. But I'll say it again: it makes no difference to us, it might even be quicker. It's cheaper at any rate, because we don't need life vests. It will only make a difference to you."

"What do you mean?"

"Nobody blames the sea for its actions. The sea is the sea. With you it's different. You are the Republic of Turkey. You have a choice."

"You too. You could stop."

"And grow old and die on your border? We won't do that. We will keep marching and force you to make a decision. You will have to decide whether we live or die."

There was silence on the other end of the line. Lionel decided to go all out: "And just so there's no misunderstanding, we're going to make your decision as difficult as possible. We're going to have the world's cameras alongside us. And the first people you'll have to kill will be our women and children."

Then the voice on the other end said, "I'll pass on this information and get back to you."

"Hey!" The bus is filled with shrieks and laughter. Lionel grabs onto the strip of metal between the two windscreen panes. A few children have hit their heads and are crying. Mahmoud turns around and shouts, "Brakes really well, doesn't it?"

He crowbars his way into first gear and accelerates.

It took them just under a week to call back.

"Let's say you weren't shot at when you tried to cross the border," the ageless man said. "What would you do then?"

"Are you talking about me, or all of us not being shot at?"

"Just you."

It was something Lionel had been obliged to reconcile himself to. Malaika, this kind-hearted sheep of a camel, would never let the two of them go on to Germany alone. "Well, I'd wait with the others until I was shot at too, something like that." He rolled his eyes and then said, "I'm afraid I can't abandon this undertaking."

He wasn't sure what was more difficult to accept:

the realisation that, for better or worse, he was inextricably connected with this refugee trek; or the phlegmatic observation from the other side. "That's what we thought. No, what would you do if you weren't shot at, all of you?"

"Surely you've seen on T.V. what we do. We just keep walking."

"And where do we, where do *you* get the assurance that you'll be able enter the next country – Bulgaria, say – at the other end of Turkey?"

"Well, I think we'll walk through Turkey and then do the same at the next border. That's when we'll find out if Bulgaria's going to open fire on us."

"And you think it's going to work again?"

"I think it'll work even better."

"What makes you think that?"

"Well, we can tell the Bulgarians that not even the Turks shot at us."

He heard a brief laugh on the other end of the line.

"I know letting foreigners into your country isn't necessarily a popular move. But you're not risking much. You're not responsible for the Bulgarians. In the worst-case scenario you'll have a heap of corpses lying around on your border. But we'll make the burial easy for you because we've got our own diggers in tow."

"They're quite something, your diggers. In fact your entire organisation is remarkable. At the moment you're covering fifteen kilometres a day. That's going to take for ever. Turkey can't let hundreds of thousands of people prowl unsupervised around the country for months on end."

"I'm sorry, but that's the structure of our march. That's our food, our water. And fifteen kilometres per day is really pretty good."

"Would you be prepared to board buses?" the voice said. Lionel told him he'd call back in a couple of days.

A man is tending a cow at the side of the road. Lionel's surprised the man isn't tending a second cow or at least a goat too. He's seen several men like this, each with one cow. He wonders how this country can be so much better off than his own, but maybe two people could share a cow and live off it, so long as there's no civil war, putsch or famine. Mahmoud hoots a greeting; the man gives a friendly but slightly apathetic wave. It almost looks as if the cow is minding the man.

He got together with Mahmoud and a few others to work out how they were going to allocate the tankers, but then the Turk said there was enough water in Turkey, provided they stayed on the move. Negotiations were carried out with "if" and "perhaps" prefixing most sentences. They would send buses with soldiers, to which Lionel replied that his people wouldn't board them unless they could drive themselves. Then the Turk said that they'd have to seal off the route using the military, to which Lionel replied that this was fine in theory, but they'd check on their phones that it really was the way to Bulgaria, then the Turk said, or Greece, and Lionel said, or Greece.

If absolutely necessary, the Turk said, it might be possible for the refugees to do the driving, but then they might have to go past a few areas where there were other refugees, and Lionel said this was nothing new, but it was already hard

459

enough keeping the payment system ticking over. And the Turk said it might not be necessary any longer because food, water, fuel and electricity could be provided, this was definitely a possibility if, in return, they were to drive past a few refugee camps. Lionel did some more calculations and realised they'd need more buses and some mechanics for repairs, if they wanted to be sure of a speedy transit. The Turk did some calculations of his own and said Lionel might be right, and in any case it was a good idea because they'd want the buses back afterwards. Then, without knowing why and off the top of his head, Lionel said, "Unless the Bulgarians need them too."

He just came out with it, but the moment the words passed his lips he was thinking exactly the same thoughts as the Turk. That the Bulgarians – and anyone else for that matter – would be far happier to let someone into and through their country if they were going at forty or fifty kilometres per hour rather than just fifteen per day. That the Bulgarians would feel more comfortable if they were given refugees neatly packaged in buses rather than in an endless, confusing procession. And if, rather than having to rearrange everything, they were able to pass on what they'd been delivered.

"Or the Greeks," the Turk said.

"Or the Greeks," Lionel said.

And that was that. Until they got to Turkey, Lionel had not known what to expect. He planned their march to the border as if those calls had never taken place, but then, on the other side, the buses were actually waiting. As the first buses drove off he called the Turk to express his thanks. The telephone number no longer existed.

Mahmoud slows down. The bus in front is braking as it has to let a man and a cow across the road. The bus is the same model and just as ugly. Sticking out from its rear is an engine block, looking like an extra-long arse, but an arse of such rare hideousness and cropped vertically. Whoever designed this vehicle must have completely lost interest at this stage and decided "the bus ends here". Then he stuck the name of the bus onto it and went home.

Mahmoud brings the bus to a halt behind the other one. "Let me out here," Lionel says. He's going to get onto the bus behind. He thinks it's better if people don't always know which bus he's in. Mahmoud opens the door and gives him a wave as he gets out.

When Mahmoud pulls away Lionel looks at the writing on the cropped arse: ICARUS.

Of course, he thinks. The name of a boy who can fly.

# 47

The minister of the interior can't sleep. He's tired, he's incredibly tired, but the moment he closes his eyes he thinks of a problem he hasn't yet solved. He hasn't had a wink of sleep for three days now. He got the hell out of Turkey as fast as he could, informing the chancellor's office on his way to the helicopter that they had to get the E.U. to club together and back Germany, securing in particular the commitment of Bulgaria and Greece. Romania's unlikely to come into the equation – the refugees want to take the land route rather than go up via the Black Sea – which leaves only Bulgaria and Greece as adjoining countries. If they keep their borders closed the problem can be overcome – the Turks will just have to be paid for the refugees. And the sum would have to be higher than what they'd save by adding tens of thousands of their own refugees to the procession.

You can always find money, but you can't find a population that will accept refugees.

The minister turns over. He's lying on the sofa he had brought over from his old office with the chairs. The furniture he sat on with Leubl just before Christmas.

Leubl.

How do you bring the Bulgarian and Greek borders under control? Because one thing is certain: if the refugees are allowed to behave as they did at the Turkey–Iraq border, the whole thing will collapse in exactly the same way. The Turks didn't do the job for us, he thinks, so nor will the Greeks and Bulgarians. Somebody else has to. Somebody representing our interests. The army? The border protection squad? Neither Bulgaria nor Greece will allow this; borders are domestic matters, and countries are mightily fussy about them. The chancellor's office is going to have to pile on some pressure. And then they can send Frontex. Protecting the E.U.'s external borders is Frontex's job. They can send German soldiers in Frontex uniforms. A sort of uniform scam, like Putin in the Crimea. Who could he call? The minister sits up and switches on the light.

The clock shows half past two. He rubs his dry eyes. He ought to have left the light off. Sometimes when you're dozing you have flashes of inspiration that turn out to be twaddle when the lights are on. He already has a pretty good idea of how the chancellor's office and the foreign office would react to his suggestion. German soldiers under the Frontex flag. By the time they warmed to the idea, the refugees would have passed Nuremberg. He has three text messages. The first two are from the domestic intelligence service. They've smashed another vigilante group, this time in Bavaria. Thirty members, an astonishingly high proportion of women. Heavy weapons, hand grenades, flame throwers. Less than six months old but already radicalised. And there's no doubting they're prepared to use these weapons – five security agents were shot dead during the arrest, and eight more injured. The third message says that they've found a database with information on a nationwide network, but it's encrypted. There is evidence pointing to dozens more groups; paramilitaries may even be heading southwards.

The minister feels as if a huge wave were washing over him. He takes a deep breath, he imagines making himself flat, as in quicksand, as with an avalanche airbag, you mustn't let yourself get buried, you have to lie flat, distribute your weight, always stay on the surface.

You have to ride the wave.

No, that's nonsense. That would mean having to deploy those paramilitaries at the border. The state has to keep control, not relinquish it. He makes a note: "Major crackdown. Raabe!" No stinting with the arrests. Let them take legal action, it's all about adopting a firm approach. The minister of justice will be on his side, he can slow down the working speed of his judges – the minister of the interior needs peace and quiet until the refugee crisis has been averted. Afterwards they can quash as many of his decisions as they like.

He scribbles "Crackdown!" He has to keep the far right off his back, even if this means locking up every last one of them. Once he's solved the refugee problem they'll calm down again. They may even make him their hero; the far right is seriously loopy, after all. If you give them a good kicking they honestly regard this as something akin to a reasoned argument.

First job, then, is to speak to Raabe. He sends a text straightaway: "We need to speak, urgently! I'll call you at 7!"

He switches off the light and lies down. He feels a twinge in his stomach: tension, he's lying there completely tense, breathing tensely, trying to get to sleep tensely. *Evangeline* said he'd become a "states-man" over the past few days. Written with a hyphen, such utter rubbish. They published "before and after" photographs of him: taking office as under-secretary, then two days after his return from Turkey. They like his three-day beard, they say he looks as determined as Gerard Butler in "300". What a comparison! Three hundred men against one hundred thousand heavily armed invaders – he doesn't know whether this distorted picture is intentional, or whether it's cheap propaganda, or whether the editors at *Evangeline* just like bare-chested men with beards.

The minister turns over. Half past three. So, with the Nazis now ticked off it's back to the refugees.

What would Leubl have done?

Actually, that's pretty obvious. So what would Helmut Schmidt have done? After all this is a kind of flood disaster too, isn't it? The Bulgarians. The Greeks. How do you keep your flank watertight? They must all realise that they'll be left with the refugees. They must realise this. They simply must.

Echler phoned to say that there are quite a few individuals in both Greek and Bulgarian government circles in favour of simply waving the buses through. Unofficial talks are under-way with all countries en route to Germany. He asked Echler about the likelihood of the Bulgarians sticking to E.U. rules. According to the Dublin Regulation all the refugees would be theirs – surely that must worry them?

Echler said nothing.

"Fifty-fifty? Forty-sixty? Come on, give me a rough estimate!"

"Based on the current situation, if our chances are 10 per cent, I'd say that's generous."

The minister's neck is aching. He's lying with his head on the armrest. Einsteiger kindly fetched him a pillow from a nearby hotel, but like so many hotel pillows it's a floppy sack into which one's head sinks like a stone. It allows him to cushion the armrest at least, but the angle for his neck is far too steep. The minister tries lying on his back.

The German border is the key. If it's credibly watertight, then the others will be too. In fact he's thought about spring-guns as well. If you're not using them to keep your own people in, but to protect the border, they're certainly worth consideration. And nobody's being *forced* to cross the border; if you tell them not to come closer but they do anyway, then really they only have themselves to blame, don't they? He even started googling all this, but then scrapped the idea. There are no spring-guns that could keep hundreds of thousands of people at bay for hours on end. In the G.D.R. they were booby traps, more or less, which went off when someone touched a wire or whatever. Bang! – and after that they were empty. No, you'd have to link motion sensors up to machine guns, but since that's never been done, it would be as reliable as screwing together parts from your local electronics outlet. The advantage? It's so beyond the realms of possibility that you don't have to bother poring over the legal parameters.

There's not a noise to be heard in the building. No

clunking in the heating pipes, no flushing anywhere. He can't hear if anyone's running a tap. No birds hopping on the roof. But no cars either. When he was small he'd always watch the headlights sweep across his bedroom ceiling at night. You were never completely alone; even in the desperate depths of night the city was alive. In his office in the newly built ministry of the interior, he can't see any headlights. Nobody's hooting, no trams rattle past.

A wall. A ditch to protect against vehicles – this is what they had in the "death strip" to stop trucks ploughing through. An open field of fire. Floodlights. Fences that can't be climbed because of the overhang at the top – like protecting flower beds from snails. Metal barriers in front of the wall. Or behind. A sort of outer courtyard, like the ones castles have. His head obsessively rearranges the components, more come to mind, towers, it's getting confusing, but the solution will come by arranging these correctly, for only with the perfect combination of all the pieces will it work. The barbed wire edges its way in again, he's doing it wrong – the barbed wire always comes last. First the ditch, then the wall, the gates, he holds them in his head like enormous puzzle pieces, but whenever he inserts one piece it's too big or it gets stuck to other bits, and he knocks the wall down, he's got to start all over again. The barbed wire gets entangled, he begins yet again, resolving to concentrate really hard this time, really slowly. First he puts up the wall, but now the wire gets caught in his jumper, his sleeve snags on the barbs, he no longer has any time, he's got to rearrange all the pieces to stop them getting mixed up, the rolls of barbed wire, the blocks of wall, the towers, the floodlights, but everything is always full of wire, the wall slips out of his hands, the rolls of wire are obstinate and keep springing apart . . .

The minister wakes with a start.

He can hear a hoover somewhere in the building.

He sits up. His eyes feel swollen, dry and sticky. He gets up and goes over to the kettle. He's going to make himself some tea.

Legally he's got more leeway now. Not in theory, but certainly in practice. Anyone trying to adhere strictly to the rules has already lost this game. Everyone acts in accordance with the principle that whoever first gets the refugees can try to get rid of them too. Of course the Dublin Regulation – whoever finds the refugees has to keep them – was nonsense. Those countries with external borders are fools. That was never going to be a solution, from the very beginning it only worked if no or very few refugees came. Once the numbers rise the injustice of the Regulation is so obvious that states with external borders will simply send the refugees on.

But then that means Germany can simply refuse to let them in. The minister rubs his neck and unwraps a teabag.

In theory the law is binding, but in practice everything here is being renegotiated from scratch. This is how it needs to be seen: an unheralded renegotiation in particularly bizarre circumstances. Like the chickie run in that James Dean film, where they both drive towards the edge of the cliff and the winner's the one who jumps out of his car last. Here the contest is: who can watch the refugees suffer the longest? Given the nature of the German population, he's stuck with bad cards.

The water boils and the minister pours some into his cup. You shouldn't do that. You shouldn't scald the tea.

The simplest thing would be to stop the broadcasting. If nobody can see the suffering, it gives you far greater freedom. But there's no way of stopping it, so they need a strategy that causes the least possible harm. A wall. But every wall needs a gate, which means they need gates like those on the U.S. government atomic bunker – steel gates. Or at least the most solid gates they can rustle up in a few weeks. And if things continue as they have in Turkey, Germany will simply have to be the country that won't open its door. That won't be blackmailed. Shooting people shouldn't be a necessity; simply refusing to open up will have to suffice.

And a fence along the border with Austria at least, if not along the Czech border too.

Unaffordable. And totally impossible in the time remaining.

They'll need simpler fences, then, and they'll have to be defended. Everything's going around in circles. Literally: the minister feels giddy, he needs to hold on to something. Apparently some of his colleagues reach for the cocaine in situations like this. But he doesn't even smoke. His pulse is racing. He tries to make himself light, and flat, like when you're in quicksand. He's sweating. Outside the birds are beginning to twitter. The minister is so tired, so dreadfully tired. His mobile flashes. A text. "Saw u in Evangeline. U look awful. Look after yourself!"

Tommy.

Knowing that Tommy's thinking about him makes him feel a little better. He goes back to the sofa with his cup. He picks up the woollen blanket and lays it around his shoulders like a poncho, before sitting down and leaning back into the cushions. He closes his eyes and tries to think of nice things. Comforting things. His childhood bedroom. The sounds. The birds chirruping. The clatter of trams as they take a bend. He's always liked trams, much more than buses. The driver raising the pantograph which then glides along the overhead cables virtually in silence. The loudest thing about the trams was always the wheels in the tracks.

The overhead cables.

The sparks in the overhead cables.

He opens his eyes wide.

# 48

He's not even allowed to express his delight.

Even though there are plenty of reasons to do so. Sensenbrink closes the office door behind him and says, very quietly, "Yesss!" It's undeniably down to him. O.K., you could say Olav was the one who gave him the information. But he was the one who made use of it.

Sensenbrink drops onto the sofa and reaches into the bottom tray on the shelf above him. He feels a bit uneasy about keeping it, but it looks so fantastic: the viewing figures from that day at the Turkish border. He yanks out the sheet of paper, but that's fine, because he laminated it. That same evening when his secretary had gone home. That in itself is quite embarrassing, but fuck it. When do you ever get ratings like these?

To begin with it was slightly disappointing – just below average, typical afternoon figures. Still extraordinary compared with the umpteenth "Big Bang Theory" repeat, but not by "A2" standards. When you're Bayern Munich you're not satisfied with winning the league; you want the cup too. Then – and how beautifully this is shown on the timeline

– a noticeable increase at the time the border is crossed. On the other channels too. They were all there: n-tv, N24, with A.R.D and Z.D.F. showing it in duplicate – you've got to spend the licence fee somehow when the other channels have poached all the football matches.

But then, on the other side of the border, everything looked very different.

Sensenbrink reaches behind him for the other graphic, the one analysing the time of the border crossing minute by minute, second by second. Ahhh. To begin with some viewers switch back to the channel they were watching before. But then word gets around that the trek is continuing. It's not over the border then STOP – now it starts motoring, literally: it's over the border then BUS. And the other broadcasters have no pictures. They don't have anything. They've finished their work, they thought that would be it. They didn't even notice what was afoot with the buses, those news experts. In town two days earlier he'd met that bonehead Klüpfel. He wanted to show off his insider knowledge about MyTV's scheduling.

"Fourteen drones? Eight camera teams? I get that the show's your big thing. Hats off and all that, but what on earth are you going to film?"

Typical Klüpfel. He's always been one of those people you don't bother trying to talk to after 5.00 p.m. And now he's deputy drip or whatever at W.D.R. But your oh-so-wonderful network of correspondents and Middle East experts are fuck-all help if they're just getting a bunch of vox pops at the border, while the real action is happening two kilometres down the road. Sensenbrink grins. They had two hours' exclusive footage of the refugees boarding buses. Two camera teams even went with them. And they're still with them, changing buses every day.

Exclusively on MyTV.

No po-faced current affairs programme is going to change that.

Well, they'd sewn it up. Once you've hooked the viewers, you've got an advantage. Of course they'll switch to A.R.D. from time to time, just to make sure that what you're broadcasting really is happening. But if A.R.D. doesn't have any pictures, what do the viewers do then?

Exactly.

After half an hour they deigned to put a scrolling banner at the bottom of the screen, which proved to be a real afterburner. It's all true, A.R.D. said, but if you want to see it, then switch to MyTV. A broad smile spreads across Sensenbrink's face. The figures were like those for the moon landings. Nobody would have thought this sort of thing possible today. Late that evening Kärrner, still ashen-faced, staggered into the office and said, "Shares aren't going to do it anymore. They've got to give us a stake in the holding company."

Oh yes.

O.K., they didn't manage to get the minister of the interior in front of the camera. But nor did A.R.D.

17–0 to Sensenbrink. "YESSS!"

And he hasn't let the viewers off the leash since. Now they're broadcasting a permanent live feed, up in the top left-hand corner of the screen, even during feature films. They're counting down the kilometres to the German border. With the refugees travelling at the speed of a bus, this countdown has become meaningful. In real time. MyTV is on constantly in most offices. It's like 9/11, but at least ten days long.

This is why he can't celebrate it. Except when it comes to the revenue.

They'd already sold their advertising space for Turkey. And now it transpires that, thanks to the buses, they've sold far more slots than are actually available in the remaining airtime. What was going to be a three-month trek has been cut to ten days. Ten days, during which viewers will be as hooked on the MyTV logo as drug addicts on the needle. A dream market: they all want to come in, but everything's full.

Olav said, we'll sell the place in the sun at moon prices.

And the broadcaster can choose who it likes, because everyone will pay. Even at three in the morning the price per minute is too high for the regular Internet whores. MyTV sells premium advertising all night long.

Kärrner sent him a box of cigars today. Cuban, forty euros a pop. Discreetly delivered to his house. Yesterday a crate of champagne. From Kärrner personally – officially it mustn't come via the firm. Sensenbrink is already looking forward to what will arrive tomorrow. It could all be so fantastic if he weren't obliged to keep his mouth shut.

Otherwise it could get really expensive.

Sure, live broadcasts can go differently from how you've planned them. Airtime can be cancelled or postponed at a moment's notice. And all this means, of course, that the programmes can go surprisingly differently too.

The key word being *surprisingly*.

Because the element of surprise could be called into question, given that MyTV just happened to be there with fourteen drones and eight camera teams *at the beginning*. Yes, that's normal for the broadcaster's biggest show. But what does it look like if you've been selling advertising space for three months of Turkey *for weeks*, even though you knew the buses would dramatically reduce this time frame? If it were to get out that you'd sold your customers a product you knew wouldn't exist?

That doesn't sound good. Yes, you can argue over whether it can be proved, or whether legal action could be taken, but these people don't like being fucked over. These people with their budgets running to tens or hundreds of millions. And so for the past few days Sensenbrink has had to go around as if he'd been taken completely by surprise. The official line can't then be: "What are we going to do with all this money?" but "Oh dear, how do I scale down the advertising slots? Woe is me, what am I going to tell our clients?"

And if someone asks, the answer has to be: "We just got lucky. It's luck and the fact that we've got a great bunch of people working here." No fucker's going to be taken in by that, but still.

At some point, in maybe twenty years, when no cocks are twitching for Nadeche Hackenbusch anymore, he'll be able to tell his grandchildren and everyone else how superbly he handled the whole affair. They'll all yawn: "Grandad Sensenbrink is going on about the war again."

What else is there?

Champagne, which he's only allowed to drink discreetly.

Cigars, which he's only allowed to smoke at home.

Two graphics, secretly laminated and shamefully stowed away like porn.

Sensenbrink picks up the graphics and holds them out in front of him. Just the thought of A.R.D. heading south! He smiles.

Cool.

# 49

"Are you serious?" Kaspers looks at the minister of the interior in disbelief. "Have you actually had a wink of sleep?"

"No," the minister says. "But that's got nothing to do with it. It's the only practical solution."

The meeting is smaller than last time. Berthold, Kaspers and Gödeke are there. Migration, international affairs and the foreign intelligence service are not. There'll be enough whining as it is.

"You know this has been carried out twice in our history already?" Kaspers opens fire. "By the East Germans and by the Nazis! I don't imagine anyone here would consider either role models."

"By the East Germans, the Nazis, and livestock holders." Gödeke's parents are farmers in Lower Saxony.

The minister puts both index fingers in the air. "Before we get carried away – the task at hand dictates the possible solutions. We have about forty-eight hours to send a clear message to Bulgaria and the other countries along the Balkan route, before they have to decide what to do with these refugees. Are we all in agreement so far?"

The trio of officials nod. Kaspers waggles his hands, then raises his palms upwards, as if to say, come on, show us what you've got.

"Good. A clear message, delivered swiftly," the minister summarises. "I see three options. One, we build a huge concrete wall. But that's not feasible, everyone knows we'd get only a couple of hundred metres up in ten days. Two, we build a fence of steel or wire, behind which we position border guards with machine guns, instructed to shoot to kill. But let's be honest, who's going to believe we would mow down hundreds of thousands like at Verdun way back when?"

"Well," Gödeke says, "they don't have to be armed with machine guns—"

"Oh yes, they do. If you try sending the same message with tear gas and water cannon, you might as well give up. I saw the refugees' faces at the Turkish border. They're not going to be stopped by a bit of tear gas. And they're not going to turn around either – they're smart enough to exert enough pressure from behind so that those in front can go in only one direction."

"That remains to be seen . . ." Berthold says.

"No, it doesn't. If we want the others to make their borders as secure as ours, they can't think, let's wait and see. They have to think, ouch, these guys mean business."

"But high-voltage current . . ." Kaspers shakes his head.

"Nothing's off the table here," the minister emphasises. "Whoever's got a better idea, should come out with it." Placing his hands on the desk he pushes himself up and bellows, "In fact you could have come out with it a while ago!" He sits down and takes a sip of water in the silence. "I do apologise for my tone just then." He can feel his shoulders and neck beginning to stiffen. "Back to businesss. There are many things in favour of using high-voltage. First, it's simple to put into operation. A wire fence is quick to erect, but it's just a wire fence, even if it's got barbed wire. A wire fence with a high-voltage current is just as quick to erect, but everyone knows it's lethal. It's very practical and therefore feasible. Second, it works automatically and it's unlimited. If somebody touches the fence the body conducts the electricity. Which means there's no reloading and, most importantly, no human factor. We don't have to expect our border guards to undertake mass killings. Third, the whole thing is ethically justifiable. It is, after all, our border. Nobody is forcing the refugees to touch it. If they want to go to their deaths, then so be it. That is their decision."

"Exactly," Kaspers says. "Like those people in the concentration camps."

The minister gives him a dark look. "I . . ." It costs him the rest of his virtually non-existent composure to assume an unruffled tone. "I want constructive suggestions here, not scepticism." He looks at the three in turn. "But before we go on, there's something else I want to say in this regard, once and for all. Because we're going to have to defend our decision, so I need to supply you with some arguments. We shouldn't forget that if these people really do end up at our fence, it's not because they're fleeing death or torture. It's because they're fleeing Austria!"

This calms the atmosphere at the table. They nod hesitantly – you certainly could look at it like that. Then Gödeke speaks.

"But you do know that's not quite so practical, don't you?"

"Why not?"

Gödeke tries to avoid another dressing-down. "If I've understood right, this is a brainstorming session where everything's on the table, yes? I mean, I don't want to get it in the neck from anyone afterwards."

"It's fine," the minister sighs, "just fire away. What's said in this room stays in this room."

"Good. Let me start by saying that I'm not a physicist or an electrical engineer or anything. But I do know some of the basics. If I'm not mistaken, electricity doesn't work in quite the same way as a magnet, where you can connect as many bits of metal to it as you like – and they're all magnetised."

"What are you saying?"

"What I'm saying is that the human body possesses a certain resistance. It absorbs energy as it flows through. And so when you've got fifty, one hundred, God knows how many people hanging onto the fence—"

"—which all of us, please note, hope won't happen . . ." the minister says quickly, partly for Kaspers' sake.

". . . which all of us hope won't happen, yes," Gödeke continues, "then at some point scrambling over it becomes about as lethal as the battery in your torch."

"Especially because fifty, one hundred, I've no idea how many people, have a certain weight too," Berthold adds. "And the moment the power is interrupted, there's no more current, and then our fence is just like any other."

The minister shrugs his tense shoulders and grimaces. "German engineers are capable of anything," he says.

"What?"

"The question is not what is possible and how," he reminds his colleagues. "The far more important question is what people believe we are capable of. Will we shoot people dead by the thousands? Or will we get a decent electrical installation?"

"Are you saying . . ."

The demoralised minister rubs the back of neck. "What I'm saying is that you're not the only one who isn't an electrician. I'm not one either. And nor are the Bulgarians. To be absolutely clear, it has to function technically, it's not a pretty solution, and we're in exceptional circumstances. But the key thing is we have a story that keeps the pressure at bay for a couple of days to a couple of weeks. That's just as important as a high-voltage fence working . . . in fact, more important than it working is that the other E.U. Member States *believe* it works. Don't forget, if the Bulgarians stop the refugees at the external border, if this whole thing grinds to a halt at *their* border, then we don't need to test our fence at all. Then the Turks will have lost and they'll have to build another refugee camp. Hard cheese!"

"A smokescreen," Kaspers says.

"Remarkable," Berthold says, approvingly. "A Potemkin fence."

"Oh no," the minister sticks his oar in. "Just so there's no misunderstanding: the fence has to work."

"The public reaction will be devastating," Kaspers says superfluously. Despite his exhaustion, the minister can hear agreement in his voice. Kaspers won't be pleased by the reaction, but he regards it as an acceptable price to pay in the circumstances.

"Maybe not just devastating," Gödeke says. "It's so unusual and so drastic that we should at least get the approval of the entire conservative right."

"Pegida down by 10 per cent would be quite something," Berthold remarks.

"It'll be better than that," Gödeke says. "20 per cent, maybe 25. A government that commands the trust of the population—"

"The reactionary section of the population," Kaspers notes with caution.

"Possibly," the minister says. "But that doesn't make us a reactionary government." He takes out his mobile, signalling the end of the meeting. Then he says to Kaspers, "Could you please turn the television on? MyTV."

Kaspers presses a couple of buttons on the remote control. The minister glances briefly at the screen, then races out of the room into his office.

"What now?" Berthold asks.

Kaspers bends to the screen and raps his knuckle on the kilometre counter, as if it were broken.

Berthold whistles through his teeth in shock. "Those arseholes haven't even stopped for a break. They're going non-stop. It won't be long to the Bulgarian border now."

"Shit!" Gödeke says. "Look at the writing on those signs. It's in Cyrillic!"

# 50

Saba isn't saying anything.

Nor is Nadeche. She wishes she had something to do right now. The T.V. crew got out an hour ago. They've been broadcasting thirty-six hours on the trot and now they're trying to edit a feature to send from the mobile unit to the broadcaster. Or they've fallen asleep. She's sitting beside a woman who's snoring like two men, and who has a small boy on her lap. Nadeche regrets offering her the seat. Two seats – what a luxury that would be now! They'd kept the double seat free for Malaika, but Nadeche refused special treatment, insisting that the woman take it. How else could she have reacted? It's incredible how jam-packed the buses are. This has nothing to do with the Turks, but with the euphoria of the refugees when they caught sight of their transport.

"If we don't have to walk, we don't mind it being a bit more of a squeeze."

An adult on every seat and a child on most adults. And the aisles full of people. The smell must be appalling. Nadeche doesn't notice it anymore, but the way her skin feels, the way

everything sticks to everything else in this bus – and everyone to everyone else – is revolting. Even Saba stinks a little,
sitting there on her lap, and Saba usually doesn't stink at all.
But her smell is not half as bad as her silence.

Nadeche runs a sticky hand through Saba's sticky hair.
She doesn't know what to do. If they were in her car she could
drive for a bit, just to pass the time, but the car was given the
elbow. By Lionel. And now that everyone's on a bus, she can't
do much to help anymore. Distributing water, aspirins – all
that's done at the service stations by the army.

Nadeche takes a filthy scrap of material from her filthy
trouser pocket. Carefully, because there's not much water left
in the bottle, she moistens it and wipes Saba's brow. Then she
makes her a hippie headband with the material. She can see
why people used to think hippies looked like tramps, but it
does keep the forehead cool.

Saba doesn't react, she just lets all this happen. She stares
out of the window. Then she says, "You didn't know either,
did you?"

"No," Nadeche said.

Saba turns and looks at her. "What about him?"

"He didn't either."

"But he must have known! And you too!"

"He doesn't tell me everything. I'm sure he knew more
than I did, but he didn't know that."

Saba turns back to the window.

"He *couldn't* have known, sweetheart! Nobody did. Not
even the Turks. The plan was different.

The little hippie doesn't react. It's hard to tell whether

Saba doesn't believe her, or whether Nadeche just isn't getting through to her. In desperation she gives Saba a squeeze.

"He told me himself. The plan was actually very different."

The plan was that the column of refugees should board the buses in the same order in which they'd been walking. Every day one section of fifteen kilometres would board. And the buses would wait until a large convoy was ready. The Turks thwarted this plan. They made some calculations and showed Lionel how it would only lead to a huge traffic jam. When a convoy comes to a halt it takes an eternity for it to get moving again. Because the buses can't all drive off at the same time like coaches on a train. The one at the front has to set off first, and only then can the second one go, then the third – this all adds up. With ten buses, if everything goes smoothly, it'll take four minutes. With a hundred buses it's forty minutes. And with a thousand it's more than six hours. So for the entire process to be quick, each bus needs to leave immediately and then keep going, on and on and on. Two drivers per bus, fixed fuel stops, fixed toilet stops, fixed water stops and nothing in between. But even the Turks thought they would board the buses in phases. They thought they could use the intervening time to drive the next buses over to the car park.

But the refugees didn't see it that way.

The little hippie lets out a sob. Nadeche can feel her shoulder becoming damp.

She can understand them. After a year and a half's trek, and seeing the people ahead of them board a bus, no-one's going to lie down after kilometre number fifteen and wait till the next day. So what do they do? They walk one more kilometre, which means they've done sixteen that day – it's not so much. And the ones behind realise they haven't stopped as they usually would. So they walk on as well, because it's only another two kilometres – it's a piece of cake after the distance they've already covered. And it goes on like this because word gets around that there are buses waiting. Which everyone automatically translates as: if we lie down now and go to sleep, the buses might all be gone tomorrow. So they up their pace. Not only that, the further back you are, the more kilometres you have to add on to your normal daily march.

Nadeche saw the footage on her smartphone. Everyone saw the footage on their smartphones. The pictures weren't from MyTV, but from n-tv and A.R.D.: people goose-stepping along the road. People overtaking others, which has never happened before on this trek. Causing those being overtaken to panic. Parents lifting up their children. Hurrying past the lorries, scooping up food and water so they can keep going, like marathon runners. Baleful figures who've been walking without a break for eight hours, twelve hours, twenty-four hours, driven on by a fear that nobody had antici-pated. Parents screaming at their exhausted children, beating them onwards. And the horror in their eyes the further back they are.

People suddenly running for their lives.

"If he'd known, he would have . . . he would have done everything differently," Nadeche whispers to Saba, even though she doesn't know whether this is true. Lionel told her that the Turks had called him. The telephone number that had vanished all of a sudden popped up again, and someone shouted into his ear, "Are your people ever going to stop, or what? We're done for today!"

Lionel called his contacts and realised he was no longer in control of the situation. Even if they'd promised everyone there would be enough buses – that they could rest for at least two hours without worry – nobody would have believed them. Nobody believes reassuring news when thousands of those dreadful, sleepless, horrified spectres wander past and just want to keep going. The fear in their faces was visible, the fear that if they didn't keep going now, everything would have been in vain.

The Turks were quick enough to realise that if they'd tried to stop people boarding at that point, it would have led to a disaster. They had their hands full trying to get enough buses onto the full roads. They must have created a new track especially. There is drone footage of the small car park. It looked like an enormous mincer in which people and buses were being combined. For when people begin to walk more quickly, they no longer arrive in a steady flow. But a catastrophe at the border was averted. In part because it had already happened, earlier on the road.

She remembers the footage of Pakka standing beside his medical supply vehicle, shattered, resigned, howling, somewhere by the side of the road. People are lying on the ground, all the way to the border crossing. The column left thousands behind. People who collapsed and could go no further. Some just have cramp, some are unconscious. Some are injured.

Broken ankles from walking carelessly, the rush, and even from being kicked by other people.

Some are dead.

Saba's mother sent a photo via her mobile.

She tried to leave Saba's father behind in a dignified fashion. She couldn't bury him, given the hurry – the fact is, she didn't know that theoretically she would have had enough time. But then if she'd known *that*, he wouldn't have rushed to his death in the first place. Dignity is relative, of course. In this case it meant dragging him out of the middle of the road. She sat him up against a bush. It did indeed look a touch more dignified, or at least a little less passive than if he were simply lying there. Did she turn him to face the wide expanses of Iraq, or the panicky sprint to the border – it's not clear from the photograph. In his arms Saba's mother put one toy from each of the three children.

Then she ran for the bus.

Nadeche can feel the dampness running into her bra. But the sobbing has stopped. From the corner of her eye she strains to look at the small, grubby head. Saba has fallen asleep.

That's something, at least.

# 51

"I've got good news and bad news," the president of the E.U. Commission says down the line.

"That's better than nothing, I suppose," the minister of the interior says. He's put it on speakerphone because he can barely sit down anymore. His shoulder is made out of wire, his neck is a vice, his back is cricked and he can only keep still if he's standing. "Let's have the bad news first."

"O.K. We haven't reached an agreement."

No surprise there. The minister doesn't respond immediately, like someone taking stock of unpleasant news they've been expecting. "What did they say?"

"Not much. But now the French are prepared to take five thousand."

"Instead of three thousand?"

"I know, it hasn't got us very far. Still, two thousand more is two thousand more."

"What else?"

"Nothing else. I reckon the French might move a little more if others gave an indication that they'd help out. But they're not. The Italians, Spaniards, Portuguese and Greeks are all saying they've done enough already. And our friends in the east are saying—"

"I know. I can only emphasise once again that *we're* the ones who'd be helping *them* out."

"They see things differently."

"The Bulgarians? Do me a favour!"

"Especially the Bulgarians."

This is nothing more than a game. It's Old Maid. It's a child's birthday party. A rich boy's been invited, and nobody likes him. All the other children are laughing and saying how funny it would be if the stupid rich boy got stuck with the Old Maid. They give each other hints as to who's got the Old Maid, and who has to pass on which card so that it ends up with the stupid rich boy. The hints become increasingly obvious. When they get bored with the game they simply slip the Old Maid between the other cards in the stupid rich boy's hand, facing outwards, without making any secret of the fact. "Go on, cry if you like!" they say. And if he does cry they're even more delighted.

"I hate to say it," he insists, "but the Bulgarians are going to have to deal with the refugees on their own." Germany may be stupid and rich, but it's not defenceless.

"That's what I already told them," the president says. "But be honest now. Do you really believe that?"

"I'm just saying it while there's still time. Any country that opens its borders has to bear the consequences. If the Bulgarians think the Serbs are going to take the problem off their hands; if the Serbs think the Hungarians are going to do it; if the Hungarians are placing their hopes in the Austrians –

that's their business. But we aren't going to do it. Last time we went as far as we could. Germany has reached its limit."

"But you're still offering to allocate them to the various countries."

"I don't think you've quite understood me. We're not offering anything. We can't offer anything. But if someone is in a desperate situation and asks for our support, we're always ready to help."

"Five thousand refugees?"

"We have a limit prescribed by law. And the job of defending our country. The principle of proportionality still stands. With a smaller number we could opt for a softer approach. But with four hundred thousand people that's out of the question. You know that as well as I do."

"Yes, you know that, I know that, everyone knows it. But the countries along the Balkan route may well be prepared to let it come to that."

"Didn't you say something about some good news?"

"I think we need more time. It's no good if every decision is taken in this highly charged atmosphere."

"We're not the ones with a foot on the accelerator, it's the refugees. And – I can't prove this, but it appears to be the case – the transit countries."

"Alright, now listen. The calculation is simple. If the borders stop working, Germany risks ceasing to be a functioning E.U. Member State. And if Germany buckles, the entire E.U. buckles too. Are you with me so far?"

"But we've already passed that point, surely. The other countries' borders are no longer functioning."

"But we can do a repair job."

"How?"

"We'll make the borders *look* as if they're functioning. If Germany voluntarily accepts the refugees, we can, for a certain period of time, continue to claim that the border is functioning. The E.U. will unanimously declare its gratitude to Germany for making a one-off exception once again."

"Unanimously . . ." the minister says sarcastically.

"Unanimously. I'll sort that out. By now you might be thinking we're incapable of sorting out anything, but I'll do it, I give you my word."

"What use to us is this 'certain period of time'?"

"It'll give the E.U. the chance to agree a refugee policy that is properly consistent."

"And you believe that?" the minister says.

"There's one thing I'm certain of: if, in the eyes of the world, the E.U.'s external border is breached, then nobody will see the need for an agreement anymore."

"The same is true of the German border. No, the only way it will work is like this: once the Bulgarians have reeled in the first quarter of a million refugees, they'll ponder whether they want the same again."

"Are you really going to put up those high-voltage fences?"

"No comment."

The story had already appeared in several newspapers and *Bild* was referring to him as "Mr 100,000 Volts". He had leaked the information himself, to ensure his plan became public knowledge as rapidly as possible. He doesn't have any political backing. Officially the chancellor's office knows nothing, and first needs to commission a review. They've made it clear that he'll have to carry the can if the plan goes wrong, if it's criticised, if there's a scandal – in every eventuality, in fact. Some experts regard the plan as completely unviable, others say it's definitely possible. At any rate, electricity is quicker to deploy than soldiers. What helps his cause is the widely held view that the Germans aren't famous for bluffing.

"In that case," the president says dejectedly, "I'm afraid I won't be able to help you. You know I'll keep trying, but there's no point in me going back to them with the figure of five thousand refugees."

"And *you* know that I can't bargain. I can say seven thousand, I can say eight thousand, but I'll never get anywhere near the numbers that would be of any use to you. I can't go back to the German people with even half the number of refugees."

For a moment there is silence on the line.

"I can't think of anything else," the president says. Suddenly she sounds incredibly tired and shockingly old. "I don't know where to begin. Clearly we're going to have to chance it."

The minister says goodbye. Standing in his office, he has to concede that he doesn't know where to begin either. Which means he might as well go and have a good sleep.

# 52

The bus has gone quiet. Not just quieter than in Serbia or Hungary, where the atmosphere was still quite jolly, as if they were on their way to a gigantic country wedding. Now everyone's fallen silent, even the small children, who usually squabble or shriek at every opportunity. It's hard to say when this began. Maybe when the mountains started looming. Maybe when they saw fewer and fewer cars coming the other way, even though it's broad daylight. Now there's nothing on the other side of the road.

The Germans have closed their side of the border and now, at the sight of the empty carriageway, the refugees feel strangely alone. Like in a Western when there's going to be a shootout and everyone vacates the saloon as fast as possible.

Lionel gazes through the windows at Austria, this astonishingly wet country. The clouds are hanging low. All the rain has made the land fertile, at least where there are no houses or roads. It's so cluttered. Everywhere you look there's something; nowhere is there nothing. He noted at once that he was right, there are no goats. It's obvious, because lush grass is growing all over the place here. Strange how these Europeans fail to come up with the simplest ideas. They're so modern and rich that they've lost sight of all the advantages goats bring. That's doubly good, because he won't have any competition. They're worried about work being taken away from them, but nobody here works with goats. Eighty million Germans and hardly any goats – if only ten Germans share one goat, it's still a huge market he can take by storm.

"Slow down," he tells Mahmoud. "Stay just in front of the guys behind."

He sees the Austrian military vehicle in front of them pull away, before it too slows down after a few hundred metres.

"More to the middle," he instructs Mahmoud. "Don't let them overtake."

"More to the middle," Mahmoud repeats like a boatswain. Lionel passes the message to those sitting at the back to signal the change in speed to the bus behind. Now they're driving across a small, astonishingly straight river. At first he thought it must be a canal, but Google Maps calls it the "Salzach".

"Should I stop?"

Lionel points at the parking signs for the next exit. "Wait till there."

He holds out his smartphone: Google Maps shows a small stopping place.

"Turn off, drive through the car park, then back onto the motorway and park sideways. I mean right across the motorway. We'll go on foot again from here."

"It's getting serious now, is it?"

Mahmoud pulls into the car park. They could have driven

on a bit more, all the way to the border, but Lionel doesn't want to spoil the image.

"When we stop, and those behind us do too, then grab a few drivers and really block the lanes. I don't want any clever Dicks sneaking past."

He's talked to a few of Malaika's television people. They say the pictures that work best on television show helpless people holding children by the hand, and they have to be walking. These same people don't look so helpless if they're travelling on a bus.

At this point the motorway takes a broad curve to the left. The cameras at the border will be able to see the people with children coming towards them from a long way off. All day long they've been swapping places to be at the front. In the fiasco at the Turkish border the young men were clearly the strongest. This upset the order, which is why they've rearranged it. Everyone knows there are plenty of young men among the refugees, but it's not something they need to emphasise. A bride makes herself pretty for her wedding.

Mahmoud steers the bus through the stopping place. He brakes on the slip road leading back onto the motorway and slowly drives it perpendicular to the carriageway. Then he opens the doors and switches off the engine, for the first time in more than a week.

The silence and lack of vibrations from the diesel engine lend a finality to the moment.

Somebody whoops, then cheering erupts, as if they'd already arrived at their destination. Lionel steps off the bus. Bushes line the stopping area. Through the bushes he can see blue lights; the Austrian police are blocking off all other routes, so that nobody gets any last-minute ideas of staying here. Aid organisations have set up taps for water and distribution points for food. The army has also secured the exits from the car park, unnecessarily as it turns out, because these are jammed with vehicles bearing the logos of aid organisations. The car park can only supply a fraction of the refugees. People who've been sitting waiting beside their cars stand up. They throw away their cigarettes, drink up from their cardboard cups and return to their vehicles to supply those sections to the rear of the convoy.

Onlookers watch from the wire fences that seal off the car park. Many are holding shapeless objects which, on closer inspection, turn out to be cuddly toys. He heard somewhere that refugees attract cuddly toy tourists like dead fish do cats. Europeans must assume that refugees need cuddly toys more urgently than anything else. Apart from in Hungary where a crowd pelted them with stones. In truth, he surmises after peering inside the bus, most people here would like nothing better than a bar of soap.

On his mobile Lionel checks the G.P.S. signal of the infant transporters. They're still fifteen to twenty kilometres away, rapidly getting closer. Malaika is on a bus five kilometres behind that. A pink zebra car squeezes past the buses and comes to a halt, and a camera team gets out and hurries over to him. He gives them a reassuring wave. "We've still got bags of time," his hands say. There's nothing to do now but wait. For the other buses. Not all of them; that would be as pointless as setting off with only one hundred people.

The cogs in his brain are still whirring away, but there really is nothing more he can do because everything has been done. His head is churning out its usual nonsense. Was this really the right place to cross the border? All of a sudden he's assailed by the thought that he's made the wrong decision. That the bridge over the Inn would have been the better bet.

But he's dismissed this idea so many times that it's easy enough to do it again now. Yes, it would have made the best possible impression in the smallest space. It's only thirty to forty metres wide, the Germans could have made every effort to seal it off, and likewise they would have made every effort to storm it. Undaunted by death and with no possibility to avoid it, with the water flowing on either side. The Germans would have had to take a decision. A nice showdown. But who would have seen it?

Where would the cameras go? The Germans weren't going to provide them with prime locations. They'd have to put the crew on boats or pontoons. And from there, below the bridge, you'd be hard put to capture faces, you'd end up with poor-quality, shaky footage. Besides, you couldn't be sure some refugees wouldn't leap into the river if things got dangerous. Then everyone would say it's their own fault they drowned. That won't happen at the Salzburg border crossing.

On the other hand, there's far more room to slip off to the side here. He can't tell how great the desire is to go to Germany and Germany alone. What if half of them were to say that in fact Austria is nice enough, thank you?

And what if the other half reckons they can manage on their own from here?

What if he sets off for the border tomorrow or the day after, and finds himself on his own when he gets there? And at the end of the day everyone has made it to Germany via detours and secret paths. Everyone but him.

Lionel massages his brow with the balls of his hands. This isn't the first time he's been tormented by all this nonsense. And on each occasion he comes to the same conclusion: how could they abandon the man walking alongside Malaika and the cameras? They'll follow him because it's their best chance of a good future.

The Germans won't shoot because they're good people. They won't switch the electricity on either. They tell these stories because refugees are tiresome – that's understandable – and they'd be glad if fewer refugees came to their country – that's O.K. too. That's why they're pretending to be angry. That's politics. But when it comes down to it, the Germans are decent.

The rain has stopped. The cloud cover has broken and the sun is making the car park quite pleasant. One of the television crew hands him a small bottle of water and something to eat. Why not? Lionel thinks.

He sits on the ground, his back against a bus tyre warmed by the sun, and gazes at the mountains. Malaika has told him about them. It's where milk and chocolate grow, she said. He told her she might be mistaken, because cacao comes from Africa. That's perfectly possible, she replied, but in Germany the chocolate normally comes from the mountains. Although in winter it comes from an old man with a beard in a red outfit.

Lionel takes a sip of water and bites into a thick slice of bread, on top of which is a bright-yellow slice that has a slight hint of mould. He chews bravely. Let everyone see how well he fits into Germany. That's all he can do till Sunday.

# 53

The minister of the interior feels as if he's in an old newsreel. Rommel inspecting the Siegfried Line. Maybe it wasn't the best idea to go for the federal police uniform. The minister is wearing a bulletproof vest, and this time he looks astonishingly good in it, determined even, as he greets the journalists. N.D.R., W.D.R., B.R., Z.D.F., R.T.L., MyTV, N24 – they're all here. They have almost unlimited access; the minister is keen to show how impassable the wall is they've constructed. Gödeke is taking him to the ramparts. He's in uniform too, but with boots and a pistol. The minister has made it clear that he wants to see people with firearms.

"Pistol, sub-machine gun, ideally both. I don't want camera shots on any of the news bulletins where there aren't at least three firearms visible. We mean this seriously! Snipers too!"

He's talked through this press conference with Gödeke several times. No affability, no friendly remarks – the message must be unequivocal. They've assembled the press in a room where they'll be easily heard, and rather than have Gödeke turn to the journalists and say, "Shall we start?", the minister introduces him, then Gödeke says, "Ladies and gentlemen, we don't have much time so please follow me."

It's all about demonstrating their resolve. He wanted the elite police unit here too – assault rifles and pump shotguns on display. He's commandeered all available special vehicles with mounted snowploughs, as if these could push the refugees away. They're chiefly for show too. More serious are the Mowags he's had unofficially retrofitted. Those who know their Mowags would be surprised. Never before have these vehicles had machine guns, let alone heavy machine guns. And anyone registering surprise might also question the legal basis for these. But the minister isn't particularly worried. In his experience journalists who are keen on weaponry are less interested in questions of legality. And journalists who are interested in questions of legality generally don't know the difference between a machine gun and a sub-machine gun. They'll assume the police must have the whole lot stored away somewhere.

They accompany the journalists to the transporters. They will have to take a detour to be able to view the border installations from outside, from the Austrian side; it hasn't been possible to drive straight for some days now. You have to go via Switzerland or Italy or, as the transporters are about to do, take one of the secret government tracks. To ensure that these remain secret, the vehicles have no windows. Mobiles must be surrendered so that no smart Alecs can follow the route via G.P.S.

He and Gödeke arrive first because for security reasons, the press have to take a few extra twists and turns. The minister gets out and looks around. The border zone, which until a week ago was permanently full of parked lorries, has been evacuated and now looks like a field ready for battle. The service stations and petrol pumps are sealed off with fences that are unlikely to hold. Some of the windows on the second floor of Walserberg service station have been boarded up. On the ground floor they're just bricked up. The large building sits tranquilly in the sunshine like a stranded ship.

As there was every likelihood of plundering, the fuel pumps were emptied to the last drop. The minister heard that the leaseholder has already sued Austria for loss of earnings. But that hasn't changed anything; even the Austrians would rather solve the problem first and then untangle the legal issues afterwards. At any rate the Austrian police and army are both here. The army can be deployed for the protection of internal security. They're allowed to use real tanks. Not that these would be particularly useful in close combat, but they give the impression of greater resolve. Or they could. In truth, the minister thinks, Austria just looks like *Sound of Music* country.

The transporters carrying the press arrive. The minister waits for the reporters to get out and lets them take in the bizarre set-up. "It's like during the oil crisis," says one cameraman who can only know the oil crisis from television. Gödeke and the minister lead the way. Together with the reporters they climb a press platform that has been constructed especially for the occasion, and which affords a good overview. They look out over the newly erected installations towards Germany.

"It's like the Berlin Wall," Mr Oil Crisis says.

"What you can see here," Gödeke begins, "are high-security fences built to the highest standard. Underpinned several times, impossible to push over. Few horizontal struts make them very difficult to climb. Protected at the top by razor wire. Each pillar is set in concrete at least one metre below the ground. The fence rises to six metres above ground level with an overhang at the top."

"Degree of difficulty?" a young woman asks cheekily.

The minister looks at Gödeke.

"We got the Alpine Association to give us their assessment. They say between eight plus and nine minus."

The cheeky woman whistles through her teeth.

"Which means you'd have to train for a few years first. Nobody's going to just climb over it. But in any case our objective is that they don't even begin climbing."

"It could look a lot more daunting," a young reporter says. "The exclaves in north Africa are better secured."

With his silence, the minister implicitly agrees.

"The appearance of the fence is chiefly down to the need for a swift response from the authorities," Gödeke explains. "It's pointless if you build a super wall right by the motorway here, but it's only two hundred metres wide and you've got a garden fence beside it. Everyone would just go to where it's easiest to get across. So rather than plumping for the most secure option, we had to go for the most secure option that we could erect across the greatest distance."

"How long is your fence, then?"

"That is confidential. But we do have the advantage that

such a large procession of people cannot simply wander two hundred kilometres unnoticed. If they change their location, so can we, and more quickly."

"Where are we here?" a reporter says. "In Germany already?"

"We're still in Austria," Gödeke says. "Officially we've just driven into Austria by the terms of the Schengen Agreement. To prevent the refugees from exploiting the opportunity that being on German soil would offer, the fence has been built right on the border."

"This is the difference from installations like those in Palestine or Mexico," the minister explains. "There people want to slip into the country unnoticed. Under Israeli or U.S. law they can't invoke their rights in the same way. So you can relocate your fence fifty metres into your country. We, however, are working on the assumption that these refugees are intending to apply for asylum *en masse*, for which in theory they merely need to be on German soil. This is what we're trying to prevent."

"There's never been a border installation like this."

"Sure there has!" the oil-crisis Berliner says.

"Certainly not," Gödeke says. "There are installations designed to prevent the covert intrusion of individuals and groups – for example in Israel and the U.S.A. There have been and still are installations designed to prevent the covert escape of individuals and groups – like the wall you've referred to. And there are installations designed to defend against armed attack – which include every castle fortification and the Great Wall of China. But to date there hasn't been a single border installation designed to withstand storming by unarmed intruders who in addition plan to claim asylum."

"Are you saying that this fence follows the exact course of the border?" the climbing woman says.

"That's correct. The electrical construction even hangs slightly over it."

"So you actually did that?" an older reporter asks.

"The state mustn't allow itself to be blackmailed," the minister says, giving his routine answer. "These people are also perfectly safe in Austria. They don't have to come to us."

"How secure is the construction?" the older reporter asks. "What we see now . . . is that everything, or is there more to come? What is the strength of the current, for how many people is it life-threatening?"

"The specifications are confidential," Gödeke says. "But I can state that we weren't able to use normal industrial protective fences because of their inadequate current. And here I'm talking about fences built to protect power plants."

"Let me assure you that any refugee who tries to tamper with this fence will face the most unpleasant consequences German manufacturing can offer," the minister weighs in.

"Lethal? Or not?" the older reporter mutters. "That's the key."

"It's a one-off experience that the person concerned will never repeat," the minister replies.

"Because they won't want to, or won't be able to?"

"Able to. In all likelihood."

"Lethal, then," the reporter notes, as satisfied as if he'd found a perfect mushroom in the woods.

"At this point I ought to clarify something. Most people think a fence should be so secure that nobody can climb over it. But that's impossible. There is no fence in existence that's impossible to surmount."

"So why bother build one in the first place?" the climbing woman says.

"A fence," the minister pontificates, "is a statement. It says that where the fence is, the path stops."

"You could do the same with red string," the mushroom collector says.

"True. The key thing about this fence is not what it's made of, but what you're going to do when somebody decides to disregard it. Whether you can defend your fence, or your string. Let me assure you that the Federal Republic of Germany has all the means and units necessary to defend her borders, and we intend to make use of these. The federal police have been in intensive training for weeks. We are prepared for any crisis situation."

"If you are so resolute," the oil-crisis Berliner says, "how many deaths are you braced for?"

"I can't give you any figures." The minister puffs out his chest. "But I was there when the refugees crossed the Turkish border. And in a similar situation the German police will not stand by and watch. If unauthorised persons try to cross the border, we will stop them."

"And if they keep trying?"

"We will keep stopping them," the minister says, and then pauses deliberately. "Until nobody tries anymore."

"You won't follow through with that," the climbing woman

says, giving the minister a stern look. "When it comes to the crunch you'll have to give in. You'll have to open the border."

"And where would we do that?"

The climbing woman turns to look at the fence. And only now does it dawn on her.

"We're not playing games here, we're serious," the minister says determinedly. "We're haven't got secret accommodation ready. And we're not going to open the border at any point. Because, as you can see, there aren't any openings here."

# 54

Nine o'clock in the morning. They thought about arriving at the crack of dawn, but that's too much like an invasion. The only people outside your house at 4.00 a.m. are burglars, enemy soldiers or the secret police. Lionel doesn't want to catch anyone off-guard. He wants to arrive on a Sunday, because that's when the Germans have their day off. Malaika's broadcaster was even able to write in the T.V. magazines: Decision Day. They will broadcast footage all day long. The drones have been in the sky ever since they set off. He's walking alongside Malaika and Saba, like a little family. Yesterday evening he went three hundred buses back with Malaika, and that's where they spent the night.

"Our last night," she said.

"The last night in this car."

Astrid was there too, and they stared lovingly at the night sky for the photographer. Not actually at the sky, but at the security lamps of a fenced industrial building. "Well, I'll leave you alone, then," Astrid said with an expression that suggested they were about to enjoy a wonderful night of passion.

For the last time they pondered whether Malaika should

stay behind. But that would be idiotic. Malaika is the only one they can be sure the Germans won't let anything to happen to. And although he wants to protect her, Lionel isn't macho enough to disregard the fact that it's much more a case of Malaika, with her fame and all the cameras, protecting him.

The plan is to have women and children first, throughout the day, then a running jump into primetime. But to start very slowly.

Each holding one of Saba's hands, Malaika and he set off at around eight o'clock. They took people with them from each bus they passed. They weren't in any hurry; this isn't an assault. "Germany is a country where everything works brilliantly," he told the television cameras, "and we are good people who work hard. But hard work is useless if your house is burning down. All we want is to work in a house that isn't burning down."

It's very calm apart from the odd Austrian. "Time to go!" they call out. Or: "Piss off!" Or: "Bye bye!" The people from the aid organisations shake their heads, paper cups of coffee in their hands. They took a small detour to a Red Cross post, where the people were very friendly and handed him a coffee. He asked whether he could have milk with his coffee: "I always drink my coffee with milk." This was a little white lie; he doesn't like coffee. But the Germans like coffee even more than they like beer, and he wants to be a good German. Let the cameras see this.

"Your German is so good!" a chubby woman says.

"Yours too," he says, principally for the television.

She laughs and brings out a carton from under the table, from which she pours milk into his cup. Lionel says goodbye to her and holds the cup up to the camera: "Cheers!"

In truth this walking is a bit unnecessary. At most they're just checking that all the women and children really are at the front, but they've known what they have to do ever since Turkey. They made similar preparations for the other borders too, even though it wasn't necessary. But Astrid said it would look silly spending the night by the fence and then just getting into position in the morning. For the camera, they have to walk up to it.

They come to the first row of military vehicles. A few hundred metres further on are barriers, which only "authorised" people are allowed through. These are reporters, police, paramedics and the like, Malaika told him, "people with authorisation. A piece of paper." Which confuses him because he's pretty sure that not one of the four hundred thousand people behind him has any authorisation or a piece of paper. Some police officers look equally unsure: how can they check the refugees' lack of paper?

Lionel is also pretty sure that some people walking alongside them would have papers. People with very light skin taking videos on their phones. But who can tell? After all, most people are taking videos on their phones – today is *the* day for it.

Malaika tugs at his shoulder. Oh yes, selfie time. She hugs him, Saba between them, then she taps and swipes and puts the picture online. Now they're passing the infant transporters. One of the nurses looks out of the open car, beside her a colleague puts a baby into a mother's arms. All four are crying. The nurses because it's a wrench to let the baby go, the baby out of habit and the mother just to be sociable, perhaps.

Here comes the last barrier. They can already see the fence up ahead. They've studied the area thoroughly – Astrid's camerawoman helped out a bit with her drone – and it is in fact the same fence here as it is twenty kilometres to either side. So they chose the place with the best view for the cameras. Right by the border crossing. The broadcasters haven't left anything to chance; they've installed all manner of floodlights for when it gets dark It looks as if they're entering a huge arena.

Lionel suddenly feels sick. It's nothing, he tells himself. You're on dry land. You're steering yourself. This is so much better than any rubber dinghy. It's been worth it at any rate. But it doesn't feel that great. He tries to find more positives. Like the fence.

It doesn't look so bad. Four or five smart, fit young men working as a team – in a quiet moment that could work rather well. But there's scant chance of a quiet moment with four hundred thousand people coming up behind. Especially as the Austrian soldiers and police officers have been most thorough in seeing to it that nobody disappears into the bushes. Not many have tried either. Those apprehended singly are soon shunted off somewhere. It's like with sardines: only the shoal offers security.

There are yellow warning signs all over the fence.

Will they switch on the electricity?

Lionel stops ten metres before the fence. Beyond it he sees a crowd of masked, armoured police officers. Armoured vehicles, machines that look a bit like ploughs. He gives them a friendly wave. They don't react. He sees a large number of firearms of every calibre, including machine guns. Glancing to his right he sees Malaika standing there. Cameras film both of them from below. Malaika looks like an angel with a flaming sword sent by God, just without the flaming sword. He sees Saba clutch her hand first, then his. He turns to the people advancing behind them. Young people, women holding the hands of children, or with children in their arms.

He turns his back to the fence and gives a determined nod. The plan is women and children first. And everyone behind him knows to go slowly, but to keep moving. Onwards and onwards. There is only one direction.

And if they can't go any further: push!

# 55

"Give me sector C," the commander says. Now the large screen is showing one of the outlying areas. They can see more young men, too many to assume this is just a random grouping.

"I think they'll be the first to try. Can I get another camera?"

The strategy simulations all showed the same thing: they will send young men up front, who will try to climb the fence and weaken it from the other side. Or claim asylum, that might happen too. They must be stopped. It's like a balloon. If the rubber bursts you can't stick it and the whole thing collapses – you have to ensure that first hole doesn't appear.

"Loudspeaker," the commander orders, "and move two water cannon over there. Keep those boys well away from the fence!"

Well away is no longer possible, however. Most of the refugees at the front are far too close to the scary electric fence. Nobody's tried to touch it yet. Some of those at the front are anxiously pushing backwards.

"Should we . . ." Gödeke asks the minister. They're standing side by side, watching the organised chaos, so that he can authorise decisions at any point.

The minister shakes his head. "Nine thousand volts is enough."

The power cables have been moved. They're working, but they're now at the top of the fence. They mooted the idea of electrifying the entire thing, but it would have been counter-productive. If such a mass of people were to push against the fence it would kill at most a few hundred before the installation became overloaded or damaged. And with such a large number of people unable to retreat, this would be a few hundred deaths to no additional effect. It would be no more than a "we tried" signal, and this signal could be given more effectively with targeted shooting. Shots are generally audible and there are fewer fatalities. And the fear of the electricity remains. It will scare them off for longer.

"We don't want to sit and wait, open up the fucking gate!" they're now singing.

"There is no gate," the minister mutters. There's only one way to disperse this crowd and that's from behind, where they can still be kept well away from the fence. Those behind would need to be driven back, dispersed into Austria, after which they could set about removing those at the fence. Then those wankers would have to scoop the refugees up again. They'd have to deal with them rather than just waving them through. But it's inconceivable that the Germans could use tear-gas grenades or anything similar on Austrian soil.

"O.K.," the commander says. "Showtime!"

Accompanied by cheers from the refugees one of the boys climbs onto the shoulders of another. "Water cannon the moment he touches the fence," the commander says into his headset. "And get ready for sector A, that's where the next attempt is likely to be."

The first water cannon spouts forth, knocking the first boy clean off the shoulders of the other, but two more have climbed up and are already holding onto the fence. These are smooth metal struts, now wet too, yet the boys stick to them like geckos, with only one arm. They reach back with the other, trying to get their hands on coats, blankets, whatever they can use to cover the electrical cables and razor wire at the top.

"Give the warning!" the commander orders. "Snipers at the ready!"

The fear of the electricity is greater than the electricity itself. As long as nobody climbs up the fence, nobody knows just how strong the current is. So the key is to keep the refugees on the ground. The commander glances at the minister and Gödeke, and when neither reacts, he says firmly, "Warning shots!"

The gunshots are clearly audible. The cameras show the crowd retreating, if you can call it that. It appears to contract, but there's barely any room. One metre, perhaps only half. The boy clings to the fence.

"He's going to get it," the squad leader warns. "Fingers or legs!"

Two shots are fired, and the boy sails back into the crowd with a scream. More shots are fired, and all the cameras show an empty fence once more. The minister fetches a cup of coffee. He saw Lionel do just that on television earlier: get a coffee. He raises his cup and toasts his absent opponent.

It could be going worse.

# 56

At some point the cameras withdrew from the crowds. To begin with Nadeche thought this sensible, as they could no longer get sufficiently far away to capture decent footage. Besides, there are enough refugee cams in the crowd. But now she feels slightly abandoned, which may have something to do with the gunfire.

She didn't see exactly what happened, she just heard the cracks. But word quickly spread that some of the refugees had been shot at. A wave of fear surged through the crowd and Saba howled with pain because someone stepped on her toes. Then the shooting stopped. "It's all part of the poker game," Lionel called out to her. "They have to do that. Our boys are only injured." Which was true, of course.

"Ooooh, it's all getting a bit like, cosy here," she says cheerfully into the microphone by her mouth. "I've been to a few discos in my time. And I've squeezed into Cologne pubs during Carnival. But there isn't going to be any dancing here!"

"You're on camera right now," she hears in her ear. "Would you give a wave? Ten o'clock?"

"Are you already on the booze? It's well past noon!"

"Our drone is coming from ten o'clock. From where you are it's quite far to the left, no, not completely to the left . . . the *other* left! Where you . . . Yes. That's it. Give us a wave!"

Nadeche thrusts up her hand, which in itself isn't easy, and waves towards the drone. This isn't very funny anymore. She's five or six metres from the fence, and up front it must be even more cramped, because the fence has less give than the people around her. From time to time some of the boys try to climb, but every one of them has paid for it by being shot at. In fact nobody is daring to touch the fence. Down below, Saba is clutching her knee to avoid being dragged away by the crowd. Nadeche bends to her as best she can.

"Do you want to go on Lionel's shoulders? Or mine?"

Quite a few people are doing this now. Children who are old enough are being lifted onto shoulders. It saves space and it's safer for the children.

"Yours."

"O.K." Nadeche groans. "But you've got to help me."

It's virtually impossible to bend over, and she can't just lift Saba up either. People are so tightly packed that she has to manoeuvre her upwards like a corkscrew.

"Press hard against me," she says. "I'll pull and you crawl your way up. Put your feet in my trouser pockets."

"I can't get my feet up," Saba pants.

Nadeche feels fingers on her bra straps, then the straps are off. The fingers dig into the sleeves of her T-shirt. The sleeves hold. A quality product.

"Everything alright?" says the earbud. "Should we send the helicopter?"

"No," Nadeche gasps as Saba's head pushes up between her breasts. "It's crunch time now! Just a little longer and they'll have to open up. I mean, surely they can see what's happening here!"

The loudspeakers are now instructing people over and over again to clear the border zone. In English, German and something else. You'll be lucky! Nadeche thinks.

"I've lost my shoe," Saba squeaks.

"Keep going, sweetie. There are plenty of shoes in Germany."

Saba's bare toes scrabble around Nadeche's waistband. Clever girl. She's realised that she can't get up at the front, so she's clasped her thighs around Nadeche like a coconut picker in a palm tree, and she's pushing herself up. She turns around deftly and gives a laugh of relief from Nadeche's shoulders.

"Hello Germany!" she squeals, waving with both arms.

"Wave towards ten o'clock, sweetie."

"That's good," the earbud praises her.

"Have you got the babies on camera?" Nadeche wheezes. "Ouf!"

"What's that?"

"Whoah, that's tight . . . I could barely breathe just then . . ." She puffs out again, unintentionally loudly. "Have you got the babies on camera?"

Hardly any of the babies are crying at normal volume now. She can hear widespread howling accompanied by that griping undertone babies put on when they've really had enough.

"Yes, we have," the earbud says. "It looks pretty mega. The viewers are getting worked up already. There are demos in Berlin and everywhere else we've put up big screens."

"H . . . ow! How many . . . vie . . . ooh! View . . . ouch!?"

"Almost a hundred thousand in Berlin, more than fifty-five thousand in Munich. But we weren't allowed to put a screen in the city centre there. Not a surprise really – where do you think the minister of the interior is from? But it's all kicked off at the border where you are too. More than ten thousand have made their way there. Your job's done, you can knock off now."

"I'm not chickening out now . . ." Nadeche moans. "That's precisely what they want!"

"You won't be able to see it, but there are masses of people coming from behind where you are. From where I am it looks pretty overwhelming . . ."

"When the going gets tough, the tough get going," Nadeche pants. "I know what I'm talking about, I come from a humble background! Bloody hell!"

"O.K., let's do a live connection then – it looks great. Right in the thick of things rather than just watching from the sides! In two minutes!"

"O.K.!"

"Maybe you should put Saba down?"

"That's not going to happen." Nadeche tries to make some room for herself, but it's not easy.

"But if we want Saba on camera we'll only just get your

head in. And if we focus on you, then most of Saba will be out of shot."

"There's nothing I can do!"

"O.K., we'll think of something. Wide-angle or whatever."

Nadeche gives Saba's knee a squeeze of encouragement. Saba squeaks. Then Nadeche tries waving to Lionel and gestures that she's about to be on camera again. Lionel gives her the thumbs up. The crowd has dragged him a few metres further away. It's annoying that the live programme is being presented by that ex-W.A.G. Didn't they want the show to be like Schreinemakers? Now it's more like Schweinsteigermakers. Forget it. When she's home she's going to take a nice chunk of time off, and together they'll write the book she signed the contract for last week. And when the book's really buzzing she'll make a grand re-entry into television, bang into Thursday evening primetime, knocking Heidi Klum off her perch.

"Ten seconds, Nadeche!" the earbud says. "And at ten o'clock!"

"Roger!" She lifts her head and says, "Here we go, sweetie!"

# 57

"This is really close to the knuckle now," Reliable Anke says. She alternates between hands on hips and clenched fists as she paces up and down. Her eyes are fixed on the screen in the middle.

"Oh, I don't know," says Olav, in contact with Nadeche Hackenbusch via his headset. "It was more extreme at lunchtime."

"More extreme?"

"To my knowledge those were the first live gunshots ever on German television."

"At least the shooting has stopped. Just look at that, it's like the Love Parade in Duisburg."

Olav scans the various screens in the control room. He shakes his head and looks at Beate Karstleiter, who's tapping one of the two technicians on the shoulder. Despite the dimmed lighting in the control room Olav is sure the technician wasn't that pale this morning. The camera zooms in to the area by the fence. It's true, people are pressed together like herrings. The women hold their heads at unnatural angles, their chins tilted upwards to snatch some air in between the taller men. It's a scene you only see on underground trains at rush hour, and it's been like this for at least an hour. People look exhausted at best.

From time to time there is pushing in the crowd, when another group of arrivals increases the pressure from behind. This pushing, these waves of pressure leave even those watching breathless. It's as brutal as it is obvious. It's not some subtle tactic; these people want to get into another country and they're prepared to die for the privilege. This time, however, they're doing it on the Salzburg motorway rather than on the Sicilian coast.

"Look at that woman there, up at the front," Reliable Anke says, and she gasps. "She's out of it. The only reason she hasn't fallen over is that there's no room. Look, her eyes aren't even open anymore."

"Are you sure? I don't know, maybe she's just having a rest?"

"Look at her! She's not having a rest. It must be thirty-five, forty degrees down there."

The door clicks open and Sensenbrink comes in. From the faces in the room he can tell at once that the mood isn't as great as the viewing figures. "What's our marvellous minister doing? Can't he see what's happening? Doesn't he have a television?"

"Possibly," Reliable Anke says. "Maybe he's on the wrong channel. Bayerische Runkfunk has stopped broadcasting."

"What's their excuse?" Sensenbrink says.

Anke points at the screens with both hands. "They're refusing to broadcast this, instead they're showing stills with an audio commentary."

"I've been dialoguing with Kärrner until just now. Last time I looked the situation was dicey, but not dire. What's happened?"

Now Anke taps the pale technician on the shoulder and he gets the shot back on screen. "Do you see that woman there?"

"Shit," Olav says. "There's another one. Christ!"

"And there," Beate says, standing up. "And there! Look!" She points at the screen.

"For God's sake, they ought to be watching out for their children if they're going to have them on their shoulders," the technician exclaims. "They're practically asleep."

Lots of children are now slumping with tiredness. Some topple over their parent's head, others fall to the side, and only some parents still have the energy to look after them.

"Don't zoom in so close for the broadcast pictures," Sensenbrink orders, then more emphatically: "I said not so close!" But the technician zooms in ever closer to a sleeping three-year-old, as if he could wake the child this way.

"Hey!" he yells. "Your little one's slipping!"

Then the toddler vanishes. He collapses to the side, then falls back head first, as if diving into the crush of the crowd.

"Shit, where's he gone?"

"He can't have gone anywhere," Olav says. "There isn't any room for him to fall to the ground."

"Rewind," Anke orders, "and let's look at the angle from camera 5."

"But for the live feed I want you to zoom out to a distance shot, do you get me?" Sensenbrink says.

The technician rewinds the film. They see the child fall back, then hit his head on a the head of a young woman behind. The woman drops to the ground, the child follows and the crowd closes above them.

"Shit," Sensenbrink says. "Fucking shit."

Anke covers her mouth with her hand.

"They've got to pick him up," the technician says. "Someone's got to pick him up. The boy *and* the girl, both of them!"

"Nobody's doing a thing," Karstleiter notes in disbelief.

"Nobody can," Olav says. "They can't move."

"That . . . that can't be . . . It wasn't like that before . . ." Sensenbrink rubs his face. "It must have escalated in the last few minutes."

"No, it's been like that for a while," Anke says.

"Oh shit! For God's sake, don't zoom in so close, none of our advertisers want to see that!"

"The girl over there!" The technician bends to the left and vomits into the wastepaper basket. Reliable Anke pushes his swivel chair to one side and takes control.

"The question is whether anyone wants to see it – oh Christ, there's another one. There! She's gone." A woman vanishes silently into the crowd like cocoa powder into a glass of milk.

"It wasn't like this earlier," Sensenbrink rants. "We can't broadcast this. Switch our feed to another area, further away. Go to a commercial break. And make the live picture smaller. How come we didn't get a heads up about this? What's our wonderful star been doing the whole time?"

"Nadeche?" Olav says. "What's the scene like with you?"

"What camera's the silly cow on, anyway?" Sensenbrink says.

"Two," the technician says, his voice shaky.

"Nadeche?" Olav tries again.

"Rubbish," Sensenbrink says. "She's not on two."

\* \* \*

The minister of the interior yanks round the steering wheel to avoid hitting a transporter. The wound on his forehead has reopened and he can feel blood running down the side of his head. They're already sending police vans back from the border – this is madness, utter madness. He needs every man up front. He reaches for a tissue in the glove box, but all he finds are cigarettes, handbooks and replacement magazines for a pistol.

Another police van races past, blue lights flashing; he almost drives the 4×4 into a ditch. He realises that he hasn't got his seatbelt on. They shouldn't pull more people out, he thinks, but he doesn't know how to give the order. He can't get to grips with these new radio devices and the mobile network is overloaded. He should tell a police officer, but there's never one to be had when you need one.

He's been at the exclusion zone, where all hell has been let loose. It's not the farmers, that much is clear – it wouldn't ever occur to the farmers. It's the furious television viewers, people who moved to the country to give their children a better or greener life, or to have a lawn to accommodate their five-thousand-euro barbecue and a playground without anyone else's children. And it's people who've driven out from the cities to demand the border be opened.

The exclusion zone was properly secured, he'd satisfied

himself of this earlier. It was no surprise that these human rights activists and aid organisations would mobilise. But nobody could have anticipated the force of the images. You can talk to Greenpeace and the others, those people are professionals. But these protesters are amateur. Worst are the outraged women. The agitation, the nagging, always in such shrill tones: "You don't have children, you wouldn't understand!"

It was particularly unfortunate that so many came. "Twenty thousand," the young police sergeant told him earlier as he was being driven there. "Twenty thousand?" he said. "Are we talking police estimates here or for real?"

The sergeant turned to him and said, "If you ask me, there are twice as many. Easily."

The twice as many saw at once that there were only a handful of officers on standby. The access roads should have been blocked, but there's a big difference between stopping demo veterans at a G20 summit and people claiming they urgently have to save lives. At a certain point they just went around the roadblocks. And then the vigilantes thought their time had come. He saw it with his own eyes, having stopped with the sergeant at one of the redundant roadblocks to get a view of the situation. Idiots in ridiculous uniforms and with extraordinary stocks of weapons emerged from the bushes and tried to fraternise with the police officers. There were at least four reports of this, all from different places. It's unbelievable how many of these loonies there are now. Some officers were even delighted – it's beyond comprehension. Via radio he ordered this chumminess to stop at once, and then he heard the shots. They weren't warning shots; those self-appointed auxiliary police officers were firing at the crowd, shouting, "Fuck off! This is our country!"

The minister shakes his head as if to banish an unpleasant thought. He watched the young police sergeant use the 4×4's radio to call in help. It was a podgy man, tattooed, with a homemade S.S. armband and a Kalashnikov, who shot the man standing beside an extremely irritating woman twice in the stomach, then knocked her to the ground with the butt of his rifle – one quick, professional, brutal blow to the side of the head, which flipped to the side as if her neck were made of paper. She toppled over like a dummy in a shop window.

The young sergeant leaped out of the car, yanked his pistol from its holster and bellowed at the minister, "Get in and drive straight to the situation centre! Get reinforcements. Go, go!" He fired a warning shot, and because the man with the Kalashnikov didn't react, he shot at him a couple of times. The Kalashnikov man fell to his knees, at which four of his fellow idiots turned around, took aim and put two bullets in the sergeant's head. No hesitation, one fluid movement – turn, raise rifle, bang – as if they did this every day. Then the minister made the engine of the 4×4 roar. Two of the vigilantes turn their attention to the screaming demonstrators, the other two fire at his departing vehicle. Several bullets tear into the metal. Something hot fizzes past his head. Soon after that he is behind a knoll and out of range.

The minister gets everything out of this 4×4 that he learned on that rally driving course. What has the domestic intelligence service actually been doing these past few months? How can these types suddenly appear out of the woodwork in packs? This is fast approaching a state of emergency; he's going to need the army. He swerves to avoid a tree growing at an angle across the road, almost ramming a police van that must have overturned attempting a similar manoeuvre. He sees officers tending to other officers and squeezes his car into the field beside the road. Hoping that this 4×4 is worth its salt, he puts his foot down and the engine roars, catapulting the car back onto the road. The minister throws himself to the side to avoid smashing his head on the ceiling. He takes out his phone and taps on it with one hand.

He should have called in the army straightaway, but then there was no state of emergency, all they could have done was to offer humanitarian aid and he didn't want to send out any false signals. The refugees mustn't get the idea that tents are being set up for them. By now he'd have had companies, brigades, everything there, hundreds of men who would just need to be given rifles. The way they do it is all wrong, and the mobile network isn't working either.

Another police van is coming towards him and the minister slams on the brakes. His weight is thrown against the wheel, he changes gear and accelerates again. Now he can see the situation centre. He drives practically to the door, a low concrete wall doing the lion's share of the braking. The minister flings his arms against the dashboard and roof, his head dashes against the steering wheel and he doesn't feel his incisors bore into his lower lip. Something light falls on his head and slides past his bloodied temple. He leans back in the seat. The sun visor is down, something has fallen out. He looks woozily on the ground, finds a piece of paper and picks it up: a photograph of the young police sergeant and a girl in a bikini. The sergeant is bare-chested, he's wearing his cap at an angle. The girl is snuggling up to him, grabbing at his cap, but one of his arms is around the girl and the other holds tightly onto the cap. She's laughing. Written on it in touch-up pen is: "My warrior for law and order".

"My" is underlined.

And on top of the "i" there's a heart.

* * *

Nadeche comes to, partly because she's lying so uncomfortably. In fact she's hardly lying. Her arms and legs are wedged between other legs, twisted at strange angles, and she can barely pull them towards her. Her face is on its side, a foot knocks into her skull and her cheek scrapes across the tarmac.

The loudspeakers have gone quiet. In their place she can hear groaning, cries for help and men's voices shouting something perhaps intended to be reassuring. She can make out a few words like "further on" and "border".

She needs to stand up.

"Olav?" she says into the headset. "Olav?"

Olav doesn't reply.

"Olav," Nadeche says much louder, because there must be a glitch on the line, "send the chopper! Now!"

She remembers that the transmitter must be under her left hip. But when she feels for it, the transmitter isn't there.

Get up. Get onto your knees and then your feet. She tries to turn over, but someone else's legs are where she wants to go. She tries to hit the legs to attract attention, but she can't even take a swing. Presumably the other person's legs don't notice any difference between her hands and all the other legs.

"Lionel!" she shouts hoarsely and then, louder, "Saba!"

\* \* \*

I've failed, Admiral Mahmoud thinks.

He's where an admiral ought to be, right at the front. He always wanted to be a proper admiral who stays with his troops, not one who hides at the back.

He tried to organise his people, but there's nothing more to organise here.

He tried to form protective rings for the women and children, but the protective rings were flattened and became useless.

He shouted at them, he appealed to their sense of honour, but now he hasn't got the puff to shout anymore. He's standing by the fence, trying desperately to prevent one of his arms or legs slipping through.

He's seen what happens to those people when the crowd shifts. Arms and legs suddenly at impossible angles, until you realise that they're no longer connected to the bones, only the skin. But the spooky thing is the silence. Because no-one has enough air in their lungs to scream.

\* \* \*

"Where are your Germans . . . huh?"

Lionel can't place the voice. It's soft but clear, and it's coming from somewhere he can't see.

"Where are your Germans?"

"They . . . they're going to open up," Lionel wheezes.

"Bullshit. They're . . . going to . . . let us . . . die . . ."

Lionel wants to give a longer answer. Something along the lines of: "This is now the key phase, we have to tough it out, we all knew it would happen like this." But he can't get enough air, so instead he says, "They . . . can't."

People are already dying. Even if the Germans pull off a miracle now, people are going to die here. And Lionel has no intention of being one of those fatalities. He can't feel his hands anymore, his legs are numb.

It's so easy to say, "We're going to risk our lives one way or another."

But in the end you only risk your life because you assume you're not going to lose it.

"Where . . . are your Germans?"

"Where is Malaika?"

Lionel can't answer these questions. And it strikes him that he doesn't care, either, so long as he survives the day.

* * *

From outside the situation centre the minister hears Gödeke bark, "How can they stand by and do nothing? I mean, it is their fucking country."

An official hurriedly opens the door for him. Gödeke is standing in the centre of the room, ranting in the middle of a group of police officers who are all staring at the screens in disbelief. Two are showing MyTV, and from the corner of his eye the minister can see the news ticker: "CKENBUSCH

MISSING +++ SEVERAL DEAD +++ E.U. OFFERS TO TAKE 15,000 REFUGEES +++ NADECHE HACK-ENBUSCH MISSING". But the most horrific news isn't coming via the television. It's the surveillance cameras on the German side of the fence – the really exclusive images. Exhausted, emotionless faces pressed by the mass of people against the wire fence as if it were a gigantic egg slicer. There's no sound, but the minister has never seen so much fear without any screaming. Arms reach through the fence in supplication, some are just hanging from it. He sees a child's head in an extremely unnatural position.

"What they're doing there constitutes failure to render assistance," Gödeke screams. "If only we could get away with that."

We already are, the minister thinks.

He looks at the police officers staring at the screens. He sees them shake their heads – this is all too much. The older ones among them can't watch anymore; they keep turning away. Sergeants, a chief inspector: experienced officers, all despondent. And whenever they avert their gaze, that gaze tends to fall on him. Slowly, one by one, they turn to face him, the last being the commander. This isn't insubordination. They're asking for help.

The minister tries to keep his composure. There must be a solution, no matter how horrendous the pictures are. What has priority? What is his most urgent task? He has to represent the interests of a country, his country, he has to act in the interests of its citizens. But is all this in the interest of its citizens?

"Minister," Gödeke says, "what are we going to do?"

Leubl claimed that this would change the Germans, that what is happening here would turn them into murderers, into accomplices to murder. He doesn't know whether this is true, but what's certain is that if he continues to let these people die, soon the Germans will be citizens of a different country entirely.

He wasn't elected so that he could change the country before the very eyes of its people.

But the country will change with more refugees too.

If the country is going to change anyway, which country should it become? He thrusts his hands into his trouser pockets and feels something, thick paper. The photograph.

The young woman. The young police sergeant.

The minister takes a deep breath. He's finding this difficult, his voice is a combination of anger, admission and resolve. His fist closes around the photo.

"Ladies and gentlemen, the objective of our operation has changed. What we see here may be the law," he says. "But it's no longer acceptable."

\* \* \*

Nobody seems to react to Nadeche's cries. She can hear muffled yelling from elsewhere. The crowd seems to surge in one direction, presumably towards the border installations, and with this movement comes a communal groan.

"Saba!"

On the ground she's useless; she's got to get up, first on one arm, then up. She tugs a trouser leg and a foot steps on her forearm. Nadeche screams. The foot twists until only the toes are on her. Her other hand feels wet suddenly, body-temperature warm, and only now does she notice that the ground is damp in several places, beneath her face too, but that's probably blood.

"I'm down here!" she cries. "Hey! Down here! Saba! Where are you?"

Painstakingly she gets to one knee, but that alone doesn't help. She's in danger of falling flat on her back, and here that instinctively feels like the most dangerous option.

"Nadeche," she hears a very faint voice say.

"Saba? Where are you?"

". . . eche!" It's impossible to work out where the voice is coming from. ". . . deeeche!"

"I'm coming . . . I'll come and get you!" Nadeche cries, and another wave surges through the crowd, people move over her like an immense swell and the mass becomes even more tightly packed. "Oof," the men say and the women scream as the air is pressed out of their lungs. Nadeche Hackenbusch yells because something heavy is burying her foot beneath her. With one jerk she tries to free her leg from the weight, now the wave moves and a sharper pain shoots through her ankle. She feels her leg give way beneath the weight, but the pain remains, it roars and drones in her ears, she gasps for air, her legs twist themselves around her, she tries to remain conscious – it hurts like hell. She feels the weight shift, only squashing her calf, but a foot is now bracing itself against her shoulder, pushing her back.

"Lionel!" Nadeche yells with all the breath her lungs will

allow. More and more feet come. They feel their way forwards, they realise they're stepping on something far too soft to be the ground, then they lift again, quickly but clumsily, as if they're struggling through a viscous liquid. They try to set down elsewhere, but there is no elsewhere, the feet feel her as blind aliens might an unfamiliar life form, and at some point they have to come down. All Nadeche can do is try to roll to the side and let the feet slide past her.

"Lionel! I'm here!"

She's not sure whether her voice can penetrate through all these bodies. In desperation she pinches every leg she can reach and tries biting into the leg attached to the foot on her shoulder. The leg shifts to her chest, it presses her shoulder blades against another leg that yields a couple of centimetres so that Nadeche slides further back.

"Lionel!" she cries out in panic. "Down here!"

Somewhere above a voice is barking orders. The legs on top of her try to coordinate.

"Hemp!" the muffled voice shouts, and then more clearly: "Hand!"

She thrusts her other hand upwards, twists it behind her and manages to push it up as far as knee-height, she can feel calloused fingertips but can't get a grip. The tips of her fingers keep groping and she manages to get them into the calloused hand, then the crowd surges again, the hand is pushed away and her arm is clamped beneath a stranger's knee and pressed to the tarmac. She feels the knee try to straighten, slowly at first, then desperately, and then it goes limp.

"N . . . deche," she hears a feeble voice. ". . . scared!"

Nadeche suppresses her panic. She's often discussed with Lionel what would happen if the border wasn't opened, and he says that there's no fence on earth that could withstand that pressure indefinitely. The way things are going here it can only be a matter of minutes before the entire fence crashes to the ground and this madness stops. Somebody small kicks her in the stomach.

"Saba, hang on in there!" Nadeche calls out. "It'll be over soon."

Her neck is painful; it's so strenuous to hold it up like this the whole time.

"Saba, can you hear me?"

It happens in a split second. As Nadeche tries to reassess the situation it strikes her as clear as day that there's no room for any doubt: if she doesn't get up in the next few minutes she will never hear Saba's voice again. She feels herself beginning to scream, no more words, she screams as loudly and shrilly as she can, louder than she's ever screamed in her life, everyone's got to understand that this is the end, this isn't about a few scratches and scrapes, this is about Saba's life. Nadeche notices she has released energies she never knew she possessed. The unbearable pain in her leg is just risible now. Nadeche pulls and tugs and fights her way up.

But she only gets as far as knee height.

A hard kneecap rams her nose, she feels it bleeding, but she can't even get her hand up to wipe the blood away. She screams, she tries to scream even louder, but her voice cracks, it's not as penetrating as before, and now she hears another woman somewhere else screaming in exactly the same way, but louder.

"Saba!" Nadeche screeches. Perhaps she only thinks she's screaming, it's hard to tell the difference because the pain in her foot has returned, and it's worse than before. A leg knocks off her wiry headset and sharp metal bores into her auricle, a foot steps on her head and slips off, across her face and past her painful nose. She senses a form of tiredness, a sort of preparatory tiredness because she realises that now she's going to need huge amounts of strength, it will be arduous, even more arduous than before, she needs to summon all her reserves. Another short rest would be good. Trying to push away these legs is so irritating and futile: the moment you've shoved one away, another takes its place. Now someone else is standing on her thigh, she rolls to the side but keeps her foot where it is, it's bearable, right now it's more important to rest, she has to protect her chest, make herself small, another surge goes through the crowd, as a result of which two feet press her to the ground, the back of her head smacks hard against the tarmac, she lifts it, more as an impulse, and suddenly the ground seems cosy and inviting, if only her leg . . .

* * *

A flashing blue hope. These are the vehicles belonging to the fire service, every fire service they could muster at the border. They're working on the fence, they're working feverishly and they're cursing because this fucking fence is made out of some kind of fucking metal that even the most powerful hydraulic cutters barely make a fucking impression on.

To start with they tried to cut too far up the blades, but the pressure wasn't great enough. You need to position the cutters as close as possible to where the blades meet, but then the blades jut out and into the people pressed against the fence. They hesitated. Referred back to operational command. Until the minister came running out of the situation centre and seized the unwieldly tool from the nearest firefighter.

Now the minister looks as if he'd been bathed in blood. He took turns with a firefighter and they cut through three struts, during which he sliced into a dead foot and a living one. Around him, firefighters are directing two diggers, trying to prevent the fence from toppling over and burying the rescue crew beneath it. But there aren't enough people, there aren't enough diggers – there aren't enough of anything. Most of the police constables are needed back in the border area. They have to ensure the fire service and other services can get through, if they're not already caught up in battles with right-wing extremists. Real skirmishes, not just Molotov cocktails, no. These are attacks by trained paramilitaries trying to get to the border to take the law into their own hands. Helicopters have been brought into operation; the Austrians authorised that, at least. Their job is to pick up refugees from the back of the crush and fly them to Germany. But the refugees don't trust the pilots. They want to walk across the border because only then can they be sure that they'll get there.

It's incredible how much the fence is sagging. Everything sags eventually, of course, every piece of metal can buckle, but anyone who saw the fence before wouldn't believe their eyes now. They switched off the current and then hastily discussed whether to invite the refugees to climb the fence, but that would have resulted in the stronger ones clambering over the weaker. The worst-case scenario would be to have the fence hanging with people like love locks on bridges; it might collapse in the wrong direction. They need to release the pressure in a controlled fashion, and the only way to achieve this is by opening the fence.

He can't hear the cries for help anymore; they don't seem to be as insistent. Since help is now suddenly being offered, some refugees deduce that the fence is no longer electrified, but those at the very front are too weak to climb it, or they're wedged in and can't move. The minister thinks they should remove the razor wire. He bellows this to the firefighters, who then argue about how best to do it. When building a fence nobody thinks about the simplest way of getting rid of it again.

Someone brings an angle grinder, which looks like a machine for cutting gigantic loaves of bread. The minister hears someone say, "Fuck it" and "Or the whole lot of them are going to die on us!" When the machine starts up it makes an ugly sound.

A small boy is lying on the ground beside the fence, looking directly at the minister. He'd feel more relaxed if this boy weren't staring at him the whole time. He's already tried to position the cutters so he's no longer in the boy's field of vision, but there's only one practicable angle. When he first saw the boy he tried to offer some words of comfort. The boy didn't respond. Now the minister has discarded his jacket.

It was as he was varying the angle of the cutter that he first noticed the boy's critical gaze, as if in surprise at the minister's ineptitude. Then suddenly his expression changed.

The minister hears a muffled bang, something misfiring perhaps. He looks up to see if everything is alright with the tools, but nobody else seems to have reacted. Clenching his jaws he presses the cutters against the metal with all his strength. The fence creaks reluctantly. They've obviously removed a substantial section at the other point, he can see the digger juddering. The driver revs the engine to push harder against the fence. The minister has one more go, then falls back and a firefighter takes over.

The boy could be eight or nine years old, it's hard to tell because only his head is visible and this head has become quite shapeless by now. Someone is standing on it, someone who has someone else standing on them. The boy doesn't care. The minister wants to look away, but that feels like a betrayal. It's as if the boy were saying, I can't look away.

With a groan he stretches his back, and then he hears it again. A muffled bang, and then another.

It's coming from the other side.

# 58

Astrid von Roëll has switched off the screen. She can't watch things like that, she's prone to claustrophobia. It's not as if she can do anything anyway. Kay is out somewhere with the drone and the agency is supplying the updates. This is how it used to be with her colleagues in sports – you just had to wait for the results. It can't be that exciting. Why should this be any different from the previous borders? Germany is one of the richest countries in the world; they'll open up at some point.

Over the past few days she's been thinking about whether she should prepare an obituary for Nadeche, just in case. It's what all the major newspapers do, the big agencies. Once a famous person gets to a certain age they have an obituary on file so they can be the first to publish when the time comes. Because these things can't always be planned. One day an actor might be treading the boards, and the very next – phut!

She's been *obliged* to think about it – that's a better way of putting it – because the deputy blockhead suggested something along those lines: "Of course this is a very delicate topic, Frau von Roëll, but we do have to be professional here . . ."

First, she's not a news agency, second, she's got enough to do as it is, third, she's a human being rather than a machine, and fourth, Nadeche might not die after all, and then the effort would have been in vain. She doesn't mean this cynically; in fact it's unimaginable that Nadeche might die, whatever the news ticker said.

And that's precisely what she told the deputy blockhead: "How can you think like that? We're talking about Nadeche Hackenbusch here! If she dies they'll have scripted it beforehand!" And this of course is doubly true for her going "missing".

In the end he understood her point. In any case they could get the intern to cobble together an obituary. If Astrid were to have any involvement at all, it would be to give the piece a personal touch: "Nadeche Hackenbusch's final hours – my own impressions."

She goes to the front, sits in the passenger seat and puts her feet up. Three young men are peering out of the back window of the bus ahead. They're laughing and making flirtatious gestures. She shakes her head reproachfully, but secretly she feels flattered. She may even miss the camper van. At least a little. How many more nights will she spend here? One? Two?

She wonders whether the Museum of Contemporary History will be interested in it. After all, one of the longest reportages in German history was completed inside this camper. Probably *the* longest reportage. As well as one of the best, as ought to be noted when they award her the Nannen Prize. Or that other one, the Theodor Thingummy Prize. The

Pulitzer might also be in the frame, but she doesn't know anyone in New York.

She feels a muffled explosion from beneath. As if the motorway had farted.

The boys in the bus in front obviously felt it too. Astrid puts on a dumbfounded, amused and innocent expression, and holds up her hands as if to tell the boys, "It wasn't me." But the boys aren't paying attention, they're looking over the roof of her camper and pointing at something. Then the ground lets rip once more. Astrid frowns. She slides her feet off the dashboard and hops out.

Her eyes follow the line of buses. There's hardly anyone to be seen, they're all inside because the sunshine makes it difficult to read off their phones. What is crucial for them is what's happening at the border. Far, far in the distance Astrid sees two columns of smoke. She turns around.

A police car is driving at high speed on the country lane that runs parallel to the motorway. She sees the man in the passenger seat gesticulating wildly. The car reverses and leaves the lane. It backs into a field and its wheels start spinning. The engine howls, the gesticulating policeman wrenches open the passenger door and runs away across the field. He takes big, awkward leaps, each time sinking up to his ankles. Astrid can't help but laugh.

The motorway shudders and roars, up ahead this time. Turning around, Astrid sees a fireball in the queue of vehicles. Another fireball, then another, another, like a ball chain, like an enormous fuse cord. She looks at the bus in front, it becomes incredibly loud, the noise swallows her like a huge dragon's mouth and then there's just a ringing in her ears.

The bus no longer has a rear window, nor any at the sides, in fact the bus has no windows at all, which is a good thing because the burning boys can climb out. They're screaming, but they must be quite hoarse already. Astrid can't hear anything anymore, or maybe only one is screaming. The other two are lying half out of the window, like duvets hanging out to air. Burning beds, they'll definitely reek of smoke.

Beds are burning, Astrid thinks, remembering the song.

She watches a woman struggle to open the rear door of the bus, but it doesn't budge; there must be something blocking it inside. She turns to scream at someone else on the bus, she bends in tears to pick up whatever is blocking the door. Then her face reappears, her mouth is wide open, she's given up on the door and is trying to crawl through the narrow opening where the window shattered. She puts her head through, then a shoulder and an arm, her mouth is open wide all the while, Astrid has never seen anyone open their mouth so wide, then her hair catches fire and a large flame rolls down the length of the bus.

The time has come.

Hot air hits Astrid in the face, but the air is much harder than air, as if Astrid had run head-first into a blistering wall. She can smell burned hair, sweat runs into her eyes, she wipes her face with her sleeve, it's painful, the sweat is dark red, she feels along her forehead and removes a shard of glass, half of which is beneath her skin as if it had been slipped into a neat little extra pocket.

Astrid decides to follow the lolloping policeman, then she collapses. Her right trouser leg is missing; it doesn't matter, she was going to throw out these trousers anyway. But there's a piece of bus sticking out of her knee and her leg isn't working quite how it was before. There's skin missing too, and she can see the parts of her knee connected to each other. It looks like chicken. Maybe it's not just her knee, maybe there's another piece of bus in her thigh. Her trousers are dripping wet, which must be a good thing with all this fire about. She's glad it doesn't hurt, it doesn't hurt at all, that's another stroke of luck she's had.

She turns to the bus behind the camper, which is still intact. The door opens, a man stumbles out, pushed by a dozen hands, he looks at Astrid, but this time Astrid doesn't feel flattered. His expression is one of horror, and she shakes her head and rolls her eyes. She thinks she can see a cigar hovering in the sky. Something comes away from the cigar, two smaller cigars, one of which is coming towards her, then her eyes are covered in blood again. When she wipes her eyes she sees the man burning, and the bus he was on is in flames too. Something burning crawls across the ground, then turns feebly onto its back and goes on burning but no longer moves.

Astrid's camper explodes without a sound.

Once, when she was a child, Astrid cycled home through a hailstorm with her best friend. It was high summer and the experience was both painful and lots of fun. The hailstones bounced around all over the place, they pelted her skin, her face, she squealed and Biggi, slightly podgy Biggi, squealed too. Now Astrid is lying on the ground, she's trying to squeal in the hailstorm, but it's a laborious gurgling, she needs to rest, she's out of breath. She allows herself to sink back, she feels giddy, lying down is much better, then the blood can run out of the sides of her eyes, carefully she raises her head, her heavy, heavy head, she sees part of the cutlery tray sticking out of her chest, two knives, some forks too, at least they won't have to look for them later, there's something stuck to her shoulder, another sliver of wood from the cutlery tray. Astrid chokes, she needs to cough, there's something in her throat, in her lungs, not that too, she's choking, she tries to clear her throat, her mouth tastes like it smells in the garage sometimes, not where they work with oil, but where the metal shavings fly around, she once had a thing with a mechanic, he couldn't stand blood, he wouldn't like her T-shirt now, even though it's wet.

Now she feels terribly cold. How weird, Astrid thinks, seeing as the camper van is blazing away. The museum isn't going to want it now.

# 59

The minister of the interior could swear it happened just when the firefighters hauled him back. A groan swept through the kettled-in crowd, the section of fence came springing towards him and the firefighter he was taking it in turns to cut with grabbed him by the collar and dragged him away from the danger zone. They watched a ten- or fifteen-metre length of fence come down as if it were as soft as wax. Then they saw the refugees burst from their confinement, a seething mass of people screaming in horror, in their panic running over and into each other. He saw that even saving them would cost lives, and he prayed that it wouldn't be many. Please let it be fewer than fifty, he prayed, or at least fewer than a hundred, oh Lord, let it be few, for it is my fault they are dying, punish me but spare them. They wanted to enter the Promised Land, just as Your people once did, and what I did to the merest among them I did a thousand times.

He prayed that the rest of the structure would give way as soon as possible, so that they didn't all have to squeeze through this ridiculous gap, and he remembers seeing the fence sway and tip over at the other end too. This completely irrational feeling of happiness, this unbelievable relief, as if there were the prospect of a happy ending after all, even though of course it won't be a happy ending because he can already predict that what they will find on this side of the fence is going to be dreadful, and not just because of the boy with the dead eyes.

Then he remembers a series of fireballs rising from the valley, glowing, yellowy-red pearls on a chain, targeted with great accuracy one after the other, as if by a particularly pedantic god. He saw them heading his way and then the kettle of people exploded in ten or twenty of these fireballs. The minister remembers a body flying towards him, circling like a dancer with arms outstretched, but with no legs or head, although in his hand was a strange, burning hat, a sort of captain's cap. Here, part of the minister's memory is missing, it seems. It must be missing, for what is happening right now doesn't fit with the flying man.

The minister is walking along the motorway. He walks past the buses, there are hundreds, probably thousands of buses, there's no end in sight, and each of these buses is in flames. Thick clouds of black smoke billow from the glassless windows, fat as gigantic, grub larvae. The seats and interior of the buses burn like torches doused in filthy oil. Some of the black bars bend in the heat, these are huge, burning cages. In the seats he can see people, their black heads sometimes tipped forwards, but mostly backwards, dark silhouettes against a flaming background. Mouths gape in skulls like vast notches in tree trunks. Sometimes he can see the teeth. From the way they're sitting, some appear resentful, but many look as if they'd just been thinking about all their efforts and privations, and then about the outcome, and as if they're laughing, loudly and bitterly.

Next to these heads he can make out smaller heads and black arms around black necks, and everywhere those open eyes, open more widely even than the mouths, those horrifically open eyes that will never close again.

People are standing beside some of the buses, watching the inferno. Some scorched figures keep trying to get back onto one of the buses, they raise their arms helplessly, they try to walk until they realise the futility of their undertaking, only to try again. The minister sees a man filming with his mobile, and a sobbing woman, perhaps his wife, place her hand on his forearm. He drops his phone and embraces her.

The air is thick with the acrid stench of diesel, burning plastic, rubber and charred flesh. Now and then the shifting wind envelops the minister in thin swathes of narcotic smoke, and people emerge from the plumes as if from an underworld. Many are missing skin, with others it's impossible to tell where the clothes end and the body begins. He doesn't know what he can do for them, without any equipment, without medicines, without water, and with only one arm he's still able to move. He ought to turn back, but he feels it's his duty to plough on; he wants to know if that terrifying god really has, with all thoroughness, turned every bus into a burning coffin.

Then the minister sees the woman and the child.

They're moving slowly, like the walking dead, but they are moving. The girl can't be older than seven or eight, but it's the girl who's leading the woman by the hand. The girl has a sooty face, as does the woman who could be her mother. She looks straight ahead with a serious expression and walks tentatively, as if here, on this motorway, she has to decide with each step whether it's worth the effort. The fuel tank of a bus behind the girl goes up in flames, she barely reacts. For a brief moment she stays where she is, a dark shape in front of the whitish-yellow inferno, then continues on her way.

The minister stops. The girl is walking with small steps, dragging the woman behind her, determinedly but with little strength, as if she were a toy. The girl stops beside the minister. She turns to look up at him. There is nothing in her eyes, no supplication, no anger, no reproach, no complaint.

The minister holds out the hand that he can still use to the girl. She hesitates, but then places her small hand in his. The minister holds it tightly and turns around. Then he heads for the border with the two of them.

# Speculation over Tauern disaster

## At least 300,000 feared dead – the search for those responsible continues

**Berlin** – Ten days after the appalling attack on hundreds of thousands of refugees at the German–Austrian border, the federal government has once again strongly condemned the action and demanded swift results in the search for those responsible. "The deliberate and ruthless killing of more than 300,000 people is nothing less than the greatest mass murder since the Second World War," the chancellor said to relatives at a funeral ceremony for those police officers, firefighters and paramedics who died in the attack. "In the name of civilisation and humanity it is our duty to bring these killers to justice."

While the authorities in Germany remain tight-lipped, investigators continue to hunt for clues. "The logistics nec-essary for such an operation reduce the number of possible suspects," one high-level Russian government official told this newspaper. "A coordinated military attack using stealth drones capable of hitting several hundred targets at the same time requires both substantial military capability as well as the appropriate technology. It is no secret that at present there are only two states in the world which have both. And Russia isn't one of them."

Experts and military specialists interpret this as a pointer towards the U.S.A. and Israel, although they describe both possibilities as "hard to imagine". Indeed, both the United States and Israel have unequivocally and uncon-ditionally condemned the attack in the U.N. Security

Council and the General Assembly. International scepticism is growing, however. Under-secretary Volker Lohm, said, "When there's a dead deer lying in the forest, it's difficult not to point the finger at the only person in the village with a rifle. Especially if it's the hunter."

With this analogy Lohm is picking up on theories doing the rounds, suggesting that Israel has the greatest interest in preventing Germany from sliding into right-wing extremism. The possible objective is to retain Germany as a reliable partner. Experts emphasise, however, that such an undertaking would require the tacit approval of all the states through whose airspace the drones flew. Groups critical of the E.U. have advanced the explanation that the aim of this action was to preserve Germany as a financially strong member of the E.U. Lohm believes this, too, is highly implausible: "That's very far-fetched. And before we leap at the wildest conspiracy theories it would be wise, at least where some of these theories are concerned, to offer up some proof. If no bullet was shot from the hunter's rifle, then no clues will be of any help."

## The logistics necessary for such an operation reduce the number of possible suspects

Meanwhile, it continues to prove difficult to establish the precise number of fatalities, although sources are now ruling out any figure below 300,000. The injured and the dead are still being recovered, as well as those who have been severely traumatised by the catastrophe. Official organisations involved suggest that the chief obstacle to determining a more accurate figure is the greatly increased willingness of the population to take in refugees and hide them from the authorities. (*a.p./d.p.a./Reuters*)

# Nadeche Hackenbusch: even in death she watches over her son

**Ex-producer Nicolai von Kraken and sweet Bonno: hand in hand, father and son are completing the life's work of this great entertainer and woman**

*kitsch!*

It's like in the film "Titanic". An incomparably bitter catastrophe leads to the greatest treasure that humankind possesses being raised to the surface from the darkest depths: the heart. Five years after the shattering tragedy on the Tauern motorway, Nicolai von Kraken, head of the Nadeche Hackenbusch Foundation for the Humans, will, at the former border crossing and now-cemetery, open the new visitors' centre designed by star architect Daniel Libeskind at a cost of 150 million euros. And even though this is a sad occasion for the widower of the unforgettable "Angel in Adversity", he cannot help but say, "Today the future looks better than we could have dared dream – and the world has Nadeche to thank for this."

It is still a practically unbelievable, almost supernatural story. In a lightning attack, bombs from stealth drones killed more than 300,000 people within the space of a few minutes, among them Nadeche Hackenbusch, the selfless "Angel in Adversity", an enchanting woman whose appearance and absolute sacrifice for the poorest of the poor made her into a Lady Diana *de nos jours*, even though Nicolai von Kraken modestly dismisses this: "Nadeche wouldn't have liked that. You shouldn't start judging one against the other. She died for hundreds and thousands of people; that British woman once put on a helmet as protection against landmines, you really can't compare the two."

Nicolai von Kraken puffs out his chest, but the pain burrowing inside him like a dog in a flowerbed is palpable. Yes, many observers were surprised when, only a few days after her death, he made it public that the divorce from Nadeche had been as good as called off at the last minute. That he and the mother of his children had fallen in love again. But anyone watching the way he gently caresses with index and middle finger the pin of the foundation on his lapel, where her happily smiling face unstintingly affords him new confidence from the hereafter, knows that it can only have been love that induced this man to abandon his successful career as a producer, to devote himself 100 per cent to the life's work of his wife, who died far too prematurely.

By now more than 15,000 people are working for the Foundation, primarily at eight camps set up by the federal government in Africa and Asia in response to the catastrophe. Language tuition and training tailored to German curricula and

the national economy are giving more and more
people the opportunity to immigrate legally. For
the first time this year, with 450,000 available jobs,
more people are being offered the chance to come
to Germany than there are applicants, because
those taking courses in the camps are now much
sought after locally too. These positive experiences
have led to two similar French and British camps
being established, soon to be followed by a
Polish one.

But, as Goethe once said on the Internet, "On the Internet"
"Every great work has petty enemies." The *is too vague.*
enthusiasm is not universal; the Greens and many
human rights groups, in particular, criticise the
dominant German culture of the camps. And *Did Goethe*
yet it is these very details under criticism, such *really say*
as German Christmas carols and forestry as *this?*
compulsory examination material, that Nicolai *I can't*
von Kraken holds responsible for the programme's *find it*
success in Germany too. "Those four Senegalese *anywhere!*
men on "You Bet!" recently, that was not a
coincidence. And it wasn't a trick either, Thomas
Gottschalk chose them blindly from 400 possible
participants. He could have picked out any four
and they'd still have trounced the A.f.D. executive
committee in spelling and waste separation. I
believe this was the first time large sections of the
German population saw how German these people
are coming out of our camps. It's not for nothing
that the video's had 20 million views."

At this point Nicolai von Kraken has to

interrupt our interview because his son, Bonno, has come into the room with a handful of documents. The golden glow of this moment is unreal. When this young man, who resembles his mother more and more by the year, whose eyes and lips have so much of the aura of Nadeche Hackenbusch, works hand in hand with his father, you fancy you can literally hear the spirit of that extraordinary woman breathing benevolently through the room. Rumours are circulating in the media that he will be continuing his mother's T.V. programme next year, but given his huge workload this remains unconfirmed for now.

*[handwritten annotation in right margin: Nice observation, but a spirit doesn't breathe!]*

Not everything is done, of course. If you talk to Kevin Kruse, former federal minister of the interior and now federal commissioner for the integration industry, you will see a man who knows he still has much work to do. "We can't hide the fact that the acceptance for refugees we see today in the east of our country isn't a change of heart. We – and I must put it this way – had to 'buy' it with all those jobs," Kruse says when we get through to him by telephone during his honeymoon with his husband Thomas Glass. "But even if people merely tolerate migrants because they're useful, there will come a time when they won't want to do without this utility any longer. Nobody in Brandenburg or Mecklenburg–Western Pomerania wants a return to the unemployment rates of the past. People living there can also see doctors are returning to the region, businesses, that the authorities and politicians have no problem justifying new post offices, shops, clinics. Just ask the inhabitants of Peenemünde."

Back in Germany, Nicolai von Kraken is making some last-minute corrections to his speech. "I have to keep on pointing out to people that Nadeche was just a very normal person," he says kindly. "That's why we made sure that the illegal Virgin Mary doll was taken off the market. This commercialisation is neither desirable nor helpful, nor does it do justice to her memory. Besides, from the beginning of Advent people will be able to buy 'Nadechemas' from our online shop." Of course it's no secret that Germany's first series of charitable toys is being expanded for the festive season. In October people will be able to purchase the pink zebra car, while with its twelve cute chocolate-brown babies the infant transporter will make the heart of every little girl beat faster. And – the special surprise! – Nadechemas will at last be accompanied by her best friend, beautiful little 'Saba'. Will we soon see a toy Nicolai too? The ex-producer gives us meaningful smile.

More detachment please! E.g. delete "cute".

Still not known is who was responsible for the attack at the border. The suspicion that Israel intervened in the interests of European stability and to prevent a National Socialist resurgence in Germany remains unproven. On the other hand, the list of states that possess the necessary high-performance stealth drones in sufficient numbers is not long.

But this is what precisely icebergs are like: half
is underwater. And often that's the larger half. *More than half!*

If only the Titanic had known!

*A ship can't know!*
*Say, e.g., "The captain of...."*

Edith von Maischenberg
Semester III

Dear Ms Maischenberg

A highly ambitious article, although there is plenty of room for improvement. As insightful as your observations are, you need to pay far more attention to research and fact-checking (Goethe!). Clearly missing here, given your focus on Nadeshe Hackenbusch as a person, is any reference to Lionel, her companion, or at any rate her assistant. At least mention he's presumed to be amongst the victims. My years at EVANGELINE have taught me that it's good to introduce a note of tragedy. The reader likes to cry too!

Overall: satisfactory

Lou Grant

ASTRID VON ROËLL ACADEMY
FOR QUALITY JOURNALISM

TIMUR VERMES was born in Nuremberg in 1967, the son of a German mother and a Hungarian father who fled the country in 1956. He has been a journalist and ghostwriter before his first novel, *Look Who's Back*, appeared in 2012. Published in more than forty languages, it was one of the most successful debuts of the decade, and in 2015 was made into a film directed by David Wnendt.

JAMIE BULLOCH is the translator of novels by Timur Vermes, Steven Uhly, F. C. Delius, Daniela Krien, Jörg Fauser, Martin Suter, Roland Schimmelpfennig and Oliver Bottini. For his translation of Birgit Vanderbeke's *The Mussel Feast* he was the winner of the Schlegel-Tieck Prize.

# LOOK WHO'S BACK

"A brilliant book" RUSSELL KANE

"Both funny and frightening . . . A powerful and important
book" SUE GAISFORD, *Independent on Sunday*

"Can we laugh about Hitler? Of course, why ever
not? . . . A better question is, is *Look Who's Back* funny?
The answer is yes" ROBBIE MILLEN, *The Times*

"Laugh-out-loud funny . . . An uproarious, disturbing
book that will resonate long after you turn the final page"
CAROLINE JOWETT, *Daily Express*

"Not so much a satire on Third Reich revisionism and
nostalgia as on the blank ironies of amoral and fad-crazy
multi-platform media. Think Sacha Baron-Cohen and
Chris Morris – but Vermes does know where he's going"
BOYD TONKIN, *Independent*

"Packed with wry, close-to-the-knuckle hilarity, and builds
to a gloriously ironic conclusion" *Mail on Sunday* (*Ireland*)

"Worryingly believable (time travelling despots aside) and
unsettling. But also very funny" NATHAN FILER

"There's no question that the novel has hit upon the key
paradox of our modern obsession with Hitler"
PHILIP OLTERMANN, *Observer*